RETURN TO INDEPENDENCE BASIN

By Matt Ellison

Send inquiries to Matt Ellison at
matt.ellison22@gmail.com

FIRST EDITION

ISBN: 978-0-9981856-0-6

Cover graphic by Betsy Ellison

Also by the author

ARTIFACT

ABANDON

THE CHOSEN ONE

SADDLE BUTTE

PASSING FOR MALE

PASSING THROUGH NEW JERSEY

NEW YORK
1979

Chapter 1

EVAN GALLANTINE STOOD at the makeshift plank stairs of the construction trailer, staring up into the foreman's flatiron face. What he answered, despite a voice well equipped to outshout the roar of heavy excavation machinery, was barely audible.

". . .makes you think. . .guy works *for me*?"

"Visiting a lot of sites like this. Talking to a lot of bosses like you."

The foreman only nodded, volunteering nothing more.

Evan looked up. Already the first of May, and high overhead, late afternoon sun creased the shaved edges of the twin towered World Trade Center, but down in the shadows, it was getting chilly, almost wintry. He buttoned up his sports jacket, then stepped up past the foreman into the trailer—despite being clearly not welcome. The staunch foreman stepped aside then back behind one of the many work tables stacked with sheaves of blueprints and engineering specifications.

It was thankfully not as loud inside.

"S'pose this so and so you're lookin for *does* work here? What's it got to do with you?"

Unlike every other hard-ass hard-hat foreman Evan had tracked down the last month, this one was truculent in his reticence, in his feigning indifference, being asked about Joe Meeks. Too indifferent. Too reticent. Such that, despite his steel plate attitude, Evan had the distinct impression he'd be a soft touch.

“It’s about a death in our family,” he said, “some related financial matters he needs to know, that kind of thing.”

“You got the wrong Joe Meeks then. The one workin for me’s got no family.”

Evan nodded. “I’ve been hearing that. Joe paints quite a picture: out on his own since he was a kid, ran off and never looked back, never had and never needed anyone. But, no, he’s not from Krypton; like it or not, he does have a family.”

Out the window a huge dragline scoop hoisted a load of dynamited rock high above as the next in a long line of patient twenty ton dump trucks rumbled underneath. The load fell onto the truck, pounding its chassis so that it quaked like a bubble toy on the mammoth wheels; the concussive shock alone shook the trailer so much Evan put a hand to the wall to steady himself.

He winced. Evan hated loud.

After the truck thundered up the earth-packed ramp to street level and disappeared in the glass and steel of the city, he re-gathered his short ponytail of graying blond. Then pulled a folded manila envelope from his jacket pocket.

“At a minimum, I need to get this to him. So if you think you can help. . .”

“Yeah?” The foreman accepted the envelope, gauging its heft. “Any money in it for him, I hope?”

Ah. Evan saw his opening.

“Money? Well, that depends.”

“On what?”

“The final disposition of the ranch.”

"Ranch? What, like he's inherited it or something?"

Evan shrugged, purposefully vague. "Something like that."

The foreman scrutinized the envelope again. "And so, who'd you say you are, again?"

Gallantine offered his business card.

"Los Angeles, huh? You're in real estate development there?"

"I'm just helping out, handling the sale."

"Sale? Of the ranch?"

"It's complicated. And a lot depends on Joe, so, if you know, and if you don't mind, I'd like to know where to find him."

"Yeah. And you're not the only one, either. How about let's take a walk?"

He flipped Evan a yellow hard-hat and led him outside. They crossed the landfill site, the grounds rumbling with construction, its buildings in various stages of completion, one already a skeleton of girders rising more than forty stories, another foundation not even fully excavated. Across the Hudson, reflected sun seared off the office building windows lining the river with such glare Evan, even with his sunglasses, had to shield his eyes to it. He hated bright, too; as much as loud.

They stopped at the largest excavation, a cavernous pit of concrete pilings and exhaust-spewing cranes, each in various cycles of hoisting a concrete block, the size of a small house, up its full height, more than a 100 meters, then releasing it, to freefall plummet down its tether of twenty to thirty stories of heavy steel cable, and hammer the steel-tubed pilings deeper into the as yet still unthawed, recently dynamited earth. Far worse than at the trailer, the ground shook incessantly, as the many cranes repeated the same process without stop. A workman here would have to grow hardy sea legs in no time. Or quit.

The foreman barked at a nearby group of workers. From among them, a jowly, enormously fat heavy whiskered man stepped out and waddled toward them. Proportionally he was as fat as the machines around him were big. Most of him was a dome of swelled out stomach that took the lead while the remainder, a hard hat and some arms and legs, tailed behind. His belt-line fell low and still only barely stretched around the enormous girth, his T-shirt rode up well shy of it, leaving a wide medicine ball of hairy flesh in between.

He gave Evan's ponytail a long once-over.

"Who's your new sweetheart, boss?" he shouted.

"Where's Joe Meeks at," the foreman shouted back.

"The fuck do I know? I'm his mother-fuckin keeper?" He squared to Evan. "Who wants to know?"

"No one, but if you know where a person might go to look for him. . ."

Evan raising his voice, shouting, yelling to be heard, he hated it; not his style, none of this to his liking.

The fat man pointed to one of the giant cranes. The only one idle.

"There's where he's s'posed to fuckin' be; what more can I tell ya?"

Evan toed his oxblood loafer against his pants leg, a scuff on the tip.

"I was more wanting to know where he actually is, not where he's supposed to be."

"Yeah?" the fat man said, reddening. "So who're you, jack, his sister?"

"Not that close. Actually, we've never met."

"Yeah? And knowin Joe, he'll want'a keep it that way."

"Maybe not," the foreman put in, "there's money in it for him."

"Yeah? For his fuckin sake, better be a shitload."

"So Joe's not working today, then?"

"Working? Oh no, hell no. Chicken Little's got better things to do than work. Na, he's too busy with how all these buildings are built poor and are about to come crashin' down any goddamn day now! How all these pilings, all of 'em, ain't set deep enough, shy by fifty feet, all accordin to him."

"Are they?"

"No and whether they are or ain't, what he's paid to do is operate equipment, not second guess the engineering." The man's meaty finger stabbed the dusty air. "I'm bettin' you got what little sense they got in that fucked up family, jack, 'cause Joe sure didn't get none. If he really does go to mid-town, like he keeps sayin, that fuck'll be lucky not to end up fifty feet under himself."

The fat man hitched his pants, raising his eyes up the open tiered adjacent tower, forty stories of open girders and concrete, each floor cordoned with bright orange safety netting.

"You afraid of heights? 'Cause odds is Joe's probly now up one of those top floors there, keepin himself company, fingerin' his navel, figurin' out how why it is he knows more'n every CE on the goddamn project an' nobody'll listen. So maybe you can catch him there. . .if a good stiff breeze don't come up and blow up and do us all a favor."

He lumbered off back behind a stack of steel casings. Evan turned his eyes to the building's, his eyes following the construction elevators as they lifted cement buckets from the shadowy recesses of ground level up into the bright, late day sunlight blasting the upper levels. Flashes of blue arc-welders burst here and there against the orange netting.

"What did he mean, if Joe goes to mid-town?" Evan yelled to the foreman.

"The managing agent. Idiot'll do it, too; you'd know if you heard half the stories I heard, like this bridge job down in Missouri, he somehow got wind of a big earthquake they'd had couple hundred years ago, and he got the highway department so riled they. . .guess you heard that one too?"

"It's possible I've heard about all of it by now. Pissed off contractors? Joe cuts a swath like Patton."

He offered a cigarette to the foreman and took one himself. He inhaled, studying his yellowed fingers.

"You haven't you fired him, though. Like all the others."

The foreman spit. "Oh I would have, all right. If it weren't for his boy."

"His boy?"

"That's why I didn't want to say nothin at first, in case you were going to make trouble for the kid."

"What kid?"

"Joe's kid. Nice boy, too. Real nice."

"What do you mean, Joe's kid? You don't mean his son?"

"If you don't know, I sure the fuck don't. A few weeks ago Joe left town and when he came back he had the boy with him. All I know is the poor kid's mother just died all of a sudden.

Joe claims it's just temporary, but I got a feeling it isn't. And Joe as broke as he is, about yay-close to getting himself fired, and probably not another site left in the country would give him work anymore. . .I don't know."

A siren blew, quitting time; almost immediately, the machinery began to stop. The shaking earth quieted, and in the immediate lull that ensued, Evan's legs felt light and rubbery.

"One thing about this ranch money," the foreman went on, "it'll do the kid good, even if it don't Joe."

He pointed out a dilapidated trailer by itself just outside the perimeter fence in the undeveloped section of the landfill.

"That there's what Joe calls home. No place for a kid, as you can see. He's there now. I'd say go pay *him* a visit. He'd be glad to help. Hell, he'd be glad just to see you, whoever you are. Joe sure don't got a clue. Hasn't even got him in school."

Evan looked up. The sun had dropped into evening, and cool dank air was now lifting out of the pit. He breathed a breath of relief. What little he'd learned about Joe Meeks made him doubt he could ever get his ear, let alone his cooperation. But with a boy to support, no money and possibly no job, well, that could very well change everything.

He crushed out his cigarette.

"Thanks for your help, chief," he said, tossing back his hard hat to the foreman. He smoothed his jacket and walked away, more of a bounce in his step than when he arrived.

Chapter 2

IT WAS LATE afternoon, almost quitting time. Wade sat on the timber steps leading into Joe Meeks' trailer, the padlocked door gleaming down at him. He twisted his fingers in his old t-shirt. It wasn't the first time he'd locked himself out.

Brian, the foreman's boy, yawned.

"God, Wade, I thought your dad would be here by now."

"His name is Joe, Brian, I told you before."

"Yeah, and I wish he'd get here already."

"He will," Wade said, wishing the same thing.

"He's kind of dickless; that's what my dad says. He said. . ."

Brian's voice was drowned out by another warning siren from the construction site. Wade stood to watch. A muffled dynamite blast rippled through the sections of twilled steel protective mesh blanketing the earth. The dozers followed hard upon, like metal tigers tearing into the loosened debris.

"What'd he get you? Anything good?"

"Brian, it's not like that."

"What do you mean? He's not getting you a birthday present?"

"Just never mind," Wade snapped, wondering why the foreman had made his boy come by. He shouldn't have bothered. They weren't friends. He was older, and homely as the Incredible Hulk.

The quitting time whistle blew. The machinery fell silent, the voices of the shouting workers died down; soon the only movement was little waves on seepage water in the sump pit, which when Wade arrived a few weeks ago had still been iced over.

"Did your dad say to wait for him or no?"

"His name's Joe, Brian."

"Alright already. Did *JOE* say to wait?"

"He didn't say anything."

"Then here; open up before I have to go." He gave Wade a wrapped present and a tied box.

"What's in this?"

Wade opened the tied box first.

"Dad told me to get you a cake too, so I got ice cream cake."

"Ice cream *cake*? There's no such thing."

"Where you been, Timbuktu?"

Wade opened the box, and sure enough, cake made out of ice cream.

"Here's candles. Twelve, right?"

Brian stuck them into the cake and lit a match.

"Won't they melt it?"

"Duh." Shaking his head, Brian set the cake ablaze, flames flickering in his eyes. "Now open up; I gotta go."

The gift was a Knicks basketball jersey, identical to the one Brian wore. Wade quietly refolded it.

"Well Jeez, Wade. You can't put it on at least?"

"We'd look funny. You want to be wearing the same shirt?"

"Don't be a dickweed. You don't like it?"

"No, I just. . .it's all right for now."

"Better than the one you got on. It looks like crap. Where'd you get it, a bum or something?"

"If you have to know, my mom gave it to me."

"Oh."

That shut Brian up. Nothing more smartass to say. For a while they both just watched the candles burn out. Wade searched the men leaving the site, though Joe rarely came home until late anyway.

He unfolded his present again.

"It's kinda chilly. Maybe I'll just put this on over mine."

"Yeah, okay," Brian said, and stepped back as Wade pulled it on. "Looks almost as great on you as it does on me." He swatted Wade's arm. "Let's eat that cake before I go, okay? Your dad can wait; you snooze you lose."

Brian scooped his bare hands into the ice cream cake and loaded his mouth with it.

"Jesus, Brian."

Brian gave him a messy grin. "Just say thanks, Wade; my Dad's waiting." His cake-smeared hand waved good-bye.

"Thanks," Wade said, waiting until Brain was gone, then plunging into the cake with his own hands. It really was ice cream cake, still frozen, pleasantly tingling his fingers, his teeth, his tongue. He stuffed some more into his mouth, smiling.

A good birthday after all.

THE SUN ALREADY setting across the river, and still no Joe, Wade set his cake under the steps, where it would stay cool for him. By now it was quiet but for the line of cement trucks on the street, mixers revolving, drivers hosing loose gravel. Spray spouted off the chutes making rainbows. The men, in huddles of burly t-shirts and hairy necks, were joking and telling stories, men Wade knew by sight now, always milling around before leaving for their real homes and real houses, Joe never among them, always too busy with work.

Catcalling and whistling broke out as two women in high heels walked by. Wade looked at the two women, wondering what men always got so excited about. He then began wondering if Joe ever got excited about women and was thinking long and hard about it when he heard footsteps approaching the trailer. He looked up excited, but it wasn't Joe. It was some man he didn't know. Well-dressed, not a worker, you could tell. The last rays of sun turned his jacket a fiery gold as he came up, stopped, and studied Wade carefully before extending his hand.

"How you doing, chief?" he said, as his yellowed fingers closed around Wade's so firmly they drew him to his feet. He asked Wade his name, then jiggled the padlock. "Your dad isn't back yet, Wade?"

"He's not my dad."

"No?"

"No, he's not. I'm just staying with him. My mom just died."

"I'm sorry."

"That's okay."

"Where is your dad, then?"

"I don't have one."

"No?"

"No. Never did."

The man seemed doubtful. And also, familiar.

"Your mother never told you about him, I guess."

"She never told me about him 'cause I never had one," Wade snapped. "I think my own mom would know, you know."

"Right."

The man stepped back. Turned around as if looking for someone. A clip holding his hair in back flashed in the setting sunlight.

"Joe's taking care of you, though?"

"We'll see. That's what he says."

"Ah. And then what, you'll go stay with relatives?"

"No. We don't have any. It was just me and mom."

"What about your dad's family?"

"I told you, I don't have a dad."

The man set his foot on the plank.

"That's right; you did tell me that, didn't you?"

"Only girls can have babies, I hope you know," Wade said.

"True enough."

"So there doesn't have to be a dad. Okay?"

The man thought a minute, then nodded. He took out a cigarette.

"You expect Joe will be back soon?"

"Maybe," Wade said. "What do you want him for?"

"Well, for one thing, to let him know his own dad died."

"Joe's dad?" Wade thought a minute. "He had a dad?"

"Between you and me?" The man leaned forward and Wade instinctively did the same. "Joe not only has. . .had. . .a father, he has a whole family. He doesn't tell people that though. He ran off from them when he was not much older than you."

"Really?"

"Oh did he ever."

Wade studied the man closely. He did look a little like Joe, only older.

"Are you Joe's brother?"

"No, cousin. I've never met him, but I was hoping to do that here."

"You want to wait? You can if you want. I have some ice cream cake you could eat."

The man looked at his big wrist watch. "You think maybe first thing tomorrow morning he'll be here?"

"I think so."

"It's very important. Can you help make sure?"

"Sure. I'll try."

"You can tell him Evan Gallantine wants to see him. He'll know of me, but just in case, make sure he gets this." He pulled an envelope from his jacket. "Tell him if he wants any of the ranch money, he has to meet me here tomorrow morning."

"What ranch money?"

"It was nice meeting you, Wade."

They shook hands again. Wade felt the man's gray blue eyes on him.

"What?" Wade said.

"Hard to believe Joe's not your father. You look a lot like a Meeks to me."

Evan smiled coolly and left. Wade sat down, smiling coolly himself. He ate some more cake. He remembered as a boy thinking twelve was so old, he would never make it. Now he'd made it. This birthday was getting better and better.

THOUGH IT WAS nearly dark, and Joe had still not returned, Wade was so excited he couldn't sit still, and went off walking. The air was thick and humid. A jelly of blue glowed around large security lights. Where the sun had just set the sky was purple; everywhere else it was oily black. The city glimmered with squares of office light, illuminating the clouds covering the highest skyscrapers, while the nearby tower construction bubbled with work lights. Wade counted; they put up another floor today. So many stories had been erected just in the weeks since he had come. How fast everything was going when day by day it all went so slow. It seemed so long ago, the days in the hospital when his mom said everything was all right. When it wasn't. He knew now she didn't tell him things, at least not everything. It was weird. Joe said don't think about it. That's how you get used to it.

On a quiet street, he passed an expensive looking restaurant and saw his dim reflection in the wide paneless windows rising from his feet to high over his head. Stopping, he looked at himself and at the man and woman inside, holding hands, talking, a white rose on the table. They smiled at him until their waitress, looking up, came to wave Wade away.

He walked back to the river and stood there, listening to the water lap against the landfill breakers. The Hudson was wide and black and flat. Wade wondered what happened when you died. Would it be like being deep under water at night? Would you go somewhere else? But if you were living somewhere else, how could it be dying? Dying probably meant it gets all black and that's it. Now that he'd made twelve, would he make twenty-one? He'd prefer to. He'd prefer to make it even longer.

A chilly gust whipped through his new basketball jersey. He dug into his pockets, hoping somehow his key would be there, but instead found something soft. The envelope. It had been in Evan Gallantine's pocket so long it was frayed, the flap almost open. By smoothing it out, it had loosened all the way. That made it okay to take out and read:

> *Leonard Meeks, lifelong Meagher area resident, died this past week of driving off the bridge on his place and drowning in the Hellwater. He was near 60. County Sheriff McComb investigated and called the death accidental as there was not too much alcohol involved. Leonard was born here in Meagher and raised on a ranch south of town, up the Hellwater Valley, owned by the three Meeks sisters and has lived there ever since, until now. His passing leaves his mother, Frances Meeks, and a sister Emma alone on the place, and the other aunt, Lillian, now named Lillian Gallantine, living in out somewheres in California. A brother Harlo survives him,*

if you call serving time in Deer Lodge surviving, and also a son, supposedly, named Joe Meeks, who is now thought to be somewheres back east. Leonard's wife died of heart failure years ago and his second son, Scotty, died at age 12, in the big earthquake of '59. Father Sterling, the new clergyman in town, offered to hold a service for the newly deceased Leonard, but says there is nothing to report on that this week as Frances Meeks still just isn't interested.

Wade read it several times, imagining this place called Meagher, imagined the Hellwater, a trough of fire rampaging down a narrow valley, imagined Joe's father, black hair and white face, in a coffin with gold handles like Wade's mother's, and the three old sisters, all in white, reaching up for heaven, and the boy Wade's age, Scotty, wide open eyes, and faceless. Wade couldn't imagine more of him than that.

A loud horn drowned out his thoughts. A ferry far out in the bay furrowed past the Statue of Liberty. God, he had never seen her so brilliant, the towering copper-green woman throwing her brightly lit reflection across the black water, and suddenly Wade felt light-headed and raw and happy. He inhaled deeply. Another flurry of wind billowed up inside his new jersey, flapping it like it was breaking into pieces.

He turned and raced back to the trailer, thrilled when he saw the padlock hanging loose. He grabbed his cake and ran inside.

It was dark, the only light leaking from under the door to Joe's room, which was shut. He tapped on it lightly. Nothing. He started to turn the knob. . .

"Hey there!"

. . .and quickly it let go.

"It's only me, Joe," he said, facing the closed door. "I have to give you something."

"Not now, Wade. I'm trying to concentrate."

Wade put the envelope back in his pocket. He kept his ear pressed to the door, listening to Joe read through his old books and write in the ragged notebook he carried everywhere.

"Joe?"

"I thought you were going outside, Wade."

"I did already."

"Okay, that's fine with me. See you later."

Wade sighed and pulled the string to the ceiling bulb; a long tailed rodent swarmed down behind the job box. He went to the front door and examined his reflection in the window. He seemed faceless, not looking as much like Joe as he'd hoped. If only there were some photographs of Joe as a boy. There were some similarities, thin white eyebrows, narrow cheeks. He pulled his wavy hair out of his face, and on impulse, got the tin snips from the job box and raised them to his hair. It took only a few minutes, and now, with a crew cut the same as Joe, there was a lot more resemblance.

He sat out on the steps, letting the breeze bristle his new hairless head, and after a suitable wait, he swung the heavy door behind him so it slammed. Went to the sink, turned it up full, let it run. Went to the toilet, dropped the seat, flushed it loudly. He went to Joe's door and pressed. It was shut tight.

"Joe, you want to do something for dinner?"

"Dinner? Like what?"

"Eat, maybe?"

"Sure, Wade; go ahead. I'll get somethin later."

Wade sat on his bed, two blankets and a piece of foam on top of the job box. He actually was hungry, and wanted Joe to be hungry too. He knelt down to the half-size fridge. Inside, there was only the boiled meat, exactly what was there before, and his cake. Wade sat on the cement-stained stepladder which was their chair, counting drips in the wash basin. He wished Joe Meeks would eat more.

Suddenly, he jumped up and grabbed his cake box. He dragged the stepladder noisily to Joe's door, sat, and dug his fingers into the thick runny ice cream cake. He smacked his lips loudly.

"Wade?"

The louder he ate, the better it tasted.

"Wade, what're you doing out there?"

"Eating my cake. Want some?"

"What cake?"

"My birthday cake."

Wade stuffed a big chewy piece into his cheeks.

"Birthday cake?"

"Yeah," Wade said. "There's a little left if you hurry."

Wade licked the candles, the frosting sweet, the ice cream rich and cold. He had never had cake so good. He could eat this kind forever, he was thinking, when the door handle turned.

Chapter 3

THE WAITRESS SPREADING their tablecloth was the same waitress that had waved him away earlier that evening when he passed the windowy restaurant and stopped to look inside.

"It's my birthday," Wade informed her.

"I see." She was friendlier now that he was a real customer. "May Day is a nice day for a birthday. How old are you?"

Wade told her. "I didn't think I'd ever make it," he added.

She smiled politely, setting two forks on his left; she was near enough to smell her skin and her bunned hair as she set tulip glasses on the table, lit the candle, adjusted the white rose. She had fingernails like pearls. She began folding two cloth napkins into birds, noticing him staring at her.

"How nice of your father, bringing you here for your birthday."

"I know, even though, I mean, he's not really. . .never mind."

Across the restaurant he saw Joe's sandy crew-cut ballooning above the sea of tablecloths and flowers, returning from the men's room wearing the black clip-on tie and black jacket the waitress had so thoughtfully offered them both. Though Joe's jacket was as small on him as Wade's was big, Wade was proud to see how handsome he looked as he passed through the sea of dark suits and gowns, nearly slipping on the white tile floor.

Joe ducked quickly into the seat opposite Wade, rattling the fancy glasses. Wade was impressed. Joe's hands were still wet from washing; Wade had never seen them so clean. And his eyelids, lavender, Wade had never seen that before either, or how they sloped across his eyes toward his cheekbones.

"May I get you a drink, sir; wine, a cocktail?" the waitress chimed.

Joe looked at his wrist as if there were a watch on it.

"No. I don't drink when I have work later."

She poured their water and left, her dark slacks rippling against her legs.

"She's pretty," Wade said.

Joe fidgeted with the top button on his tight collar. "You couldn't pick someplace a little fancier, I guess?"

Wade leaned nearer.

"You like her?"

He downed his water in one swallow. "Who?"

"The waitress."

"Nothing the matter with her, I guess."

"What do you like best?"

"I don't know. I don't like anything better than anything else."

"Know what I think you like most about her?"

"What?"

Joe stopped fussing with his collar and sucked on his ice, interested. Wade looked from him to her as the waitress returned.

"Her tits."

Joe's eyebrows flung up his forehead and the ice stuck in his throat.

"Here we are, gentlemen," the waitress said, arriving with menus as large as posters. "May I tell you about our specials?"

"No. . .um, thanks anyway," Joe said, clearing his voice.

"What specials?" Wade said.

"Well," she began, and as she recited, Wade studied her carefully.

"I think she likes you," he said after she left

"It's her job, Wade." Joe tugged his jacket around his shoulder. "What are you going to get to eat?"

"What are you?"

"You go ahead. You're the birthday boy."

"Anything?"

"Yeah, I guess. Get whatever you want."

"Thanks, Joe," Wade said, beaming, deciding this was his best birthday ever. Once he finally got Joe out of his room, Joe had asked what he could do for Wade's birthday, and Wade knew exactly what: To eat at the windowy restaurant, the two of them, and when Joe said okay, he felt so happy, he couldn't stop smiling. Joe standing shirtless at the wash basin cleaning up, he had looked so strong, Wade thought, running his eyes down Joe's knobby long back, swirls of hair on his arms, his neck, his knuckles, the bristle of his crew cut. Wade hoped to look like that one day. Maybe when he was twenty one.

Wade closed his menu. "I want that special honey duck thing."

As much as Wade savored the sweet-sounding dish for

himself, he wanted it even more for Joe Meeks, eager for him to eat something besides boiled meat for once.

"That only comes for two, Wade; don't you listen?"

"I know, but if we both. . ."

"We aren't that hungry."

"But it has honey, Joe. It's good for you."

The waitress returned again, this time with a basket covered with a dark green napkin. Wade opened it; steam from warm bread rose out, and suddenly it felt days since he'd eaten, weeks, months, years. He felt hunger inside in a way he never felt before. He seized two rolls and pressed them into his mouth.

"Are we ready to order?" she asked.

She held her pen on her pad, polite, waiting. Neither answered.

"Would you like some more time?"

Wade shrugged, mouth full of moist bread, and looked at Joe.

"Well, just that duck then, that's all," Joe said.

The waitress snapped her pad shut and collected the menus. "Very nice choice, sir; I personally think it's our best entree."

This made Joe Meeks relax a little, and she leaned over to whisper something Wade couldn't hear. She leaned back and Joe nodded.

"What are you guys talking about," Wade said. "Making sex?"

Joe's face purpled; the bristle of his hair rose.

"Well, no," the waitress said, glancing at Joe, "no, it was just something about dessert."

"Oh." Wade slumped back in his seat.

"Are you sure you couldn't use a drink?" she said to Joe. "I might know just the thing."

He rubbed the bridge of his nose, nodded, and she quickly left.

Joe's eyes lifted. "What'd you do to your hair, anyway?"

"You like it?"

"It's a little funny looking, isn't it?"

"I thought it looked like yours."

Joe felt his head. "Yeah, maybe so."

Wade fingered Evan Gallantine's envelope in his back pocket.

"Joe, do you think you could tell me some things?"

"What things?"

"You know, sex things."

Joe leaned quickly forward. "No, for crying out loud."

"Why not?"

"Well, because it's not up to me, that's why."

"Well who is it up to then?"

"Your mom," he said, then winced. "I mean. . .she went over it already, didn't she?"

"Not everything."

"Not everything?"

The waitress appeared with a frosted glass full of mint-colored drink. Joe sat back and pulled his hands into his lap.

"Yeah, like how come when you get a hard-on. . ."

"Thanks!" Joe exclaimed, knocking his knife into his lap and knee-jerking the table. "Thanks again; that'll be fine."

She looked at Wade, nodded graciously, and quickly left. Joe took a long drink. He took another.

"Well?" Wade said.

"Well what?"

"You know, about sex."

Joe fingered the condensation on his glass. He drank again.

"What's got into you tonight, Wade? You weren't this feisty before."

"I wasn't this old before. I need to know some things."

"Well I'm sure no kind of expert."

"Well, you are compared to me."

Joe mulled that over, feeling the drink spread inside him.

"What's there to know? It just happens, that's all. . .it's just that. . .see, the man has the, well, his seed, and he. . ."

"Seed?"

"Seed. You deaf? Seed, like, well, like anything."

"Like a plant?"

"Like that. That's all there is to it."

He lifted his glass to find it already empty. He picked up a piece of bread and mopped up the dregs.

"Then what's the seed do?"

Joe sucked the drink out of the doughy bread.

"Every man is given, well, a staff, so he can sow his seed. In the womb."

Womb. The word tumbled in Wade's mind, somber, dark.

The waitress, in passing, noticed Joe's empty glass. "I was right about that drink, wasn't I? May I bring you another?"

"You mean like a vagina, Joe?"

"Please," Joe said quickly, "one more, thanks."

Joe waited for the waitress to leave, then finally unbuttoned the collar button that was choking him. He cooled his forehead with his water glass.

"Joe, what's a womb exactly?"

"It's like. . .you know, a soft place in a woman's belly, where if the man sows the seed there, it grows up, um, into a. . ."

"Baby?"

"There you go. That's all there is to it. It's no big deal."

He found he had two pieces of bread, one in each hand. The waitress returned with his drink and two salads.

Wade mulled over his new data quietly for a while, eating his salad, then looked up.

"A man has to sow the seed in the woman, right? That's the only way to make a baby?"

"Right. Now can we just drop. . ."

"So I really did have a dad, didn't I?"

Joe began picking at his salad, avoiding Wade's broad smile.

THE FIRST PLATES of food began to come, sidetracking Wade's inquisition as he devoured them ravenously, while Joe watched at first, then picked at a piece of crisp skin, then knifed at a piece of leg, and eventually was forking duck as fast as Wade, smothering it with the sweet, lathery sauce.

"You sent mom money, right, Joe? Those envelopes?"

"I helped out now and then. I never need much."

"Were you boyfriends with her or like that?"

"Let's just eat up and show a little more respect here."

"But didn't you guys ever, you know, make sex or anything?"

"Wade, you don't ask things like that about your own mother."

"'Cause why?"

"'Cause you don't. Just try and not worry anymore about her."

"But I'm not. I'm worrying about you now."

"Well, don't. Here, look at this here."

Dessert arrived, a slice of cake with candles and two singing busboys. Wade smiled, seeing Joe's mint-colored drink reflected in his eyes. Wade wondered if now was a good time to give him the envelope.

"Joe, do you miss your dad?"

Joe dipped the last scrap of duck into the congealed sauce.

"Never had one."

"Yeah you did, everybody has a dad. You just said so."

Joe coughed. "No, I meant I never knew him."

"But didn't you ever want to know?"

"Wade, does it really matter all that much?" Joe said, suddenly reddening. He picked up the check and stood up, digging a few crumpled bills out of his pocket.

"Damn," he said, counting them, "This was supposed to last me the rest of the month."

Wade went to the door to wait, pondering the reflections in the wide glossy windows, of dark couples talking, of golden sconces festooning the walls, of smoky air, wavering. Joe paid and they began the walk back to the trailer, Wade's body full of dinner, his head full of ideas.

"How come you never got married, Joe; don't you like women or something?"

"I just never cared all that much one way or the other."

"Not even my mom either?"

"I didn't say that."

"How did you guys meet?"

"Oh, I was doing a highway job in a little town in Iowa, and used to eat in the diner where she worked. We went to a few movies. When the job was over I moved on."

"Did you ever at least kiss or anything?"

Joe stopped. "I mean it, Wade; this's getting on my nerves."

"Okay."

They continued down a long street of warehouses. Wade noticed they forgot to return their ties and jackets, and now he and Joe seemed like a pair of something, clowns or dancers or hobos. He bounced up the steel stairs to a loading dock, liking walking alongside Joe, being on different levels. For the rest of the way, he bobbed up and down the various platforms the rest of the way home.

"How come you came when mom went in the hospital?"

Joe unlocked the trailer.

"She wanted to make sure you got looked after."

"What did you talk about?"

"Not much. She mostly slept."

Joe still hungry for some reason, ate the remainder of Wade's cake, while Wade lay on the job box looking up at the metal struts of the ceiling.

"I wish I knew everything that was ever going to happen."

"Yeah, and I guess it's about time we found a place for you, too."

"What place?"

"Somewhere better than here. An orphanage or whatever. We can't have you always hanging around like this."

Suddenly, the metal struts felt like iron bars, and Wade sat up.

"Joe, do you think you'll ever want to know about your father? What happened to him?"

"Wade, I warned you about that, didn't I?"

"But wouldn't you want to know?"

"Wade, for crying out loud, I don't know anything about the guy."

Wade leapt up. "I do!" he announced.

"What d'you mean you do?"

"I mean I don't, but Evan Gallantine does."

Joe jumped. "What do you know about Evan Gallantine?"

"He came by earlier. He told me to give you this."

Wade handed over the envelope. Joe read it. Read it again. He looked up, his mouth thin.

"He told me to make sure you're here tomorrow morning," Wade explained. "He's going to come by and talk to you about the. . ."

"Time for bed, Wade."

Joe walked to the door and stepped out. Wade followed and stood in the open door.

"Joe, I don't think I can sleep now."

"Why not?"

"I keep wondering about my own dad."

"Your mom told you didn't have one."

"But you said I did, and I believe you."

"I didn't say that, Wade. I said. . .oh never mind. Just get to bed."

He walked down the step, and Wade quietly followed him.

"Joe, you said we need a place for me. I was thinking, what if we could find my dad? Maybe he'd still want me. Maybe. . ."

"Dammit, Wade!" Joe yelled, exasperated, whirling around so fast Wade lost his balance, and fell from the stairs onto the ground where his head smacked onto a large chunk of rock. Wild light shot across his eyelids; his eyes exploded with leopard spots, flashing sparklers and exploding starbursts, mysterious shouting reverberated in his mind. As he blacked out, mumbling "fireworks", Wade realized one last thing, even one more thing to be happy about. The most dazzling birthday ever.

Chapter 4

AFTER JOE CLEANED and dressed his eye out and went to bed, Wade lay in a kaleidoscoping darkness, all night his body a long peninsula of limbs, a short walnut shell. He would float. He would see across the screen of his eyelids first flickering then flashing then throbbing lights. There was a dull black knot behind the swollen eye where he had struck his head, where if he trained his mind he could soften the knot and a strange blindness would come over him; then he could sleep a while, before it began all over again.

The next morning, at daybreak, he was vaguely aware of Joe slipping out and tried to wake up but couldn't. Later, as daylight filled the room, he got up. In the glass of the front door window, he examined the yellow bruise over his left eye. With his new short hair, his face was unfamiliar in the wavery glass; he seemed smaller, shorter, weaker, then larger, taller, stronger. For a second his mother's face ghosted across his reflection, how she looked in the coffin, then his hurt eye burned as warm salty fluid ran down his cheek. He closed his eyes.

He heard tapping. Opening his eyes, his reflection was replaced by a familiar-looking adult standing outside the door, rapping his knuckles urgently on the door.

"How you doing, chief?"

Wade recognized the face, but couldn't quite remember who it was. The man opened the door, and as Wade stepped back, slowly remembering, Evan Gallantine stepped in.

"He's not here, is he?"

Wade shook his head, which made it hurt again, and he put his hands to his temples.

"Sorry," he said.

Evan sighed. "What happened to your head?"

"I trimmed it myself."

"Looks good, too. I didn't mean your haircut, though. I meant the swelling around your eye."

Wade thought for a minute. "I guess I fell."

Evan examined his eye more closely. "Did anybody look at it?"

"What for?"

"A concussion, for one. You have any dizziness? Blackouts?"

"No."

"No flashing lights?"

Wade shook his head again. Evan felt his forehead.

"Did you try putting ice on this?"

"We don't have a freezer."

As Wade closed his eyes, Evan's hand left his forehead.

"Wade, I need you to think hard. Where can I find Joe?"

Wade looked up. "What day is it?"

"It's Sunday."

"There's one place we could try, but I'd have to take you there."

"Fine," Evan said, "it's a nice morning for a walk."

A THIN FOG had settled in during the night, and as Wade led Evan toward the new tower where Joe might be, early sunlight fell on the mist making everything fresh and clean.

"Wade, has Joe said any more about what he has in mind for you?"

"We think I should go live somewhere like a cemetery."

"Cemetery?"

"Orphanage, I mean."

"Couldn't you stay with him?"

"Okay with me, but it'd be hard on Joe."

"Still, I imagine something can be worked out."

Wade smiled, running his finger in the moisture beading on the fence, less nervous about taking Evan Gallantine to Joe.

They walked among several truck trailers parked around the loading platforms and came out at the elevator cages. Wade pressed the call button, and one of the cars suspended high above began its descent. At least being Sunday, there was no one on site but security guards, who knew him and no longer paid much attention. Or even noticed as he walked Evan into the lift car when it stopped at his feet. He slid the door shut, click, and the car lifted rapidly, as fast as if it were falling.

As it rose above the fog, the air felt bluer, the sun warmer. Wade closed his eyes; bright red-orange swarmed inside his head as he ticked off the floors with each clank of the elevator, 37, 38, and at 43 his finger pulled away from the button, so at the next floor, they stopped.

At that altitude crosscurrents of air whipped across the open floor. In his feet, Wade could feel the building's subtle sway in the concrete. A wall of plastic swelled from the steady wind on the south side. Wade pointed to it; Evan nodded, intuitively quiet. He leaned to speak in Wade's ear. Above the rush of wind Wade understood he should give the two men a few minutes alone. As Evan went through a splice in the plastic wall, Wade sat against a cement pillar, where he was less exposed. Hoping it was all right to come here.

A PLACE OF rest. Joe Meeks on the 44th floor. Where you stood above it all, the firmament to yourself. Rising sun in full flare; strident magenta east, the west, dark. Sky, earth, sun, and air. Layers of it; thick and sooty near the earth, benzene pink then pallid green then above that aqueous swirls of blue, and above it all, the sun, as always. What things it must have seen, eon after eon, Joe thought.

North, the curving horizon, the round highlands, the crest of the Palisades and the Hudson, flat and burnished green. At his feet, the brick and steel city, a lichen feeding on the island bedrock. And hundreds of yards straight down, the excavations, the microbe machines, and those concrete pilings, toothpicks in sand.

He leaned against an outer column, feeling the tremulous sway of the entire structure, mere steel and concrete against the living earth, a furnace which could split ocean floors, spread continents, fold hundreds of miles of granite like a soft towel.

No one cares, he trumpeted to himself, proud nonetheless for going to mid-town yesterday though no one listened. He was used to that.

Behind him, the elevator clanked, and he stood motionless,

eager to be unseen. Through the murky plastic, two figures, one short, one tall, come onto the open floor. The tall separated and emerged through the protective plastic.

Eyes met.

"The door was open," Evan said.

Joe looked away.

That was the introduction. Evan expected no more, and walked to join Joe Meeks at the edge.

"Quite a cathedral you have here."

Joe didn't reply. Below a large tug boat nudged a solitary ocean liner slowly up river.

"I hear you think it won't be stable."

"When it settles. Just a matter of time. Same as happened in Boston with that skyscraper there. Probly worse. At least no one can say they weren't told."

Their eyes met again, looking one in the other for familial resemblances.

"Don't the engineers make allowances for settling?"

Joe scoffed. "Sure they allow for it, but enough? These pilings are only set down in man-made fill, when not fifty feet below that is solid bedrock. They could avoid a big catastrophe, that's all I'm saying."

"Probably hard to prove that kind of thing."

"Maybe I can't, but time can. Three months, a fraction here becomes an quarter inch there. Six months they occupy all the offices, load up every floor, an inch, two, three or four. A year, better part of a foot. Floors buckle, windows break out, elevator shafts warp. Proof enough? A hundred years from now? They oughta've done it right. I did what I could."

"You went to mid-town, you mean. To the managing agent."

Joe crossed his arms.

To the west, at Newark, a jet drifted into a landing while simultaneously in the east, at Kennedy, another rose in takeoff.

"So what now?"

"Now nothin. I move on."

"What about Wade?"

"Wade? We'll get him into a good home somewhere."

"But he's your son."

Joe toed the cement's edge where it fell squarely into space. "What makes you think that."

Evan laughed. "I'm a sucker for the obvious."

"Well just because his mother died doesn't presto chango make me a father."

It grew quiet as the wind let up. The Hudson became a sheet of liquid metal in which an ocean liner spread a wake of veiny ripples.

"I never should've agreed to it," Joe said.

"Agreed to what?"

"To any of it, even to going out there. I mean I hardly even knew her. It was only those couple months. Things happened, but we both of us knew it was never more than that. The work ended, I left, and we both figured that was it, except, then it wasn't. By the time she was able to get hold of me, she'd already decided to raise him on her own. And she didn't want anything from me, just to use me on the birth certificate because she thought it'd make things easier for him. Which was fine. I said I'd send her money, and I did, whenever I had any, though she never even asked for that. All this time she never asked for anything, until now. In the hospital."

Joe stared into the slowly undulating plastic screen, and saw her looking up at him, her eyes dark, waxy, her face feverish, her hair falling out, her veins yellow. Saw her trying to talk, saying all those things, how they were both people who neither one ever cared about much, how she'd been lying for days thinking it over, feeling worse about that than she did about even dying, how she said Joe should marry her, before it was too late, right then and there, she said, so they couldn't orphan Wade, so Joe could still have the chance she never did, and how she grabbed him, saying deep down it's what he needed, and as he tried to tell her there was no way he could all of a sudden start being a father, she leaned up so fast he thought she'd yank the tubes out of her arm and said, You don't need to be a father, Joe, she said, you need to be a human being.

He watched the ocean liner disappearing peacefully upriver.

"I knew she wasn't all that healthy, but up to the last I sure never imagined it was that bad. She didn't even make it past that afternoon. I wish I'd never listened. Wade would be better off if I'd done nothing at all."

Wind caught the splice in the plastic, whipping it open, revealing the boy himself. Joe shook his head and walked over to him.

"Look at him, Evan. I'm no good for him. He needs some of those government offices to put him with decent people who'd know how to take care of him, not a harebrained misfit like me."

"Good luck on that, Joe. People who take in nearly grown boys do it for money, tax breaks, that kind of thing, not because they want a son."

"Look, Evan. I got the envelope. Why are you here, to lecture me about Wade?"

"Not exactly, although if you had better finances you wouldn't need a lecture."

Joe spit over the edge, and followed it as it fell to oblivion.

"You mean money?"

"A lot of money."

"And the catch is it's got to do with Frances Meeks, I suppose?"

"It does."

"You know I don't have anything to do with those people."

"It's no problem. I can deal with them for you."

"Why, because you're the top vulture now?"

"I think it's time that land did everyone in this family some good."

"Bravo for you."

"You included, Joe."

"Sorry. Not int'rested."

"Not even for Wade's sake?"

Joe felt Wade's eye on him. His injured eye.

"No, but I'm curious. What is your angle, anyway?"

"There's a group of lower valley ranchers who have a consortium called the Hellwater Reservoir Corporation. It formed many years ago, in an effort to get the Hellwater dammed."

"It already is damned."

"The point is, they finally got their dam site approved."

Joe's eyes flickered. "Where at?"

"Bitterroot Gap."

Joe laughed outright, then stepped back, suddenly feeling loopy and too near the edge.

"What's so funny?" Wade asked.

"Nothing, really," Evan said, "it means the dam is going to inundate the entire upper Hellwater and the Meeks ranch with it."

"What's inundate?"

"Drown it. All of it. Buildings, fields, sheep, cattle; the only livestock that place will produce then will be lake trout."

"Better than ratty sheep and shit-ass cattle," Joe said. "As far as I'm concerned, they couldn't put that ranch under enough water if they built a dam right on top of it."

Evan shrugged.

"If it's going to drown, how could there be any money?" Wade asked.

Joe looked at Evan. "Wade must have read my mind."

"There's a way," Evan said, biting a cuticle.

"Have a seat, Wade," Joe said, sitting down, "this oughta be good."

"It's fairly straight ahead," Evan began. "The HRC will have to pay compensation for any ranch their dam floods, but only at fair market value, which for upper Hellwater land is next to nothing. Those ranches are just subsistence operations, and the families are old and gone away, so HRC expects to pay very little. What they can't afford, though, is to have any of those old timers stall on selling, or they lose time and eventually, if they can't show progress, they could even lose the dam site itself."

He squatted on his haunches, drawing imaginary figures on the floor.

"If I can offer them the entire valley, uncontested, they'd save a mint in legal fees getting those old timers out, and in exchange, they'd pay a premium for the land."

"Good plan. Too bad you don't happen to own the entire valley."

"I spoke to all the ranchers involved, explaining the plan very carefully: They legally consign their ranches over to me, using my company as sole proprietor, which in turns sells to HRC. Once the money changes hands, my company then divides the profits among all the families equally, less expenses and a small fee."

"You been in the California sun too long. You'll never get those ranchers to agree with you."

"You'd be surprised. Between Leonard and myself, we already have most of their agreements."

"My dad? He was all for this?"

"As much or more than I am."

"Huh; I never thought he'd do anything practical in his life."

"In fact," Evan said, "there's only one hold out."

A wry smile spread across Joe's face.

Evan sighed. "If Leonard had owned the Meeks ranch, this would all be over and done with. Unfortunately for us, he never did."

"There you go," Joe smirked, "that's the Meeks family for you. If I know Frances, you'll be as old as she before you ever get her agreement, let alone that ranch."

"She's the most intransigent ninety-year old I ever had the pleasure to deal with. If it weren't for her, I wouldn't even be out here wasting your time."

Joe looked up. "What do you mean by that?"

"She said she'd never agree to give up that land while there was still someone left to work it. But your father was the only thing close to an able body left on the place, so now that she drove him to his death from sheer frustration, she claims there's still you."

"There's still no one, then," Joe said. "Me take over where my dad left off? You can set her straight on that right now."

"The sooner the better. The minute we get you out there and. . ."

"Ho no," Joe cried, jumping up. "Go out there for what? The only way I'd go out to that Godforsaken place is to bury her in it."

"It's the only way. She's has to see for herself. Joe, it'll take two or three days. We'll cover all the expenses. All you have to. . ."

"Nothing doing. No way, no how."

"Joe, it's easy money, and think what money could do for Wade. You could afford the best boarding school in the country. Think it over, Joe, you could. . ."

"Evan, it's nothing to think over. Good luck on your plan, but include me out. I don't need one red cent of money from that ranch. Never did and never will."

His eyes flashed. Evan studied the floor a long time, then crushed out his cigarette and buttoned his jacket.

"I don't go back to Meagher until tomorrow. You have until then. I delivered my news and I'm done. If you choose to be as intractable as Frances, it's not worth any more of my time to try and help this poor family."

Joe folded his arms, rocking steadfastly on his feet.

"Then let's leave it at that," Evan said. He turned to go, then turned back. "Here Wade, my card with my hotel on the back. In case something should change your father's mind."

He patted Wade's head. "Good luck, chief." He parted the plastic drop and disappeared.

THE MORNING ADVANCED; a warm breeze quietly ballooned the plastic. Deep in thought, Joe looked up at Wade, sun on one side of his face, the other in shadow.

"How's your head, Wade?"

"Good. I do like you said, try and not notice it."

"I said that?"

"Yeah, remember? When I would feel bad about mom, you said growing up is learning not to feel things."

Joe shook his head. "I got to watch what I say around you; you get me all backwards."

"It works, though. I don't feel it now."

Joe leaned his forearms on the safety netting, gazing over the limitless city, peaceful at this elevation. Wade leaned forward on his forearms too. Joe suddenly laughed, and Wade asked why.

"Frances always said the Gallantines would turn up one day to try and get the place. I don't think a day went by she didn't worry about somebody gettin the ranch away from her, and it was almost always Lillian that was going to be the one to do it. In her mind Lillian's sole purpose was to one day come steal it away from her."

"Who's Lillian."

"Evan's mother. The youngest sister. See, there were three Meeks sisters in all; Emma, Frances, and Lillian. Lillian's been in California since she was twenty, but who knows, maybe she did hear about that dam and sent Evan to wrangle out whatever he could. They ought to know better, though. Next to their mother, who homesteaded it, nobody worked that place like Frances. She'll never let it go; she runs it like it was hers."

"I thought it was hers."

"No, that's the funny thing. Before their mother died, she put the whole place in Emma's name, with Frances as guardian."

"What's funny about that? She was the oldest, wasn't she?"

"Yeah, but Emma was born simple-minded; never had the sense of a six year old. Still, of the three girls, their mother left it all to her. I don't know if anybody knows why, but that's how it was. After that, Lillian took off, but Frances stayed. Maybe she thought she'd eventually get it if Emma died. Looks like Emma never cooperated, though. Now with that dam, Frances never will."

"Do you really think Evan's trying to steal it from her?"

"Ah no, but I bet Lillian did send him. Evan Gallantine never set foot even close to Montana before this as far as I know. He doesn't even seem like a Meeks to me. He seems more like a normal person, or a Californian, at least."

Below, a bird's wings blazed white among the shadow and sunlight of the city's quiet buildings.

"Imagine what it looked like to him. Things he must of seen then."

"Who? Evan?"

"No, Peter Meeks, the father of the Meeks sisters. My great-grandfather. He came through after he stowed away clear across the ocean by himself."

"Why'd he do that?"

"To get away from home, I suppose."

"Like you did."

"Yeah," Joe said, looking at Wade like he'd only just realized it himself, "I guess like I did."

"What happened to him, Joe?"

"He went out west, first the Black Hills, then up the Hellwater to a camp in Independence Basin. He died early, leaving his wife and those three girls to eke it out on the ranch, that's where the whole problem started, I think. It's too bad. He must've been a hardy man. When he stowed away, he was only twelve or thirteen at the oldest."

"Man, I wonder if I could ever do that."

"You're too young."

"You guys weren't."

Wade looked up, smiling. Joe smiled back.

"You're a funny guy, Wade."

They leaned together, watching the city come to life. The sky was cloudless, the horizons far and clear in this air. He breathed deep.

"Don't you love it up here; no fumes, no dirt, no noise."

"Yeah, it's great, Joe."

"Air and only air."

Joe turned. Wade was so near, he could smell his fine hair. The soft skin of his cheek. And how there was always the corner of a smile in his mouth, tempting you to smile back. It had never occurred to Joe before, but how such a person could come from nothing, all that youth, the eyes, the hands, the perfect head, all out of nothing? You couldn't help wanting to run a hand over his head.

"Listen, Wade, you know it's not that I don't like you, don't you?"

Wade nodded quickly. "I know."

"It's just that it'd be better. . ."

Joe's eyes wandered off.

"What?" Wade said.

"I was thinking Evan might be right about that ranch for once doing somebody some good."

"You mean you'll take the money?"

"Hell no. I meant maybe it isn't a half bad idea, that boarding school place he was talking about. I guess they must have places like that, where they take kids off your hands and do the right thing with them. Sounds like just the ticket, doesn't it?"

"Not really." Wade brightened. "Don't you think it's probably too expensive."

"How much could it cost? I could just keep hard at work and the money can go to one of these live-away type schools and in a couple three years, you're out and on your own. Now there's a plan for you, right?"

He rose and started off to the elevator.

"Come on, let's get back. Think about it, Wade. The best part is you get your schooling and don't have to live with the likes of me."

Joe was all smiles in the elevator, while Wade stared at the floor, the rush of air whispering in his ears. Back on the ground, they stepped out into shadows protecting the last of the morning haze that hugged the ground. Joe skipped briskly toward the trailer, but Wade lingered, liking the misty vapor watering his cheek, soothing the hard throb in his eye.

Chapter 5

THE TRAILER DOOR flung open, the bottom hinge snapping like a dry leaf.

"Where's that fucking goldbricking greaseball?" a heavyset man in a rumpled suit roared, red about to burst from his face. He stormed inside.

The foreman, his square forehead sweaty, his skin vermilion, was right on his heels. "Joe," he called, "the G.C. wants to. . ."

"Meeks!" the other man bellowed, the trailer rumbling with his weight. As Joe ran out from his room to see what was going on, the man hurled his hardhat at him so hard it bounced off the wall, leaving a hole, and narrowly missing Wade, who was lying on the job box.

The man, seeing Wade jump up, stopped short.

"Who the hell is that?" he cried.

No one answered. The man, one of the general contractors and the foreman's boss, looked from Wade to Joe and back again. He seemed to lose some of his steam then, and stood there like a panting bull, glaring at Joe with caustic eyes.

He turned to the foreman. "It's not enough this idiot goombah dances into mid-town with a ten mile string of bullshit on my fucking time and then has the balls to ask for a raise; no, on top of that, he's raising a family on my construction site? I ought to . . ."

But he couldn't finish, and speechless with rage, he let fly with profanities so venomous Wade shrank down behind the job box for safety.

"Take it easy, boss," the foreman said.

"I'll take it easy, alright," the man yelled, then walked to the foreman as if to crush him. "Listen to me and listen good. Get Eddy or Spinelli or whoever on the biggest dozer we got and raze this shithole trailer to a pulp before tomorrow morning. I tell you now, if I find this insolent son of a bitch asshole anywhere near my site after today, he's Joe fucking History. If you give him one red cent of his back pay, Jimmy, you're fucking history too. Got it? Now get the fuck going."

He shoved the foreman aside and barreled out, slamming the door so hard it ripped off completely. The foreman watched him go, then picked up the hardhat which had almost hit Wade. He looked flat-faced, his face ashy, except for the ridge of his scar. He turned to Joe, started to say something, then shook his head and left.

It was several minutes before Wade's ears stopped ringing, and several more before he dared come out from behind the job box.

The whole day, once Evan had left and he seized on the idea of a boarding school, Joe had been bustling around the trailer cleaning up and making plans. Wade had never seen him so chatty and lighthearted. Now he stood silently cutting up the last of the boiled meat.

"Might as well eat it up," he said, offering it to Wade. Wade shook his head. "What? You're not hungry for a change?"

"Joe, what are we going to do?"

Joe sat down with his plate on his lap. "Don't worry about it, Wade. It's not like I've never been through this before."

Wade wrung his hands in his pockets. "But I never have."

Joe looked up at him.

"Do we have any money?" Wade asked.

Joe put his plate of meat aside. "No, I guess we don't."

"Do you have any ideas?"

"Well, no, not at the moment. I was expecting to. . ." He looked at Wade. "Why, do you?"

Wade pulled out Evan's card. "I have one."

"Yeah." Joe rubbed his ear and took the card. "I figured you might."

EVAN GALLANTINE WAS paying for his Chinese food in the lobby when he saw them arrive; they passed the front window like two homeless drifters. He retrieved them and shepherded them up to his room, where Wade plopped on the bed in relief, while Joe went to the window. The balcony looked out over 23rd street; below, cars flowed in a river of headlights.

"But nothing's changed, Evan. I'm going for Wade's sake, not mine."

"Fine," Evan said, spreading out an array of white cartons full of steaming mysterious-looking food on the dresser near Wade.

"And whatever I get out of the ranch goes for Wade's live away school. All of it. I don't want anything to do with it."

"However you want it," Evan said, unwrapping his chopsticks. "Wade, I've got more than I can eat, feel free to help me out."

Wade, needing no further encouragement, plunged in with

his fingers since there were no utensils, just another package of wooden sticks. Evan picked at a few bites, then leaned back and fluffed his pillow.

"And I want something legal," Joe continued, "in writing."

"As soon as we have her commitment, I'll have the contracts all ready to go."

"I mean before I go. To make sure I'm not wastin my time. Say Frances still turns us down, then what?"

"Impossible." Evan took a liquor bottle from the bed cabinet. "She's nearly ninety. She can't even make the drive down to Meagher anymore. How would she ever keep a ranch going?"

"She might find a way. There's always Harlo. What about him, anyway?"

"I don't think he's a factor. He's in prison."

"Prison?" Wade lifted his head out of the food.

Evan removed the plastic covers from three hotel glasses and poured each glass full of the clear liquid from his bottle, then took a lemon and sliced thin wheels into each glass. Beside him, Wade's eyes fell on two chocolate mints which for some reason were lying on the pillow.

"Joe," Evan said, "what you need to do is relax. Eat something. Did you leave him any food there, chief?"

Wade looked sheepishly at the empty cartons. He had about decided he'd better offer Joe one of the chocolate mints he wanted when Evan clinked a glass and passed it to Joe.

"There's a sauna and hot tub in the hotel; why don't you take your drink and go soak your bones? Take advantage of the place."

Joe took the glass. He felt oily and filthy, and the thought of immersing his entire body in steaming hot water was more than tempting. While Evan gave him towels and directions, Wade helped himself to the mints and stepped out onto the balcony.

The noise of traffic surged below. As he was finishing the first mint, Evan came out with two glasses and sat down. He pushed Wade a glass, a perfect slice of lemon floating on the surface.

"Sake," Evan said, "It's a Japanese drink."

"Thanks."

Wade sipped, curious. For a second, there was no taste, then his mouth turned to cotton, then erupted as if in flame. His eyes gushed; he couldn't breathe. Trying not to gasp, he turned to wipe his lips so Evan couldn't see, then sucked quickly on his chocolate mint to clear the taste.

Evan was quietly thinking to himself, a pleased expression on his face. He finished his glass and poured them both some more.

"It must be all very strange for you," he said thoughtfully, "all at once having a family you never met and never knew you had." He nodded to himself. "It's too bad it had to have been this particular one."

"How come Joe doesn't want to go back?" Wade said, his voice cracking, his mouth feeling acidized by the sake.

"I don't know. I wonder if he knows himself, anymore."

"Who's that guy Harlo?"

"Leonard's brother, Joe's uncle."

"He's in prison?"

"In and out."

"How come?"

"He apparently regards writing bad checks, grand larceny, and auto theft as a viable career path. Typical Meagherite."

There was one other thing Wade wanted to know.

"Do you know how Scotty died?"

"Scotty?"

"Didn't Joe have a little brother?"

"That's right, the slow one. I don't know much about Scotty, only that he was buried in a landslide set off by an earthquake, and apparently Joe was. . ."

His voice trailed off. Wade looked up. Joe stood behind him, his hair waxy clean, his face shiny and still damp. Wade smiled up at him.

Evan stood. "You look a lot better."

"I don't know, Evan. I was thinking about things. What if Frances. . ."

"Joe, forget about Frances. Once you set her straight, she knows there's only one option."

Joe sighed and looked down into the whirlpool of traffic below.

"Well then, if I'm doin it, I'd like to do it get it over with."

"I do as well, before we lose the edge with HRC. I've booked you on a flight tomorrow. The one I'm taking was full because it's the Monday morning business crowd, but I'll wait in Billings for you. I have things to do there anyway."

"You already booked us? You sure didn't waste any time."

"I expected you might change your mind. Is there a problem?"

Joe shook his head. "It's just happenin so fast. You only told me about it this morning."

"And you only just told me you wanted it done and over with."

Joe looked at Wade, who nodded.

"We'll probably have it wrapped up in a matter of days," Evan said, "after that, you and Wade can leave whenever you want."

"Wade?"

Evan looked at him. "Joe, you can't very well just leave him."

Joe looked down. A police car wailed past, and behind it the stream of cars became a torrent.

"Besides," Evan went on, "look at it this way. It's a vacation, and you can make the most of it. You two can get better acquainted."

He downed his sake.

"And who knows," he mused, "a trip home might bring back some fond memories."

WADE YAWNED. THEY had been travelling since that afternoon, and it was very late, almost dawn; he had trouble keeping his head from falling on Joe's shoulder.

The plane from Denver to Billings was tiny, a sixteen seat prop. As the final passengers boarded, the stewardess squeezed up the aisle, her nylon legs swishing with static. Wade drowsily raised his eyes to see if Joe Meeks thought she was pretty, but he was staring out the oval window, looking worried. Even on the big jet from New York to Denver, Joe had seemed very nervous about flying, and Wade felt he should keep him company, but he couldn't keep his head from drowsily folding deeper onto Joe's shoulder. When the propellers started and the plane lurched, and Joe instinctively grabbed the armrest which included Wade's arm, Wade didn't really mind. He was blissfully close to sleep.

Wham! Something struck him on the head, right on the swollen eye, and he woke seeing pinholes of red, seeing black stars, seeing a thicket of wheat-colored hair and under it a lanky teenage girl. She had swung the satchel that had whomped him up into the overhead, and shoving it in, the back of her t-shirt hiked up, exposing the most woman flesh Wade had ever seen so close up: White skin taut around her ribs, the upslope of her hips, a triangular lace of blond hair in the small of her back; he knew without turning Joe was looking too. The girl, when she noticed, pulled the choppy bangs from her eyes and glared at them both. She had a surly lower lip, which was about to snarl something at them when the young guy behind her crowded up to intervene for her. She turned on him instead.

"Just sit, Squash, and let me be; Christ anyways."

She pointed to the seat behind her, cheeks flushed, and the young guy Squash stepped back, gangly and awkward, as though the studs in his jeans were little bolts that held his clumsy assemblage of limbs together. He looked around, but their side of the little plane had only single seats, and he had no choice but to take one a few seats behind her.

"And you might take off your damn hat once," she added.

His cowboy hat was scraping the low ceiling, cramming down over his head. When he took it off, stray flips of mouse brown hair fell across his forehead. Giving Wade and Joe his best mean look, he sat down.

As the girl sat down, a feather leaked from the old vest she wore, and landed on Wade's cheek. He was about to hand it to her when a man in a business suit and silver-tipped cowboy boots rose out of the seat in front and bumped him in the head again.

"Sweetheart, it's goin to be a bucky ride," the man said, pouring liquor from a pocket flask into a plastic cup. "Let me offer you a little high altitude medicine," he offered.

The young cowboy was back up in a flash, his fists sticking like unpruned shoots out of his jeans jacket.

"Anne, this man botherin you?"

"Squash, didn't I tell just you to quit sheepdoggin me?"

Rebuffed again, Squash stumbled back as the propellers wound to a scream and the plane began to shimmy. The business man, feeling bolder, steadied himself and leaned further toward her, the seat of his pants right in Wade's face.

"Where you headed for, honey?" he prodded. "Cody?"

She ignored him. He chuckled.

"Well then I guess it's Billings, kitten, 'cause those are the only stops. There's a nice place in Billings, you and me could have a little. . ."

"Fistfight?"

She half rose out of her seat, and Wade saw tiny foam in the corners of her eyes. Taken aback, the business man fell into his seat, spilling his drink in his lap. He swore, fishing away the ice from between his legs.

The girl eased back into her seat and let her leg roll out. Wade was captivated. She seemed tough for a girl; though her cheeks were young and her pants too loose on her frame and the ragged legs crumpled up at the bottom and her cracked cowboy boots two sizes too big, you got the idea it was so she had room to swell up eight feet tall if she wanted. He feigned sleep as the stewardess requested everyone to fasten seat belts and the plane began to taxi. He watched her, eyes secretly parted, as they taxied, and though Joe, still thinking it was the arm rest, squeezed his arm even harder, Wade hardly noticed. As the plane sprang up airborne, he let his leg roll out, so when the plane jounced, his knee touched the girl's, and he pretended to wake, radiating her with his best smile.

"Christ, you too?" she said, rolling her eyes and turning her back to him.

WHEN THEY WERE aloft, sunlight came streaking through the window, spangling the soda in the plastic glass the flight attendant had served. Wade, ravenous, devoured the flaky breakfast roll that came with it, and had his eye on Joe's, who had his eye out the window, staring obliviously. Wade helped himself, stuffed it in his mouth, and sent flakes flying. The girl next to him blew air into her bangs, peeved, making a point of brushing his jetsam of crumbs off her leg.

Wade smiled.

"Hey," she snarled, "how bout just keepin your eyes to yourself."

Wade leaned closer. "'Cause your boyfriend will get mad?"

"Boyfriend?" She glanced back at the cowboy looking guy who had fallen asleep. "Squash Maloney? He ain't no boyfriend."

She picked up her own breakfast roll.

"Where you from?"

Wade shrugged. "I don't know. Nowhere, really."

"Yeah. Tell me about it. What part of nowhere?"

"New York. The city, I mean."

Her eyes brightened. "No shit?"

"Uh huh. Really."

He felt important, pleased to be getting her full attention.

"So what's he do?"

"Who?"

"Your dad, Mr. Burrhead there next to you."

"He's um. . .a construction engineer." Wade lowered his voice. "We're on vacation. What about you?"

"I went with Squash while he visited his uncle's big fancy creamery outside Denver. I wanted to go along and see a big city. It was somethin else."

She fell quiet, leaning back, looking dreamily into the ceiling, her knees splayed, brushing Wade's.

"You like livin in New York. . .the city?"

"Yeah, it's okay," Wade bragged. "It's just another town only bigger."

She leaned up. "What happened to your forehead? Your dad brain you for bein a wiseass or somethin?"

"No."

Again she looked from him to Joe and back again.

"Hair don't grow any too long in your family, I guess."

She zippered her vest, ducked under her hair, and turned into her seat like an animal bedding down.

THE PLANE LISTING up then down, he and his body seeming to separate, Joe fought to rise out of his semiconscious doze, his temples sweaty, his head pressed into the seat, his eyes like cold, weightless balls.

He did wake, when he felt his shoulder jostled by the person next to him; his eyes opened a slit, expecting Wade, but seeing it was not, it was the wheat-haired blond girl, he started. And realized his hand was entwined with hers.

"Bad dreams?"

Joe yanked his hand away. "Sorry," he said, reddening, retracting his whole body from touching her.

"Your boy switched with me; wanted to sit by a window."

She proffered Joe a flask.

"Drink?" She indicated the sleeping businessman. "It's on him. I helped myself."

Joe shook his head, then replanted his face in the window.

ENDLESS CLOUDS FORMING continents of their own, porcelain blue sky, soothing drone of propellers. The plane rising, falling, as it pierced the intermittent pockets of turbulence.

The captain announced that due to some weather

smothering the entire northern Rockies, the Billings airport was socked in, the plane would need to circle 'just a bit' until the sun could burn off enough of the low-lying clouds, and he still anticipated an on-time landing.

On cue, turbulence increased. The businessman woke, looked irritably at his watch. Joe's stomach tightened a little in, a little out, as the high altitude cross currents wafted the plane a little up, a little down. He wished he could at least see ground, suspended above a bank of clouds. Unmoored.

Joe closed his eyes.

He opened them. The girl was leaning across him, looking out the window. Her hair was thick in his face. He noticed how it rose with the plane, momentarily weightless, revealing her earlobe, a bud fleeced with tiny white hair. Then gone.

"Bet you could jump right off from this plane and land on that pile of snow."

Joe followed her look. A mountain peak now loomed out of the clouds, so close the wing seemed to touch it. Further away, several other peaks stuck out; sunlight pointing them like needles.

"Can I see?"

Wade standing in the aisle, leaning in.

"Sure thing."

The girl rose and they changed back their original seats. Joe leaned back for Wade to see, noticing, on the window, the vaporous imprint of his cheek.

They took turns gazing out over the topography of cloud-studded mountain peaks, the weather as though swarmed over everything clear to every horizon.

"Do you recognize anything, Joe?"

Joe shook his head. "Not in this weather."

He wanted it to clear, he said. And wanted it not to.

"Look at that one, wow."

Joe leaned and looked out. The place was circling a tall ridge of a mountain, majestic, towering, but for its ruptured north face, a massive fault scarp. All so restful at this altitude, the sharp arêtes softened by the feathery blanket of weather.

"Mount Contact, must be. And that down below, that'd be Independence Basin."

And Meeks land, somewhere underneath that.

And that one night, the earthquake, the massive landslide, and under it, the one victim.

"The gold mines? Where Peter Meeks worked?"

Joe nodded, almost seeing like infrared traces the footsteps of his past, faint but visible after all this time. The yearly hunting trips, all of them—his father, his uncle, his brother—on the frozen dirt of the old sheepherder's cabin, breathing the breath of sleep, shivering, wintry gusts lashing the cracks in the timber logs. Wearing all your clothes in your sleeping bag, little warmth against the below zero cold, the night air frosting your breath, breathing in and out, in and out, and outside, the snap of the icy brook, the trickling wintry source of the Hellwater. The cold. The cluster of rifles, his own stacked among the others. Lying awake, thinking of morning, how he'd spot the first elk, fire the first shot. Take the first kill. . .

. . .The quiet. Then movement. Scotty, slow silent brother,

who everyone said got Emma's half-wit genes, with a mind of his own nevertheless, only ten at that point, curling his legs out of his bag. Soundlessly lifting the iron shank of the door. Sneaking outside. Like the night before.

Only this time, Joe out after him. Scotty nowhere to be seen, under high black stars popping with arctic cold, fastening his parka, Joe began to walk, breath-cloud in front of him, eyes inventing light. Radiant starlight infused snow powdering his steps. Air so bone-cold you could hear sound with your cheeks.

Reaching the blackened abandoned buildings, fallen down sluices, snowed over tailings of the Independence mine. Ghosted with the rough men of the mining camp, years before, among them Peter Meeks, his bushy moustache, dirty black bowler. Only that one picture of him, circled in ink, the company photograph of the camp and its men.

No Scotty, but not far beyond, Joe walked into a field of slow boiling geysers sweltering with hot mist. Picking his way between the sulfurous pools. Carefully; the travertine crust could cave in, boiling your feet. Engulfed in the heat, gazing up through the swirls of steam to the pulsing of stars and all around the large black outline of the Absaroka range.

He felt more than heard it. And again. A large sound; a sibilant jet of air. A wild smell curled his nostrils. The feeling of sudden fear. He turned back, and directly before him, a few yards away, was a mammoth-sized bull bison.

It snorted, snorted again, lowering its head. Joe petrified and motionless, but the animal did nothing. Then it turned, its profile etched in the steam, and took a tenuous step. Something strange. Another tentative step, and immediately Joe realized: blind. The old bull had sought out the treacherous grounds for warmth but now couldn't find its way out.

A wispy shape. Scotty. Slowly walking to the animal. Face to face with it. A long time that way, then reaching out his hand onto the bull's massive flat forehead. A step backward. The bison, after a great shudder, took a step ahead. Then another, then another, following Scotty, his little hand. In some time, they reached the safety of the trees. The bull disappeared.

The next morning, Joe walking a ridge, Scotty tagging at his heels, his father and Harlo working the timber. They met up at the divide emptying into Independence Basin.

"Looks like we're goin back empty," Leonard said.

They had seen no elk, but now Joe didn't care. Glad the hunt was about over.

"What the hell?"

Harlo lowering his field glasses. He pointed to a large dark shape on the slope below.

"I'll be damned. Thing must of strayed out of the park."

Scotty fiddling with his toy binoculars.

"Acts blind or somethin," Harlo said after a few minutes.

"What do you think? He ain't inside the park."

"Rangers won't never come up here."

"If it's blind, maybe we oughta take it."

"Maybe so."

"Joe?" Leonard turning to his son. "You got first shot. If you want it."

Scotty made a high-pitched squeak when Joe shouldered his 30-06. As he took aim, he was aware of Scotty churning the snow, whimpering. He unshouldered his rifle.

"Here now, Scotty," Leonard said, "Harlo, get Scotty calmed down while Joe gets his nerves together. Joe, take your damn shot now before you lose it."

Joe reshouldered his rifle, closed one eye to sight with the other, and held his breath, squeezing slack from the trigger. In the crosshairs he saw the mighty forehead. He counted. His finger trembled.

"Hell," his father said, "Guess I need to take the damn thing myself."

Joe fired. The concussion walloped his ears, and through the flames that filled his scope, he saw the old bull buffalo sink to its front knees. He ejected and reloaded, but felt Harlo's arm hold down his barrel. Leonard fired. One shot to the head. The animal moved no more.

"Nice shootin, Joe," his father said.

"Damn lot of work to dress a buffalo, though."

Harlo started down the hill. Leonard started after him.

"Joe, get your brother there."

Scotty had flung himself down and was thrashing in the snow.

"He's pretty upset."

"Scotty don't understand these kind of things. Bring him along; he'll be all right."

Joe went to his brother. Glad at least that Scotty couldn't speak. He didn't want to know what he was thinking.

THE CAPTAIN ANNOUNCING preparations to land, Joe

realized that the cloud-cover had parted. Below, though still only early May, he saw ground, and on it, snow. A sprinkling, enough to make the earth wet brown. Freshets of runoff cut into the tawny grasslands, ribboned with white. Land and nothing but for miles. In it, Joe searched for Meagher, the two street town along the Hellwater below where it spilled out of Independence Basin. For the scratch of road leading high up to the Meeks place. For the lane, the bridge, the barn, measuring his approach, unhurried at first, faster and faster as his thoughts hardened, Leonard shrinking back, Joe towering over him, his blood pounding, raising a hammer-like fist to drive him to his knees with one single. . .

"Joe? You all right?"

Joe sat up. Sweating profusely. His shirt sticky against his chest. They were streaking down into a thick swirl of clouds. The vast blue sky turned quickly black. He gripped the armrest.

"What am I doing? I oughta get on the first plane back."

As much as he hated flying, he hated even more what lay ahead.

"Go back?" Wade asked. "Why?"

"Better to let sleeping dogs lie, that's why."

The wheels jumped onto the runway.

As the passengers deplaned, Joe made no attempt to get up. Wade, eager to get out and see everything, nervously hoping Joe wasn't really going to turn right around and go back.

"Have a good vacation, burrhead."

The wheat-haired girl, Anne, leaving with the guy who was not her boyfriend. The last to deplane.

"Joe, shouldn't we go? Before Evan leaves without us."

"Don't give me ideas."

Joe exhaled, and stood, and bumped his head on the low ceiling of the plane.

Chapter 6

WADE SAT BETWEEN Evan and Joe in the pickup Evan had rented. True to his word, Evan was right there to pick them up when they landed, and now, several hours after leaving all the farm equipment lots of Billings behind them, he turned onto a gravel road heading into the mountains. A stinking odor filled the air.

"Man," Wade exclaimed, "What is that?"

"Mineral pots," Joe said, "It's why they call it Hellwater, Wade."

"It sure does reek. How do they stand it?"

"Don't worry, it's clears up before Meagher."

"How far is that?"

"Long ways yet."

"Especially in this," Evan said.

The sleet that had locked in the airport had turned to snow as they gained elevation, and heavy snow, burying everything but the newly leafing cottonwoods lining the Hellwater River and the spring grasses along the knolls of red rimrock. Ahead, the road vanished in an ocean of white; the same in back, except for the twin tracks behind them, their own. Clearly few people had any reason to drive to or from Meagher, even in the best of weather.

Evan looked at Joe staring glumly out the window, looking for something, some sign, some landmark, but there was only white, only old fence posts lining the road, a bead of fine snow running along each strand.

"Look familiar, Joe?"

"Can't tell."

Evan nodded.

"Where we staying tonight, anyway?"

"The Grand."

"That run-down old dump?"

"Oh, you'd be surprised. Marly Croft? I don't know if you remember her, but she's getting it a lot different than what you might remember."

Joe shot him a look. "What's Marly got to do with it?"

"Marly owns it now."

The pickup swerved; Evan took the wheel with both hands, the snow a constant pull on the wheels toward the road edge.

"I understand you and Marly were something of an item back in the day. Have you even seen her since you. . .left?"

"No, and don't intend to. I came to get this business done with, not to look up everyone in town. Stay wherever you like; I'm not staying there."

"It's the only place in Meagher, Joe. Period. Unless you want to drive up and spend the night with Frances."

Joe snorted. He rubbed a hole in his icy window. "You told Marly I was coming?"

"No. I didn't know if you were."

"Well then, don't."

"We need to let Frances know, though. Since we need to go up first thing. And speaking of that. . ."

He reached for the carphone that came with the pickup. As he slowed to a crawl, he dialed a number, then handed it to Joe. "Given her low opinion of me, it would go better if you spoke to her. Sooner rather than later."

Joe shook his head but took the handset. The rings crackled one after the other.

"Not home."

He was about to hand it back when he heard a click and a hiss of static filled his ear. Then a cough on the line.

"Anyone there?"

No reply.

"Frances? Can you hear me? This is Joe."

"Joe who?" a raspy voice cracked.

"So, uh, how are you?"

"Not too goddamn well. What d'you care?"

Joe looked at the phone.

"Uh, so, guess I'll be comin up tomorrow. To. . .um. . .visit."

"Goin to join up with the rest of the carrion, are you?"

Then for a time neither spoke. Then,

"Leonard died a while back," Frances finally said. "That'd be your dad, you know."

"I heard."

"Can't think of nothin else to say then."

The line went dead. Joe passed the phone back to Evan. Wade asked who Frances was.

"Joe's grandmother."

"I can't wait to see her."

"You maybe can't. I can."

Joe rubbed at his window some, still nothing but endless greening hay and a tundra of snow.

Evan slowed to a stop. "This snow is too much for the wipers. Joe, you mind clearing the windshield for me?"

Wade bounded out after him. He saw along the fence a band of sleek deer, their big mule ears on alert. When Joe slammed the door, the herd bounded the fence and bolted up the ridge. All but one, a little one, which went under the fence and got wedged into the barbed wire.

"Hey look," Wade cried, as the fawn struggled desperately to get free, only to lodge itself even tighter.

"Goddamn thing."

Joe went over to separate the wires but the frightened animal kicked too hard for him to get near enough to free it.

"What are we going to do?"

"I don't know, Wade."

Evan called from the truck, "Joe, just forget it; it's going to be dark soon."

Joe stood, looked back at the pickup, then the sky, then knelt again. He started bending the strands of wire back and forth. He told Wade pull to give him more slack. As he did so, he could feel the heat of the wire in his bare cold palms.

The deer continued to kick, but was weakening. Its walnut eyes rolled in their sockets. Its tongue hung out, clenched between his teeth. Wade looked away, to the fields, then to the sky. Strips of blue opening to the north.

Heard a faint 'pop', felt the wire pull through his hand, cutting him. He quickly let go; the broken wire flew apart. For several seconds, nothing moved. Then the fawn sprang to its bony legs. Joe flailed his arms, and the deer ran off to where the others had run and were standing, waiting, at a safe distance.

"Man alive, Joe! We did it!"

Wade licked his cut hand, cold but elated, watching the deer vanish.

"Was it a baby?"

"Yearling."

"How can you tell?"

Back at the pickup, Joe opened the door for him.

"From how it didn't stick close to its mother."

"How come?"

"How come? Well, sooner or later all things got to go out on their own, Wade."

A flake of snow had landed on his eyelash, and as it melted his eyes seemed to sparkle. Wade laughed.

"What're you laughing at?"

"This is going to be a good place, Joe. Right?"

Joe wiped the snow from his eye.

"No; this's going to be hell, Wade."

THEY ARRIVED IN Meagher well after dark, when there wasn't much to see but the pulse of a lone traffic light on the few dark buildings. In those yellow intervals, Wade saw a statue, a mounted cavalryman dripping with melting snow. Then dark. Then yellow again, swirling a broken saber over his head, charging full bronze gallop, his sculpted hat rolling off his shoulder. Then dark again, then Wade read the engraved stone: MJR. THOMAS F. MEAGHER. And dark again.

Evan stopped outside a stone block building, with a large sign "Grand Hotel". Next door, a sign in the window lit with blinking neon letters: "Mint Bar".

"How's dinner sound, Wade? If she's still open."

"Good to me." Wade jumped out. "Come on, Joe, you hungry too?"

"I'll be there. You go on."

Joe lingered until Evan and Wade went into the hotel, then walked off. He wandered down to Second Street where it crossed First Street. The town's only real intersection. In all directions, there was nothing else. No one else.

Meagher. How in just two days could a person be in the one place he'd tried not to think about for twenty years?

A car passed, slowly, full of dark shapes, and stopped in the alley behind the Grand. A lanky kid in oily jeans emerged, shoved out by exhortations from those inside the car. He reluctantly walked to a window and rattled the screen.

"Hey Anne. C'mon drinkin, why don't you? Anne?"

He stood nervously wriggling his hands in his pockets. Joe walked a little closer. The kid stepped back to the car.

"She says she won't c'mon."

"Why, what's wrong with her?" a voice in the car said.

"Nothing's wrong with me," the window barked. "I have work

tomorrow."

"So do we."

"Real work."

"Don't mean you can't c'mon drinkin like usual."

"We all thought you were a big girl now."

The car chorused with chortling and a rattle of beer bottles.

"Maybe she's savin herself for Squash now that she went to Denver with him?"

"He must of wooed her pants off."

A louder burst of chortling.

"You assholes."

A screen door slapped open and shut, and the thick-haired girl from the plane came out. All four doors opened, three more bottle-drinking kids emerged and one put his teenage arms around her. She shook them off.

"Just let me in and get me a drink fast before I change my mind."

She tilted back her head and took a long drink from the nearest bottle. The wolfish boys piled in after her, and the car quietly drove away. Joe watched it turn west on First Street then south on Second, headed out of town on the Upper Hellwater road.

Joe caught himself walking south himself, following instinctively. He stopped. What are you doing?

BACK AT THE Grand, Joe looked inside. As though stepping

back in time he saw: The ring-up cash register on the cracked glass counter mended with the dried tape and under it the ragged cardboard boxes of copper-tipped bullets next to the seedy fishing flies and hard candies covered with dust that had been there since he saw them last.

There was one drunk at the bar. A couple people eating in the booths in the rear. Recognizing no one, no one who was going to know him, he went in, looking for Evan and Wade.

Lining the walls, stark black and white photographs: sheepherders in woolly chaps, shadowy young cowboys in dusty corrals, black-whiskered miners at Independence. Someone's old wagon and team. A photograph of the Grand itself. Another of the view south, the mountains of the upper Hellwater. One, a prominent view of the northern flank of Mount Contact. It was unbroken, solid, eternal. Joe stepped in closer. The date scrawled across the corner: "1940".

It had yet to strike.

"Joe, look."

He had been so engrossed in the photograph he hadn't noticed Wade in the booth next to him, cradling a hot cup of coffee. Evan was not with him.

Joe sat down. "What are you doing with that?"

Wade sipped importantly.

"She brought it."

He meant a woman with thick red hair tied in a kitchen towel just coming out the swinging doors, slinging off her apron. As she came, the drunk at the bar swiveled on his stool and threw his arm around her.

"Buzzy, damn you, I'm in a hurry here."

She pushed him away but the rebuffed drunk affectionately ran a hand down her blouse.

"How bout we dance a little and you advance me a couple beers, Marly; what d'you say?"

She pulled him out of her blouse. "If Tyler made your payday today instead of tomorrow, you're part on; otherwise you have to make do with imagination, you randy bastard."

She laughed and continued to Wade and Joe, buttoning herself.

"So you're Evan's latest prospect?"

She tilted her head, to get a better look, Joe keeping his face down.

"Aim to stay long?"

"Couple days only."

Joe fingering a set of initials carved in the tabletop.

"That's longer than most; hell, we'll be old friends by then. I'm Marly Croft, owner and chief bottle washer. Expect you had a nasty drive up, so I won't bother checkin you in till tomorrow. Take any room upstairs where you find a key in the door, none are any better than any other. Whatever else I can do, go on and ask."

She pressed her hip into the table.

"Feel free to come by the bar later; we'll get you even better acquainted with this town. What d'you say?"

Joe, stymied for how to answer, turned dark, while she turned to Wade.

"Our menu, such as it is, is posted there behind the bar. We're out of a few things but I can't remember what the hell they are right now. Go ahead and take your time; I'll come right back."

She left back for whatever was behind through the swinging doors.

"Man o man, she's sure friendly, right, Joe?"

Joe looked up, and around. "Where's Evan, anyway?"

"With those guys, over there."

The booth in the back corner was dark; it took Joe a minute to recognize Evan. He was sitting with two men, Asian looking, obviously trying to look western, Stetson hats and new Levi's tucked in embossed calf leather boots. The three leaned over the table intently.

Joe reached to have a slurp of Wade's coffee, then wiped his lips.

"I wonder about him."

"Wonder what?"

"Just wonder, that's all."

He started to get up when Marly Croft reappeared, this time with three steaming plates on a large tray. The drunk at the bar rattled his glass at her.

"Jesus, give me a minute; I ain't got but one of me."

She handed the plates to the men with Evan then returned to Wade and Joe.

"So what'll it be, you two?"

She stood expectantly. Neither answered.

"Lotta folks go for the antelope plate."

She lifted her arms to retuck some wisps of her red hair; her breasts swelled.

"Or you might give the rainbows a try. They're fresh as rain. Guy from the survey crew caught a slew of em just yesterday."

"Just coffee's fine," Joe muttered.

"All right." She turned to Wade. "You look like you need a bit more nourishin; right, sugarbeet? You the big eater in the family, I bet?"

Wade wiped his mouth of some saliva. "What are rainbows?"

"Rainbows; you know; trout. It's a fish, honey. If you never had rainbow, well, hoo boy are you in for a treat. I got a nice three pounder; how about I give you that? You could use it more than these local rascals anyway. Just watch the bones is all."

Wade looked across the table. "Okay, Joe?"

Joe rubbed his face in his hands, nodding.

"Rainbow it is. And you eat it all, sweetheart; your dad had his chance, right?"

She winked at Wade. "What happened to your eye?"

"Oh. . .I just fell, I guess."

"Uh huh." As she leaned over to wipe off the crumbs and dried glass rings, she got her first close look at Joe Meeks. She stood up, swinging the hair out of her eyes.

"You sure do look awful familiar, fella. You ever been through before, maybe on a pack trip, somethin like that? I'd swear either I know you or you remind me of somebody, I just can't think who it. . ."

She stopped mid-sentence, backing away, wavering. She

backed up, rubbing her hands on her thighs, then quickly walked off toward the kitchen.

Wade watched her leave, then leaned toward Joe, sipping carefully at his coffee.

"She likes us, Joe."

"Don't slurp like that. Sound like a sewer."

"It's so hot though."

"Then get used to it."

Wade sipped again, this time noiselessly although it still burned. Evan and the two men with him walked by, smiles bright as their big silver belt buckles. Evan saw them to the lobby, then returned. He clapped his hands, sat next to Wade, and lit a cigarette.

"Gentlemen, how's everything?"

"Who're they?" Joe asked.

"Potential investors." Evan waved away his cigarette smoke. "What are you two having?"

"Rainbows."

"Good choice, Wade."

Evan held up Wade's coffee cup. "Marly, when you get a chance?"

Marly, now cleaning the booth in back, nodded back blankly. Evan folded his arms, watching Joe a while before he spoke.

"Joe, I have a problem with tomorrow. I have to drive back down to Billings to meet with those two and their big boss. Which means I can't go with you up to see Frances. I still want to make sure. . ."

He looked up. Marly hovering over them with a tin pot, from

which she filled Wade's cup, then Evan's. Then making it clear she wasn't leaving.

Evan stood. "Joe, let me introduce. . .or re-introduce, maybe I should say, Marly Croft? Marly, you remember Joe, I imagine?"

She nodded, the sparkle gone from her eyes. Joe nodded, but said nothing.

"Been a few years, Joe. You back for a while, or just long enough to run off a second time?"

She reached out her hand.

"Nice of you to drop by and visit us anyway."

Joe reached out his hand, which she shook once and dropped.

"You don't look too worse for wear. Your boy looks good at least. He looks a lot like you used to, now that I think about it."

She smoothed her blouse.

"Why don't you sit down and join us," Evan said. "I was just about to ask if you could maybe help us out tomorrow."

"Help you out, huh." Marly sat, guardedly, next to Wade. "With what?"

"Joe needs to get up to see old Frances Meeks, and something's come up, so I can't drive him like I'd planned. We only have the one vehicle, so. . ."

"Well I can't, but he can ride up with Annie. She's workin with the survey team just above there."

Joe about to ask, "Who's Annie?" but Wade beat him to it.

"Annie's my big baby girl." She took Evan's cigarette and smoked from it. "Surprised you didn't run across her; she'd of been on the same flight from Denver." She exhaled grandly and stood up.

"She leaves early, so anyone wanting to go along with her, get down here even earlier."

She left. The table was silent a while.

"I feel half poisoned," Joe finally murmured.

"How? You didn't anything."

"By this time tomorrow, it'll be all over, Joe." Evan got up. "Come on, let's us two go find a room and let the boy eat in peace."

EVAN HAD ALREADY booked two rooms upstairs, one for himself, another for Joe and Wade. It was small. It had only one bed. Joe, exhausted, lay down on it, but only a few minutes. Restless, agitated, he had to get outside again.

The night sky had cleared; there was weak moonlight while he walked. Both thinking and trying not to, he was surprised to realize he was over a mile outside town, on narrow Hellwater road. Where, in the dark river bottom, choked with fallen cottonwoods, he could make out a sod cabin. Sheepeater Croft's cabin. Marly's father. Still there, where it had been as long as Meagher had been a town, if not longer.

As he stood thinking, a car pulled up. The car with the teenagers he'd seen earlier. Someone got out, laughing coarsely. A female voice. Anne, Marly's daughter. She stumbled over a lodgepole pen disturbing its two goats who began bleating loudly. She cursed them, then threw a rock at the cabin door so hard it rattled.

"Hey you old geezer in there!"

"Shut up, Anne!" A nervous boy's voice from the car. "That old sheepfucker is liable to blast you."

She laughed them off. "Hey you! Old sheepfucker man! Come on out and tell us some stories. Tell bout how my mom. . ."

A fiery explosion burst from the cabin; a shower of pellets whooshed over Joe's head. The car was peeling out even before the rock salt landed. Anne staggered drunkenly backwards and fell into the sheepshit and straw of the pen. The two goats banged into each other and fell on top of her. She batted them off and stood.

"Come on out, you old shithead," she yelled again. Laughing again. "Your goddamn granddaughter wants a goddamn word!"

Silence.

She resumed her way toward the cabin, brushing her pants, when suddenly the night erupted with another blast.

"You cocksucker anyway!" she yelled, this time stumbling back into the trees.

All was quiet again. But the air was redolent of cottonwood and gunpowder.

Joe shivered. It was cold. What moon there had been was now gone. He lingered a while, in total dark, but that was it. Nothing else happened. Anne had either somehow left, or passed out.

So Joe left too. On the way back, he wondered about what the girl had expected. The old man was loony, everyone knew that. He'd been gassed, in France, serving in the Canadian Army. Then somehow ended up in Meagher, with nothing but a sheep wagon. Thereafter he spent his life drunk, herding sheep, menacing town kids, and harassing everyone and anyone without end. Including his daughter. A wild, feral, loony herself.

Marly.

Lunatics. All of them. Thank god he'd soon enough be rid of them again. And he smiled. Thinking about the girl, Anne.

She certainly seemed to be her mother's daughter.

Chapter 7

THE ROOM WAS dark but for the rhythm of the amber traffic light, quiet but for Wade's restless breathing. He lay next to Joe, stiff and unmoving, so not to keep Joe awake, but, with jagged streamers flashing in his eyes, head pounding, heart racing, it wasn't easy.

"Wade?" The sound of Joe's voice lighting up the darkness. "You ain't asleep?"

"No," Wade said weakly. Then, "I have sort of a headache."

"Oh." Some more silence. "I got one too. Probably the high altitude. Try and sleep; get used to it."

"Yeah, okay." Wade feeling a bit better just knowing he wasn't the only one.

"Joe? You see don't any flashing lights, do you?"

"Flashing lights?"

"Uh huh."

"Yeah, I do."

"You do? Really?"

"That traffic light, is all. Just close your eyes."

"Okay. Thanks."

Though Wade could hardly tell any difference, opened or shut.

More time passed. Faint light washing through the curtains. Wade rose, head spinning, and walked a twisted course to the bathroom. Shut the door. Quietly knocked his forehead against the tile. It helped. He dressed. He felt close to normal.

He stood at the bed. Joe groggily lifted on one elbow.

"What're you doing, Wade?"

"Want to come outside with me? See what everything looks like?"

"It's Meagher, Wade. It doesn't look like anything."

"Okay."

Wade remained, shifting from foot to foot.

"Joe, but, you'll get up, won't you? To meet that girl for our ride."

"Yeah. I know. We got some time."

He fell back into his pillow, slept a few minutes, then got up. Out the window, a red glow etched the horizon, seared a few wispy clouds fiery pink. What looked like a storm became a front of black-blue mountains with flanks of sandy grasses, peaks glistening with snow. Town was still dark. No one about. Except. . .down the street, there was Wade, standing under the traffic light. Looking to the end of every street.

Time to face the music, Joe thought, and went down to join him. They waited a while, sitting on a bench under Major Thomas. F. Meagher. Sunlight began to slowly break across town. They watched the stone facade of the Grand brighten top to bottom, the high cornices, then the black windows, the rotted sashes caked with paint, and finally the granite cornerstone, glittering black and diamond. Having settled a little south, the building leaned like a plant looking for more light. They watched the statue gradually come to life, and the newly budding aspens surrounding it. They watched sunlight wash the chalk-red pickup parked outside The Grand, rust around its wheel wells began to shimmer, chrome blisters on the bumpers began to gleam silver, the bald tires and the few remaining lug nuts shone like new.

Wade looked in the cab. He saw a familiar looking tattered vest on the driver's seat, feathers coming out of its seams.

The sign in the Mint Bar switched on with its own light. Wade, curious and impatient, got up and wandered inside. Marly was clattering pans in the kitchen. Two squinty-eyed ranchhands came in. An old woman with two kids. Four men, one with a badge and a gun, and one, a young guy with a large cowboy hat. The guy from the plane.

As they entered, Marly greeted no one, though her eyes kept coming back to Wade. She set four plates on the counter, then yelled over her shoulder.

"Annie? Serve these plates on your way out, will you?"

A voice from up the stairs, "I got work now, remember?"

"Honey, please; before they get cold."

"I'm later'n hell already. Can't they get their own damn plates?"

"Just do it, sweetheart. I'm too busy to argue today."

Wade heard a ruckus above him, then clunking down the stairs. A disheveled girl stormed in, boot laces flying. She grabbed the plates, swore, blew on her fingers, snatched a towel and took them to the back, snapping, "Okay, who gets what here?"

Wade couldn't believe it. Of all places, the girl from the plane. Anne. Annie. About to call out to her, he heard a snicker pass among the four men at the counter.

"You'd think she'd maybe at least wash up once't."

"Oh now be careful, Chuck. Squash here thinks she hung the

moon, don't you, kid?"

This man elbowed the guy in the cowboy hat, and Wade now remembered him too: Squash, the guy on the plane. Who wasn't Anne's boyfriend.

"I'd think she'd be more appreciative bout that, then," the first man said. "Other'n Squash, most boys don't think much of her but a quick roll in the hay."

"Wonder where she gets that from?"

The older man with the badge and gun turned to them all. "Somethin wrong with that?"

That shutting up his companions, they all now fell to looking down at their food.

Anne grabbed a sweatshirt and pulled it over her head. Wade watched mother and daughter eyes meet eyes. Marly's face darkened. Then Anne left, letting the door slam behind her.

Wade followed out. She'd stopped to tie her laces, lifting one boot then the other to the pickup running board, the soles of her boots as bald as her tires. Then she noticed Joe leaning against the cold stone of the Grand.

"Goddamn if it ain't the burrhead from New York. So you're the contractor goin to polish up all that old marble then."

"Marble? This here? This ain't. . ."

Anne yanked the door handle of her pickup. She yanked harder with no better luck. "This goddamn thing!" She threw her hip into the door and pulled a third time. Nothing.

"This isn't marble." Joe scratched his nail on the stone wall. "This's quarried dolomite from up the Hellwater."

"Okay, you're the engineer, and me, I don't give a damn. If some guy named Joe Meeks comes lookin for his ride up the

Hellwater, tell him it left without him. I'm later'n shit."

She kicked one last time and the door popped open. She jumped in.

"I'm him." Joe ran up to the pickup. "Joe Meeks."

She squinted at him. "Then either get in or stay here before you make me later still."

Joe yanked the door handle on his side, expecting it to stick, but it didn't; instead, it flew open and struck his knee. He yelped, but jumped in; Wade right behind him.

Anne turned the key; the engine merely clicked. She jumped out, calling out, "One a you get behind the wheel. When you hear it turn over, give it the gas."

Wade, sensing urgency, jumped back out and raced around behind the wheel. Anne lifted the hood, grabbed a screwdriver sitting on the battery, set it across the starter contacts. The pickup roared. Wade, not sure which pedal was gas, pressed them all. "More!" He jammed down his right foot, and the pickup shook, surging against his feet, shuddering the steering wheel. "Pump it! Up and down!" Wade pumped his foot. Anne slammed the hood and came around; Wade slid to the middle, breathless. He had never felt such a thing.

"Wade, what're. . .you aren't going," Joe exclaimed.

"But. . .why not?"

Anne hurled the pickup into gear and barreled out south on First Street.

"He's goin now."

THE PICKUP TWO-WHEELED in and out of the hard curves south of town, raining gravel and mud in its wake. The gearshift battered Wade between his knees, but he wasn't aware of it. He was watching every shift she made, every pedal she pressed, wondering if someday he would ever know how to drive.

"You rotten sonuvabitch," she yelled as she roared past the sod cabin of Sheepeater Croft in the cutbank below.

"Can you slow it down, please?" Joe said.

"Hey, I didn't ask for driving lessons, did I?" She floored it harder. "Ain't you the one wantin to get to the Meeks place."

"Yeah. In one piece."

"Relax. You ain't the one that's late."

"Well I wasn't the one up all night drinking and tormenting a crazy old coot. Is why you're late in the first place. Far as I can tell."

She threw him a look, downshifting so hard gravel flew forward of the tires.

"What the hell d'you know about that?"

"Slow down!" Joe braced both arms against the dash. "You're scarin Wade."

"You, you mean; you're as bad as you were on the plane, for Christ's sake. Here, want to hold my hand again?"

"All right. That's it! Stop it right here."

"Sure thing." Anne hit the brakes, and even before the pickup completely stopped, Joe had flung open his door and jumped out.

"Have a nice walk!" she called roaring off without him.

"Oh man, don't say that," Wade groaned as Joe vanished in a swirl of dust. In about a mile, Anne slowed down somewhat.

"You know, who's he think he is, your old man, comin out actin like he knows everything. Big shot New Yorker, fuck him."

"No but he grew up out here."

"What? No way."

"Yeah, he did. Can't you tell?"

"What d'you mean, can't I tell? And move over, we ain't on a date. How could he of grew up here?"

Wade shrugged. "Well, I mean, you know Leonard Meeks? That's his dad."

"You lie."

"No. Really. That's why we're going up to see Frances. And maybe Joe can save the ranch from being undulated and she won't have to sell it. We only just found out."

"Old Frances Meeks is his grandma?" Anne slowing down even more. "No wonder he's such an asshole."

She stopped. The pickup idled. Anne went silent, thinking.

"He sure does act like a Meeks, give him that."

"Do I act like one?"

She seemed not to hear. The road stretched ahead ribboning through fields of yesterday's evaporating snow.

Anne finally sighed, slowly letting out the clutch, and turning around.

When they spotted Joe again, she pulled around and slowed alongside Joe as he walked straight ahead. Wade rolled down his window.

"Just get in, okay?" Anne called.

He ignored her.

"C'mon, dammit. Okay, I'll drive slower."

Joe kept walking; she kept pace.

"C'mon. Or I'll get fired."

"I'll get there on my own."

"No way. That'll take you forever."

"Let it."

"Yeah? What I think is, you don't even really want to see her at all. You're scared a her."

Joe continued walking, then stopped. He looked back behind, then ahead, then, without a word, got back in. Anne pulled out, a little more gently. The bickering ended, as abruptly as it began.

No one spoke as mile after mile, gravel clattered pleasantly against the wheel wells. The valley deepening the grassy hummocks of the bench where Hereford steers grazed the lush green timothy and purpling alfalfa. Tractors already summer fallowing the river-lining hay fields. These lower valley ranches had not only survived but clearly had prospered. Lanes paved with red clay, lined with poplars and scotch pines led to modern split-level houses with fancy mailboxes: the Tylers, McKenzies, Moores. These were the HRC ranchers, thirsty for irrigation, to add third and maybe fourth cuttings to their haying season, to add oats and barley and rye and soy to their crops, dairy cattle and hogs to their livestock. It wasn't hard to understand. All this fertile alluvial soil, a promised land of richer and richer crops, given enough water. It all made sense: Dam up the upper valley, with its plentiful water, but where no amount of irrigation would ever generate bounty out of the sparse grass, rocky meadows and dense timber thickets. Land that was nothing but a boulder strewn purchase for immigrants like the Meeks. Who had arrived last and who would only ever have least.

"Tell me one thing," Joe breaking the long silence, "what are you surveying for when the dam site's already been filed and approved?"

"Don't ask me. I just started. Ask Norman; he'd know."

"That's your boss? Norman who?"

"God, I'm later'n hell again, ain't I?" Anne biting her pouty lip. "Well so what? If they fire me, least it'll make mom happy, her and her big ideas for me at the Grand."

Joe looking out the window, not answering, so Wade did. "But seems like you like survey work though?"

"Yeah, maybe I would, if surveyin's what I was doin. But all Norman lets me do is lug chain and tape for those asswipes from Roscoe. They sure don't work any harder'n me, and I know I could learn how to do what they do, but he only gives me stupid work, probly 'cause I'm just a girl and from Meagher to boot. He's such an asshole he shits sideways. I oughta just quit anyway."

"Quit? A job on a survey team, though, and specially young as you are?"

"I'm eighteen. That ain't young. Least out here it ain't. Maybe back east. . ."

Joe ignored her. "There's worse things than bein late. Instead of sulking in like you are now, you could show up all ready and eager to work. Attitude goes a long way."

Wade saw Anne about to erupt, but whatever she was going to say, she thought better of it.

Joe went on. "Ten to one your boss don't even know you're int'rested."

Anne grunted, focused on threading Twenty Mile bridge, its silvered girders bristling with rusting old rivets, shaking from the choppy meltwater. Once across, she geared down, beginning the steep climb up Bitterroot Gap.

"Joe, you could help her learn, maybe. You could teach engineering. Couldn't you?"

Wade didn't see why neither of them seemed to get what a good idea that was. They just went all quiet.

After a while, Anne eased up on her grip. "So. . .Wade told me you grew up out here, I guess."

Joe looked at Wade. Wade shrugged. She went on.

"Kind of hard for me to believe."

"Why's that?"

"I just never knew anyone to ever leave, let alone come back."

"I didn't 'come back'". Joe's voice rising. "It's only to get Frances to sign over, like everybody else is doin, get a halfway decent price so for once make that land pay for all that got put into it, then—I don't know about anyone else, but I leave. First chance I get."

In the narrows of Bitterroot Gap, the previously placid river, high with spring runoff, was now a thundering whitewater torrent.

Wade looked to see what Joe was looking at. In the blue above them, three red-tailed hawks hovered in a heat thermal. He watched them too, then noticed Anne stealing a look Joe's way.

"Joe knew your mom from before too, you know. Right, Joe?

You knew Marly?"

Joe, not listening, or looking like it, eyes fixed above on the lazily soaring hawks.

"Well, did you or not?" Anne asked.

"I knew of her, yeah."

Joe turned in his seat. The road had opened into the Upper Hellwater headlands. Sun streaks between the broken clouds fell on the acres of wet sage brush turning it a gleaming mint. From this vantage, at the crest of the Gap's hard limestone ridge, the delineation of upper from lower valley was stark: Below, verdant and fertile; above; sparse and rocky. Little of it arable. Through this the road continued up the elongated bowl of valley, stretched miles beyond, capped by a field of glacial debris called Sweetgrass Moraine. Above that, the wilderness of Independence Basin, uninhabitable in the extreme, of value only to hunters, mineralogists, and sheepherders, at least in the warmer summer months. Above it all, the remnant skirts of yesterday's storm, the occasional grumble of thunder, vapor laden clouds snagged trying to rise over the Beartooth peaks.

They passed the surviving ranches, the Burchard's, the Gustafsen's, and on toward, at the high end of the valley, the Meeks. Marked by the field where the first homestead burned down. The charred stone chimney standing like some archeological site in the middle of nowhere.

Middle of nowhere, Joe thought. Where people who aren't from anywhere are from. From nowhere you left and to nowhere you return.

At the Meeks turnoff Anne stopped.

"Changed much?"

"How could it?" Joe opened his door. "Wasn't much when I left. Thanks for the lift."

"Stay put; I'll drive you down."

"You'll be late."

"Yeah, maybe. But for the last time."

Seeing her smile, Joe noticed, in the coral of her cheek, a constellation of small moles in the flat next to her ear. A smile formed in response. Anne turned onto the road; Joe turned his face into the cool clean air rushing in his window. The lane, grooved with ruts and gullies, bounced the pickup and passengers, and along with that, the storms in Joe's head. Somehow clearing them up; all the worries—people, places, things that had happened—it was all past, all behind him.

What was there to really be worried about?

What could go wrong?

Chapter 8

JOE STOOD ON the platform bridge, the swollen Hellwater roaring underneath. He hadn't set foot on its rough planks since. . .since the morning he'd left.

Across the bridge, the rambling timber farm house, sheltered under several old cottonwoods. No sign of Frances. No sign of anyone. Just bleating livestock in the fields out back.

He imagined, in the rampaging waters, his father returning home, late, drunk, raging at his obdurate mother, and her tight-fisted grip on his life, plunging his car headlong off the bridge into freezing cascades. And in imagining that, Joe felt another wave of reluctance to cross. Felt fear of making the same mistake.

Wade, waiting alongside, watching back up the road where Anne, having dropped them off, was racing to work.

"Hey Joe? I think Anne. . ."

"What, likes me? You on about that again?"

"Well, yeah, but I mean, I think she does. Don't you?"

Joe picked a blade of grass somehow growing out of a split in one of the bridge planks.

"Come on; let's get it over with. You finally get to meet you a real Meeks."

Once across, a pair of dogs, a large golden and a smaller black, pushed off their hind legs and came up barking, but for all their bravado, they were quickly curling at Joe's feet, then Wade's, pawing and sniffing and rolling between his legs until he couldn't walk.

"*HEY* you dogs!"

A harsh voice broke the air. At once both dogs scrambled to their feet and sidled toward the porch, tails nervously awag. A figure emerged from the shadows, propping itself with both hands on a cane. The big golden's rear end hung back as his front cautiously curved up to her. His smaller black companion cowered behind him.

"Get back t'your hut damn you!"

Their tails stopped midair. They hesitated. The person flinched her leg. They shot off instantly for their hut.

Descending the porch steps, whacking them one by one with her tightly gripped cane, head fiercely upright despite her stooped shoulders and round back, heavy black dress over work pants, face hidden under a torn felt hat, chopped white hair blazing out in back, Wade had never seen anyone quite like Frances Meeks.

Not sure what to expect, everyone waited in place: Joe, Wade reverently behind him, the dogs at their hut, the golden with one forepaw crossed elegantly over the other, the black resting his jaw on the golden's neck. Their tails flicked, their eyes darted, but both stayed fast as Frances haltingly caned her way, not to greet them, but to an old silver jeep parked on the grass.

"You wanted to see me?" Joe finally said.

"Now I seen you."

Frances hoisting herself into the jeep, which took a few tries. She knocked Joe's hand away when he tried to help. She started the engine, backed into the road, then paused a minute, eyes front.

"You've looked better."

She ground the gears and rattled off in her jeep out to the back pasture.

Wade looked at Joe, puzzled. "Are we going out with her?"

"No, *we* aren't."

Joe watched the jeep leave, then walked back through the yard to the orchard behind the house.

Wade followed, eyes everywhere at once. His feet crunched fallen apples, his hands brushed the white blossoms clinging to the few unbroken branches. The dogs ran bounding through the waist-high grasses; the golden pounced on him, knocking him down, whereupon the black joined in, grappling and nipping. When Wade got to his knees, the golden flipped on his back. Wade scratched his belly, a tangle of long hair and burrs.

"It's so beautiful here, right, Joe?"

Joe raised his palm against the sun. What he saw wasn't beautiful, it was a barren infestation of brome and leafy spurge and blossoming dandelions. . .the perfect plant for Frances, one surly root going down ten times its size, sucking up the last drop of moisture, leeching the land for everything it was worth.

At one point, Wade's movement through the grasses released a flight of insects with dusty green wings.

"What're all those? There's hundreds of them."

"Grasshoppers."

"Are they good for anything?"

"Yeah, they're good for nothing." Joe wiped his forehead. "Whatever's useless, there's always plenty of it up here."

Walking only a few steps farther, Wade spooked up a flash of brown that vanished into a nearby gulch of juniper and chokecherry.

“Ring-neck pheasant, Wade.”

“Man!”

Wade ran after it, the dogs racing ahead, inspired by Wade more than any interest in prey.

Joe went into the stackyard, what there was of it, mostly just strands of barbed wire hanging between fallen down posts, which left the measly hay unprotected and ravaged by deer. He toed a loose bale, and the rotted twine snapped, spilling its sheaf of moldy feed. A bull snake moved sluggishly under another bale, rattling annoyance.

Wade came back, brandishing a thorny branch thick with blackish red berries. “What’ll happen if I eat these?”

“Nothin. They’re just pretty bitter is all.”

“Okay, here goes.” As soon as Wade bit, the pulpy berries sucked the tissues of his mouth dry, coating his teeth. He spit out.

“Ugh, worse than medicine.”

“That’s why they’re called chokecherries.”

Wade looked at the juice stains on his palms. “You think Indians used them for war paint?”

“What Indians? Meeks are about the only people dumb enough to live up here. It’s one god-awful waste, you ask me.”

The rest of the morning they sat in Frances’s house, waiting. The air was heavy with mildew from the pasteboard walls. Every so often, Joe got up from the bentwood rocker and paced. Examined the old shotgun stacked on a rack of antlers.

Fingered dust off the mangled antenna of a dead Motorola. Held up a pearl-glazed coffee cup, remembering the hard black coffee he'd drunk from cups just like it, morning after morning, sitting at this same table, even before his legs were long enough to reach the floor.

A hall door opened. Joe looked up, expecting. . .he didn't know who, but certainly not the ghostly woman inching her heavy shoes step by step toward the swivel chair next to the table. As she walked, her head bobbed up and down from the loose skin of her sternum, as though her neck had been removed. Her face was sallow, her dress worn. Flesh colored stockings bagged over her ankles. Eventually reaching her destination, she wheezed, then in weary stages lowered herself into the dirty cushions cladding her chair. She seemed to age with every breath.

Once seated, she noticed Wade, and her face wrinkled with a dark smile that opened around her three or four rotting teeth. Wade smiled back, trying not to gape; he had never seen anything so old yet still living.

"This is Emma, Wade. The oldest Meeks sister."

Emma croaked, Wade not sure whether it was words or guttural cleansing. She smiled again then fell dead asleep.

Joe, finding a pair of binoculars, spotting out the window, saw Frances standing over a large red-brown fallen lump.

"The hell with this waiting for her."

"Wait up, I'll go too," Wade called, following Joe out the front.

"Just stay put for now, Wade. I mean it."

Joe headed through the corrals out the gate into pastureland, already hard and dry again from a morning of sun baking out all moisture from yesterday's snow. Here and there, a few scrawny head of cattle grazing leftover winter stubble, eyeing him hopefully, sickly calves, heifers chewing dirt, sheep gouging thistles along the far off fence corners. All of them marked with the familiar three-iron brand: Bar Slash Heart. Frances's brand.

Good riddance to this soon enough, Joe thinking as he headed toward Frances. Nice to imagine all this land—hardened by bitter winters, remorseless summers, and leathery humans—lying under the enormous reservoir of a Bitterroot dam. He agreed now, one hundred percent: best thing for everyone was for Evan Gallantine to get as much as he could for it.

When he reached Frances, he saw the red-brown lump was a bull, dead so recently its belly had not yet bloated. A lariat was lashed around its back legs, and on the other end was Frances, sitting in the shade against the back tire of her jeep. Sweat jewels gleamed in the folds of her forehead. She either didn't hear him arrive or chose not to.

"Looks like it just died last night."

"You come here to tell me that?"

"What d'you think it was?"

"Probly just he got fed up eatin nothin but thistles."

She worked her way to her feet and tied off the rope to the tailgate. Watching, Joe remembered her hand, where there should have been three fingers there were only swollen knuckles grown together. The same disfigured claw he'd seen day after day hooking haybales, milking cows, tossing lambs like sacks of flour.

"You can't let your hired man take care of this?"

"Him? He quit."

"How come?"

"Ever know a man who didn't?" she said blackly.

"Well did you ever try paying him? That sometimes helps."

"You think a man'll work for what I could pay? Even the drunks and old time sheepherders don't bother anymore."

Joe leaned against the wheel well, the metal hot on his back.

"Maybe it's time to call it quits, then."

She turned. "That's what you come to tell me?"

"I came to make clear; I'm not wasting my life stepping in where dad left off."

"You think I'd let you? You'd be even less help than him."

"Still, you can't run all this livestock yourself."

She pulled a thistle from her dress. "That's why I'm sellin em."

"Selling em?"

"Truck's on its way even now. Here I figured at least I'd get a decent price on this bull. Now I don't even get that."

Her steely eyes found his. He looked down. Frances waved her bad hand at the fields.

"Look at it. Even burdock hardly bothers comin up anymore. Buyin feed costs more than I get for the few calves I do manage to get. Half the herd is too old to calve anyway. It ain't worth draggin withered alfalfa mornin and night to keep a few steers and heifers alive. How'm I goin to keep at it, when I can't even feel my feet half the time, I'm so damn old? And there sure ain't no one else gonna do it for me."

"Well whose fault is that?"

"Oh? Think you could'a done better, that's why you're here? Back to run things right? Well maybe so, maybe you'd do fine, for the coupla months you'd stick around."

"I'd stick around if there was the least reason to."

"Oh? Whose side're you on today, or did you forget?"

Joe toed the ground, exposing white tendrils of new growth, life struggling on. Frances got in the jeep; it stalled before budging the carcass even a foot. She tried twice again with the same result.

"Why don't you just leave it?"

"Why, as a callin card for coyotes and timber wolves? It's about the only thing hasn't overrun the place as it is."

"It'll be under a hundred feet of water before long anyway."

"Ha." She tried hauling the bull again, racing the engine so it wouldn't stall, but now the tires only spun uselessly and a cloud of smoke and dust spewed over Joe.

"Untie him then," she said, sliding to the passenger side, "and drive me back; I'm sick've this whole damn. . .everything."

Joe sighed, untied the bull, and got in, placing his hands on a steering wheel grooved to years of her holding it. This wasn't the conversation he wanted to be having. Had he come all this way for nothing, he wondered, staring at the cows who began to circle the jeep, dumb-faced and expectant, as if he'd brought food.

"What's the hold up, let's go. You forget how to drive anything but bulldozers?"

"Maybe so," Joe said, and took off, wheeling through the litter of white boulders and hungry animals. Back in the corral, as he stopped to open the gate, Frances saw Wade standing at one of the pens.

"Now who in hell is that?"

Before Joe could answer, she was out caning her way to Wade like a three-legged bull herself. Joe trailed after. In the pen was a sickly cow, lying on her side, belly distended, eyes glazed and ringed with thick puss, panting and weakly bellering. Wade had his hand through the rails soothing her white forehead.

"What's wrong with it?"

Frances looked her over long and hard. "She's way overdue with her calf. Though doubt she'll make it, way it looks."

Joe shook his head. Was there anything on this place not dead or dying?

"He'll make it, though, won't he?" Wade asked.

"Who he?"

"Her baby calf?"

Frances turned to Joe. "Clear this ain't your boy. Way too optimistic."

She asked Wade his name and offered him her hand. Wade took it, staring at the white and blue flesh where three fingers were missing. He was about to ask her what happened when the cow bellered and kicked.

"Shouldn't we do something?"

"Bout only thing is to shoot. . .put her down."

"You mean, like, with a. . ."

"There's the trucker comin," Joe said, seeing a long livestock tractor trailer navigating the lane toward the house, followed by a pickup pulling a horse-trailer. The semi moved painfully, inching its way carefully on the ungraded road.

"Who's that?" Wade meant the butternut horse with burnt

orange mane standing in the shade where the river ran through the corral.

"That's my sorrel filly there," Frances said.

"He looks like a real good horse."

"Sure she is. Should get a good price for her at least."

Wade, taken aback, said, "You mean, sell her? Why? Don't you, you know, need her for something?"

"No good to me; I got no one to finish breakin her. Though if I remember correct, your dad there could."

"They're here."

Joe pointed across the river, the semi backing up to the bridge, too unsound for it to cross, while the pickup driver let out a saddle from the trailer. Frances waved him over, directing him to the beer she had waiting, gesturing toward the pastures, and what he was to round up.

While her disfigured hand flailed instructions, the sorrel filly sauntered near the saddle horse, a large bay stallion, and the two began to nicker. When she began nipping at his flank, the stallion reared. The cowboy tried to slap her away, but the filly was not about to be put off. As he led his horse out of the corral, she tried to follow. When he closed the gate on her, she banged her sides against it until the cowboy rode out of sight.

Frances scanned the hillsides, its glistening streaks of shade and snow, as though it was her gaze more than the sun doing the melting. Joe opened a beer, more for something to hold than drink.

"Frances? So what happened with my dad, anyway?"

"Leonard?" Frances scoffed. "I'll tell you what. As soon as

they announced that dam, that lackey Gallantine shows up, sweet-talks Leonard, gets him so worked up he couldn't see straight. Yellin about everything, carryin on, drinkin. He'd be in the Gulf of Mexico now but the car he drove off the bridge got snagged between river boulders."

"All Evan's fault, I guess."

"Well it wasn't me killed him."

"You might as well have, holding out like you are. All he ever wanted was to finally get something out of this damn place."

"It ain't mine to give away, Joe. It's Emma's."

"You're custodian. You have the right."

"Meanin I have to do what's right." She lowered her beer can. "Don't s'pose you went to pay him your respects yourself, though. At least I did that much."

"Like you ever had any. How come you haven't roped in your other son by now? Or don't he count?"

"Harlo? That drifter, he's better off in prison. Knowin him he probly prefers it."

Something caught her eye and she looked off. "Damn surveyors."

Joe followed her look. Far off, in the rocky mass of Sweetgrass Moraine, sunlight sparkled on a red pickup.

Anne's, Joe realized.

"Why're they surveyin that far up? No Bitterroot Gap dam would back up a reservoir that far."

"Dam?" Frances spit. "There's gonna be no dam there."

"There sure enough is; why else is everyone but you sellin out?"

"Sellin out?"

"Evan said once I'd made clear I have no interest, you'd finally deed over like Leonard wanted. Like Burchard and Gustafsen already did. So, in case I wasn't clear, I ain't int'rested."

"That don't matter; the last thing I'd ever do is give over this place to any Gallantine."

"You don't have a choice."

"I see you sucked up Evan's crazy ideas just like your dad. There ain't goin to be no dam. It'll never happen. Those HRC folks don't got the money now any more'n they ever did. There's no dam and no reason to listen to any kin of Lillian's." She caught her breath. "I half wish there were, just to be done with it. But I run the place, long as Emma's still with us, that's how mother wanted it and that's how it goes."

Cattle had begun to throng into the corrals, driven by the cowboy, who rode up out of the dust and noise, hollering. Wade leapt off the fence and soon, copying Joe, he was raising his arms, shouting, darting like the well trained dogs, flailing to keep the calves at bay while the cowboy drove the mothers back outside the corral. Once the calves were separated, they did the lambs, then when they were done, they and the dogs forced the jittery bawling yearlings across what they sensed was a treacherous passage. Beyond which waited the menacing hulk of the semi.

When the last of them were loaded, Wade sauntered back, joining Joe and Frances in the corral. Thirsty, helping himself to a beer, to which he clearly felt entitled, though having no idea how it might taste, he sipped it gingerly.

"Is that cow in the barn going too?"

Frances shook her head. "Don't think she's quite up for it."

"Good."

"Good, huh. What d'you mean, good?"

"I want to see a calf born."

"So you think it's gonna make it after all?"

"Why wouldn't it?"

"No reason, I guess."

Wade nodded. As he walked off to the river, Frances drank on her beer, then pushed back her hat.

"Somethin about him at that. Kinda like havin him here." She looked at Joe, then back to Wade. "How he sees things; that look in his eye. Makes you wonder."

"Wonder what?" Joe asked.

"If he were a little older."

Jesus, Joe thought, but kept silent.

At the river bank, Wade ripped a handful of grass and patiently held it out, to get the sorrel filly to come to him. She approached, cautiously stretched out her neck, sniffed. Then suddenly her lips parted, her teeth shot out, and the clump was gone from his hands. Wade jerked back, which startled the filly. She bolted quickly away. Wade, disappointed, went for more grass.

"Frances?" Joe squatted. "Anybody ever say much after I left?"

"What was to say? You did what you did."

"Didn't it matter to anybody? No one ever wondered?"

"What difference did it make? You're the one ran off, not us."

"Sure I did," Joe said, his voice rising. "Because you sons a bitches never cared about anything but this pile of rock dirt."

Frances tamped her cane free of the mud and manure balled up the end.

"You oughtn't go talkin too loud yourself. I ain't so sure you treat your own kid much better yourself."

She planted her cane and hoisted herself up.

"Guess I oughta go invite that horseman to some lunch."

She left. Joe remained, and in the dust and manure and riversmell and bawling cow unable to give birth and mothers crowding outside the corral smelling for their calves and the carcass of the dead bull shimmering in the distance, he remembered again why for sure he never should have come in the first place.

Chapter 9

WADE BROWSED AROUND the house while Frances served the cowhand his lunch; there was little to do and much to ask, most importantly the story of Frances's bad hand, but it wasn't a good time. Joe was out walking the river, Frances staring out the window, the plain-faced cowhand eating a deer sausage and potato salad lunch, and old Emma asleep. No one had much, had anything, to say.

He found some old photographs in a kitchen cabinet, when they were alone, Wade took them to Frances. On top was a photograph of rough miners and primly seated women. He asked about the black-bearded man circled in ink.

"Peter Meeks."

Next was a photograph of a pack horse being struck by lightning, grazing unsuspectingly in the instant of its death; a jagged bolt creased the dark sky to the saddle horn, electricity crackling around the horse's body the way you would imagine but never think it would really appear.

"Just some accident," Frances said, disinterestedly.

Under that was a reaping team of two swayback horses, a wagon of loose hay and four gaunt, climate-hardened figures standing stiffly for the photographer. Wade could identify all but one, the glum young boy with the lowered head. He guessed aloud that the old woman standing to the side was the mother, Peter Meeks's wife. Frances nodded. He guessed that the woman on the buckboard was Emma, seeing in her eyes even then the same black circles she had now. The one holding the team, a young girl in a long dress, he guessed was

Lillian. So the glum young man, he asked, was it Frances's husband?

"Husband? What made you think I ever married?"

Then who was the father of Leonard and Harlo?

"Accidents themselves," she said, her eyes not leaving the window.

"Why? Don't you like men or something?"

She never gave them much thought, they never stick around long enough to bother with anyway.

Then who was that other man in the photograph?

It was no man, she said, at last turning to him. "It's me myself."

Wade looked again and realized it was so.

Just then, through the window, Wade saw the sorrel filly start rampaging in the corral, her sharp hooves thrashing up wet loose manure. With her hind legs she began pummeling the chute where they had penned the stallion saddle horse, who was now heaving himself against the posts that confined him. His efforts excited the filly even more; she slammed the chute with the full weight of her body.

The cowboy flew out from where he'd gone to wash up, racing into the corral, Wade right behind him. With humans on the scene, there was a short hiatus; both horses, male and female, panted, stock still, their flank muscles twitching. The cowboy eased open the chute to pull his stallion out and get him away, but the horse reared and wouldn't come, and the rejuvenated filly tried to get at him with renewed ardor.

The stallion moved after a hard kick in the flank, and while the cowboy dragged him across the bridge, the mighty animal twisted and churned and tried to bite the halter. His shod feet hammered splinters out of the planking, and his neighing sent the filly racing around the corral in frenzied circles, ears down, head horizontal, her bulging eyes wide with desire, oblivious to anything in her path, which happened to include Wade, who stood watching her, transfixed.

"Wade! Get the hell out of there!"

Joe's running up from the river roused Wade out of his trance just in time to make the fence as the filly thundered past him. She halted at the gate as her stallion, fearful of the turbulent river beneath him, forgot her for the moment and nervously allowed himself to be led across. The filly strained her neck over the fence, panting and smelling the air.

Wade felt Joe Meeks grab his arm.

"Better we head back, Wade."

Wade nodded. Midway across the bridge, he stopped.

"What were they doing, Joe?"

"What do you mean?"

"The horses. They weren't fighting, were they?"

"Um, well. . ." He saw the cowhand had loaded his mount and was leaving. "I thought Frances meant to sell that sorrel?"

"I did too, but told me she's keepin her after all."

"She say why?"

"Said she changed her mind is all."

The filly's neighing pierced the silence, as the pickup pulled the trailer, and its stallion, away.

The afternoon passed, the sun waned, cooler air wafted up

from the river. Wade sat with Joe out in the shade of the stackyard while they waited for Anne. Joe, restless, just to pass some time, began to lift some of the fallen bales back up on the stack.

Wade got up to try too; he bucked one up on his knees the way Joe had done, and—to his surprise—found he could raise it above his head.

"Hey Joe. It's lighter than hell."

"It's so dried out, weighs less than feathers. And you can stop with that swearing while you're at it, Wade."

Was he always so tall, Joe wondered, as Wade slapped his hands clean and stepped back to admire the bastion of straw he was restoring.

"Bet you're an expert at this, Joe."

"Yeah, I probably stacked and unstacked quite a few by your age."

"Maybe this summer I will too."

"Except soon enough, they'll build that dam, and you'll need a motor boat instead of a Farmhand tractor."

The stack sagged at the center like a starving animal, old posts jabbed into it to prop it up. Joe gave one a swift, impulsive kick. The rotted post shattered and the entire stack gave way, avalanching them both in dust and hay.

"Holy shit!" Wade cried, thrashing out of the mess, brushing clots of hay off his head and daddy long leg spiders out of his mouth. Joe burst out laughing.

"What's so funny?"

"You," Joe chortled, "you looked so. . .surprised." He laughed harder, and harder still; he couldn't stop. He sunk to his knees in the loose hay, still laughing.

"Well what about you?"

Wade's voice broke; frustrated, he threw a wad more of hay on Joe's head, but the sight of the hay jiggling from his laughter was ludicrous, and Wade felt his own laughter removing the insult he felt he had taken.

"Frances will be mad as hell though, won't she?"

"Tell her," Joe Meeks squawked, tears streaming down his face, "we went for a roll in it."

And so they remained, the stack and dust and hay shaking with their laughing, though it made no particular sense, which only made it more funny. It was a long time until Wade could breathe again, and when he could, he lay under the fibrous mound chewing a fat stalk of clover.

"Joe," he said after a long silence, "I get why you ran away now."

Joe sat up. "You what?"

"'Cause this was such a shitty place to grow up. Right?"

Wade flashed him a toothy grin.

"Yeah, and what did I say about you swearin, Wade?"

They both turned, then, hearing a pickup work its way down along the gulch.

"Anne's here. Joe?"

"Yeah, I see."

But Joe, in his mind, wasn't seeing Anne's pickup, he was seeing an old black Studebaker, one hurtling down that same lane twenty years earlier, and remembering how he had stood up then as he did now, clearing his eyes of sweat and hay dust. He had been high on the haystack helping get feed to the yearlings, Frances with him, cursing for the hundredth time Harlo's slowness returning with the farmhand. But she stopped when she too caught sight of the car. It pounded across the irrigation ditches, barreled up to the stackyard gate, and sprang to a stop. A barefoot person, a girl, flew out, red hair flying. She hurled her door shut and stood, looking all directions, her eyes white. Joe had no idea who she was or why she was there; no one ever came to the ranch, especially no girl. He stood up, twelve tiers above her, naked to the waist. A trickle of dirt and sweat forked mercurially down the small of his back; he shivered ecstatically, despite the heat. Her sickle-sharp eyes darted up to him.

"What're you gawkin at?" she yelled.

He swelled his chest. He felt bold, and didn't answer.

"Feed wagon's due there," Frances said, "so you better get your damn car clear of that gate."

"I know that!"

The girl kicked her car so hard a hubcap rolled off. She kicked it again. She slapped her fists on her hips. "And Harlo ain't gonna get rid'a me so easy as them others."

"Damn him and his little shit-ass females," Frances muttered. She looked to the heavy ball of sun, then threw her old legs over the ladder to climb down, and though that meant quitting time, Joe hardly noticed.

"Look at you," Frances snapped at him, "you barely got your skin on, never mind a shirt, and here there's a female around. You're worse'n a goat in locoweed."

She shook her head, descended and left. Joe watched her thread back to the house. In the shadows back of the barn, a stoop-shouldered statue, his father, stood pressing the brittle teeth of the mower sickles into a grinder. A fireworks of sparks bounced off him. Joe felt dread suddenly, of summer and its hard labor, but even more of the fall. Even as his first year of high school was ending, he dreaded the year to come, and the year after that. . .nothing but cranky teachers and pimply smart-alec town kids for the rest of his life.

His heart sank, and he looked back down. The girl was slumped against her car. She had come for Harlo, Joe didn't know why, but now he felt sorry for her. Far afield, he saw the spurt of black tractor smoke behind the ridge, then just as it came over, the farmhand stopped. When the girl saw it, she trembled.

From his vantage atop the stack, Joe saw what she could not, Harlo sneaking off the tractor and down the gulch, which concealed his route to the house. No intention of letting her find him.

"What d'you want with Harlo anyway?"

"Forget about Harlo."

"What if he don't come?"

She ignored him, sticking insolently to the car, and suddenly Joe knew who she was. His uncle Harlo, who was nearly thirty and still a bachelor, sometimes went to dances in Meagher, and though Joe had never taken any interest before, this last time he waited up to hear every word, so to better know the ways of town kids. But all Joe could get from him was that town girls kept getting so young and spare that he finally just got so drunk he even went after Sheepeater Croft's girl. "She's so ornery, I'd of had better luck wrasslin with his sheep," he had told Joe.

"I know who you are," he said brazenly, "you're Marly Croft."

"And you're a shitkickin steer-fucker!"

Her red hair flashed, a tangle of knots. Her chest rose. She raised up a dried piece of cow dung.

"I'll stuff this in your mouth, you ain't careful."

"Whyn't you come up and try?"

Joe's heart galloped. He teetered on the bale. She glared at him. Neither moved. Late afternoon sun sparkled between the pines along the ridge, leaving a feathery light on the range. The fencelines were green with thistles and the field creamy with last year's fallow straw.

Marly Croft sidled into a slice of sun; her red hair gleamed. "You come down here."

"What for?"

"So I can give you what I meant for your older brother."

"We ain't brothers. He's my dad's brother."

"I don't care if you're cowlickin assholes, just come down here. You afraid of me?"

"Nah."

Joe looked away. He saw his dad had finished sharpening sickles; lights were on in the milking barn.

"Don't you even got a shirt?" she sneered. "How'd you like it if I went around without a shirt?"

"Suit yourself."

She swore, then started up the ladder. Once up, she was taller than Joe expected. And obviously a few years older. He stared at her, she stared back.

"Your dad's Sheepeater Croft. Harlo told me."

"Piss on Harlo." She spit to the ground. "You ain't so shitless yourself. An what're you lookin at?"

The light darkening but clear; her eyes sparkled. Harlo had called her a gap-toothed skag, but she didn't look that way to Joe. Her teeth flashed white and her lips opened, exciting him.

"Don't get any ideas. Kid."

"What ideas?"

"I'll show you what ideas."

She shoved him, and he fell on his back. The hay was sharp, but with the broiling sun all day welding sweat and hay dust like a second skin to him, he felt nothing. He lay waiting for what she would do next. She straddled him. He tried to wrestle her off but she was strong. She sat. "Give this to Harlo," she cried, then all at once she began punching his shoulders like a wild animal, scaring Joe but exciting him more. He held her arms at bay, and she started yelling at him, crying, laughing, he couldn't tell which. Her ratty blouse fell open, baring her breasts, and then Joe, going somehow numb to everything, stopped holding her back altogether. She was rocking back and forward on him, her breasts swaying. Joe no longer cared. His eyes rolled shut. He shuddered, shuddered again, continued to shudder until where she sat on him flooded in a warm wet quaking spasm.

His eyes opened, his brother's burly sheepdog sniffing his head. Joe batted him away, and he yipped, scampering away. There was a head sitting on the edge of the stack. The head with a young boy's face, Scotty, who had trundled up the ladder to stand and watch.

Marly, sitting on Joe's thighs, panting, trance like, glared at him, to go away, but Scotty stepped up another rung, staring back, neither speaking nor leaving.

Joe sat up. "What d'you want, Scotty?"

Scotty pointed to the barn.

"Yeah, okay. You just get on back. I'll come milkin in a bit."

Scotty remained.

"How come he don't say nothin?"

"'Cause he ain't quite right, is all. Scotty, quit starin and get goin."

But only when Joe stood did the boy and his dog quickly vanish.

Joe swayed on his feet, hard to hold steady, his ears humming loudly. Marly blouse-less, hay-dusty, sweaty, smeared her forearm across her mouth.

"Lookit you. All puffed up. Like you stole something Harlo probly never even wanted anyway."

She snatched up her blouse, flung it at Joe, and climbed down. Joe stood at the stack edge as she drove off, then lay back. The hay bristle gouged his back; he was not feeling so thick-skinned now. He lay a long time, weak and pleasantly tired. In no hurry to go get his whipping. It could wait.

He put Marly's blouse over his face and breathed.

ANNE'S PICKUP PULLED to stop; she waited, the engine idling. Joe momentarily forgetting who or where he was, took a deep breath. His lungs swelled, his nostrils singed, the odors of earth and decay. He stood, tenuously, echoing with daydream afterimages, then followed Wade, like a weary cavalcade of two, to the pickup.

On the drive down, Wade feigned sleep. The center of his vision was disappearing again, but he hoped maybe this time the raging headaches and flaming lights would not follow.

For what seemed hours, Joe as silent as Anne, Wade off and on realizing he'd let his forehead roll onto her shoulder. Which was comfortable, and she didn't seem to notice, but it occurred to him it must hard for her to steer, so he leaned away. And off and on realized it was lolling onto Joe's shoulder.

In time, it grew dark. Ranch house lights miles away, blue and luminous, the sky ticked with stars, an impending quarter moon etched the eastern ridge.

"Might want to turn on your headlights now."

Anne wordlessly switched on the lights. Wade saw their reflections, all three, curling up onto the black windshield. She turned on the radio, which only crackled with static, signals lost to the stellar confusion that was night over the Hellwater.

"Guess you weren't fired after all," Joe observed to the window.

"What makes you think that?"

"You seem different."

"Differnt what?"

He didn't answer. She turned off the radio.

"You were wrong about one thing anyways. About Norman. Son of a bitch chewed me out first thing. Said one more stunt like that and it'd be my last."

"So what'd you do, scratch his eyes out?"

"Just about. I started to get all riled but. . .I don't know, I just bit my tongue. Told him I was sorry. Wouldn't happen again. He just nodded and walked off." She took a deep breath. "Thinkin about it, it makes me nervous now."

"How come? He didn't fire you."

"At lunch, instead of eatin by myself again, I sat near him. He eats by himself too, only but a few minutes, then starts to work again, so, this time, stead a takin the full half hour, I kinda just got up when he did. He didn't seem to mind, or even notice, me standin there, while he was readin figures from the log books each team keeps, makin some calculations, then writin other numbers on one of those big maps. I never paid much attention to em, but all of a sudden I recognize the section where we'd been workin. It just leaped out at me, all the coulees and the notches, like a picture developin right under my eyes. Next thing I know he's got me readin from the log so he don't have to look back and forth, and he's snappin at me just like he does the other guys. When it occurs to him I'm s'posed get back out haulin chain, and he sees everybody else still lazin away on their half hour, he said to pair up with him, and let those Roscoe boys carry chain. So all day I got to work the, what d'you call it, that telescope thing."

"Transit?"

"Yeah, transit. Then after work, I got up my nerve to go let him know I was int'rested in learnin more, like you said this morning. And how much I'd liked helpin out that day. He asked if I meant it. Well I did, so he gives me a book, and tells me he'd appreciate it if I'd read a certain section of it. 'Cause if I learned more or less of it, it'd help free him up for other work he wanted to get to."

Anne had started to speed while she was talking, nauseating

Wade as the pickup zoomed headlong over the gravels quick rises and low troughs. Joe asked, politely, if she'd mind slowing down. She did, and apologized, and the rest of the drive was as smooth as it was dark.

Despite, or because of, the grinding flashing lights in his head, Wade gradually lost consciousness, sleeping the rest of the way to Meagher.

SOMEONE SHAKING HIM. Wade tried but couldn't raise his head. He wasn't asleep, but wasn't awake. Someone spread a coat over him. It smelled of Joe.

"We'll just let him alone, then," Joe's voice.

"Leave him here?" Anne's voice.

"Yeah, well, you can see he's dead out."

"Can't you just carry him up? I'll help."

Silence.

"I'll just do it."

Joe's arms around him. Tugging. Lifting.

"Gettin bigger'n I thought."

More lifting. Grunting. In the end, Joe needed her help.

Chapter 10

IT SEEMED EARLY; it seemed late. Joe lay on the floor watching the yellow traffic light blink on and off. Wade asleep on the bed where he and Anne put him after carrying him up.

Some headlights pooled slowly on the ceiling, then swept down the wall to the floor, then gone.

Maybe hours, maybe minutes, Joe lay awake, thinking about the day with Frances. How coming back hadn't made no difference. Worse, after only a day out here, he felt like he'd never left. More than ever in his life, he did not know what came next.

Dim noise from The Mint welled up through the floorboards. The flat thump of the jukebox. The click of billiard balls. The banter between old timers. Marly, her words indistinguishable, but not her laugh.

Headlights passed a second time. Joe looked out his window. The same car from the night before outside Anne's window. And again, too, sounds of whispering boys. Clinking bottles. But this time, no answer. No window arguments, no screen door slapping shut behind her. In a while, the car left. Empty handed.

Joe sat in the chair, propped his feet up. Maybe he slept, mostly he churned. Marly's laugh kept waking him up. Sleep just not a possibility, finally he went out and down the lobby stairs. A loose tread screeched, announcing his entrance.

Behind the bar, a man in black vestments and a clerical collar was washing a hi-ball glass. He filled it with gin and sipped, licking the hairline mustache on his upper lip. Seeing Joe, he poured another, which Joe declined, so the man shrugged, disappointed, then downed both glasses almost instantly. In the mirror behind the bar Joe saw Marly come out of the kitchen, straightening her hair. In the neons of bar light, it gleamed of red honey.

The man in clerical garb greeted her with a cheek kiss. "Arrivederci," he gurgled, nodded to Joe and left, chanting to himself.

Marly continued behind the bar.

"What'll you have, Joe?"

Joe stood up. He sat down. On the chair, but only the very edge.

"Joe, for Christ's sake, it ain't a trick question."

Someone guffawed, a one-eared man standing at the end of the bar, wearing the fold-down rubber boots of an irrigator.

Joe surveyed the bottles stacked against the mirror and saw one with liquor the color of her hair.

"I'll try that there."

"Rocks or straight up?"

He looked at her. "Rocks?"

"With ice or without?"

"Oh. I guess it don't matter."

She sloshed a glass full of the liquor, slid it to him, and slung herself up on her bartender stool.

"You're up kinda late."

"Oh, yeah." He looked at the gold-plate flower-work clock reflecting reds and blues of the neon beer sign in the window. "You probly want to close up."

"No, finish your drink. Stay late as you want, I can just leave you help yourself. Week nights I won't have much business now."

The one-eared irrigator abruptly belched, tipped Marly good-night, and stumbled out, leaving Joe the lone client. He sat, drinking whatever it was, feeling it warm his insides. Marly cleaned a few already clean glasses; Joe studied the sanctuary of liquor bottles stacked against the mirror. It was an old mirror, its silver peeling, and everything it reflected looked worn and dirty. Including him.

Marly poured herself a silver cup of scotch.

"You're about the last person in the world I would of ever expected for a guest last night."

Joe nodded, toying with his glass, which she thought meant he wanted another. She filled it until liquor overflowed on the bartop.

"You look like maybe it didn't go too well with Frances today."

In the mirror, he saw what she meant. Haggard. Low down. Worn.

Cup raised to her mouth, Marly looked at him, then drank. The liquor glistened on her lips.

"Funny thing just came to my mind seeing you now."

"Yeah. I can probly guess."

"Nothin bad. Just how you still wear a crew cut. I realized I never known you with hair."

"And I never known you without."

She laughed and untied her hair, making it longer, making it redder, making it thicker.

"So. . .what's your old lady do?"

"Old lady?"

"Well since you got your boy along, I figure there's a mother in the picture somewhere."

"Well, no. I mean. . .see, his mother only just died, and he's not. . .I'm just trying to help out."

She looked at him. A flash of blue neon across her eyes.

"Well, it's none of my business anyways. Speakin of hair, it's time for me to get out of yours."

She rose, to leave. And didn't. Instead, she poured each another round. Leaned forward, arms on the bar.

"Six months from now, you won't recognize this place. Already got a stone man contracted to come shine up the marble outside, and that's not even the beginning of it. Once that dam goes up, the business'll be rollin in. Evan was just this morning talkin about how attractive this valley'll become with some development. Hollywood north. Ha. But I guess it could be, so many big shots nowadays that need a place where they can all get away and be normal rich people together."

She leaned closer, lines winking around her eyes while she pointed out the timber beams and tin ceiling and how rich people liked all that nowadays, looking around like her Grand was the eighth wonder of the world. "Here's where I clip out all my dreams," she said, pulling out several hotel trade magazines. She ran her fingers on the glossy photographs, murmuring about conversations with Evan, how clever he was about finance and real estate and renovation. How her Grand would soon be swelling with engineers, surveyors, earth-movers, and in a year how corporation retreats, celebrity ranches, condominiums and ski slopes would bring bags of money to Meagher.

"Joe, it's what we always imagined but a thousand times over. Remember us wantin like crazy to go out into the world, and now look, I don't have to go anywhere. Here it is comin to me."

All the more Marly rhapsodized about it, all the more Joe felt blue about it.

"And so good for Annie, especially. You know she's—well I guess you wouldn't know, would you—how she's always had a mind of her own. . .like with this waste of time survey job, but she's got to learn it don't last. It's been hard with her, droppin out of school, actin like she don't care about anything but boys and booze, but she'll see. One a these days. What a great opportunity this is. She's a good kid at heart. You'll see."

Joe nodded, realizing what a small speck in Marly's life he'd been, A few summer months. Out of all her years.

"One thing I could never understand, Joe. How you could ever leave all this? There's days I'm crossin the street, I look up, there's peaks glistening any which way you look, and I just can't imagine why would anyone ever want to go anywhere else."

"Yeah, it's. . .somethin," Joe said, spirits falling. What could be better than the place she described?

"This town is goin to boom, Joe; I hope you appreciate what Evan's doin here."

"If it's gets Wade a good home, that's enough for me."

Marly tossed back her head and drank.

"Imagine you might feel a little sad too, though. Losin the ranch and all. Too bad you couldn't somehow keep it."

"Yeah, well Marly, it ain't even mine to keep."

Now Joe stood to leave. And didn't.

"Joe?" Marly touched his fingers. "I am glad to see you again." She withdrew her hands and folded them in her lap. "We all felt bad after Scotty died too; nobody ever said it was your fault."

"Maybe they never said it."

"What they said was, why did he go and run off, anyway. That's what nobody can understand. Least of all me."

"What's to understand?" Staring into his drink. "There was nothin for me here."

Joe noticed the anger in her eyes as they flashed up at the clock.

"No, I guess not, was there?"

She rose to flick off the neon signs, darkening the bar even more.

"Can't blame a man for wantin to get out in the world. And. . .you found what you wanted, I guess."

She walked to the front to lock the main entrance, then headed to the back and up the stairs.

"Help yourself to anything, Joe. Just kill those lights when you're done."

JOE SAT TIMELESS time. Fingerpainting in the film of liquor under his glass. Feeling small when he had meant to be big. Purging persistent thoughts, of Marly now, of then, of the days following their encounter on the haystack. . .then like now he could think of nothing else. . .

. . .the red-haired Croft girl, how her heat had steeped his sunburned skin, had thickened sweaty cilia on his arms. Unwashed, he fell asleep with her scents at night, woke to her each morning. His daily dread of town school gave way to eager fantasies, anticipating a second vision.

For three straight days, the school bus stopped at the cut bank along Sheepeater Croft's place; for three straight days, his daughter didn't appear. Then she did, the fourth morning, at the last minute, bolting out of the adjacent sheep wagon, half-dressed, just in time.

As ever, in the same soiled incompletely buttoned ankle-length dress, she walked the gauntlet to the back, past all the other ranch kids, knotted in unwelcoming groups, of girls covering their giggles, of boys pelting spit-wads and catcalling animal grunts. But this time Marly Croft didn't hiss back like always, bubbles of drool in the corner of her mouth, eyes rolled back her eyes show only the whites, didn't lift her dress to flash herself, and cause uproars of girls shrieking disgust and boys howling obscenities. This time, she was impervious to the rain of insults, silently ignoring them, continuing with purpose toward the back, all the way back, to Joe Meeks.

Where she stopped.

Different, cacophony quieted in puzzlement.

Where always before she was just another scourge to avoid,

now visions of her nakedness, her young womanhood. . .he couldn't look but at the floor.

So it stood, strangely tranquil, different, the cacophony quieted by puzzlement, until she sat down next to him.

When pandemonium erupted. Word spread like fire. When classes let out that day, Joe found himself surrounded by a weaving tribal circle of town kids, which opened only to deliver Marly, goading her with sticks as though afraid to touch her, shoving and kicking her together with Joe. "Kiss, lovebirds!" they chanted, "Kiss!" It was a new dimension of torment, and Marly went crazy, leaping headlong into her attackers, scratching and grabbing hair. Joe, whirling and spinning and lovesick, tried to get her away, delighting the raucous town kids even more, and they jeered with redoubled viciousness.

The next day, it all ended. That morning, as the school bus passed Sheepeater Croft's, their motorized sheep wagon headed south into the mountains. Marly did not get on the bus that day, or any day thereafter. Joe found out that every spring Sheepeater Croft awoke from his long winter's drunk to herd some lower valley rancher's sheep to the summer meadows of Independence Basin, yanking his daughter out of school to help him with his labors.

Those last days of school Joe spent listlessly looking out windows. He had never missed another living thing like this in his life.

THE MINT, THE hotel, the night, dead quiet. Joe by himself. Behind the bar. Sampling shot by shot each bottle lined up on the back counter, left to right, front to back. None of which, so far, had made a drop's worth of difference.

"You're still at it, Joe?"

He saw her first, a granulated apparition, wavering in the mirror.

Marly again.

"Here she is." Joe took a soap-stained glass from the sink, sloshed a honey-colored liqueur into it.

"One more round for the lovely first star of morning."

She stayed her ground, kept back, next to the pool table, smoothing a rip in the threadbare green velvet.

"Not in a drinking mood, I guess?"

"In the mood to get somethin off my chest."

Joe nodded, tipped his glass to her, woozy, light headed.

"You had me going that summer, Joe, you and all your plans, all the ideas you had for us. Even after you took off without me, I knew you'd be back. You'd work out whatever you felt, Scotty dyin, and be with me soon enough. Years I figured that, Joe. Then after that, years I hated you. Not till today, I never saw it no other way." She folded herself in her arms, looked down, then up again. "Now, I can only say thank you. One way or another, whatever happens, or don't, the waitin, the hatin, is over. I'm sorry, Joe. Don't hold it against me."

Joe reached for another bottle, and its dark green syrup contents.

"Fortunately for me, bartender, I'm all drunk," Joe said to his mottled looking self in the mirror. "These people; drive a man to drink. Here's to feelin no pain."

He saw, thought he saw, Marly gone. He drained his glass,

dutifully fumbled and found and switched off all the lights, made his way to the lobby. Stopped at the foot of the stairs, sensed more than saw her, inches from him, but nearly invisible. As though it could see in the dark, her palm found his cheek. Resting there, familiar, warm, steadying him in his swaying stupor.

Then gone. Footsteps up the stairs. The light creak creak on their loose treads.

Chapter 11

WADE, WHEN HE woke, dreamily dreaming, his headaches were gone.

And so was Joe.

Not in the room, not down in the lobby. Not in the cafe, the bar, not up or down any street, the sheriff's office, the filling station, nor any other place Wade found open. He stood out on the pre-dawn street, kicking gravel back and forth, wondering: had Joe left him. Had Joe actually really finally gone and left him.

Back in The Grand, Wade sat in the booth in back, weighing his options. He'd be okay; he just needed attitude. Like Joe told Anne. It was all about attitude. He'd just need to think of something, so he thought what that something could be. For instance, in only one day in Meagher he already knew people, so like, for instance, Frances; he could feed animals and stack hay for her. Anne; he could help carry chain for her. Marly; clean or do dishes, trading for food.

Thinking of food, he realized then that, first, he was famished, second, he didn't have any money. When at the same time, he felt a hand tousle his hair.

"How's it going, chief?"

Wade looked up. Through the cloud of cigarette smoke: Evan Gallantine. And Wade sat back, happy.

"I'm all better; I have to ask you something."

"That's the ticket. Good man."

Evan taking a seat, when Anne came out, rushing to and late for work, but seeing Wade, she stopped. Taking in that it was just the two of them.

"Where's Joe Meeks at?"

"He's gone."

"He ain't goin up the Hellwater with me today?"

"No, he's. . ."

Noticing her mother heading toward them, Anne glanced at the wall clock and took flight out the front. Evan crushed out his cigarette, souring the air with the after burn.

"So actually, where is the better half, Wade?"

"Wade *is* the better half, ain't you noticed?" Marly joining them, toweling her hands. "Joe's up sleepin it off no doubt."

"No, Joe's gone." Wade leaned toward Marly. "I have to ask you something."

"What d'you mean, gone? Gone where?"

"Just gone, you know; gone gone."

"No, Wade," Evan said, "we only mean where did he. . ."

"Really, you guys. I mean, he's not upstairs, he's really just. . ."

"Never mind." Evan rose. "Now I get you. Come on, Wade."

THE PICKUP SPED across the open meadows where the Hellwater meandered along the lower basin plateau before plummeting down the front range into the great eastern plains. Wade in the passenger seat, leaning almost into the windshield, scanning for any sign of Joe Meeks.

"He can't be far," Evan Gallantine mused, "though he made it further than I'd imagined he would. He must have left in the middle of the night."

"Maybe he hitched a ride."

"Not a chance. Not since, back several years ago, a local ranch hand picked up a couple young hitchhikers on this same stretch. Those freaks befriended the poor guy, led him to somewhere remote, then ate him."

"Ate him?"

"Uh huh. Bludgeoned him, cooked him, lived off him, then disappeared. A game warden found the leftovers, but not those two. They got caught long after, completely by accident, picked up in some unrelated drug sting in Colorado. When they had to empty their pockets, cooked fingers spilled out. There's no chance Joe hitched a ride."

"Yeah but I bet Joe doesn't know, though."

"No, probably not. A lot of things he doesn't know."

Wade spotted him first, standing in a turnout of windswept spruce, lit by the first rays of sun, jutting his thumb out at them.

"Look at him, Wade. Would you pick him up?"

Certainly he looked unsavory: Matted bristle of hair, unshaven face, his shirttails out. Evan pulled over; Joe shuffled up, then stopped short.

Evan rolled down the window and called back, "You forgot something, Joe."

Wade jumped out, but stayed by the pickup, Joe keeping his distance. Evan rested his arm on the window, letting the standoff run its course.

"Evan? I hope you know by now, there's no more reason for me to stay here."

"Oh? Why is that?"

"Frances's never goin to sign on to it. No how no way."

"Is that a fact?"

"You bet it is. Why should she? There's no dam ever goin to get built. And no premium for her to sell that land."

"She showed you her crystal ball?"

"Hellwater Reservoir don't have the money and never will."

"Wrong-o potato head." Evan got out. "They not only have the money, they have a hard deadline. I'll tell you why. The reason I had to drive back to Billings yesterday? A meeting, the HRC board with Arapahoe Oil, a huge regional energy company. Arapahoe owns most of the recoverable soft coal rights all over the front range. Turns out they've done millions worth of R&D on a new technology that converts this coal to liquid fuel. Which means now they can transport it straight to the Gulf by their own, existing pipelines. Not railroad. Which means? They're going to make a goddamn killing."

Evan shielded his brow, the orb of rising eastern sun directly in his eyes. Joe reached down for a handful of gravel and began to toss stones one by one. A lone eagle dipped in and out of the cottonwoods lining the Hellwater.

"This conversion technology though, it needs water. A lot of water. So, enter Hellwater Reservoir Corporation. As of yesterday HRC is under contract to Arapahoe to provide that water. This dam, Joe? It's not just some puddle water for a few hard scrabble ranchers needing irrigation. HRC has three months to start work. Or the deal ends."

Evan leaned against the hood.

"Joe, take your time, let that sink in, so to speak. But that dam is going to be built and built soon. Hundreds of millions are at stake. Meaning, once I package it all up and bring everyone in, which at this point means only Frances, all that land will get far fatter prices than I first thought."

Sunlight rose in layers over the mountainsides, turning the sage brush meadows turquoise. Shadows of dew twinkled black then blue then silver. Joe threw some more stones at nothing in particular.

"It ain't Frances's land, Evan. It's Emma Meeks's."

"True. God only knows why. But that means nothing now. The state already granted contingent approval, which means eminent domain law takes precedence. It's only a matter of time" He lit a cigarette. "We're not asking Frances to like it. Burchard and Gustafsen sure didn't, and they're just as ornery and obstinate. As Emma's custodian, Frances has no other choice."

Joe toed the gravel. "She don't trust you, Evan. She still thinks Lillian's usin you to steal it all away from her. Like she always meant to."

"Just because my mother is equally entitled to her share doesn't mean she's stealing anything. We're a family and we have to act like one. If it weren't for me. . .whatever, but I'll tell you this: Every one of us—including that old goat—will get a whole lot more than that wasteland will ever be worth."

"You're all heart."

Evan threw down his cigarette, opened his door, didn't get in.

"Joe, I'll go with you to talk to Frances one more time. Once she knows just how much we stand to make, you can't honestly think she won't listen?"

Joe gazed over the open range around him; watered by the recent snow, lush migratory greens now covered the land all over except where red rimrock chiggered its surface. He could picture the water canals to come, lacing the fields, winding around slopes, oblivious to property. Water never had trouble knowing which way to go.

"I oughta just go back to work," he muttered. "The hell with all this."

"But you don't have a job, Joe," Wade said. "Do you?"

Joe guffawed loudly enough that the antelope grazing nearby raised their wary ears.

"Joe, give it some more time; no reason to leave just yet."

Joe, clearly lost in thought, tossed another few stones, then cast them all away.

"All right. One more day. After that, I don't give a damn; I'm leaving."

He walked to the pickup.

As Evan pulled out and turned around, his two passengers watched the antelope, their hides and the grasses under them rippling with capricious breezes stirred up by the early morning exchanges between earth and sky. Wade sighed.

"I sure would've liked to be the first human to ever come here, right, Joe?"

The lone eagle he had been watching came to roost in a tall cottonwood.

"Far's I can see, Wade, you might just be the first."

JOE, ALONG WITH Evan, arrived that night, Frances already at dinner, sawing at a chop of mutton, rusty boning knife clutched in her two-fingered hand. Emma in her rocker, head lying flat on her old bosom, legs splayed, black-ringed eyes closed.

"You two may's well sit down and eat her food; she ain't goin to. Where's that boy'a yours?"

"Stayed in town. Tired out I guess."

Frances braced herself, got up, hobbled into the kitchen. She returned with a blackened skillet, from which she tore out three remaining chops and put them on a plates, then drained skillet grease over them.

Evan took a chair and lit a cigarette.

"Smells just scrumptious, Frances. But much as I'd like to, I have to decline. Because of my ulcer."

"Suit yourself. Joe might still know what's good for him anyways."

She pushed the plate to Joe, who in fact was very hungry, and immediately ripped into them. While he ate, no one spoke. Evan smoked. The only sound was the occasional beller of the pregnant cow across the river.

Emma twitched suddenly, gasped faintly, then was quiet. Frances went over to her, looked at her, then sat back down. When Joe finished, she cleared the food and took scraps out for the dogs. Through the porch door, he saw the dogs sniff the bowl and back away.

He gauged Frances to clearly know why they had come, yet she seemed uninterested. To have softened somehow. And Joe began to feel a little more at ease. He glanced at Evan, who winked as he smoothed back his hair over the crown where it was thinning.

"Frances? Joe and I have a lot of respect for the responsibility you feel for this place. That's why. . ."

"Why we figure you might listen to reason this once," Joe added.

Frances raised the part of her forehead where an eyebrow used to be. "When I hear some I will."

She pushed him a pan of chokecherry-rhubarb pie, the center fallen, the edges baked away from the tin, the crust wooden, the filling sour, but Joe devoured it anyway, spooning a gob of cream from the crock to cut the sharp bitter taste.

Evan rubbed at the yellow film on his nails. "What I need to explain. . ."

"Save your breath, Evan. The place ain't mine to give over to anyone. Even if I wanted."

"Actually, as custodian, you have the legal right to do whatever is in Emma's best interest."

"Till she dies." She drummed two fingers on the oilcloth. "Years ago when mother made up her mind leavin the place to Emma, since Emma would never have no mind for that kind of thing, she also made up her mind that when she went, the place went to Leonard. Him and only him. Nobody else."

"Only him?" Joe demanded.

"It's what she said. So that's what goes. Since you're his son, and since he's dead, well, I guess that leaves only you, don't it?"

Joe pushed back from his seat.

"See there, Evan? We should've known better than think we

could talk to her like a normal person."

"I wasn't talking of normal people, as I recall, Joe. I was talkin of you. Not someone with any common sense."

"As if she had any," Joe said to Evan.

"If you had some yourself, you'd get it straight, Joe. What side'a the fence you're on."

Frances caned over to Emma, planted herself behind the rocker and looked straight at Joe.

"Joe? I guess it's time you might as well know. Emma here was Leonard's mother. Not me."

Evan stopped in mid-inhalation. Joe threw up his hands. Stood. Sat.

"Goddamn! Is there any end to this bullshit?"

"No need for your damned cussin, if it's all the same to you."

Evan leaned forward. "What do mean? Leonard was. . ."

Frances spoke flatly to the window. "I raised Leonard from a baby, same as his twin, Harlo. But the sorry fact is they was both Emma's. The way Emma used to sneak out in the fields, we figure it was some old sheepherder; they're the only ones low enough to take advantage of a simple girl like she was. She never had but the wits of a child, let alone a mother. So obviously there weren't much choice but to raise the child myself. Even so, Emma bore Leonard, which makes his son Joe here her only surviving heir, not me, and that's how it is."

"My god." Evan took a flask from his jacket and drank. "So. . .Joe would own the ranch. . .if. . ."

"I knew better than to come back. I never should'a. . ."

Joe, holding the wall, feeling light-headed, abruptly walked outside for air. Despite the day's heat, now it was cold out. When he came back, Evan was helping Frances wash dishes in the galvanized steel tub. Joe sat back at the table. He stared at Emma. He got up and stood beside her rocker. He nudged her.

"What they hell're you doin?" Frances said, wiping her hands.

"Wakin her up. I want to hear it from. . ."

"Don't be a damn fool."

"I'm not a damn fool."

"Seems to me you are. Can't you see she's dead?"

Chapter 12

WADE WOKE DURING the night; laughing downstairs in the Mint. Marly. Evan. Not Joe Meeks. He woke again, and quiet. And so, several more times, each time, not sure where he was, each time a bit scary, until he made himself remember. So much had happened, all in a few weeks: his first big city, his first birthday party, his first plane ride. His first ranch. His first real relative. His first vacation, really, and with his father too. He had gone from the worst day ever, his mother's funeral, to the best. More excitement in the days since Evan Gallantine had shown up than in his entire twelve years. He felt so lucky he felt guilty. Just thinking about it he couldn't go back to sleep. When he saw it getting light, he went downstairs.

Anne under a bright lamp in the lobby, pulling her hair, intently reading. Lamplight shone on her neck; Wade followed it down the milky white curve within her half-buttoned shirt. Pretending to browse the phone book, he stepped nearer. Anne looked at him, then went back to reading. He moved nearer still.

"You mind?"

"Are you reading the surveying manual your boss gave you?"

"Mine to know; yours to find out. Joe comin this morning?"

Wade didn't know.

"Annie? That you?"

In one movement Anne swept her reading material into a satchel as the stairs creaked and Marly appeared.

"You're up this early, honey?"

Noticing Wade, Marly turned to him. "Joe stayed up the Hellwater last night, sweetheart." She gently felt his forehead above his injured eye. "Old Emma Meeks died yesterday."

Wade nodded, not really listening; her hand cool, soothing. Marly went on.

"Evan's sure tickled, that's clear. I didn't quite follow it all, but turns out somehow Joe owns the ranch now. Guess he can't get away quite so soon as he wanted. Lucky us, huh Wade?"

Wade nodded. The lobby door opened. Squash Maloney walked in. Half asleep, but not so much he couldn't throw Anne a hurt, angry look.

"What's he doin here?" Anne asked, suspicious.

"I have to get help from somewhere, honey. Since you're up, I want you. . ."

"I'm goin in early, Mom; I can't."

"Not till six thirty."

"No, I'm ridin with Norman today; he'll be pullin up any minute."

Marly started to raise her voice when two guests came down the stairs, the two smiling Asian men Evan was with their first night in Meagher. A third, much younger, in a suit like the others, carried their luggage. Evan met them outside and the four got into a waiting black sedan and drove off.

"Listen, Annie," Marly said, "Push is comin to shove here, so this surveyin business is gonna have to end sooner or later. I just cannot do without some help."

"Fine, you got Squash now."

Squash, despite the oscillating bewildered looks from Marly to Anne, was for the most part still asleep.

"No, not fine. I need a partner, Annie; like I told. . ."

"Well I ain't that partner."

She stood up defiantly.

"I could help," Wade interjected.

"There. There's your partner, mom. Use him."

A horn sounded out front; she grabbed her satchel and ran out.

"I thought maybe I could help Joe out, Marly, and start taking care of myself."

Marly sighed. She put her inside wrist on Wade's forehead again.

"The swelling's gone down. It's gettin better?"

"Just some headaches now and then."

Marly poked Squash in the arm; his eyes fluttered open.

"All right, Mr. Maloney, let's get you goin; there's half dozen highway department people stayin here tonight, and their rooms need to get ready."

She nudged him toward the cafe, turning back to Wade.

"Since you and your dad might be around a while longer, I don't know but that we couldn't work somethin out. But first, young man, you get yourself over to the clinic. Have Edna give you somethin for those headaches. This afternoon, once I get Squash goin, you come start by helpin me out upstairs. Okay by you? Partner?"

"Okay by me," Wade grinned.

A MAN WITH a clerical collar and black clothes approached the clinic as Wade was going in. Wade recognized him from the Mint, though it wasn't until now, close up, that he realized that the line of dirt along his upper lip was in fact a narrowly cropped moustache. The man deferred to him with a grand sweep of his arm.

"After you, my lamb."

"It's okay, you go ahead."

"No, no; I insist. For unto us a child is given. Please. Go in."

Inside, behind a counter, was a very, VERY fat woman. She sat on two rolling chairs lashed together in tandem. Her flesh spread over every side; though she pressed her thighs close together, her knees could not get within a foot of each other. Her two beady eyes scowled up at Wade over a pair of bifocals, then forgot him altogether when the religious-looking man stepped in.

"At last," she cried. "You'd be the new clergyman Sheriff McComb said might stop by. We have the hitch-hiker he collared right back here, Mister, um, sorry, I don't recall your name."

"If you would," the man said, "I prefer to be addressed as Father."

"Well of course; my pleasure, Mr. Father," she said, all excited, "and such a nice name, too. Now if you'd come straight back with me, you can have your look at him, but I do want to tell you," she whispered, leaning forward as much as she was able, which wasn't much, "he's quite suspicious looking. I'm thinking—and see if you don't agree with me on this—that he's way more than a run-away. No sir, he's most likely a dangerous escapee. I sure doubt you would ever want such a renegade as him to be your acolyte or what have you. I myself told McComb he ought better lock him up before he does something gruesome. Such characters we get around here; you'll see, Mister Father."

"I'm sure I will, Mrs. . ."

"Maloney, Mrs. Maloney," she beamed, "but Edna's just fine."

"I'll have a look just as soon as you administer to my anonymous young companion, Mrs. Maloney. Inasmuch as he was here first."

He sat on a waiting chair, leaving Wade standing alone before her.

"I see," she said sternly.

Weathering her fearsome glare, Wade supposed she was Squash's mother, since they had the same last name, and now he felt sorry for Squash, understanding why he might have problems when it came to girls.

"If you're here about your head, young man, it looks fine to me."

Her flat puffy nose jiggled when she spoke. "I know," he said, "but Marly. . .Mrs. Croft. . .told me to tell you to have the doctor give me something for my bad headaches."

"You can't deceive me as easy as you presume. First off, she ain't married and ain't no "Mrs." part of the Croft name. Second off—which Marly knows as well as anyone—there's no doctor here."

"But isn't this the clinic?"

"Of course it is, but before I call Billings and request a

visitation, I must first deem it necessary." She rifled papers at him. "Here, fill this out and this and this too."

"No, it's all right," Wade said, turning to leave. "It's nothing I'm not used to."

"Hold on there, young man; where do you think you're going? You may not just walk in here and leave, a complete and utter stranger. We need to know what's going on here."

She flailed the forms at him. Wade filled out what he could, using Meeks as his last name, just to show her he was no complete and utter stranger.

"What's this?" she said, pointing a fat finger at his sheet.

"Meeks. Capital M, little e-e-k-s."

She hmphed as she read it. "Wait here," she commanded, then rolled on her two squeaking chairs through a frosted glass door. Behind it, Wade saw a skinny young man with a scraggly goatee and an unshaven face. He wore no shoes, his feet were black, and he was picking his bare toes and licking his fingers. When he noticed Wade, his eyes widened into large brown marbles. Reminding Wade of the eyes of the fawn Joe had freed from the fence.

The glass door slammed and the fat woman rattled back, a manila folder quivering in her massive lap.

"I happen to have a file here, surname Meeks, Christian name Joseph," she said. Wade reached for it, curious, but she snatched it out of reach.

"Excuse me, we don't let just anyone walk in and see our records." She wedged her bifocals up her nose. "In this folder there is only one item, a bill for the delivery of an eight pound three ounce infant named Meeks, Joseph. From the date of the charge, I can be certain you are not he."

Her eyes widened, bugging out of the folds of flesh surrounding them.

"Furthermore, this fee has never been paid," she said menacingly. "You may not leave, not until we have payment for this birth."

Wade walked to the door.

"Young man!" she cried, clutching the phone in her meaty fist, "I warn you I'll have Sheriff McComb here before you can spit."

Wade ducked out the door and walked quickly away, hearing her chairs clatter frantically, hearing her shrill voice yelling into the phone that she had discovered another possible felon for the sheriff to apprehend right away.

WADE FOLLOWED SECOND Street out to where it narrowed to a lane lined with wooden fence. The lane led him to a bluff and a gate built of river rock. He was resting there when a pickup drove up, Meagher County Sheriff Department stenciled on the door, and a man, an older man, with silver stubble and a sinewy neck, got out. He was quite slender and wore his cowboy shirt skin tight. He had a badge pinned to his hat, and the handle of a revolver stuck out of his pants.

"Lo," he said.

"Lo," Wade said back.

"Seen any young trouble makers here abouts?"

"Just me."

The sheriff nodded, looking around like he expected bandits to appear at any time. "Got business here in the cemetery?"

"Cemetery?"

Just beyond the gate, in the sage brush and chest high weeds, Wade saw a sign marked Meagher County Cemetery.

"I came to see my grandfather," Wade said. The sheriff nodded again. He leaned next to Wade and picked some tall wild wheat to chew.

"What's with your head there?"

"Oh yeah. I walked into a wall."

The sheriff tugged at the fabric around his armpit.

"Spaced out, no doubt," he deduced. "I figured you for a soft-headed city type right off. From now on, pay more attention and you won't be walkin into any walls." He hiked up his pants several times as he spoke. "Well I see now you got some sense, comin out here, at least," he concluded. "Hard to run into much of anything here."

He swung back up into his sheriff's pickup.

"Excuse me," Wade said, "Do you know where the Meeks graves are?"

"Oh, well let's see. I think Meeks they got over that way. Yeah, see where they're diggin a new one? That's for the old one just died." He pointed to a backhoe scooping new dirt from the ground. "Never thought either of them Meeks women'd ever die. Now with her gone and that dam comin, I bet old Frances ain't far behind; that place means more'n life itself to that woman."

He drove off. Wade walked toward the backhoe.

Close by the new grave for Emma Meeks was a mound of new grass and dirt, a less recent grave. To the head of it lay a headstone. The name: Leonard Meeks.

Wow, Wade thought. Below him lay a grandfather, a grandfather until a month ago he didn't even know he'd never known. Wade felt lucky that, even though he was dead, he had finally met his real grandfather. He picked up a small chunk of earth to put in his pocket and turned to leave.

"You're new to this hamlet," a voice called. The man in the minister's clothes stood out in the sage brush. "You're Wade Meeks, I assume; my name is. . ."

"Father Sterling."

"Well, well; youth knows, of course."

"I read it in the Meagher paper that had Leonard Meeks's death in it."

"Indeed." Father Sterling picked a branch from the tall sage and held it to his nose. He inhaled.

"You have headaches, I understand."

Wade nodded.

"The bane of adolescence, headaches," he said. "You know what causes them?"

"What?" Wade said, interested.

"Hormones. Toxins fouling the young corporeal vessel, the unrelenting onslaught of adulthood. I had them too, you know."

"Toxins?"

"Headaches."

"The flashing kind?"

"God awful ones. Blinding visions. Bile in my eyes. Knives of light stabbing my brain. Good Christ if I wouldn't retch and reel so bad I passed out. Even now, I have remnants in my eyes, black globules floating across my sight, clouding my vision." His dark eyes flicked back and forth. "But you adjust. Over time, they abate. Now here, breathe deeply."

He handed Wade a sprig of the sage.

"Clears the mind, I should hope. Now then, the import of all this. I have a question for you."

"What question?"

"An easy one. As congregations have increasingly become liberal with their conservatism, my calls have inversely become abbreviated. By now a maverick reputation for unorthodoxy precedes me everywhere, and parishes will no longer accept me."

"You can't get a job?"

"I see not only brevity but also youth is the soul of wit. No, I can't keep a job, to be more precise."

"Why not? Do you cause trouble?"

Wade wondered if he had a problem like Joe.

"I'll be glad to share my philosophies with you at the appropriate time. As for the matter at hand, I have been reprieved to this remote Shangri-La to begin a parish, only because no one else was indigent enough. Thus I, like you, am new here myself. I am alone in this missionary endeavor, and therefore have need of an assistant. An acolyte. Someone to accompany me in my services, someone like. . ."

"The guy in the clinic?"

"Perhaps. My question to you, however, is whether you might not be interested yourself?"

"Does it pay?"

"Blunt. That's good. Pay? If it must."

Wade brightened. Though his immediate obligation was to Marly, it was good to have alternatives.

"It kind of depends."

"Of course," Father Sterling said. "Give it some thought, take your forty days, wrestle your devils. Afterwards, come find me; more than likely I'll be in the Mint. In the absence of a congregation, I go there frequently. To rest and resuscitate my soul."

Father Sterling then went further out into the sage brush, hands clasped behind his back. He walked slowly because he had on no shoes.

OH NO, NOT again. The sidewalk reeling under his tired feet. His vision fraying; whispers chorusing in his ears. Back at the Grand, Wade sunk down into the swirling lobby sofa, its corduroy fabric speckled by years of cigarette burns. He closed his eyes, breathing air musty from the chill stone walls.

Someone walking the floorboards upstairs. Wade went up and found Marly in one of the rooms, smoothing clean sheets and whipping a worn white bedspread across the mattress. He silently began to help; she silently let him. They went to one room, then another.

Marly first seemed to have things on her mind, then she became more conversational. She asked if he had got Edna to help. He nodded. She asked him how he liked Meagher. He liked it. How much? He'd rather stay here than get sent to boarding school.

"Boarding school?"

Where you get your kids taken care of if you can't do it yourself, Wade explained. That's why Joe wanted the ranch money.

"Hell, why not just go to school in Meagher?"

Wade admitted that was a good idea. But he wasn't sure about Joe.

Marly fell silent again. "You father ought to quit driftin through life and settle down," she said after a while.

Wade didn't answer. He felt far away. She asked was he alright, he looked a little peaked. He told her he had a headache coming on. She said she'd run him a bath, which had always helped her feel better.

He lay naked in the tub, listening to the water softly rise. The light was off; the door open. Marly changed bedding in the adjoining bedroom.

"Why didn't you ever get married?" he asked the darkness.

"No reason to."

"But so who's Anne's dad?" his own voice said.

"Oh that don't matter." Marly believed what mattered was a good home and a decent upbringing. Then they stopped talking a while.

Wade slid down in the tub; water submerged all of him but his head. He looked up. Marly leaned against the bathroom door, her red hair backlit and radiant. She could see all of him, but he wasn't ashamed.

"What was your mother like, honey? If you don't mind my askin."

Wade said she was okay. Not very happy.

Marly supposed he missed her quite a bit?

Not anymore. Nor more than he should. Especially since he had a dad now.

Wade sinking further in the tub, letting the hot water ease over the pounding in his eyes, and soothe the echolocating in his ears.

Marly sitting on the toilet now. He asked if she knew what happened to Joe Meeks's mother.

"She was a frail thing, I realize now; pretty much a ghost." Her words muted by the water over his ears. "Barely surviving ranch life to begin with, then Scotty came and turned out simple like Emma, she went over the edge herself. Eventually, not long after Joe left, her heart gave out."

"What about Scotty?" Wade's own voice sounding submarine.

"Oh he got buried in the avalanche from that big earthquake. You mean Joe never told you?"

"Was that why Joe ran away from home?"

"You probly ought to ask Joe about that, Wade. It's not for me to say. Anyway, it's time to go check on Squash."

Her departing footsteps echoed in the water. Wade got out, his head steamy. He moved down to the lobby, where, as a few guests came and went, he felt less alone. He lay on the sofa, his long body shivering.

EVENING.

Marly walked up the stairs, hitting the loose tread.

"There's that bright stair," a quiet voice said.

"Wade?"

She came back down. He stirred. His eyelashes were shaking, his face glistened.

"Smells dark in here," he said. "Could we turn off the lights?"

"There's none on, sweetheart. Are you alright?"

"Maybe I should lie down."

"You are lyin down. Why don't you move up to your room?"

"No, I like the company."

"You're cold though. Want me to bring you something hot? Soup?"

He said no to soup—the notion of food turned his stomach—but said he might like some coffee.

Marly put her hand on his chest, listening to his breath. In. Out. Then on his forehead.

"No temperature. Or no feeling in my hand." She stood. "Don't worry, Wade; Evan'll get things worked and Joe'll be back soon. You sure I can't get you anything?"

"No. That's plenty."

Wade smiled his wet face. Liking the sound of his voice.

Chapter 13

MARLY'S EYES WENT to the gold plate wallclock. Only Father Sterling remained, edifying her on the finer points of his doctoral dissertation on Kierkegaard and ruing the golden days of seminary glory, while she thumbed her restaurant magazines and um-hmmmed, interrupting occasionally to ask whether he liked this or that decor.

Squash Maloney came out of the kitchen. Unexpectedly, Squash had taken to kitchen work with a vengeance; though it was well after midnight, he was only now finishing up with the stoves which, on his own, he had undertaken to clean. As he went by, Father Sterling, getting an idea, beckoned him near with an offering of gin.

"I don't drink," Squash said. And left.

"Ah well, never mind." To Father Sterling, that disqualified anyone as a possible acolyte.

Marly looked up from her magazine. Sheriff McComb sauntered in.

"Lo, churchman. Marly."

He took a seat next to Marly. McComb, a life-long loner, had only late in life developed a regularly blossoming desire to lavish all his never used affections on someone, and to such purpose, once a month, he came to visit Marly. He liked to put his arm around her waist and smell her hair and enjoy being in love with someone.

McComb took the dice cup and rolled for a drink. Marly bettered his six and one with two fives. He slapped down four bits and she pulled his beer.

"You read in the Gazette about that Arapahoe Oil buyin in on the new dam, Marly?"

She murmured she had.

"Like that Evan Gallantine's been sayin, looks like Meagher's goin on the map after all."

"Especially if they upgrade that Hellwater road over into Yellowstone Park. We'll be up to our eyeballs in tourists."

"That road? It ain't had hardly anyone but sheepherders on it since the Independence mines give out, has it?"

He began to finger her ear, which usually she allowed, but tonight her mind was in a hundred other places. She batted him away.

"McComb, I have so many ideas but meanwhile, just look at it." Her glossy imagination faded into dusty moldings and splintered floorboards. "If you could only see how it looks in my wishes."

"I will do." McComb ran his finger along the back of her arm. "Whyn't you send this priest character packin, Marly? No offense, churchman."

"And none taken."

Father Sterling was busy translating a Hank Williams line about lonesome whippoorwills into Greek, testing his gin hazed memory.

"I think you both should go," Marly decided, "I feel like closin up for some reason."

"I hope it ain't your notion of progress," McComb grumbled, scratching his stubble. He stood and tossed back his drink. Father Sterling drunkenly clasped an arm around him.

"Constable, the night's young and we've still got four legs between us. Let's us good shepherds go partake of some homebrewed vitamin A."

"What do I need vitamin A for?"

"A for alcohol, sirrah. I have a sacristy full of it, every drop guaranteed holy and fully consecrated. Avanti."

McComb let himself be weaved out. "Guess you're better company than none," he said, with a parting glance at Marly, who was staring at her ceiling like she could see the stars through it. "Civilized man like you oughta get him some shoes, churchman," he said as they went out.

Marly sat a while, her mind running, then closed up. In the lobby she found her daughter under the desk lamp absorbed in her book. Too late to hide it, Anne closed it shut and walked wordlessly to her room. Her door closed. Her light went on.

Marly started up too, then in the quiet, she heard short pffts of sleep. Looking down from the banister, she saw Wade asleep on the sofa again. Waiting up for Joe, in case he came back. He'd been days up at the Meeks ranch—his ranch now—and all the business that came with Emma's dying.

Marly continued up but then down the dark hall toward the guest rooms, not toward her own. And found herself in Joe's room, on his bed, her weight rippling the nappy bedspread. Her thoughts continued turning, endlessly. . .

. . .about Annie, about her wanting all this. . .whatever it was, it wasn't 'this'. . .when it was everything she needed. Right over her head. If she only knew. How much she had. How much she'd been spared.

. . .about Meagher. All the impending changes; the dam, the visitors, Joe. About what it meant now that he owned the ranch? About whether there might be any change in him? A strange coincidence, how what was to come had brought back what was long past. And thinking of that, and her own past, it hardly seemed her own anymore. So far back in time, that summer high up Independence Basin, herding sheep, milking ewes tethered to the wagon wheels, slaughtering lambs and cooking stews. So alone, rattling pails to scare away black bears and singing songs to charm grizzlies, since not much anything scared them away, yet, after all that mayhem at town school, the relief of the solitude of high altitude wilderness. No one to make fun of her, taunt her, provoke her into fights. The companionship of a wet lamb when it rained; the trifling fantasies of her own unencumbered mind. Where (other than grizzlies) her only fear was impending imminent intolerable autumn, when they would head down, when she would live again outside town, when she would endure the hooting gangs of teenagers and the rants and raves of her shell-shocked father, reeking in his skin of discolored long underwear father, crazed by his impoundment in the habitats of other people. When high up high here she had her pick of many drafty cabins of the abandoned ghost town remnants, where even demented war veterans were at peace, free of their fear of other people's habitats. When their wild untamed daughters could be freely alone in a paradise of high sunny meadows and cool shady buildings as the thriving herd grazed on silky lupine and stoneseed and brome grass. Here Marly made house, made it the way she otherwise wouldn't down in Meagher, scouring empty jars and burning tin can refuse left by unknown elk hunters, breaking out boarded windows so that sunlight sparkled on the decaying timbers, covering rusty bed springs with wagon canvas for a bed, picking bouquets of Indian paintbrush and pasqueflower and mountain laurel, assembling a dining set from chipped pottery strewn among the ruins with which she set a table of goose berries and cattail root tea for Joe who, in her daydreaming, came to search for her, or—sometimes, for variety—a handsome stranger who had strayed from his hiking tour of Yellowstone and, lost, and, finding her, grateful for the luncheons she would graciously serve, who, every time he strayed, every time became lost, would come to adore her.

In one old building she found a battered piano with a few wires still strung, so in the evenings, while her mad father outside his sheep wagon home across the basin howled old Scottish ballads and sucked on his canteen of Everclear, she plucked the heavy piano wire, hummed plaintively with the vibrating rust, and—occasionally—imagined: if only Joe Meeks could only see her now.

In the slough above the mine she discovered a mineral hot springs pooled in kettle holes of glacier-gouged travertine, hard as porcelain, where she could discard her rough, floursack clothing, bathe for hours, then sun herself in the tufts of surrounding moss. It wasn't long before she started and ended every day walking naked to her pool, and it was there, after plunging into her private spa, that she first encountered Vaughn Marlowe.

It was late afternoon. A strange man was soaking himself in the reeds. With only his head above water, and in the lengthening shadows, Marly didn't notice him at first. She performed her regimen, scooping the mineral sand from the bottom, pressing it to her face, letting it leech her skin clean, lingering in it, smelling its hot sulfurous aroma. When she did notice him, she froze, mistaking him for a wild animal, then a madman, but she didn't cry out. He was also naked; she could see in the limpid water his body hair swaying like dark algae. He had curly dark locks and a beard, that could not conceal his florid cheeks nor the fiery tint of his eyes. Eyes—now that he'd spotted her too—smiling at her, and looking at her, and she looked where they looked, which was at her breasts. They swelled, buoyed by the gaseous velvety water, flanked by the tips of her wet red hair, and she was astonished by the fullness of her own womanhood.

Then she became crazed with fear and self-revulsion and shot down through the marsh to her cabin.

Where she sat out the waves of fear then confusion then curiosity then disappointment. Here was the stray lost tourist of her imaginations, and here was she, unfriendly and not at all gracious. Eventually she walked back up. He was dressing under the glittering aspen that overhung the pool. He put on his backpack and was gone.

THE SMELL OF motor oil. The sound of an engine idling down in the street. Marly heard it shut off. She got off Joe's bed and moved to the chair in the corner. Closed her eyes. For a long time, no sound. Then someone creaking up the stairs. A silhouette of shoulders at the door. A tired man flopping onto the bed. All was dark. All quiet. But the sound of sleep breathing.

"Joe?"

But Joe was already asleep, and Marly let him, while she, sunk into the chair, let her eyes close, let magazine visions pour from her mind, her Grand in elegant architectural renderings, its exterior stone polished white, new soffits enclosing all copper plumbing and furnace ductwork and silver circuitry, the high tin ceiling reshaped by expert tinsmith hands, the inlaid teak bartop gleaming with polish, the lobby's cut glass chandelier softly illuminating davenports of umber velvet, halogen sconces casting shadows on royal green carpets, an ebony handrail crowning a balustrade of wrought iron swans and flowers, the stairway spiraling around a column of bronze, gold-capped rods retaining the carpeting as it flowed up the oak treads to a skylight rotunda, where quiet guests read international newspapers, and the chatter of foreign tongues rose over the soft parade of movie stars and entrepreneurs, walking to their dormered rooms with canopied beds and thick cream-colored comforters, floor to ceiling windows, mahogany bureaus and Morrison tables, bathrooms of dark blue porcelain and double glass showers.

"Joe?"

A sudden urge, to lie alongside him, to run her fingers in his hair, moved her to the edge of his bed. Asleep, Joe turned over, his warm mouth landing against the flesh of her inside arm. Cool moisture where his lips touched her skin. He shifted so his head came to settle in the cusp of her lap. She smoothed his cheek. Wondered what he'd do if he woke up. Wondered what she'd do.

Later, he turned, rolled, His back to her, Well, she thought, why not, and kissed his neck. She smelled her breath mix with his skin, heated. Her lips whispered.

"Joe?"

Dead asleep, but, wasn't he aware in some way, listening for her, waiting for her hands to grasp him as they once had, eager for her warm fingers to slip inside his shirt, his pants, secret their velvet oil, entwine him with her arms and slick flanks. His hips shifted, wasn't he maybe reciprocating the flourish she herself felt inside, the wondering, the desire to know, what it would feel like—after all these years—to weld body to body, glossy flesh against flesh? Would it be once again like it once was then, rippling her every fiber, touching the liquid nest between her hips the way he had once done? She took his hand. She placed it to her face.

He shot up with a start.

"Wade, what the. . .?"

She pulled her hand away. He looked at her. Not sure who she was. Or who he was.

"Marly? Where's Wade?"

"In the lobby, waiting for you."

Joe rubbing his face, she swept back her damp hair. Asking herself, Jesus, what are you doing?

"I, uh. . .what's. . .are you all right?"

"I'm fine."

She patted his hand. Straightened her blouse. Rose and went to the door.

"You know, Joe, when things ever do repeat themselves. . .maybe they're even better the second time?"

Fumbling for the door, she left and went to her own bed, where she slept alone.

WADE PUSHED OPEN the door to Anne's room. Her dark female shape lay asleep on the bed. A long time he stood over her. Sunstorms flared in his eyes. His body clattered sweat.

"Wade?" Anne lifted her head groggily. "What're you doin

here?"

"Someone was in with Joe."

"What time is it?"

"You want me to go?"

"Wait a minute." She sleepily sat up. "You caught me naked."

"I know." She was remarkably naked; he could sense that even as the pounding screen of his vision washed green then red. He sat beside her. "I'll take my clothes off, if you want."

She pulled on a t-shirt and propped a pillow against the wall. She stretched. Yawned. Shook her head.

"Wade? You ain't quite all there sometimes, are you?"

He shook his head, placing his hands against the rim of his eye. He could see only a large oval nothing surrounded by a lace of jagged lights, or turquoise pain flooding his eyes, beautiful to watch, actually, or a speckled frenzy of microscopic globules. Distant conversations, everything Chinese, mute gongs and flutes.

His rested his head in the pocket of her shoulder, her chest soft, her arm feathery. He felt her heart beating. Stroking his choppy hair; blue lightning flickered from her fingers. His body became long, dizzyingly long; his legs dangled off the end of the bed out the window across the street. Nothing was touching him now, not even his own hands holding back his face. His eyes glazed. Sleep, he thought, floating; ethereal and white. Delirium receded into the dark room with no center. Breathing the inside of her arm, a black veil swept the storm from his eyes.

When he woke again, Anne was at the window, arms folded around herself. He turned on the lamp. The parchment shade threw a smoldering brown on the walls and a hot white oblong on the ceiling. Almost how it looked right before a headache. In the dark light Anne's skin blended into the faded paint of old walls, leaving the outline of her body glowing.

"I couldn't sleep."

"Join the club."

In the drawer of the rickety cabinet where the lamp sat, one crinkled color photograph. He viewed it askance, not all of his vision back to normal yet. It was a girl and a boy, he couldn't tell who, the light so brown, his eyes so frayed, the colors so faded and washed out.

"Who's this? You and your boyfriend?"

"Me and my boyfriend? Are you blind?"

Wade squinted harder. The boy and girl familiar looking, but holding one another so closely, hard to even clearly tell them apart. Just behind them, a small single prop engine plane, its door flung open, its propeller invisibly whirling, obvious from how its gusts furled the girl's long hair into ribbons, some of them flying across the boy's mouth, which was wide open ringing with laughter. What *was* clear was how excited they were; whatever it was about, you could tell that much at once.

"You look so happy."

"I do, huh? Take a closer look, why don't you? I wasn't even born when that picture was took."

Wade squinted. Looking more closely, he realized—because she looked so happy—he'd assumed Anne was the young woman, but it should have been obvious from the red hair who it was.

"I know. It's your mom."

"No shit, Sherlock."

"And so. . .that's your dad with her?"

"Oh God no." Anne laughed. "I don't know who it is. Not that I ain't asked, all the time, but all she'll ever say is, it's just some boy, she forgot who, no one important."

"He looks important to me."

And familiar looking. Wade closed his eyes, feeling sure that any minute he was going to know who it was. He looked once more, and now, sure enough, he did know.

He looked at Anne with a cocky grin. "You *sure* you don't know who?"

"What's your problem?" she said, annoyed.

"Try looking again." He put the picture next to his own face. "Don't you think he kind of looks like me?"

Anne sat up, took the picture, looked carefully.

"Holy shit! I don't believe it."

"Told you so. It's Joe."

She ignored him. She stared a long time.

"Holy shit!"

Chapter 14

IT RAINED. FOR days the heavens deluged Meagher, delaying Emma Meeks's burial. On the fourth morning, a streak of blue appeared in the sky but by the time they gathered in Sheriff McComb's office, the black firmament reopened and torrents descended with redoubled fury.

Wade was cold; it had been a long wait. Burchard and Gustafsen, huddled in rumpled suits, slept upright on the bench along the wall. Vapors clouded their faces as they snored asynchronously with each other. Joe sat on an old chair near the door, nervously bouncing his knees, worrying the frays of the cushions.

Duffy, the sheriff's deputy, came in from the dingy hall carrying in a tray of coffee and cups.

"Frances'll never make it, now with that road the way it gets. She's probly stuck already."

"She'll make it," Joe Meeks said, "even if her jeep don't."

"You put it off three days now already, why not another, at least until this weather lifts? She's out of her flippin mind to drive down in this."

"Who's out of her flippin mind?" Evan Gallantine ducked in the door, rain gear crackling as he shook off the water trickling down his face. He turned to Joe, apprising the situation. "You're actually going through with it then?"

Joe nodded.

"And you know I can't be here, right?"

"Why would you be? She's only family."

"I'd take umbrage at that. . .if it weren't raining so hard."

Joe didn't find it funny. "Glad one of us is in such high spirits, 'bout our 'generous stroke of luck'."

"I'm sorry, Joe, I didn't mean it that way. It's more that I've been in high gear than high spirits. At least the coffin made it."

Outside, a frilly white brocade casket stuck out the back of Duffy's pickup, covered with a plastic tarp that was collecting large pools of rainwater. Evan had arranged for it to be sent from Billings, where he'd been day and night with lawyers, since no coffins were to be had in Meagher.

"Frances is sure goin to have something to say, she lays eyes on that over-stuffed Styrofoam go-cart."

"It was all they had on such short notice. I was lucky to get that one."

"That's a coffin?" Wade had expected wood and little gold handles, like his mother had, not something all covered with white crinkly fabric. "I thought it was a sofa."

Joe blurted out a laugh. Evan shrugged. "Frances shouldn't look a gift horse in the mouth, my humble opinion."

Wade wondered what a gift would be doing in a horse's mouth, but stayed silent, seeing Joe, jumpy, agitated, biting his lip and pulling off flecks of chapped skin.

"Joe, by the day after tomorrow, this will all be behind us. All that's left is to put your pen to paper. You need something to really worry about? How about that it's already getting late for getting Wade into a good boarding school."

Oh great, Wade thought. To himself.

"So, it might help to know I had my office assistant in L.A. look into it. If anyone knows how to pull strings, she does. We'll get him in." He lifted his watch. "I should leave."

Joe peered out the rain sheeted window. Just as Evan drove off, an old silver jeep parked out front.

"She's here," he announced, standing, zippering his jacket.

Frances hobbled in, rainwater cascading from her hat brim, thwacking more from her overcoat. She stomped her boots so that deltas of mud streamed at her feet, rousing Burchard and Gustafsen, who struggled gallantly to their feet, stoop-shouldered and baggy-suited. Their chivalry went unacknowledged, as Frances gave the sheriff's office the once over.

"This place don't look any better'n when I sat here years ago."

Duffy neatened his desk, wanting to ignore her, but galled nonetheless. The old coot never failed to remind him that she—a woman—had his job long before him, during the war, and here he was, nearly forty, a grown man, and still only a deputy himself. It was only due to the shortage of men, he assured himself, but privately he believed it was because Frances wasn't a natural woman in the first place.

Evan stood at the door. "Frances, I'm sorry to say I can't be here, but if we could just put this off another day until the weather clears? We could move you into the Grand for a. . ."

"Even better," Frances cut in, "whyn't we just wait'll I die myself, then you can bury her'n me all in one shot?"

A shadow of silent contempt crossed Evan's face, but without further comment, he smoothed his hair—its wetness revealing its actual thinness—and left.

Frances peered out the rainy window. "What's that gaudy canoe you got in your pickup, Duffy?"

"That ain't a boat, Frances," Duffy said, with poorly concealed smugness, "it's Emma."

Frances poised herself over her cane, staring at the coffin.

"Why, we goin to put her in the Hellwater and float her down to the Gulf of Mexico?" She turned to Wade. "Promise me you won't ever let no one stuff me in a thing like that."

Wade shook his head; she nodded. Duffy offered her coffee, and the room relaxed when she accepted it. She sat, whereupon Burchard and Gustafsen took the opportunity to quit being gentlemen and sit themselves. In no time they were back to sleep. Frances nodded off herself, then woke with a start.

"You so-called men might get a move on any time now."

"Plaggemeyer should be over any time now," Duffy said.

"Plaggemeyer, what do we need that wastrel for?"

"Well, as justice of the peace, a course."

"Ah damn." Frances switched her cane from hand to hand. "I hate this waitin. Got no cream for this coffee?"

Duffy shook his head. "Guess you have to make do without."

"Don't see how it matters what I make anymore." She poled herself to her feet. "I'll make water, least I can still do that. It's back this way, if I recall."

On her way to the back, she stopped to poke open the jail room door; Wade, ever curious, followed to have a look. In the holding cell was one prisoner, the shoeless unshaven young man Wade had seen in Edna Maloney's clinic.

Frances noticed Wade. "Well, this don't look like a half bad place; maybe I'll come here once they boot me off my land. What crime you think I could do to get me a fancy cellroom like this?"

Wade laughed. Though no one else seemed to, he found her very comical.

Frances gestured at the prisoner with her cane. "Who's this monkey they got in here?"

The prisoner grabbed the bars. "This ain't a zoo!"

Duffy leapt to his feet to get between them.

"What'd he do? Kill somebody with his smell?"

"Nobody quite knows." Duffy squeezing past Frances to close the door. "McComb says he's a possible felon, so we're checkin him out. He no doubt done somethin."

Frances ignored him. "You in there; what'd you do?"

"I did nothin!" the possible felon shrieked.

"Then you got what you deserved."

Frances left to do her business. The commotion from the cellroom woke a befuddled Gustafsen.

"The only one comfortable at these damn burials is the stiff," he grumbled when he remembered where he was. "Next one I'm comin to won't be till my own." He smirked at his dozing companion, Burchard. "He looks like hell, don't he, young man?" he said to Wade. "Damn no-good. Pissed his life away and looks it too, don't he? His suit ain't even pressed. And you see how he's aged?"

Satisfied with his observations, Gustafsen settled down to sleep again. Almost immediately his twisting and churning roused Burchard, who also took a while to get his bearings.

When he did, he tapped his companion. "Gus," he said, though Gustafsen was fast asleep, "remember years ago we all of us took that graduation trip? You recall? We went to some big city or other. I remember realizing how us Meagher people sure are a world apart, ain't we?" He nodded vigorously, impressed with his wisdom, then resumed tapping Gustafsen again. "Even so, I'll tell you somethin else. When it comes to them Meeks's, they're in a whole 'nother world altogether."

As Frances returned, the phone rang. Duffy answered, listened, hung up.

"Plaggemeyer says he ain't goin to preside over any burial in this kind of rainstorm."

Frances sat down, winded. "The hell with him."

Duffy poured her more coffee. "An he wondered if you heard the news about Harlo?"

Joe started. "Harlo? What about him? He's getting out of prison?"

"Already is out. They released him yesterday."

"I'll be damned."

"So will he, I have anything to do with it," Frances said. "Hell with all this. Joe, you go get on with it, without Plaggemeyer and without Harlo. And me as well. I 'bout had my fill of this all."

She sat down and was soon herself asleep.

Duffy buttoned his coat. "Joe, that casket weighs more'n a lead submarine. Us two ain't enough to lift it down."

"There's Wade."

"Still ain't enough. Doin it another day is out of the question?"

"You don't have to come, Duffy. Suit yourself."

Joe went out, soaked before the door closed behind him. From the back, another rounds of yelps from the possible felon gave Wade an idea.

"What if we take along that guy? The guy in jail?"

Duffy looked out as Joe disappeared into the bleak pouring rain. "Well, now you mention it, ain't any law says the scrawny s.o.b. can't do a little community service, that I know of."

As Duffy was letting him out, the prisoner, sensing his new status, refused to leave unless Duffy removed his handcuffs. "I'll go barefoot, though, that way you know I won't leave. How far could I get without shoes?"

"That's true," Wade said.

Duffy considered it a minute, then took off the handcuffs. The three trooped out together splashing across the inch deep street water. The prisoner tilted his head, slurped at the hard rain, and laughed like a jackal.

"Come on, you." Duffy yanked him into the pickup cab. Wade joined Joe in back alongside the plastic-covered casket, and the funeral procession, such as it was, began. Slipping and sliding, coated gray by the alluvial Hellwater mud, the pickup spun up the lane, a one car caravan through the monochrome drizzle. The rain was so dense Duffy located the cemetery only by its windbreak of poplars, which drooped under the rain, looking just as lost as Duffy felt himself. Unable to locate the grave site, Joe jumped out to look, while Duffy continued to circle, cursing in despair of ever putting poor old Emma Meeks to rest, when Joe banged on the cab.

"This's it. Stop here."

"What makes you think so?

"Those mule deer there; they're eating the new grass. Must be Leonard's plot, so hers'll be right next to it."

Duffy and Wade joined Joe; the deer vanished, ethereal specters. Sloshing to the excavation, the black loam sucked at their boots, the outsized raindrops pelted their jackets. It fell in a frenzy, so hard it bounced so that it rained up as hard as down. The grave itself was full of loess-laden water, its walls rife with broken roots washed white by the liquid air. At the far end, the excavated earth had reservoired a large pond of rainwater behind it.

Duffy tugged at Joe. "Come on, let's go get her and get this over with."

Joe nodded but didn't move, puzzled that such sandy loose soil could dam such a sizable body of water.

Duffy tugged again, then suddenly broke into a run. "Shit'n'ay, he's gone!" he whooped, throwing open the pickup cab door and looking inside. He ran circles around his pickup in a futile search for clues where his prisoner might have run, cursing blinding condensation that had disguised the escape.

"Why didn't you stop him?" he yelled at Wade, swearing and lamenting, leaping behind the wheel and spinning out in hot pursuit, bouncing Emma's casket out into the mud so it landed just shy of everlasting repose. Wade ran to it, Joe right behind him.

"He said he just wanted some mud between his toes," Wade said. He got no response from Joe, who just stood, shaking his head in resignation. Wade didn't know what to do, but didn't want the coffin getting waterlogged, knelt to push it, and to his surprise, with mud oiling the way, he had the strength to move it. He yelled to Joe, who, though even more surprised, joined him, and together they quickly slid it up next to the grave.

Where they then abruptly stopped. A biting odor hung in the air, and a weasely looking thing floundered in the grave. The thing became the possible felon, who continued leaping at the sides, failing to get a handhold, and sliding back down into the watery six foot depths.

"What are you doin in there?" Joe cried, "Get out! "

The trapped man wiped the mud from his face. "I was walking in those poplars there when this muddy skunk sprayed me. I ran off this way and fell in. Gimme a hand, okay?"

"Damn you!" In his frustration, Joe kicked the pile of excavated dirt, and slipped, and fell, and the impact sent a shudder through it, and as they all gaped in astonishment, a channel broke the mound's surface. The entire pond burst through in one moment. And as silty water flooded down upon him, filling the grave, and buoying him, in this way the possible felon was able to scramble out.

He joined Joe, and Wade, and all three stood wiping cold rain from their faces.

"Now what, Joe?"

"The hell with it."

Joe bent down over the casket and gave it one big heave. As though by design, the bulky coffin slid home and came to rest in the grave, where it bobbed sublimely, slowly displacing the water and sinking to the bottom.

All three stood silent, possibly in reverence, Wade blowing onto his hands, the possible felon grinning absurdly. Joe, in time, began to feel an odd serenity come upon him, as he imagined, in time, a long time, soil would reclaim the chintzy casket and its corporeal remains, and the mineral-laden water would soak into her marrow and crystallize, petrify, and eventually preserve her, forever. And in time, he would—maybe—get used to the idea that he, through Leonard, issued from Emma, not Frances. And that—maybe—he, like his little brother Scotty, had receive, from Emma, those witless Meeks genes.

The prisoner was the first to stir. "I ain't goin back," he vowed. "I didn't do anything."

Joe turned to him. "You didn't?"

"Hitch-hiking's no crime."

"Hitch-hiking? To where?"

"Independence."

"Independence Basin?"

"I met a man. He told me, if you're going nowhere, it was *the* place to go; that's why he was going there." He squeezed water out of his stringy hair. "I said to myself, that's me, all right, and that's where I'm going too."

"But you didn't even know this guy?"

"He had a look to him. Like, man, this guy knows. He just knows."

Joe shook his head, sucking heat into his fingers, which were blue with cold.

The possible felon poked Wade. "I see you're gettin too big for your shoes. You should try doing without. Like me."

Wade looked at his feet; his toes had broken through his worn-out sneakers, and were coated thick with freezing mud.

"They're better than. . ."

But the prisoner was gone. Wade caught only a glimpse as he disappeared into the poplars, a shadow in the rain.

"Hey! Where you going?"

The shoeless spirit pointed somewhere between straight ahead and straight up and was gone.

Chapter 15

THE NEXT MORNING, Evan Gallantine, briefcase armed with packets of contracts and title transfers and appraisals to be completed, knew as soon as he joined Joe Meeks for breakfast he had a new problem. Not sure what it was, but he knew; the way Joe was sullenly drawing circles on the damp tabletop, he read like an wide open book. Evan sighed. No doubt this kind of indicative behavior many an irate construction manager came to know only too late.

"So, Joe. What's on our mind this morning?"

Joe lost in thought. Or ignoring him.

"Having second thoughts, maybe?"

Joe sipped his by now cold coffee. "Just that maybe I oughta talk with Harlo, get his read on things, you know. Before doing anything further."

Evan leaned back, taking a long thoughtful draw on his cigarette. "You even know where Harlo is?"

"I have a good idea. I was thinkin of goin up to see him this morning."

Evan exhaled a sheet of smoke between his lips. He looked toward the kitchen, Marly keeping her distance, to prove she couldn't be less interested. She caught his look, and brought the coffee, took her sweet time pouring it, and—though Joe waved his palm over it—thoughtfully filled his cup anyway. Slowly. To the brim.

"So, you two got the HRC deal all squared away?" she said with grand indifference.

"Close." Evan looked at Joe. "But not just yet."

"Problems?"

Joe fingered one of the decorative cattle brands burned into the wood paneled booth.

"Just I'd like to find out Harlo's thinking on things, that's all."

Marly gave Evan a look. "I s'pose that only makes sense, don't it?"

"I'm sure it does," Evan said, with no enthusiasm, accidentally spilling coffee on his dress shirt.

"Sorry about that," Joe said, as though it was his fault. Like everything else.

"Here, Evan, let me."

As Marly wet a napkin and dabbed at the stain, Wade arrived, rubbing his eyes, ready for breakfast. No one greeted him, not even Marly.

"Joe, one thing to think about." Evan smoothed the wet but now clean wrinkles on his shirt. "About this pattern of yours. How trouble follows you, job to job? Inconvenient, maybe, but it was only ever you affected by the consequences, right? Up to now you always had the luxury of just drifting on." He set his hand on Wade's shoulder. "Now though, I just ask you to bear in mind, it's not only you that'll suffer from any ill-advised ideas you get into your head."

He drained his coffee cup and rose to leave.

"Just a word to the wise. See you later."

MARLY BROUGHT WADE'S second plate of hotcakes and eggs

and sat down.

“So Joe, you really are goin to give Harlo a say?”

“I thought, yeah, maybe I should.”

“I’ll go too, Joe, okay?” Wade said just as Anne walked up.

“Go where?”

“To talk to Uncle Harlo.”

“Harlo? That no-good. . .you mean they actually let him out?”

“Why is he no-good?” Wade said, but no one answered. Marly reached to wipe gooseberry syrup drips from his mouth.

“You can take along some of my loganberry wine. You’ll want to lubricate them dried up vocal cords’a his.”

“Good idea, right, Joe?”

“He’s probly on probation; I doubt. . .”

Just then a clattering racket of pots falling came from the kitchen.

“Good Christ, there goes Squash again. Every time you show yourself, Anne. Poor love-sick kid.”

Marly quickly ran back to head off more trouble. The table fell silent, listening to her yelling at Squash to get his mind off her daughter and on his work. Anne, leaning against the table, reluctant to leave, unsure whether to stay. Wade noticed that her hair was brushed and tied back with a blue scarf, and that her face was washed and shining, and her work shirt ironed. So pretty looking, he thought, wondering if Joe noticed too, how he looked at her when she wasn’t looking, and wondering if she was wondering too, how she looked at Joe when he wasn’t looking. Weird, Wade thought, no one looking at anyone. He went back to eating.

"Joe, if you want," Anne said after a while, "I guess I could drive you to find Harlo."

"You don't got work today?"

"Too wet. From all that rain."

"Well still. Maybe if I could just borrow your pickup. No reason for you to have to go."

"I never let anybody drive my pickup; too temperamental. And anyway I don't mind at all. Got nothin else to do."

"Knowin Harlo, I should probly just go myself."

"All right, take it or leave it. Be hard findin that rascal without wheels though."

"Guess that's true enough." Joe shook his head. "Ain't really sure why even go. What would it change, except to make things worse."

"Joe, I think it's a good idea," Wade said, "and plus I'd like to meet Uncle Harlo. Why can't we just go anyway?"

"*Uncle* Harlo?"

"Well, I mean, uncle, meaning your uncle. That'd be fun, don't you think?"

"Fun," Joe muttered. He pushed his half eaten plate aside.

"Well, so go get you a jacket then; ain't exactly hot as hell up at Independence."

ABOVE THE MEEKS ranch, the Hellwater road leaves the open upper valley and becomes an old mining access, climbing the spruce slopes of Sweetgrass Moraine. For a few miles it parallels the cataract falls of the Hellwater. Here, the air cools under the towering lodgepole pine, whose crowns split forest sunlight into dusty angular planes, and whose redolent needles carpet the twin ruts of the road. It is quiet but for the serene tumble of whitewater over the falls. Above the cirque behind Sweetgrass Moraine, the mining road begins ascending the series of switchbacks which lead to Independence Basin.

Joe noticed the falls were already low, despite the heavy rains of the week before. His arm dangled out the window, brushed by undergrowth. Anne smiled at something, he didn't know what; he smiled reflexively. Mountains sharpened by sunlight beckoned here and there through the trees.

Wade, eager to see Independence Basin, because of what the possible felon had said about it, pointed at the majestically glaciated peaks and broke the tranquility.

"Just like New York, isn't it, Joe?"

"Just like New York?" Anne said. "You kidding? What does that even mean?"

"How in the morning the skyscraper tops are all sunny and down below the streets are still dark."

"Y'know," Joe nodded. "It kinda is how it looks, at that. You know?"

"No, I don't know. How would I?"

Wade, riding next to her, felt her stiffen.

"What's wrong?"

"Nothin's wrong. What's wrong with you?"

"Nothing, I just thought. . ."

"I know what you thought. You think I can help where I'm

from? And it don't make you better'n me, so how about you stop always rubbin it in?"

"Rubbing what in?"

"I don't have anyone to take me places like New York like you. I'm stuck in Meagher, just like my mom, just like everyone I know. How far you think I'm ever goin to get? Nowhere, that's how far. You guys don't even know. You guys can just leave. Any time you damn want to."

"That's not quite true," Joe ventured. "I mean, well, you have a job. And no tellin where that can get you. You give it time."

Anne vented a jet of breath through her lips, but said nothing.

The road wound down into an aspen hollow, then back out into sky and open scree, where it sliced up again along a hanging wall of rock and scrub pine. As the air rarefied, so did the mood in the pickup, Anne thinking of her work again, how for days now she'd lived and breathed nothing else, the transit and standard, the calibrations and math, the transcriptions and field sheets. How she'd wanted to give it up that day she was late. She looked sidelong at Joe now. A real engineer, but who'd grown up here same as her. Then thinking, what had happened, why'd he leave, and why not her mom? Then about that photograph, and whatever happened, and that happy looking guy. And how now, here he was back here, with her, flesh and blood.

All at once the pickup rose onto the windblown barren saddle of the Absaroka divide; Joe grabbed the dashboard in fear, as though the earth was about to end and they were about to fall to their doom, as suddenly, below, the terrifying spread of Independence Basin, and above, the soaring peaks of the Beartooths, Mount Contact foremost of all.

Anne gasped; Wade in turn.

There was no mistaking it. The landslide lay like a slain dragon fallen across the narrow sunlit cirque. The entire north face of Mount Contact as if frozen in time and motion avalanching down the valley wall, a fallen citadel plummeting across the basin floor and careening of its own megalithic weight halfway up the opposite slope, burying everything in its path. Chunks the size of barns lay strewn miles from where they had been wrenched loose. The fragile network of headwaters damned by the slide into a pristine tarn of shallow transparence, studded with now dead drowned tree tops, leafless bone-white sticks rising from liquid blue.

"God," Anne said, "I never had any idea."

"Let's get out, can we?"

Wade nudged Anne and they walked to an overlook, then stepped back, feeling vertigo. After a while, Joe followed them out, faceless as a ghost.

"Wow, right, Joe? That was some earthquake."

Joe's gaze rolling over the scene, the morning haze like the dust of that cataclysm still settling twenty years later. So little changed. Here and there, fringes of pioneering aspen interspersed with colonies of Sitka spruce, but in the thick swath of the slide itself, not a blade of grass nor sprout of juniper had been able to root. It was an unhealed wound on the side of Mount Contact.

Wade looked up. "Was that where Scotty died?"

Joe nodded.

"Did you see it happen, though?"

"Yeah. I did. The morning we planned to leave."

Long minutes he stood, eyes reliving the stupendous flow of rock, the naked flank of Mount Contact, its interior secret,

Scotty entombed under the debris. In the high blue above, a jet's fan-tail iced a white line through the sky, streaking east into the sun.

"Who's Scotty?" Anne asked.

"Joe's brother," Wade whispered.

"He got killed?"

"Yeah but we don't like to think about it."

"What's to think about; you can see for yourself."

Joe coughed. Wishing he were back on that jet overhead, headed away, looking down upon this from on high, free, and unaffected, above it all. Superior to the elements of calamity, upheaval, change.

Anne took Wade's arm and pulled him to the pickup. Something about leaving Joe alone.

So they waited. While Joe stood a while longer. Sweaty in the mountain air, shivering from the hot sun. A breeze fluttered up from below, whipping his sleeves, the kind of slow weathering it did on all that he overlooked.

Then he realized he was alone. And returned to the pickup.

CONTINUING DOWN THE pass, the Hellwater road frayed into indistinct marmot trails into raw meadow; it was off road low-gear maneuvering to find a way to the grassy bottom along the lake, avoiding rocks and dead ends and trees, laden with a wet veil of snow still surviving into mid-May in the innermost boughs. In time they reached a timber cabin that obviously predated the quake triggered landslide and the lake it created, and now was settled half in the water, half out.

"This is that hunting lodge you told me about on the plane, isn't it?"

Joe said it was. White smoke feathered from the tin pipe in the roof.

"That'd likely be Harlo."

"And maybe the possible felon, if he made it," Wade said.

"Wait here." Joe walked to the cabin. He poked open the door. Inside, nothing but black.

"Figured you'd find your way here 'ventually."

The voice husky and eerily familiar. Joe widened the door, enough to make out a man, Harlo, far to the back. Continuing inside, ducking the dank and sagging timber beams, Joe had to feel more than see his way through slits of sunlight streaking between cracks in the mud-fill seams, to the back room, the floor of which was half hard dirt, half black liquid of the intruding lake water.

Harlo was sitting on a salt block deeply grooved by sheep tongues, his big grin knife-like and white. Joe went to the one boarded window, knocked a plank loose, jarring loose a soft flour of dust, which sparkled brilliantly in the bands of sunlight.

"What're you now," Harlo cracked, "the bank examiner?"

Joe saw Harlo more clearly now, how he looked older, his face weathered, his mouth more jowly. A drinker's red-veined nose and old timber teeth. Though obviously he could still turn up that same infectious grin. That made it hard for Joe to keep withholding his own smile, at being so glad to see him.

At which point Wade burst in, followed by Anne.

"We brought something for you, Harlo."

Wade proffered his gift, the label-less dark filled bottle of homemade wine Marly had given him.

He had waited long enough.

ALL THE REST of the morning the four sat on the dirt in the splinters of sunlight, sipping and passing the wine. Harlo grooving the floor with his boot heel, practiced in doing time, listening to whatever there was to listen to, the breeze on the lake outside, the rustle of the newly budding red alder. Joe settling lower and lower into the dirt and its memories, forgetting why he came, if he even knew. Anne, loving the mountain air, napping then waking. Wade, resting his chin on his fists, extrapolating on the end of speech, the last word ever spoken, if there were to come a time when everyone on earth decided to wait for someone else to talk, how no one would ever talk again.

"It's pretty chilly, right?" he said.

"Yeah, Wade; imagine it is for you city slickers. Why not let's move outside then."

Harlo stood. Pantomimed a stately 'ladies first' bow for Anne, who went out ignoring him. Walking after her, his left leg swinging limply behind the right, Wade realized Harlo must be partly lame.

Outside, Harlo hiked himself up on the woodpile. "Guess you come up to see Scotty then, Joe?"

Joe shook his head. "Nope, not why I came, Harlo."

"So you say, but I bet ya for a fact it is."

Harlo nudged Wade, to watch, as he reached to tickle the back of Anne's neck. She batted him off. She seemed familiar with Harlo, but not fond of him.

"The reason I came was about the ranch. Now that Emma's died, things've all changed around. Where, now, legally, I own. . ."

"Don't waste your breath, Joe; air's too thin. I heard all about it, and so what? I never expected nothin from that place, and was I right or was I right? Hell, what d'ya 'xpect, when even your own mother ain't your mother. Myself, I think, perfect end to it, The only one of us sorry assholes to get the place is the one who ran away from it. And even funnier? Even you don't get nothin, not really. They're goin to flood the hell out of it. So Joe, I don't see what's left but for you to get your money and leave again."

"Which is why I'm here. I'm not sure that's what's right."

"Rat's ass you ain't sure. End of the day, money is what's right, and we all know damn well that's what you come for. Same as ever'one else; you ain't no different'n Leonard or me or Frances. Get right down to it, we're all of us just jackass Meeks's. An always will be."

A flash of alpine air fluttered the sun-dappled aquamarine lake water. Joe dipped his hand to drink.

"What about I don't sell it, Harlo? What about, if I had a little time. . ."

"What the hell? Sell that damn place and live it up, for Chrissake. You really want my opinion? Don't think twice. Whatever money you can get you're welcome to."

"Come on. You always wanted that place. Now I'm supposed

to believe you don't anymore?"

"Damn right. What in high heaven would make me wanna go back bein a two-bit sheepkickin cowpunchin rancher? Hoo boy, Wade. Runnin off didn't improve your old man's sense any. He never was much good knowin which side his bread's buttered on. Am I right?"

"I guess so." Wade liked this, a criminal uncle, and how he teased and joked with everyone.

"Sure as shit you guess so!" Harlo laughed. "Your boy's got your number there, Joe."

Joe, getting exasperated, kicked loose a mound of wet moss, then went back in the cabin. Harlo stretched out his legs.

"So Anne, how's my girl? Drinkin your fill of good wine like this here, what're you now, eighteen or so? Wade, last time I seen Anne, she wasn't near so filled out."

"Harlo, just shove it."

She walked off, away from the cabin, then reversed, and went inside after Joe.

"I guess she doesn't like you so much?"

"Ah it ain't nothin. Been like that with us since she was little. It's 'cause I never settled down with Marly like everyone kind of expected. Maybe I should of, but with all my rodeoin and wild ass ways. . ."

Wade leaned back, basking in the high sun. "We met a guy that wanted to come up here and find you. He said you told him how great it was here."

"Oh yeah, that scraggly barefoot homeless kid? Na, I ran him off the minute he turned up. He don't belong here; he belongs in Warm Springs with all the retards."

"I liked him though."

"Well you're somethin then, Wade."

Harlo picked his teeth.

"Harlo, where's that old mine up here? Joe said. . ."

"Independence? Hell, it got buried by the landslide; the whole damn shebang." He pointed to the landslide. "One hell of a grave for a ghost town and one poor little kid, ain't it?"

"Were there any other people here?"

"Nope, not a soul. He was the only casualty."

Harlo jammed his stick in the dirt, bent it till it snapped and flung a divot of black dirt in the air.

"Only one that died, anyways," he added.

ANNE FOUND JOE in the dark of the back room of the cabin, pungent of rotting wood, lit only by the small square of rusty window sun light that fell on the water. She took off her boots, rolled up her pant legs, and, ducking the jungle of tendrils hanging from the ceiling underside—roots of the mountain grasses flourishing on the roof—waded to an old rotting dresser along the far water-side wall. On it, a bouquet of tinder dry stems and thistle flowers, which became a puff of ash at her touch. Alongside, a piece of clear glassy stone. Which she held into the beam of streaming window sunlight.

"What kinda rock is this?"

Joe only then realized he wasn't alone, and in turning to answer, didn't; instead, in turning, he was struck silent, by Anne, by her standing in the blaze of sun, the sapphire in her eyes, the luster radiating off her skin. Struck dumb, standing still as stone and held in sway by the fullness, not just of her but of the moment, all of it, how it all at once revived resuscitated resurrected that young watershed summer so long ago, all its fear and joy and desire and passion, all that they had had then and there, here, he and Marly, in this interior of this cabin, all that for a few short months they felt and shared, and felt how it felt to share, and shared how it felt to feel. Thunderstruck by all of that, that he had left, left on that final day, in the hours and aftermath of that fatal landslide, because how it felt to him, then, on that day, was that leaving, leaving it all, was the best thing, the right thing, the only thing to do. How he felt so sure of it, that day and ever since and all this time, that it had to be done, leaving, but now, here, so stunned by all that was suddenly standing there facing him, not Marly but her flesh and blood and same aged daughter, both collapsed into the here and now and then and there. . .only now, this time, Joe standing and wondering. . .*Was it*? Was it the right, the best, the only thing to do? To have done? And in wondering that, for the first time ever, Joe was no longer all that sure. Not sure at all.

"Calcite," he replied.

Anne waded toward him, the clear colored calcite flat on her extended palm.

"Look, it reflects things double."

She held the translucent rock over her finger and Joe noticed, first, that she had put a ring on her finger, and only second, how that ring's golden red image refracted in the calcite into a double image.

"Actually, that kind of crystal calcite, they call it refracting calcite. It's not really a reflection. . .it's more like, you know, a window. . ."

Third, he noticed her shoulder brush his arm. And he stepped back a little, rippling the lazy sunlight so it rose prismatically rose-like from the water.

"What are you guys doing?"

Wade standing in the low door—even he had to duck—grinning, startling Anne; a highly visible blush colored her cheeks.

"Just looking around. Bout done though."

Joe sloshed to the door, and forgetting to duck, knocked his head on the low frame as he was leaving. Wade remained with Anne; they played with the calcite, focusing it to split the sunlight and make rays of color dance on the walls.

Harlo greeted Joe when he came out again.

"I ever tell you, I put up a plaque for Scotty?"

"No," Joe said, shaking his feet dry, rubbing his head.

"Yeah, I did. Go on up and have a look. It ain't much, but it's somethin. Visitin him might help get your thoughts straight better'n I ever could"

Joe looked up. In the vast blue sky, he saw two new fan-tails, one laced across the other, their intersection a solar cross, as though marking the earth where a mountain fell.

When Anne came out, Joe was already hiking up the rubble of the landslide.

WHEN IT FELL, the collapsing mountain wall smothered the basin floor and mauled its way up the other side; at its furthest reach it left one particularly enormous block of dolomite. To which Joe intuitively climbed, intrigued even more by flashes of metal that the monolith appeared to emit. Nearing it, three big horn sheep, who'd been eyeing his clamber up, abruptly fled, jostling the nearby white pine, its few branches glistening of the last snow still clinging to the short needles. Reaching the boulder, he saw that the flashes were glints of sunlight off a license plate affixed to a cleft in the rock by a lariat that had been flattened into a kind of makeshift tablet, on which an epitaph was embossed with crude cuneiform lettering cudgeled by a cold chisel:

HERE DIED SCOTT M MEEKS 1959

In the shade of the monument, on less than a square foot of the thousands of tons of naked dirt and blonde rock that had shattered like a bad tooth from Mt. Contact and fell in cascades that awful morning, Joe sat estimating the magnitude of the slide at, oh, a mile long, and maybe, oh, four or five hundred yards wide, at a depth of, say, a couple hundred feet, at least. A sizable tomb measured by total cubic feet. Imagine such a thing as a spirit, and if say there is one, and a young one at that, how was it supposed to get out from under all this? You lift a small rock and under that was another, and. . .how long would it take? Some peoples didn't use graves; they wrapped the body in animal skins and lifted it on a platform of lashed together branches. Which made sense. Being raised into the sky, that seemed a lot easier way to give up the ghost, to get free, to get away, than dig out from a pile of earth.

Though maybe, sometimes, you don't even get away even by dying.

The platinum disk of sun encroached on his plot of shade, an emulsion of visions mixed in his head. Suns, earth, crosses, graves. In one or two eons a body melds and fuses and compresses and what's left? Some Great Spirit, a few bones, a flattened petrified fallen down cabin, or maybe nothing; it all turns into nothing but more rock. Maybe, in the future, archeologists would dig up buried Meekses just like they did apes in Africa, millions of years old. Maybe the geologists or priests or whatever of that age would find the bony record of Scotty's microscopic life and make theories about the existence of humans just how nowadays they took dolomite made of hard-shelled sea life and guessed about the teeming primitive life millions of years ago, from just one bone a million years old could tell how it belonged to a young male and how old he was and how it was he died.

Joe stood up. Too bad you couldn't live that long, he thought. He watched the two jet fan-tails scatter. Too bad you weren't airborne, in sky and brilliant sun. Too bad you didn't know everything that was ever going to happen.

WADE WANTED TO follow after Joe, but Harlo had advised against it.

"Wait here an try this instead. You ain't to too young to take a hit of weed, I s'pose."

Harlo pinched some fibrous dried plant matter into a square of paper and one-hand rolled it between thumb and forefinger into a white crayon-like cigarette.

"I got me a little boo garden over in those alder there. Figure to train me a mountain lion to scare off anybody might come mess with it."

"Mountain lion?"

Harlo lit a stick match off his muddy boot.

"I got one like to come skulkin around now and then. Checkin up on me. I leave him a little somethin in return. You just come back in a few weeks an see if we ain't partners by then."

He smoked and passed the bone white cigarette to Wade, who mimicked his every move. The first taste thickened his lips. His pulse skipped. He coughed. He swirled. He spun. Anne reached to take the cigarette from him, a pretty King Arthur spell-casting she-witch wordlessly thinking her thoughts, Harlo a Cheyenne brave sitting spraddle-legged against the cabin, idly peeling off dead bark from the timber wall, his prison haircut grown out into brown mongrel hair, thick as dried moss. To Wade, in no time it seemed hours sitting, the three of them, like hired hands on break, like drunk miners, like trail weary cowboys, rawhide hands sticky with pine pitch and dust.

Harlo relit and gave the cigarette a hard suck, making it pop. "Yeah," he said, holding his breath in, "no way I'm goin back down, getting involved, nope, no way, not for nothin. Wade-ster? Too bad you're a Meeks, though you seem kinda differnt, so let's hope you ain't only one."

"Why not?"

"A Meeks is a son of a bitch. No matter what. Come whatever, he's a son of a bitch if he stays or if he goes."

He closed his eyes, and the long exhale smoothed the unshaved crags and creases in his face. Smoke streamed out between the gap in his front teeth like waterfalls.

"What happened there, Harlo?" Wade indicating the bulbous contortion on Harlo's forearm.

"That there? Must be where I broke it, years ago, fallin off my horse."

"Does it still work okay?"

"Works better'n ever, actually."

"As opposed to the rest of you." Anne's first comment in some time, an exit line, as she stood up and meandered off into the trees.

"How'd you fall off your horse? He bucked you?"

"Na, hell no. My beat up old saddle had got so wore out, the goddamn cinch broke. Matter of fact, it happened right up on the divide there. Crossin Slough Creek. Gizzard, that was my horse then, he just all up and stopped. I give him a good kick in the flank, and he goes, okay, you're the boss, and takes but one step, then, Bam. That saddle spin upside down, just like that, an next thing you know I'm flat on my back lookin at my the wrist end of my arm twisted near perpendicular to my elbow part, wonderin what the hell. See, Gizzard known the whole time the cinch had broke."

"What did you do?"

"I look up and see Scotty's took off like a banshee to get Joe, who'd got way out ahead'a me. Damn kid, I remember how he'd been mopin around weeks, barely doin chores, not ever sayin a word—which I admit I kinda liked, up to a point; hell, I near had to tie him on his own horse to get him to come up movin the herd, then we're no sooner up here and he's gone. I found out later, what happened was, he'd spotted young Marly, up here watchin out over them rat-ass sheep of her crazy old man, an off he took."

"Did it hurt?"

"Not bad. Times like that, the body takes over, you go into a bit of shock, take a step outside yourself. Some ways I kinda enjoyed it, just lyin there. Wouldn't a been a bad way to go at that. Someday way down the road some hiker or hunter or alien finds me. Wonder what become a me. How'd I get here?"

Harlo rubbing his thumb against his chipped front teeth, Wade loved how they sparked when he talked.

"Goddamn Joe. After that, he come up here near ever' day for Marly, couldn't keep him away, her and that maverick geologist up here lookin for chromite. Scotty too, followed Joe up here like a damn sheepdog. Hadn't been for that, Scotty probly still. . ."

A cool wind whipped eddies across the lake. They were in shade now; Harlo stood and stretched his arms. "I feel like havin me a hot bath on mother nature. What d'you say, Wade-ster?"

"What about Joe? And Anne?"

"They'll show up. C'mon."

Harlo headed out into the field of newly forming bear grass bulbs.

"Ugh. It smells like rotten egg stuff," Wade said when they came to a quietly steaming hot springs pool.

"Last one in *is* a rotten egg then."

Harlo shucked his clothes and picked his way whimpering about the stony accretions surrounding the pool. His naked mangled muscle-y limbs the story of his life, Wade wondered if his own body would ever harden manlike like that.

"C'mon, Wade, what're you waitin for?" Harlo walrused into the simmering turquoise water; steam bubbles frothing his torso of graying fur. "Oh man, if this ain't the life."

Wade hesitating, seeing Anne who had appeared, did not want to strip, and show his own body, with no muscle, no tone, no hair. So he just sat.

"How come you limp, Harlo?"

"Too much rodeoin. And that black ass Brahma which't got a hoof in my groin and did me some damage." He stretched wide. "Man, lookit me. Gimp leg, busted teeth, broke arms. Bet there ain't much left that's not been broke." He shook his head at his reflection. "How'd I ever make such a wreck of my own self?"

Anne moved closer, sitting against a young dappled aspen.

Harlo sank to his neck. "These last couple days, thinkin about things. All that time gone in the big house. Then bang, I'm out. An my life more'n half over. Now what?"

"Maybe kill yourself," Anne suggested.

"Hah. Yeah, maybe so. Do the world a favor."

"How about the ranch," Wade said. "You don't want it either?"

"Oh man I sure used to. Ask Joe. I was younger, I'd go on and on, how if it were mine I'd do this, do that, gravel the roads, fertilize, rotate the fields, buy out the Burchard place. I had big plans, and Joe loved to hear em. Till that last summer. Marly took over after that."

"Took over?" Anne said. "Took over what?"

"Hey, damned if she don't talk after all. C'mon, Anne, get your ass in here. What do you got to be ashamed of?"

"Who's ashamed?"

She jumped up, pulled off boots, threw off jacket and blouse, dropped jeans to ankles, and walked naked and painlessly across the same travertine grit Harlo had yelped over, but stopped short, at water's edge, to consider her reflection.

"There now, Wade. Ain't she a sight?"

Not sure he was allowed, Wade wasn't about to look, and moreover not sure he wouldn't be called on next.

"She looks even better outa the wrapper, don't she?"

"What wrapper?"

"Harlo, you're such a bullshit artist. Think I can't tell that?"

"Damn these modern girls, think every little thing's wrong with em when there ain't, not even one damn thing at all. . .'xcept they won't take no man's word for it. Wade, get the hell in here; don't make me come after you."

Knowing Harlo would not let it go, with guarded maneuvering Wade stripped, just to his shorts, and slipped hurriedly into the water.

"That's more like it. Now tell me this ain't heaven."

And so they soaked, and talked, or not, and Wade liked how the gloss of water colored their submerged bodies, Harlo's rippled umber fur, Wade's sheathed skinny white, Anne's brown areolae and auburn triangles.

Harlo noticed Wade's smile, and grinned himself. "Lookit us. We look like morning glories floating in a lily pond."

Anne, looking over her own reflection, said, "Harlo, can I ask you somethin, and get a serious answer?"

"Hard to say. Probly not."

"Outside of around here, which don't count, how would I look compared to New York City girls?"

"Anne, you don't know the half of it, how pretty you are. Hell, lookit Wade. Can't take his eyes off you."

"I'm serious, Harlo."

"So'm I. Course you are. Prettier'n any city slicker girl."

"Joe's been in New York, he don't seem to think so. At least he don't act it."

"Aw Christ, Anne. That's just differnt."

"Why?"

"Ask him yourself, he's right up there."

Which Joe Meeks was, sitting on an outcrop above them. Harlo, then Wade, called to him but he didn't answer.

"The hell with him," Harlo said.

"How come he was able to get away, Harlo?" Anne asked.

"Get away? He only just left. Have to do more'n leave, you want to ever get away from this shithole."

"At least he made somethin of himself."

"Not enough; lookit him up there. You can't tell?" He cupped his hands to his mouth. "Hey you damn eaglet, c'mon down here. You too good for us?"

Joe continued to ignore them. Anne became irritated.

"What's wrong? We ain't attractive enough for you?"

Harlo chuckled. Wade laughed too. He had found a corner where his youthful skinny body was not so public, and he felt safe from any possible teasing from Harlo.

"Well, you comin or not?" Anne yelled again, and this time Joe answered.

"I will when you're decent."

Harlo laughed, grinning at Anne, daring her.

"Here's decent for you then."

She moved to the shallows, stood up, stood in full view, water falling in pearls from her naked skin, hands on her hips, head tilted tauntingly to the side. She felt cocky. Sure of herself.

Joe looked away.

JOE LOOKED AWAY, but couldn't stop seeing, couldn't avoid the memory, the flood of them. . .

. . .those weeks after she stopped riding the bus to school and the urges he felt—and hated that he did—for Marly. She became an obsession like he had never known. He didn't know or care why. From the day Harlo broke his arm and Joe first spotted her in Independence Basin, he woke very morning to wanting only to go to her again. Each school day he could, he skipped the bus, slipped out back, saddled Loner, and spurred him the three hours to the Independence mine, pressing against the saddle, squeezing Loner's mane. Once there, he dared approach no closer than the rocky outcrop overlooking the mineral springs near her cabin. All day thereafter he did nothing but wait and watch, impatient for the next glimpse of her tangled red hair and sun-browned arms. He kept cautiously hidden though was well aware Marly was well aware of him, well aware even as she undressed to bathe in the springs, well aware of his breathless anxiety. He stayed too long. Only when she dressed and returned through the reeds to her cabin—the same cabin the winter before when he had shot the blind bison, only when the dusk began to fall, did he leave.

So it was until, one day, she wasn't alone. A black-haired man, not old Sheepeater Croft, a grown-up young Joe had never seen before. He sat across from her in the water, naked but for his sunglasses. Whoever he was, or why he was with her, he shouldn't be. She shouldn't be either. Joe burned. He sulked. He walked circles around his lair like a wounded cougar cub. He raged, jealousy boiling over in him even more after he mounted Loner and left.

The next time, it was only Marly again, the man of the time before nowhere around. This time young Joe approached her, this time he meant to sit across from her. But he didn't, at first. Nor did he speak. He squatted and threw stones, letting fly his heartsick foolishness.

"Get in, why don't you?" she said.

He savagely took off his boots, nothing else, and waded in. His dusty pants fizzed in the hot mineral water. He felt dizzy, from the heat, from the craving, from the anger, from being helplessly lost. At which point a sheepdog appeared, Scotty's dog, sniffing the pool.

Joe stood, furious anew, yelling to the trees, where he knew his brother was shadowing him, ordering him home, threatening a beating, pleading to be left alone. Knowing Scotty couldn't understand, let alone obey.

"You oughta treat him nicer." Marly rose out of the pool. "He just wants your company."

It was late; she left for her cabin. leaving Joe at a loss. So he decided to leave, he felt so jealous; he decided to stay, he felt so lonely. She was no help, making no invitation for him to follow her, no command not to. He racked his brain. He felt senseless. He climbed on to Loner and rode home.

Thereafter Scotty openly joined him, careful to trail well behind, never too near, but always in sight. For all that Joe swore and cajoled and threatened and pleaded, Scotty would not go back. He might retreat, dawdle, hang back, disappear, but every time, when Joe looked behind, there was Scotty. Always Scotty.

And so it went, the next day and the next. Joe more and more wanting to tell Marly that. . .that something, he didn't know what, but something. It was never any different

And then one day Joe turned and he was back, that man, standing over them, hair sweating, sunglasses gleaming. He set down his backpack, took off his boots, and soaked his feet.

Joe ignored him. Marly did not.

"So. You 'bout finished up there I guess?"

Joe heard hurt in Marly's voice.

"Not yet. There's a formation the other side of Mount Contact there, the Stillwater Complex. My company wants another look at a quartz monzonite vein that cuts into there."

"For gold?"

"Oh no, for PGM. Platinum Group Metals. Palladium. The Russians have most of the known sources, but they're getting depleted, so, palladium's worth a lot more than gold about now."

In his face, his rutilant eyes, his short black curls, Joe saw the devil. The man caught that look.

"Don't get all worked up, now, fella. I won't be staying. By the way, I'm Vaughn Marlowe."

Joe shrank into the water, furious that his mind had been read.

"Then where, after that?" Marly asked. "Alaska still?"

"Or Alberta. Wherever they want me."

"Vaughn, I said I'd go with you. You ain't forgot that."

"No, but Marly. . ."

"You said I could."

Joe looked at her, lonesome. His stomach rolled with grief and despair.

"Marly," Vaughn Marlowe said, "I didn't say that. How could that even happen?"

"I told you," Marly sighed. "I want to get out. Of here. I want to see places, and things, just like you done."

"See things? But it's all here, right under your feet. This is where I'd want to be, if I could."

Vaughn shouldered his pack. He smoothed Marly's hair.

"I'll be back," he added, and he left.

Joe, beside himself with hatred for Marly, could no longer contain himself.

"You do it with him, don't you?" he cried.

Not denying or acknowledging it, she stood.

"He's nice to me. Nicer than anybody else ever was."

She stared at her feet then left for the cabin. Joe, enraged, started after her. Stopped and came back. Dressed. Paced. Started down after her again. This time going inside, into her home, past the table with its flowers and tablecloth, into the back room, where she was sitting, on her canvas covered bedsprings. Hands on her knees. Sad.

He didn't know what else to say and left.

The next time, he also smoothed her hair. She said, "That's nice." She smiled at him and touched his fingers. This scared him; he felt this was not the Marly he pined for, this was another girl, a new one, and he left.

And came back the next day and the next time after that he held her and she held him and the next time he held her harder, and she held him harder too. His heart pounding, his breathing difficult, his arms stronger from holding her tight; her arms just as strong from holding him just as tight. He stayed later, too late, nearly to dusk, aching, knowing he was learning from her what she could have only learned from. . .him. He decided he didn't care. He lusted for tomorrow even as he left today, already aching for her, smelling her hair and the back of her arm.

A few days later, Vaughn was back, sitting outside the cabin, reading. The black in his hair shone blue in the bright midday shade.

He smiled when Joe arrived. "You look like you not only ate the canary, like you ate quite few of them."

"What're you doin here?"

"On my way back down to Meagher. Don't worry."

Joe sat down. Scotty limped to the nearby wood stack, the dog taking his side.

"That dog have a name?"

"Scotty don't talk, you know."

Vaughn nodded.

"He has a name for him, just that we don't know what, since he can't talk either."

"His mind is somewhere else altogether, must be."

"Just that he ain't all there. That's all."

"He's your brother?"

Joe nodded.

"He likes it here."

Joe picked at some grass. "He likes it okay, mostly, I guess."

Vaughn went back to his reading.

"What're you readin about?"

"These? Geological abstracts." He showed Joe. "This one about the Greater Yellowstone supervolcano."

Joe glanced at it. "Guess you must find that in'eresting?"

"Are you kidding? Fascinating."

"How come?"

"God, how to begin. Well, for example. Take this place. Simply speaking, we're right here and now sitting atop one of the thinnest stretches of continental crust in the world. And since the mantle right underneath is unusually near the surface, it's unusually molten. Most likely there's a big vault underlying the park, and it's like an underground chamber that over the eons fills up with magma. Eventually it starts to blister under all the pressure. That makes for quite a supersize lava dome. Given time, over thousands and tens of thousands of years, the dome has to give. It literally blows its top. Blasts the crust to smithereens, shoots fiery gassy magma a mile high, burns the sky, then cools back into particles, and what doesn't get blown by upper winds all the way to Kansas all collapses back down and makes what's called a caldera. Monstrous floods of lava smother every crook and valley in its way. The research in this particular article is about how new carbon dating indicates this has been recurring here more or less once every half million years. Which could mean there's a cycle of some sort."

"When was the last time?"

"Exactly the right question. That you asked it is interesting. How about that the last occurrence was 620,000 years ago."

"So we're goin to get blowed up again then?"

"We're overdue for it, that's for sure."

"So how come you don't leave then?"

"Well to make you miserable." Vaughn laughed; his eyes twinkled at Joe. "And that, being a geologist, you can't help wish to be just once in the right place at the right time. This certainly the right place. The time, though. Volcanic time isn't exactly like clockwork. So what do you think?"

Joe spit the tall grass blade he was chewing and picked another. "That you're full of it."

"Think so?"

Marly came out to sit with them, but she didn't join the conversation.

Vaughn picked up a white gray piece of rock. "What if I were to tell you that this dolomite, which caps almost the entire top of Mount Contact, is made of the skeletons of diatoms, teeny almost invisible creatures that fill the ocean, billions and billions of them, over millions and millions of years. When there's no ocean within 1500 miles of here."

"Really full of it," Joe said, "up to your ears."

He leaned lazily back against the cabin wall. Marly smiled, tucked her hands between her legs. Vaughn returned to his reading. And with his attention diverted, Joe reached his hand out to take Marly's.

Shadows lengthened. The time to go came. He couldn't. He wanted to never go. Nor did she want him to. She smiled, sad. He lowered his eyes, to hide his desires.

Eventually, though, he had to leave. Or suffer another whipping from his father. Which he wouldn't mind, but so would Scotty too. He stood.

"Might see you around," he said to Vaughn.

Vaughn stood to extend his hand. "Could very well be."

"C'mon, Scotty. Gotta get back for chores. Get your dog too."

Scotty stood up. As Joe walked to him, he noticed his eyes, how they seemed hollow and ringed with black. Like old Emma's. Making him look old beyond his time.

HARLO ALONE IN the mineral springs, sunning his face in the light bouncing off the water; Anne, and Wade as well, had given up waiting for Joe to come down and join them. She dressed and together the two walked down to her pickup.

Not long after, Harlo opened his eyes to find Joe kneeling next to him.

"So what's goin on, Joe?"

"Wonderin what you want to do, Harlo?"

"Soak a while, then try'n catch some trout."

"I mean, about when you come back home."

"Home?"

"You can't be a mountain man the rest of your life."

"Yeah, that much you got right. I don't know, what the hell, get some kind of job. Though I doubt anyone'd hire me. For now, anyway, I'll just lie low, keep to myself, live and let live. Hole up here till somethin better shows up."

The sun fell behind the trees. Harlo groaned as he got out. He pulled on his pants and boots, then stood up.

"I ain't the one to say I told you so, Joe, but you shouldn't of took him up here with you."

"Wade?"

"Scotty, you son of a bitch."

Harlo took a cigarette from his jacket, dropped it, and when Joe bent down to get it, Harlo stomped on his hand.

"What the hell, Harlo?"

"That's either for runnin off, or comin back, I ain't sure which."

He laughed, took the cigarette, and lit up.

"Guess you had something to get off your chest about it after all. After all these years."

"And now it's off. Done. Over an out."

Joe sucked dirt and blood from his knuckles.

"Seems like everyone thinks the best thing is sign over to Evan and let him get the most he can get for the place."

"So what if you do? Yeah, count me with him. Get what you can get, Joe. What I'd do anyway."

"Even if there's a way to keep it."

"Dang. You're bad as your old man."

"You don't want to even try."

"Hell no. Haven't for years."

"I don't know. It's. . .hard to believe."

"Joe, you're soundin more like Frances Meeks than Frances Meeks herself. If I'd ever thought there was a chance I'd get even part of that ranch. . .but forget that shit. I knew from day one I never would. And so'd Leonard, though he couldn't ever admit to it. Joe, I don't want the fuckin place. No one does. Somethin is tellin me that you wantin me to is more to do with you wantin it yourself."

Harlo looked away, inhaling, exhaling. His shirt was buttoned crooked; the opal inlaid snaps flared chaotically in the last of the sunlight.

"What's the M stand for, Harlo?"

"Say?"

"The M you put on the plaque for Scotty. I never knew he had a middle name."

"I never either, I just made it up. Looked more official that way."

"You got the dates wrong."

"Yeah, I probly did. I never was good with figures. Let's go."

Harlo threw his stub down between them and they walked down through the bands of evening light lacing the trees.

"You got a good kid there, Joe."

"Don't necessarily make me a good father, though."

"No, it don't."

"You're either cut out for it or you're not."

"Agree with you there."

At the grassy flats Anne and Wade were waiting by her pickup. Harlo squinted, first at Wade, then at Joe.

"Helluva resemblance, though. You two."

"Maybe there is. I don't see it though."

"Oughta have another look. 'xcept for Wade, we're about extincted, us Meeks."

Harlo clapped Joe hard on the shoulder.

"See you around."

He took off back into his cabin, his lame leg flying.

Anne backed her pickup around, Wade turned around as he was about to get in.

"I hope he'll be okay, Joe."

"He'll be fine. He doesn't do it very often, but one thing Harlo can do is take care of himself."

When the pickup reached the divide back down Sweetgrass Moraine, Anne pulled to a stop. They all as one turned to look out the rear window. The last sunlight swept the peaks like a cold fire, while below tree line, evening had already fallen.

Anne sniffed and turned to Joe. "I bet that ain't how evening looks in New York City, anyway."

"Hard to think that. At the moment."

"You'll just have to go see for yourself, Anne," Wade said, making Joe laugh.

"I will," she retorted, stretching her arms long. "Just waitin for the right guy to ask me."

"What about. . ."

Wade looked at Joe, who looked away.

And so they sat, quiet, softly smiling, enjoying the vista of their high altitude perch.

Chapter 16

JOE AT THE table, drinking Frances's boiled coffee, he'd come again that morning, not so much to see Frances as to take refuge, to avoid Evan, to have a place and some head time to sort things out.

His chair turned to face out the window, in the many many long long lulls between any words being exchanged, he furrowed his gaze back and forth, like he was tilling all that he saw, turning it over and over and reviving it into fertile lush arable land.

When he did speak, Frances only scoffed at him, and what she called his idle speculations.

"Maybe at least, if you had someone move up here with you, help things out? For a while anyway?"

"I'm fine on my own, same as I ever was. Now Emma's gone and it's gone over to you and all outa my hand, suit yourself. I don't care. Do whatever you damn please."

"Maybe if we invested in better irrigation; we'd get more yield if we had more water."

"Maybe we invest in a pig, we'd eat more pork and beans, if we had any goddamn beans."

She sipped from a Bell jar full of her homemade syrupy chokecherry wine.

Whatever in his mind he wanted to see as a possibility, what he actually continued to see were slopes of parched range and fields of paltry hay, sparse tufts choked by steel-green thistles, the thorny purple flowers of which the last few head of cattle had already grazed off. He saw one hungry cow go for the teats of another, receiving a swift kick in the head for the audacity.

And he saw Wade and the two dogs coming out of the barn where they'd been checking up on the ailing pregnant cow.

"Maybe Harlo would want it. He says not, but if we gave it to him, he probly would."

"Harlo, hah. Never did and never will."

"It might make sense, though, to wait and see for a bit."

"Wait and see about what? What the hell for? No point in it."

Joe nodded. "That's Harlo's opinion, too, I guess."

"It's no opinion. It's plain fact."

She tapped her fingers in a blot of wine she'd spilled. Her empty jar now joined two others stuck in their drippings on the oilcloth. She set her cane down to get up.

"Can I get you something?" Joe said, rising. "You don't have to do everything yourself."

"Then how bout go to the john for me, you want'a be so helpful."

Wade shooed off the dogs and came in the front door. Frances, distracted by the commotion, forgot her original intent and returned to the table with yet another jar.

"You oughta lay off, Frances. You'll be sweatin that stuff before long."

She wiped a trickle from a fold in her chin with the back of her scabrous hand.

"Keeps me goin just fine. You might better have some your ownself."

Wade reached for the jar. A kind of over-fermented steam clung to the top. He sniffed at it.

"What is it?"

"Ain't for kids," Frances said.

"That's okay. I'm not a kid."

"Is that so?" Frances pushed the jar to grinning Wade. "Here you go, then."

He drank guardedly, then grimaced.

"Not good enough for you?"

"Tastes like Kool-aid. But. . .kinda moldy."

"Wade, drink enough of that and you'll grow bigger'n a horse, you'll be smarter'n a whip, and you might even outlive your dad. Way he's actin, I'll probly outlive him myself."

"Outlive anybody you want," Joe said. "Serve you right."

Wade pushed the jar back to Frances.

"Maybe we should give some to that sick cow. She's having her calf now."

BY THE TIME they got to the stall, the long suffering cow had delivered. Her calf was scrawny but alive; the mother just barely. She was on her side writhing in pain, all of her insides along with the afterbirth spilled out onto the stall floor.

"She pushed out more than just her calf," Joe said.

"Got no damn choice now."

Frances sent Joe to get her shotgun then sent Wade out to the corral with two fraying felt blankets to swaddle the calf. Who was not so weak he couldn't kick and squirm and cover Wade with newborn calf goo. But he did his best, tending to this new chore, while Joe returned to the barn with the shotgun and ended its mother's misery.

As the ear splitting gunshot died out, Wade sat with his calf, rubbing mucus from its eyes.

"Wade, you look as proud as if you'd delivered him yourself," Joe said when he came out.

"Told you he'd make it."

"Seems healthy lookin." Joe knelt, squeezing open its mouth, examining it. "He'll be fine, looks like."

They readied a pen with what good hay they could salvage from the stackyard. Wade poured milk into a pail with a rubber nipple. When he offered it through a feeding opening in the gate, the runty calf shied away.

"Maybe back away a little, Wade. He's scared of you."

"Me? What for? I'm not going to hurt him."

"Well, you're a bit bigger than him for one thing. I swear you grow bigger by the minute." He tugged down Wade's t-shirt which no longer reached below his navel. "See there?"

"Maybe it's Frances's cooking."

"Maybe it's the way you eat everything in sight."

Joe took the milk pail, pumped the nipple so a stream of milk shot onto the calf's nose. Interested, he stretched out his neck, sniffed, then lunged and went at the rubber nipple ravenously.

"There he goes, Joe. Look, he's sucking it dry."

"Look out he don't suck that nipple right off and down his

throat."

In no time the bucket was drained. Wade wrestled it away, leaving the calf bawling for more, his nose stuck between the fence rails. Joe scratched its wet snotty nose.

"Now I got two hungry mouths on my hands."

"No. I'll take care of the other one for you."

"Yeah? And how long's that goin to last?"

"Till his gets on his own two feet."

"Yeah, very funny. But you go and get attached, Wade, what happens come fall? When we have to sell him."

Wade looked up. "So we get to stay till fall?"

Joe shook his head, then tousled the thatch of Wade's growing hair.

"Man o man, Wade; if you aren't some piece of work. I'll say that for you."

He sat against the fence. Wade squatted next to him. It was late in the afternoon, Anne would be coming by to pick them up, so they had nothing to do but wait.

"So what do you think, Joe?"

"What do I think? I think, well, it's bout time, and so what's got into me, that I don't get this over and done with. Can't just sit by and wait."

"I don't mind."

"You don't mind, but you don't gotta deal with getting you into a boarding school. You forget about that?"

"Not till fall though."

"No sir, Evan's right; we gotta start now. He's probly right about everything else too."

Joe fingered the soil.

"Just that, there's something about him. Like if you struck his bell, he wouldn't ring quite true."

When Anne picked them up that evening, she was full of questions about the surveying books she'd been reading. Joe explained what he could, from the little he'd picked up on his various jobs. Now and then he would suddenly tousle Wade's hair again and laugh at him.

"So Wade kinda likes it here. Thinks he's staying till fall."

"Why?" Anne said, "you mean he ain't?"

"Well he sure would if he had any say in it."

"You say it like he's the only one wants that."

"Yeah, Joe," Wade said, "you can't blame only me. Right, Anne?"

She nodded, Joe laughed, then the cab fell silent for the long ride to Meagher.

ON THE AFTERNOON drive up the Hellwater, Evan Gallantine rode in front, using hand signals to give directions to the non-English speaking driver, while over his shoulder he amicably highlighted the many features of the country to his clients in back, Mr. Kato, the rather obsequious executive, and Mr. Harada, the poker-faced owner. Though he spoke equally to both, he was sure that Kato was already 'sold', though Harada was a holdout. InterPacific, the American division of Harada's export company, was rapidly expanding operations to raise Kobe beef for the highly profitable

Japanese markets back home. Aware that they were looking at several options, Evan also knew that Harada himself coming in person revealed serious interest. Whether Harada wanted to show it or not.

So Evan was careful to avoid any hard sell, while he casually extolled the value of property as they drove through it, now and then alluding to the reasons a big footprint here would be so profitable. How it "went without saying," he said several times, that "time is of the essence." How, addressing Harada's concern that the "numbers" were too high, just for the ROI capital alone, the valley's real estate was "dirt cheap." How they should bear in mind, after all, who was better able than Evan—with deep roots in the valley—to evaluate its real and potential worth? How of course they could at least all agree on how well-positioned InterPacific would be over its competitors. No need to explain to them, he explained, the hidden values to be unlocked once they owned the land and water rights. Pointing out how the remoteness would be a perfect shield from negative publicity sensitive to foreign takeovers. Reminding them of the proximity to the major feed lots and shipping yards. Not to mention, he mentioned, that land value would easily increase tenfold. . .twenty. . .fifty fold because of the dam.

Evan stretched out his arm over the seat. Enough of business, he said. He asked them to just envision the valley, like he did, in one, two, three years to come. With the new access road to Yellowstone, think of the recreational investment potential: ski-slopes and summer resorts. The brand association with the many high-profile Americans—he didn't need to name them—corporations, movie executives and stars, owners and players of major league teams. One only had to compare this valley to similar country in Colorado and Oregon where smaller properties were selling for three and four times his price. He said proudly that he would take pride in selling to a company that had need of it for what it was best suited: cattle. That's why he felt no need for a high pressure sales pitch; for the kind of operation InterPacific had in mind, the land he had to offer was unequaled, and would easily sell itself.

Finally Harada spoke. Said he had a concern. "Arapahoe Oil? I understand it has already purchased this new dam's water rights. Is that not correct?"

Evan turned around. Harada's face was hard to read. He had young features, smooth skin and light beard, much smoother and lighter than Evan's, yet his hair was much grayer than Evan's, and Evan knew they had more in common than age.

"Mr. Harada, as a principle in the negotiations between Hellwater Reservoir and Arapahoe Oil, I can safely assure you that deal does not interfere with ours. In fact it will be so stipulated, and ensure that you have guaranteed unlimited irrigation waters." He smiled wisely. "Look around, Mr. Harada, you'll never see an opportunity like this again. At the moment, which won't last, this is bargain basement land."

This evoked a wry smile from the executive, and Evan knew he could stop talking. He rode the rest of the way in optimistic silence. Unlike when he first arrived, Harada got out when the black sedan pulled up at the Grand. Evan detected a warmth Mr. Harada had not previously allowed, this time speaking more freely, expressing admiration for the valley's beauty. He took time to show off his new western wear: cinnamon leather boots with black piping, an engraved rawhide belt with sterling silver belt buckle fashioned as a Lazy S Heart, the brand he had just recently registered with the state. When he left, he shook Evan's hand, pointedly using the American custom, and said that though there were many options, he looked forward to their next meeting.

Waving as the car drove off, Evan saw Joe walk into Goosey's Drug.

A STRING OF tin chime bells clanked as Evan pushed in the screen door. He took a seat on a cracked vinyl soda fountain stool, next to the cash register where Joe was paying for some suntan lotion for Wade.

Evan all smiles. "Long time no see, Joe."

"Who's that guy you were talking with out front the Grand just now?"

"He owns a Japanese export firm. He's looking to buy land, and I said I'd see what I could find to turn his way."

"Must have money to burn then," Joe said, "or no sense."

Joe got his change from the acned boy behind the counter, but as he turned to leave Evan swung his legs to block his way. He patted the stool next to him, asking the counter boy to bring two cups of coffee.

Joe sat down.

"So tell me about your visit with Harlo, Joe. I've had my hands full the last few days. How is my recidivist cousin?"

"He always wanted the ranch, Evan. I was only makin sure."

"Of course. Oh and by the way. I was talking to the foreman from the Tyler place. Tyler's running so many cattle now he's started up his own trucking operation. He needs good drivers, and one thing led to another, I brought it up, and he said he'd be willing to hire Harlo. We might make an honest man out of Harlo yet."

Joe didn't comment.

Evan took one of the coffees the counterboy brought for them. "So now that we're straight with Harlo, can we get on with the matters at hand?"

Joe bit his lip, and Evan reddened.

"Goddamn, Joe. What now? I just can't figure you out, you know?"

"Yeah. Makes two of us."

"I put myself in your shoes. I imagine if I'd ended up with our family's ranch in my lap, I might have second thoughts too. I imagine I might want time to think about it. Whatever. The one thing I really can't imagine is that I'd ever get the crack pot idea into my head that it might make sense, any sense at all, to keep it."

"I don't like rushin into things, if that's what you're getting at."

"I don't know." Evan added a spoonful of sugar to his coffee. "Look, if you still want more time to think about it, Joe, think about this too. It's not just about you. It's about way more. Your own friends and family. About Frances. What's she supposed to do when Arapahoe Oil backs out. Do you think anyone would pay even a fraction of what she stands to receive? What about Burchard and Gustafsen, when the sale falls through? What about a home for Wade? What about Marly? There goes her plan for the Grand. What about the whole town of Meagher and its future?"

The screen door tin bells jangled again. Anne. She caught Evan's hand waving her away and took a seat at the far end.

"Joe, I'm sorry, but if you get out of control again, pull

another one of your stunts, this time, damn you, it's on you. For once in your life you really need to think about the harm you do if you drag this down. It's not just on you. And the hell with you if you do."

Joe started to say something, then stopped. He was already an open book to everyone anyway.

Evan rose and put down money for the coffee. "I don't have anything more to say. I have to be back in L.A. for some company rah rah. You may want time, but you don't have any. This deal is complex, and if it's not in place when I get back, we lose it. All right? And you, Joe, you're the only missing link. I really hope you understand that."

Joe nodded. Evan went out, the screen door, and the string of bells, clapping behind him. Now only Joe, Anne and the boy behind the counter Joe put his palm against the screen door to leave. Anne swiveled on her seat.

"You don't want to sell it now, do you?"

"I don't know." His hand remained on the door, pushing it half in, half out. The tin bell chimes clunked both ways. The counterboy wiped his hands, giving Joe an irritated look. "I don't have much choice, the way Evan talks."

"Wade'll sure feel let down if you do."

"Yeah, I'm sure he will."

"He ain't the only one, either."

"You mean your mom?"

"Well, yeah, her too. I meant me, though."

He pressed the door reluctantly, sounding the bells once more.

"I better get going."

"I'd appreciate it one way or the other, mister," the counterboy said.

Joe nodded. He looked out over the street, then turned back to Anne. "Maybe another couple days, till Evan gets back. What could it hurt?"

"Not much. Pick you up tomorrow mornin as usual?"

Joe nodded and went out. The bells clattered resoundingly.

"Thank God," the counterboy muttered.

Anne laughed as she finished her pie.

Chapter 17

ALL WEEK ANNE drove Joe, and Wade, to the Meeks ranch on her way to work, drove them home after.

She didn't say much, but neither did Frances seem to mind as Joe began repairs: the barn's crumbling rock foundation, its timber where there was rot, the fences where wire was rusty or loose. He fashioned a splint for a broken strut in the gas tank tower, replaced all the sheared bolts on the mower sickle. To sharpen the few brittle teeth, he resoldered the switch to the grinder.

Wade, meanwhile, kept hard at it with the animals, 'his' animals, the rambunctious dogs, the white-faced calf, and especially, the sorrel filly. Three times each day he approached her, holding out a bucket of oats and old fruit from the orchard, a halter behind his back. With his face in her warm neck, stroking her sweat, talking in her ear, little by little he got her familiar with the leather until he could drape it over her head and get the bit between her teeth. Though he was excited about taming her, he felt bad about her loss of wildness, and that's really why he named her Sorry, though he told Joe it was because it was short for sorrel.

Afternoons, Joe walked. One day he walked downriver and found a few Bar Slash Heart cattle that had been missed the day Frances sold them. The Hellwater had already exhausted the spring runoff and was now so low they had forded across onto Gustafsen's land. The cattle eyed him stupidly, then bolted as though he had appeared out of nowhere. Joe squatted down on a dry boulder mid-river. The brackish flow of water barely covered the gravel; it was now more a moss-choked ditch than a river.

It was unavoidable. Irrigate this land? With what? To have water, the river had to be regulated. If you dammed it at the only logical site, Bitterroot Gap, what land would you have left to irrigate? The hell with it, his daily conclusion. Let them have their way. And let them be damned.

The fourth day, heading back, he saw a figure silhouetted against the sun-baked ridge: Wade halter-breaking his horse.

THE FIRST TIME Wade brought Sorry to the fence and tried to slip onto her back, the jumpy filly sidestepped out of reach. "Whyn't you acquaint her with a saddle first?" Frances advised, watching from the branding shed. It took all his might to lift the heavy saddle on her back, and when he had, Frances spoke again. "She ain't goin to take much to all those burrs diggin in her side," she said. Wade muscled the saddle down again, picked the burrs off, and hefted it back up. When the sorrel realized the clunky leather was actually fastened to her, she kicked, bucked, thrashed and chewed, and rubbed against the barn, but nothing got it off. After two days, she had resigned herself to it, and Wade brought her to the fence again. This time, when he sprang onto her, she stood still, momentarily puzzled. Wade sat up straight and turned to Frances, proud of himself, when suddenly the horse shot off in a dead run. Caught by surprise, Wade instinctively flung longer arms than he thought he had around her neck. "Use your damn knees!" Frances hollered, "Grab her mane!" Joe ran to help, but he was too late. Sorry drove toward the pasture in a full out flat-backed gallop, then abruptly stopped short, catapulting Wade forward. With his arms locked around her neck, he felt his legs then hips then torso fly forward of his head, and with exquisite precision he lit squarely on his feet in front of her, landing like a stunt rider. Joe broke out in a laugh and started whistling between his teeth. Frances waved her old black hat. Wade spun in a circle. He was the most exhilarated he had ever been in his life.

THE HIGHEST POINT of the ranch was at the far end of the upper Hellwater valley where Meeks land ended and the long boulder and rock ridge of Sweetgrass Moraine began. From that point, a person had a full view of the entire valley below ... even a glimpse now and then of the survey crew down below the falls of the river. And the longer he sat there, the more Joe began to wonder. Would a dam site located somewhere besides Bitterroot Gap, would that maybe allow Meeks land the water to irrigate without being inundated, without being 40 thousand acre-feet underwater?

WADE SAT WITH Frances at the table. She was drinking her wine and had nodded off. When she came to, she began to paw his head with her bad hand. His hair was growing out, and he liked her touching it.

"What happened to your hand, Frances? Your missing fingers hand."

"Them? Damnest thing. I lost them when I socked a guy years ago. I was on duty that night, and some vagrant had wandered into town and was on a nasty drunk in the Timber Bar. I had to go on in and inform him he better either call it a night or get himself locked up. He started to put up a fuss, goin on about how no woman could make him quiet down no matter if she was a sheriff. I knew better'n to start something inside, so I just told him again what I'd told him before, and that I was done talkin; if he wanted to continue I'd be waitin outside. I hoped that'd be it, but sure enough, the son of a gun followed me out, and the one thing sure was, I didn't have no chance if he tried anything, so while he was least expectin it I walloped him with my right fist. Got him square in his jaw, too."

"Really? You knocked him out?"

"No, but I got it done. Lucky for me he was so snockered he buckled down into a heap; I sure couldn't of used that hand to hit him again. That point, there was two of his broken teeth lodged here in my knuckles. Well I pulled em out and didn't think no more about it, but a few weeks later my fingers turned all black. Son of a bitch bastard had give me the gangrene. So they had to cut off the black ones. Said I was lucky not to lose the whole arm. But fact is, I never seemed to miss em all that much. Them fingers."

"I never met a real sheriff before."

"Na, I wasn't a real sheriff. I was pickin up night work durin the war. It was some hard years up here back then."

Frances left and came back with some old newsprint. She handed it to Wade. "There's a picture, if you're still int'rested."

It was a faded, one page issue of the Meagher Chronicle, a blurry photograph of a stiff, black hatted figure on the front—Frances. The headline read "Man Killed Robbing Goosey Drug."

"You killed somebody?"

"Can't you read?"

"Well yeah, but did you really?"

"Wasn't much to it. I was just out on my walk like always. That particular night I had a funny feelin passing Goosey's. There was a set of stairs around back going down to the basement, and I stopped there to listen. I didn't see or hear anything, but still, I stepped to the side and waved my hat out in front of me, callin down into the dark that I knew they was down there and to come on up or else. The whole time I was hopin no one was around to see what a fool I was, talkin to myself, when all of a sudden the stairwell roared with a gunshot and my hat blazed right out of my hand. That about startled me to death, and I got so riled I drew my revolver and reached it around, took blind aim down the stairway, and waited. Once I heard the stairs creakin, I fired off my shot. That's how it happened. It's all in the paper there, ain't it?"

"Not like what you just said."

"Well that's how it happened. I heard a body thump down the bottom stairs, then a little while passed and up comes this whisper goin, "Don't shoot no more, I'm comin up now." When he got up I stepped right behind him and put the barrel to the back of his neck. I was still shakin from bein spooked like that, so I took it pretty slow, explainin how it was right there where the spine enters the skull that was the best spot to shoot a animal for slaughter, and asked him was he aware what it was makin that cold feeling on his neck. He said he sure was. I asked him was his friend dead, and he said dead as a doornail. He was shakin like a leaf, so I eased off a bit and told him to turn around. I asked him what he thought he was doin, which he said was nothin, he and his pal heard they could make easy money in a little town with a woman police officer. I told him he was clearly mistaken, but that I was sorry about his pal, and he said he was grateful and thanks for not killin him too."

"The paper says there was only one robber."

"Yeah I know. That's 'cause I let this other one go."

"How come?"

"He didn't seem a half bad guy, just needed a scare throwed into him. Besides, I had another problem. Meagher never had its own judge back then; just one who come up only as needed. He was an old timer and cross as hell too; his own father had been a vigilante back when they just hanged up a robber right then and there, no questions asked. This judge hated like the dickens havin to come up to Meagher, and he'd of probly fired me for wastin his time when I could of shot this bastard in the first place like I did his partner. I figured my best bet was let this guy go. I explained the situation to this robber I'd apprehended, addin in a few things for effect, holstered my revolver and made a big show of peerin right at him, my face right up against his. I told him I was burnin his pitiful face into my mind so when he come around the next time, which criminals'll do, I'd then deal with him my own particular way. What was that, he wanted to know. I said I'd take him up into Independence, tie him naked to a tree and coat him with honey, that way, what the coyotes and grizzlies didn't get of him the Hellwater winter would. He said I wasn't a natural woman, and I told him he was damn right."

"And he never ever came back, did he?"

"Yeah, he did as a matter a fact. After the war ended, he showed up wantin to know was I married. He said he'd thought it over and wanted to marry me if I wasn't already." She fell silent a while, thinking about it. "But I seen he was a bit confused, like was he wantin me for bein a woman or for keepin him outa jail, but by then Meagher'd hired a real deputy, so it wouldn't of worked out either way. I said no, thanks all the same, and sent him on his way." She looked at Wade. "That might of been as close as I ever got to marryin."

SWEETGRASS MORAINE. BEAUTIFULLY still. All sound muted by the thick timber. Broken only occasionally by shouts of surveying crew. Even the cataracts, where in spring the torrent of meltwater raged and tore and gouged deeper into the glacial ridge, were quiet with the river level so low.

Down valley, the hard metamorphic ridge of Bitterroot Gap, blue black from this distance. The valley this side of it so dry already that the harsh angle sun reflected from it like from a dammed up reservoir already. No getting around it; Bitterroot Gap had to be the ideal dam site. How it laterally bisected the valley, like nature itself erected it to host a dam. Just pour cement into the mold of the Gap. A beautiful, satisfying project. Joe took pride just imagining it.

Evan, and the HRC, and everyone else, they were right. Which implied Evan was also right about Joe. That every job he had ever had inevitably had got to the same point. Sooner or later, he found fault. They were doing it wrong. Their plans were off. He knew better. Even literally found fault, like that Missouri bridge and the mayhem he got into about earthquakes. Each time, every time. At bottom, the pattern of loony unkempt imagination. That he kept repeating, even though, where had it ever gotten him? Except out of a job? And now what? Let all that money, and all the good it would do, drain through his hands? Rather than do what anyone in their right mind would do, do pronto and be done with it.

Nearby, a red tail hawk that had been completely hidden in its perch in a fully leafed cottonwood, burst into flight and soared away, it's cry hanging in the calm of the tree rimmed pocket.

Anne.

Walking up the ridge, picking her way around boulders and pine, sunlight sparkling intermittently on her face.

Joe stood up. "What're you doin up here?"

"Gee thanks. Nice to see you too."

"No, I mean, why aren't you at work?"

"It's 6:30; we have what they call 'quittin time'. Never hear of it?"

She sat on a low bough of pine.

"Noticed you up here all afternoon. What're you up to?"

"Just thinking."

"And keepin an eye out for me?"

She smiled at him; he didn't.

A pool of spring water bubbled in the flat of pine needles between them; Anne knelt down to dab some on her sweaty face. Her neck. Down her front. She pulled out the tails of her work shirt.

"That's more like it."

She dusted herself off and sat again, this time alongside Joe.

"Evan's due back soon, I guess. Know what you're goin to do yet?"

Joe cleared his throat.

"You came up to ask me that?"

"No. I got somethin else I meant to ask, though."

She took a photograph from her shirt pocket and handed it to him. Recognizing nothing, about to hand it back, Joe looked again. Two young people, embracing, hair swirling, mouths laughing. This time, though he'd never seen it before, he knew now. Like it had happened yesterday.

He turned it face down and handed it back.

Anne turned it face up. "All I just want'a know is, what happened with you and mom?"

His knee began to bounce. His lips moved, but no words passed.

"Come on, how come you can't just tell me about it?"

"Anne, it was one summer; not even. It was years ago."

"So? I never seen mom look that happy, never in my whole life. I never seen anybody ever look that happy. Not in Meagher, anyway. I just want to know about it."

"What do I know. Can't you just ask her?"

"You think I never have?" She sat down, chewing on a strand of her hair. "Since before I can remember I was askin her, who's this, who's this, who's this? What happened to him? What were you so happy about? But would she ever tell me one word about it? No, except to lick me for naggin her. I know you were in love, that's plain as day. So what happened that stopped it?"

A breeze flickered the higher tree tops. Shadows lengthened.

"There's things people do you just can't undo. You live your life and try not to get too strangled by what's past."

"I don't care whatever I feel lookin back later on, if at least just once I'd feel that happy about something."

She stood up and walked off, her boot steps puffing up dry pine needle dust; she walked back, shaking her hair out of her face. She took the photograph back.

"God I've wanted to meet a boy made me feel like that. I thought if only. . ." Her voice cracked, sucking in a cry that came back out a big laugh. "So here I finally meet up with him, and wouldn't you know, he only turns out to be only you."

Anne so sorry-sweet looking, Joe reflexively reached for her hand, then thought better of it. It was, all of it, just too much and he didn't want to remember. He didn't want to explain; he felt like he could more easily take flight like that red tail hawk than explain it. Any of it.

For a long time neither said anything else. The sun setting, the hollow darkening. The sound of a truck.

"Hear that?"

"That's probly Norman, still workin."

"I don't get what it is he's surveyin this high up for."

"For the new dam," Anne sighed, grooving her boot into the dirt.

"How could that be? All the surveying would have to get done before any site'd be approved."

"Then ask him if you don't believe me. I just map out terrain, I don't make it."

Joe considered this. "Maybe I will. Tomorrow. You can bring. . ."

"Not tomorrow I won't. It's Graduation Week. I'll bring you the day after. Norman's been wantin to meet you anyway; you should hear me go on and on about you." She threw her arms around his waist, pullin him to her. "I think I love you, Joe. You know that?"

"Aw c'mon, Anne, don't."

He leaned back from her, startled by her irresistibility. "Come on, let's go get Wade."

"Asshole."

She pushed him off and took his hand, not letting him let go, until she stopped and pointed. "Hey look."

Far below, Joe saw Wade was riding his horse Sorry in the corral.

"He looks like he belongs there, don't he?" she said.

Chapter 18

HIS DAILY SCHEDULE of facilitating contracts and expediting agreements made Evan Gallantine a familiar face in Meagher: at the Timber Bar, at Treasure State Bank, at Goosey's Drug and Maloney's Dairy-Gold creamery. At Hell Gate Printing.

Hell Gate was run by Jack and Ruth Loomis, and was housed, like its owners, in Meagher's one-time railroad depot, a Romanesque Revival clay-brick building built at the turn of the century to be the terminus of a railroad spur linking the booming Independence mines with the smelters and refineries and markets of the mid-west. No sooner was it built than the mineral bearing veins gave out, whereupon, one by one and as though overnight, those mines went bankrupt. Whereupon the railroad terminus went belly up. Hoppers of ore were abandoned in place and left for dead, their cast iron wheels welding in conjugal rust with the steel rails on which they expired, dead weighting the underlying oil soaked ties into embankments swallowed up by invasive milkweed and spurge that overran the gravel ballast and hastened its dispersion into high entropy disorder. And so, for the decades ensuing, the widowed depot sat off by itself, left at the altar, weathering and withering, gown gone to weeds, windows boarded, mortar eroded, wrought iron rusted. A living dying monument to bygone prosperity and to the daily inevitability of ruin and decay, testifying to the natural order of rise and fall, to the collapse of all things, of Meagher and, in some ways, of humankind itself.

Evan first made overtures to the Loomises in their capacity as progenitors and dead-earnest publishers of The Meagher

Chronicle, their periodical which now was a clarion broadside of saturnine reportage and embittered op-eds, a monthly organ of gloom that like a low-pressure cyclone, stirred up regularly recurring pestilences of woe in the tiny but heedlessly suggestible community of Meagherites.

In contrast to all other local establishments, it was slow tending for Evan, cultivating a relationship with the Loomises, who had by this point given up on life's rare joys and intermittent pleasures, which they once enjoyed, even in the dark years of America after the war when they were both, Jack and Ruth, due to their being idealistic and left-leaning journalists, driven to this far end of the interior seeking refuge from the many red-baiting and black-listing pilers-on who were then in vogue throughout the country. And continued to enjoy, well after those first days in Meagher and the birth of their one child. They purchased the abandoned depot, mounted their Air-Stream out back, and staked their future and that of their son to the admittedly insignificant but happy enough life they envisioned spreading out ahead of them. Their hopes were simple then, to expand their newspaper and raise their son, and so they did, happily enough, as his 18 years passed and time stood still. They did so, that is, more or less, until one drunken night, carousing with cohorts, that very son and his boyhood friends in one spontaneous burst of pride mass enlisted in the army, for honor to their people and service to their country. And an all-expenses paid passage to Vietnam. With great fanfare these young men signed on and shipped out, and with no fanfare at all, one of them, that particular son, came back, in a small black box, wrapped with a polyester flag, and a photostat letter bearing the signature of the, by then, lame duck President Johnson.

That wan afternoon forward, unsurprisingly, the simple

hopes of the Loomises were leveled, every joy vaporized. For them, life was voided of even its most minimal riches, as fast and as completely as the mother lodes in the mines that predated them. The moderately virtuous circle of their outlook turned viciously downward, precipitously bottoming out at a dead low flat line of the deepest bitterness. In time, as the amputation of life numbed them, they reverted to vacuous asceticism, withdrew into the empty patriotism of the Silent Majority. They channeled their accreting despair into the Chronicle, disseminating its recurring pall of increasingly pathological indifference. Day by pointless day, in step with their depot and its history of erosion, as another LOVE IT OR LEAVE IT sticker was pasted on their Rambler, as garish posters of American flags papered the shop walls, they withdrew into a self-enveloping shell of grief gone sour.

But Evan endured the hard eyes. With his growing connections throughout the area, he was able to foster a small but steady trickle of advertising, trade the Loomises had long neglected. With patient, persistent visits, in several days' time he little by little won Jack's grudging alliance. The information Evan let drop about the progress of the dam began to revivify the spiritless articles of the Chronicle. He had found an opening the Loomises had forgotten to seal. The old waiting room of the depot, filled with its out of date jerry-rigged presses, began to crank with the sound of new business.

On the first of June, the morning of Graduation Week, Evan arrived at Hell Gate early to pass along more news about recent developments. Jack raised his head from behind an offset type machine where he was spooning dollops of congealed black into the inkwells. Amid the clank of cams and joggers, his greeting was lost, but Evan saw levity in Jack's hands as he beckoned over his gloom-infused wife.

Ruth stepped out from the back, her sullen face enhanced by black-smudged cheeks, and exhaled a plume of cigarette smoke most foul into air already palpable with solvents. No matter how encouraging Evan's news, Ruth never had happy hands or a good word.

But again, Evan disregarded the carapace of Ruth's outer disposition; as ever, he knew eventually he would find some kind of inner angels lurking within her. He returned a smile that hadn't been given as Ruth grudgingly dragged over a large skid of paper stock for him to sit. . .and left.

Joining Jack, Evan pulled a newly minted supplement from under the spurts of drying powder. He carefully reviewed the information he had supplied the day before.

"More news?"

Jack sat on the skid and opened his daybook expectantly.

Evan nodded, considering what best to say and how best to say it, when surprisingly, Ruth returned. Shedding her grimy printer's apron, she offered him cinnamon donuts and coffee. The coffee with an oily based film on it, the donut a sugar hardened stone a hungry man could be guaranteed to flint a tooth on ... but Evan welcomed the unexpected gesture nonetheless. And noticed something like a grain of light in Ruth's otherwise dead eyes.

"You tell him?" she said to her husband.

The couple exchanged what might have been a smile.

"Yep. Fact is, Mr. Gallantine, we're planning to go to twice't a month now. Um hmm."

Evan was truly floored. "Well, congratulations. That's great to hear! Bigger news than mine, that's for sure."

Ruth raised her palm. "An there's one thing more."

"We're lookin to build a new house," Jack cut in.

Evan nodded, inwardly rejoicing, that even pillars of salt like Ruth Loomis were not immune to the renewal properties of hope. He dunked his impervious torus of a pastry into his inky coffee and 'ate' it with great ceremony, a pantomime of delighted chewing, as though the most delicate of French eclairs, while discretely ejecting the offending morsel from his mouth into his palm to scatter on the greasy floor. But this was not his being deceptive. This was the very reason Evan loved this work. There was as yet not a pinch of earth broken, not a yard of concrete poured, no laborer hired, no blueprints except in draft, and yet the merest possibility of renewed growth had seeped into even the hardest veined Meagherite and taken root.

And so in such high spirits, as he returned to town, he perceived a new vitality whistling the air, a lightness in peoples' step pervading the street. In the bar, the cafe, outside the bank, passing the statue of Major Thomas F. Meagher. In the people's visiting, drinking, playing pool, eating. In Arnie Beiber leaving Goosey's Drug with his two illegitimate sons, each laden with comics and cokes. In the ornery widow Nadine Much gabbing with the staid and female-averse Sheriff McComb. In one couple then another walking hand in hand and arm in arm. Evan imagined inside the homes the hearths rekindled, the husbands' clean-shaved, the wives' earrings sparkling.

And in the Grand.

Going inside, Evan remembered it was the first day of Graduation Week. The establishment had become, by some unvoiced decree, a hub of spectators brimming with anticipation for the annual parade. Person after person greeted him with nods and monosyllabic murmurs, howyadoins and nicetoseeyas. A white-haired couple danced to invisible music. Steaks sizzled in the kitchen. Balls clacked on the pool table.

Joe Meeks nowhere to be seen.

AVOIDING THE HUBBUB, Marly kept to her room, as had been her wont more often, of late. With Squash working full time now, she had less cooking and waitressing, cleaning and bartending, to tie up her time. And with more idle time she had begun to spend more time idling through décor and design magazines, pouring over architecture and remodeling digests, pondering and revising her many expansive plans for renovation. Along with and in darker counterpoint to that, she found in her new down time old ways to worry, more and more finding folly in an idea as soon as it came to her, uncovering two reasons why not for every reason why, each day lending credence to a more colossal fear coalescing in her imaginations: That, one way or another, the tidal wave of change coming at her from all around would surge and swell and in some as yet unknown way sweep everything away from her, unless—if she could only think how!—she could find a way to hold on.

It was all the worse for feeling left alone with these worries. Marly was also becoming increasingly apprehensive about her daughter, about her clothes soaking in softeners in the sink, her new shirts hung and drying on window sills, her work boots resoled and re-heeled. Marly could not see these welcome signs of Anne's budding self-image without feeling the anxiety of losing her own. A new strand of gray, a slow sag in her breasts, an intermittent presence of lines when—more like if—she smiled. At breakfast, with orders of lamb's liver frying on the stove, the meat sweating, the blood sizzling, inadvertently burning her fingers seeing Anne about to leave for her job, Marly volubly sighing, "Whoo boy, I don't see how I'll keep up much longer," Anne left without a word. Late evening, rubbing the blistered backs of her hands, leaving the bar crowd's laughing and drinking and North Dakota jokes to trail Anne half way up the stairs to her room, Marly advising, "Honey, just make sure not to put this surveyin job ahead of your future," Anne wordlessly nodding and quickly shutting her door. At night, Anne on the lobby davenport buried in her books—surveying books!—Marly twisting knots into her red hair, speculating almost woefully, "Honey, you know I just can't help look around and feel so happy that you have so much I never had," Anne slapping shut her books and straight up to her bedroom.

During the night, Anne woke. Something in the dark. Sitting on the edge of the bed.

There was a long silence until Marly spoke.

"I don't know, Annie, I really don't understand. When there's so much for you here."

"Like what, mom? Waitressin and changin sheets?"

"No, no no. We'll have help for that." Marly staring into the dark as her vision began to play on its screen. "You know, there's talk of a summer theater here. There'll be actors, and actresses, and audiences." Straightening the comforter over Anne despite the summer night's heat. "We'll have gourmet dinner theater, Anne. Such fancy candlelight meals, oh, it'll be. . .it'll be so . . ."

"Yeah Mom; I get it. It'll be nice, for you, to finally have what you want."

Hearing Anne's quiet brush off, Marly's chest fell. It's come to this? Anne not even bothering to pitch a fit?

"Honey, I don't get it. Why don't you want to be happy?"

"Mom, you think I don't? You think I don't want that more than anything?" She turned over, murmured into her pillow. "Maybe it's more the other way around, an you're the one that don't want to be happy."

As she rose to leave, Marly noticed new curtains hung on Anne's windows. She could not tell what pattern, or see what color.

AND INCREASINGLY AS well, Marly was angry, angry that she was angry at Joe. Angry that she could not stop finding reasons, every day, that all the good fortune coming her way would be lost and would be all because of Joe. Would be all his doing. Again! And after all these years! Fool me once, she chanted in her mind as it fell into restless sleep.

She rarely saw him now. He no longer stopped in the Mint at night. He didn't come when she left word about dinner specials she knew he'd like. What she did see of him was when, late in the day, Anne dropped him out front on her return home. She noted they sat in the cab before he got out; she timed how long the pickup idled before Anne pulled it around back. She noticed Joe's slow walk and how he turned to look back. She detected how Joe was in Anne's thoughts when she stopped by to look in on her, knowing how a mother knows that her child, despite the feint of not answering, was not asleep.

Marly went to bed, eventually to sleep, in fits, arm clutching her pillow. She felt alone when she had never felt alone in all the years before. So many years, so comfortably, and now, so much inexplicable dread. What could cause such anguish when before there was none? What but Joe Meeks?

One day, leaving Squash all in charge, Marly wandered into Joe's room. His mattress was crooked, his sheets in tangles, and she felt a bit better knowing his night was as fitful as her own. She sat on sheets still warm with his heat, spread her hands on the contour of his sleep. Her breasts ached like they hadn't since Anne was born, reminding her of the insatiable longing she felt then, nursing this infant, this newborn, this living creature suckling her breast, utterly trusting and dependent, as Marly had never been allowed to be.

Ah Christ what's happening to me, she moaned, and laughed, and rose to go. She noticed, on the floor, a photograph. She picked it up and stared at it, into it, beyond it, its image of a windy-haired laughing girl in the arms of a laughing sandy-haired boy, slow to reconstitute her memory. She felt it though, her detachment, like when you touch fire, the feeling delayed. For an instant she felt such joy, remembering.

Then joy became anger, realizing the photograph was only here because Anne brought it here. Dropped it here as she sat with it here, Marly held her breath as it dawned on her, what was happening, to her daughter. With, of all people, Joe Meeks. And what a mistake it would be, such a big mistake, and worse? Her mother was the last person Anne would ever want to hear it from. The last one she'd ever believe.

The woman who knew it best.

TO TAKE FULL advantage of the impending Graduation Week celebrations, Father Sterling planned a major service for that

Sunday morning. He hoped for heavy attendance, and with good reason. It had not escaped attention that, soon after his arrival, on the mere occasion of his making an insignificant inquiry about how he might best procure a source of cheap ready red wine for the Eucharist, how word of it spread like prairie fire. Now here was a man with the auspices to sanction the consumption of alcohol on Sunday. The full import of what this meant came in lightning-like epiphany: No person in Meagher would ever fail to give full unqualified trust and support to a such man. And whatever such a man were to proclaim and hold forth, they would believe to their bitter end.

Already, come that Sunday dawn, he was witness to even more than his most optimistic expectations: throngs of young and old and men and women filing into the black granite church. By ten o'clock, there was not an empty pew in the house.

In preparation for this particular special occasion, Father Sterling had enlisted Wade as an acolyte. And, initially, Wade was very enthused. They rehearsed the ceremony day after day in the week before the service. During that time as they enrobed in the vestry, Father Sterling took advantage of the young ears at his side, and mused at great length upon his past. He recounted, glowingly so for Wade, the halcyon years in the seminary, where as a philosophy wunderkind he first acquired his passion for Kierkegaard. He spoke, if not miserably, then somewhat less glowingly, of the dark ages thereafter, when life devolved into an endless ministry of frustration. It was more than a pastor, none more than he, could bear, that otherwise ardent and devoted Christians would refuse to open their souls' minds (as he had opened his own) to the apotheosis of philosophical achievement that Kierkegaard had attained, that no matter how much his own ardor consumed him, his laity asked meekly, again and again, for those parochial words of God they were used to. As parish after tiny parish proclaimed itself at wit's end, seeking simply enlightenment and salvation, not deeper understanding, Father Sterling earned a reputation such that no parish, no matter how small, would accept him. Finally he had no other choice: he accepted the final offer from the bishop and volunteered for Meagher, where for years the diocese had been unable to find a clergyman willing to establish a congregation where none had ever before been able to find purchase.

Wade, completely enthralled with Father Sterling leading up to that service, was miserable when it came to pass. Like in a bizarre dream, Father Sterling transubstantiated from a soft-spoken philosophical oddball into a furnace fusing manic apprehension into a fiery cold sweat. His droning of the liturgy reduced into a stew of incantations, the frenetic orator spewing forth more and more spittle as again and again, he forgot his place, and covering himself in a swoon of redoubled jabber, intoned a vehement mix of Saint James English and bastardized Latin salted with pidgin Greek. He rushed into the ritual blessing of the wine, his hands quavering so violently Wade couldn't help but slosh the wine as he valiantly tried to pour from the silver urn into the jittery chalice. Less than half full, Father Sterling maniacally clutched the sacred cup and gulped it down in one vast open-throated swallow, while Wade tried to remember which sacred cloth to drape over his left arm and which over the right. It was all too much, and that was even before the reeling minister pivoted abruptly, to raise the holy cup to the high cross, when his entire holy raiment swept around, knocking both the tray of wafers and the wine from each of Wade's hands before they could transform into the blessed

Body and Blood. Father Sterling, aghast, peppered Wade with a farrago of profanities, beseeching him to run quick to the sacristy for more, forgetting that he himself, with Sheriff McComb, had finished the entire supply the night before.

So informed, Father Sterling turned to the congregation, facing what was by now a scudding sea of rough faces and thirsty throats. He majestically raised his pastoral arms, a gesture of calm to mask his predicament, and only Wade could observe his small frantic eyes roll in circles, only Wade could hear the hissing plaint to God beseeching Him to magically turn something, anything, into more wine.

Wade, desperate to end the frenzy, whispered a sudden proposal to use gin instead—he had seen an ample supply in the cabinet—but Father Sterling decried the suggestion. It would be a travesty of celestial scale, and besides, he could hardly pass off juniper based swill as the blood of the Lord. So Wade expanded his solution, and dashed without approval over to the Mint, where he obtained a jar of sheep's blood which he knew Squash was using to experiment with sauces. A quick addition of a few drops to the gin made it swirl into an oily liquid, that was not unlike red wine. Father Sterling, taking hope, seized it and drank heartily. His eyes slammed shut then sprang open; his neck swelled and chest heaved. He coughed, gagged, then, miraculously, drank another. Dabbing his lips with Wade's frock, he nodded and quickly took point in the sanctuary, where he snapped into a posture of utter divinity, turning to the congregation and beckoning them forward. While Wade mixed, the aisles of supplicants came a second, a third, a fourth time to his altar.

Soon Father Sterling was trembling in joy. After years of failures, this was clearly far and away his most successful service ever. As the multitudes sat gabbing and chatting in the nave, Father Sterling extolled upon ethics and angst and existentialist faith and the subjective relationship between the individual and the God-man Jesus in an articulately abstruse mashup of a sermon.

At noon, after everyone had stumbled out into the sunlight, after Father Sterling had passed out in the vestry, swaddled in his robes, Wade shucked his gown and vowed never to acolyte again, no matter how desperate Father Sterling became.

YEARS BEFORE, WHEN automobiles began to be generally available to the young, a phenomenon not uncommon to many of the state's towns began to occur in Meagher, and became a sinister ritual of its youth, who, on the wavery cusp of adulthood, and like the generations before them never shy about spiking their juvenile bodily vessels with a toxic brew of Lemon Hart 151 and sloe gin, began lemming-like running those 4-wheeled parental hand-me-downs headlong over rocky embankments or piling them into one of the many dangerous curves of the Upper Hellwater road. Statewide, each successive class was yielding a greater number of celebrational high-speed car crashes, one more gruesome than the previous; the roadside markers that tallied each fatality at the location of these wrecks grew thick with the accumulating leaves of white cut-metal crosses. Finally, to bring a halt to the deadly rising parabola of such incidents, one wizened Meagher old-timer put forward a motion to the Chamber of Commerce (which briefly existed at the time) that, to thwart the efforts of the local young to die that way—young—the town would sponsor a week-long stay-put all expenses paid drunk, with all graduating seniors taking up residence at the abandoned state hatchery on Castle Creek, where all during their bacchanalian revelry they could be corralled and contained and, most especially, kept off the roads.

And so it was decreed, the first annual Meagher Graduation Week.

This year as before, the high school band kicked off with a ceremonial march through town; this year again setting a new record, two dozen straggling underclass boys and girls, including many who could read the music, and several who could also play it. As always, as they rounded unevenly onto First Street, the honored seniors in ill-fitting gowns merrily jeered and pelted the band with the odd crab apple, then fell in line behind. As ever, the parade stopped in formation, of sorts, at the Major Thomas F. Meagher statue. There, thick hands of applause exhorted them to play more, because, though they played the same song they didn't play it the same way, and so they impressed the crowd with their seemingly unlimited repertoire. Homemade fetishes waved, boots tapped in the street, husbands and wives two-stepped in the dirt. Graduates were called alphabetically to cast up their diplomas and tattered caps, ticker-taping the sky, all to the raucous cheers of all Meagher and the occasional curious visitors, whereupon the acned rabble continued on its way the two miles to the hatchery, blazing their path with the breadcrumbs of discarded liquor bottles.

And thus began their final saturnalia of childhood. For the seven debauched days thereafter, with the last blush of innocence on their cheek, these rookie adults would drink themselves into oblivion, fighting and singing and necking and diddling in the box elder brush with abandon. All week Castle Creek would flow with beer foam, adolescent vomit, and alcohol-clarified urine, male and female commingled. All night angry beaver tails would slap the pond waters in vain as the pulchritudinous youth invaded their dams to clumsily, though ardently, enact their human copulations in the soft and accepting mud, secreting into it their robust human fluids. And inevitably, afterward would come the small rash of pregnancies, the frenzied claims and counter-claims, negotiations in front seats of cars, and hasty marriages as a consequence of vaguely remembered pleasures. In this way as well, the local population decline was reversed, as the incidence of adolescent autocides declined, and the bounty of last year's crop of spring wheat babies bouncing on their grandmother's hips rose, every bright-eyed one as uncertain of its fathering as positive of its vacuous future.

VERY LATE ON the first night of festivities, the Mint finally emptied, Marly's only remaining customer was Father Sterling, ruddy faced happy in the aftermath of his largest service to date. Wade was shooting pool with Squash, learning the complicated shots developed by ages of bar flies to effectively utilize the long stitching where Marly had repaired green felt with patches of old hats.

Helping himself to more peach schnapps, Father Sterling took Wade's arm while Squash lined up a bank shot.

"Son, you are unquestionably the most talented acolyte I have ever had the chance to encumber. You must not quit. Not now at least. Please, tell me you will not."

Wade shook his head. "Why don't you try Squash?"

"Aw no, that poor post-pubescent soul? I can't abide a boy whose face looks like it caught fire and was put out with an ice pick."

Father Sterling cackled his way back to the men's room, but Wade himself envied Squash's face, pocked as it was with spontaneously bursting whiteheads. Wade's own face still remained clear as a boy's, and though in truth he had a rash of pimples on his shoulders, what good was acne where nobody could ever see it?

Squash wasn't saying so, but it was obvious to all that he was staying late waiting for Anne, who had left town to spend the day off with her boss and his family. Earlier in the day, Marly Croft had sat him down and force-fed him beer. . .despite that he didn't ever drink. She told him she had been doing some thinking about careers, his in particular, she told him. She told him she was considering, eventually, giving him a share in The Grand, along with herself and her daughter. Listening to her coaxing words, he saw his future coalesce: what with inheriting the family creamery, and the expansion coming to Meagher, taking over the Grand as well? He would easily become town's most prominent entrepreneur. It didn't need any hinting by Marly, who better would ever come along for Anne? She was destined to be his, whether she knew it or not didn't matter. What better option did she have?

Now, idling at pool with Joe Meeks's kid, Squash had real objectives to contemplate: Maloney's Dairy-Gold, Marly's Grand, Anne's hand in marriage. His expanded creamery, with spotless aluminum equipment like he had seen on the visit to Denver, rows of separators gushing white milk and thick cream, the gleaming stainless steel churns and automatic packagers. He foresaw himself as the clean-faced smiling Mr. Lowell Maloney arm in arm with Mrs. Anne Croft Maloney, beautiful of buttermilk skin and mellifluous voice. All a delicious end of life under the tutelage of the overbearing Edna Maloney and the humble homely Charles Maloney.

When Anne did return, she passed by humming to herself as though lost in thought and as though he, Lowell Maloney, were just anybody. But Squash knew better now. He knew their destiny. He knew them as the envy of every Meagher has-been or would-be bride, their lives the fruition of two childhoods of solitude and deprivation. He stood. Indomitable. Unwavering. He took fire, anticipating the day when he could dish it out to Anne like she had dished it out to him. As she went past him, pretending she wasn't at all aware of him, he took her arm.

"Hey!"

Anne whirled, then saw it was only Squash.

"Damn you Squash, just 'cause you work for mom now doesn't mean you can grab-ass as you please around here."

"Anne, your mom don't say what I do or don't do. You neither. I say."

"Then tell yourself to do somethin useful, like go wash your face."

She pulled her arm back but he held on tighter. "I think you better try bein nicer to people. It's time you faced facts. Even your mom sees how we're a good match. But I won't always be here for you."

Enraged, Anne yanked free, yanked so hard she fell into the cue rack and broke it. Chunks of plaster fell to her feet. Wade stepped out of harm's away as she seized a cue stick, her face burning with the low hanging pool table light.

"Squash, I swear, one of these days."

Despite her brandishing the thick shanked cue, Squash

advanced on her, impressed by his own audacity.

"I ain't backin down to you no more, Anne."

"I don't care what you do. We ain't married, in case you ain't noticed."

He grabbed her waist. "Not yet, maybe."

Anne went white. Suddenly it was not Squash clutching her, it was fate.

"You asshole!"

She swooped the cue stick down across his shoulder. He fell back as another blow immediately followed. Father Sterling, returning from the bathroom, turned to Wade.

"Ten bucks that she'll skunk him thoroughly this time."

"Anne honey?" Marly came around the bar. "Please don't tangle with our help. Sweetheart?"

Anne ignored her, raining successive blows on Squash, who backed away to the door, smarting not from the beating but from the surprise, genuinely astonished that Anne wasn't behaving the way Marly led him to expect, not whatsoever at all, and he wondered, was he premature in his proposal? Then with one look into her wilding savage eyes he all at once understood. Her anger was no different than his own. It was not at him, any more than his was at her. It was bigger. It was at the boys who scoffed behind her back by day then plied her with booze by night. At them having their way with her and worse, letting them, worse yet, daring them. At the inevitability of their common Meagher fate. Deflecting her pummeling attacks, Squash understood they shared the same futile rage, and he silently cursed heaven for its determination to forever keep her from him. Then he stopped fending her off, dropping his arms, exposing himself.

"All right," he shouted, "go ahead; have it your way! But one of these days you're gonna realize I'm the only one who don't deserve it."

He flung open the door and left. Anne glared after him, lowering her now broken cue stick.

Marly stepped wearily, and hesitantly, toward her daughter.

"How come you got to be so hard on him? He's been so nice lately, as far as I can see."

Anne turned. "You put him up to it, didn't you? Part of your big plan, right?"

Marly took the cue from her hands. "Anne, you could do a lot worse."

"And if maybe I want to make my own plans?"

She was breathing heavily, trying to contain herself. Then turned to head up.

"I know I sure couldn't do no worse than you ever did."

Chapter 19

WADE, WHO HAD eaten one breakfast in town already, was in Frances's kitchen making another. Joe sat with her at the table. He looked at the clock. Anne, after she had dropped them off, said he should give her boss Norman an hour to get his crews out, then he could come by to meet with him.

The phone rang. Joe acted like he didn't hear.

The phone rang again.

"What about that phone?" Frances said.

"What do you mean? What about it?"

"What about why don't you answer it?"

"It's your phone."

The phone rang again.

"Well?"

"Joe, ain't nobody'd callin me anymore."

Joe stood up, not to answer the phone, but to walk quickly to the door.

"I need to borrow your jeep."

"Why ask me? Jeep's yours. Like everything else."

Wade came in proffering a heaping plate of bacon and eggs he had prepared. The phone rang again, and he picked it up. By then, Joe was gone.

"Evan's on the phone," Wade called outside.

Joe opened the jeep's door. "Tell him I'm not here."

"I already told him you were."

"Then tell him I'm not."

He climbed in and took off in a ball of exhaust, Wade left holding the door. One of the dogs, the golden, lumbered up the porch. As he scratched Butter's ears—Wade had first christened him Buddy for his chumminess but revised it to Butter for his tawny coloring—the jeep roared back and lurched to a stop. Joe rolled down the window.

"You want to come along, or not?"

Wade shrugged, like it didn't matter to him but okay if you want, but he immediately went to get in. As he opened the door, Butter jumped in ahead, swatting Joe's face with his burr-studded tail. Joe slapped his rump, and Butter sat appreciatively; in all his dog days he'd never been allowed in the jeep. His large mouth panted with gratitude and bad breath.

Joe pulled out, the engine sputtering.

"This gutless thing."

"You're not supposed to use second gear," Wade advised.

"What?"

"When Frances and I were driving she told me make sure I don't use second gear. She said to save it."

"Save it? Hah. That's Frances for you. No wonder this clunker cuts out."

He shifted hard into third, throwing Butter happily into Wade's lap, where he was better able to stick his snout out the window.

"Wade, what was that you said again? About Frances and you? Driving?"

Wade leaned his head out with his dog. The river of air blew the long hair of Butter's ears in his face.

"You aren't thinking you're old enough to be driving I hope. Hear me, Wade?"

"Oh man! Evan was on the phone, and I forgot to hang up."

Joe gave Wade a sidelong glance, which Wade avoided returning.

"Wade?"

"Goddamn. I didn't eat my bacon and eggs."

Joe sighed.

"Oh and now you're using swear words now too?"

He drove the rest of the way in silence.

THE SURVEYING WAS trig-leveling halfway up Sweetgrass Moraine, Anne working at a plane table. When Joe pulled up, she smoothed her hair and ran to the jeep.

"Norman'll be here any minute; he said make sure you stay so he gets to talk to you."

She quickly leaned in to kiss Joe's ear, then returned to her plane table.

Wade hopped out to go look over her shoulder; Butter bounded out after him to mark his new territory, but Joe stayed put. After a while he got out, stood shielding his eyes in all directions as though making his own kind of survey, then inched his way over to Anne.

He was impressed, how she was contouring, plotting transit readings from notebooks onto topographical paper lined with a light blue grid. Looking over her work, he recognized the transposed topography of the cirque above Sweetgrass Moraine, its dry creeks and spidery ridges like the venation of a palm-shaped leaf.

Two boys from the crew returned, dropped all their transit equipment and staked out space for a break in the shade of Norman's quarter ton pickup. Norman appeared a few minutes after.

He was younger looking than Joe expected, despite his wiry frame and bristle of white stubble, a no-nonsense man in earnest but not aggressively so, going straight to check Anne's work. He rubbed his chin, made a correction, reminded her to darken every fifth contour, then initialed her worksheet. That done, Anne pointed; they both laughed. The boys had already fallen asleep.

Norman turned to Joe. Joe nodded; Anne grabbed his arm, pulling him nearer.

"This here's my Joe."

Norman shook Joe's hand. "Dang glad to finally meet; she's told me plenty enough about you."

"Yeah; Same here."

Norman's bony fingers still held his hand.

"So I been hearing around that you're holding things up."

"Don't see a reason for the hurry, that's all."

"Sure can't blame you for that. Inheriting a place only to turn around and lose it. But what about how Anne's saying you have questions about the dam site itself."

"Well no, not exactly, I mean. . .anybody could see how down below at Bitterroot Gap is the perfect site for it. All's I said to her was I didn't get why you're surveyin up here in Sweetgrass Moraine. A reservoir from Bitterroot Gap wouldn't flood this high up."

"Na, heck no. That Bitterroot Gap site was all done before me. I'm doing a timber survey."

"Timber survey? For who?"

"Hellwater Reservoir Corporation."

"HRC? This is all state forest land though."

"Yeah, till a month or so ago. HRC traded some of its lower rangeland for this entire tract. I guess to bring in a big lumber operation here."

"Timber here? It's mostly all spruce; why trade valuable grass range for scrub trees. You wouldn't make anything on it."

Norman nodded. "I don't see why either, but all the pressure they're putting on us, I guess they need it whatever. And quick."

Joe bent over the chart again; the longer he studied it, the more he puzzled over it, the more he could begin to trace out a saw-toothed image, of a lake, formed by, and fanned back upstream of, Sweetgrass Moraine.

In the midday quiet, Butter, hot from his territorializing, took up a spot at the feet of the boys in what little shade they'd not taken over.

Joe straightened up. "Thing is, to me anyway, just looking at it, you get the idea that Sweetgrass Moraine, with this big cirque behind it, would make a pretty sizable reservoir, deeper and not as long as at Hellwater Gap."

"Oh I know what you're getting at, Joe," Norman said, folding up the chart, "but why waste the time on it?"

"Maybe for a backup to Bitterroot Gap, in case for some reason, it don't work out?"

"I don't see why it wouldn't. They didn't start me here till a month ago and that was after Bitterroot Gap was already approved. Nobody'd fund a backup site when the primary's locked in. Knowing those HRC folks, I imagine they are just making sure they got every kind of survey they might need."

Joe nodded, but thinking about Emma's grave that rainy burial day, the way that rainwater dammed so fast behind the loose excavated soil.

"Might be a lot cheaper though. The way Sweetgrass Moraine makes a natural earthworks itself, all's you'd have to do is close up the channel where the cataracts are. Wouldn't need the heavy concrete work you need at Bitterroot Gap."

Norman swept back a shock of his white hair. "I suppose that might explain the profile leveling then; they'd need it to size up water area and volume. But it can't be right."

"How come not?"

"Well then it's a heck of a different story altogether. So I don't see how that's what's going on. If it were, you'd want the Corps of Engineers in here right quick." He looked off, thinking, his face reddening. "Then again, the way they've been pressuring me to finish up, I think I better go down and get this all straightened. . ."

"Hey, hold on," Joe exclaimed, "I was just saying. I'm no expert."

"You're an engineer, aren't you?"

"Not, you know, exactly. I mean, not that kind of engineer."

"It's engineer enough for me, because now you mention it, it does make a certain amount of sense. Never hurts to clear things up."

Butter yelped. The dog had been sniffing the rich smelling boot of one of the sleeping boys and that boot had suddenly shot out and kicked him. He loped back to Wade and sat, getting his head patted distractedly.

Norman reached for Joe's hand. "Thanks for coming by, Joe, but I gotta get these lamebrains going on the next station, before I drive down to town."

"Norman, I. . ."

But Norman was off rousing his crew and running them up the slope. Joe stood worrying his fingers into his temples, and didn't notice Anne beside him until she leaned her hip against him.

"Joe, if you're right, maybe you don't got to sell."

He shook his head. "You don't understand," he wanted to say, but it felt pleasant, her closeness, the sun, the quiet rustle of timber, so he let it go. A breeze fluttered the papers on the plane table, and he looked them over again.

"Anyway."

He became aware of Anne, her arm around his own and her head against his shoulder and the smell of her hair mixed with the rich scent of pine. A sense of well-being swept through him, like that of a man feeling sure of his ground.

"Evan got back yesterday, and before he jumps all over me, I better get down to see what he's got to say about this."

Anne squeezed his hand, then wordlessly went to roll up her work. Joe started off for the jeep, then stopped. Wade stood behind him, smiling, Butter's rump on his foot.

"Don't see what're you so lit up about, Wade; I still think I oughta clobber you."

"What for?"

"For inventin that engineer story, that's what for. Getting me in over my head."

Wade shrugged, scratching the dog's ears. Butter looked up, a drooling toothy dog smile, his tail beating the grass.

EVAN WAS AT the home of Einar Leeds, one of the attorneys representing Hellwater Reservoir Corporation. The sky was full of fast moving clouds; their shadows zipped across the browning lawn. The two men were moving out to the porch when another shadow, a silver jeep, raced across the dry grass toward them. Joe Meeks got out and approached them.

"Evan, is HRC surveyin for a second dam site?"

Evan removed his sunglasses, his eyes squinting, making him look oddly haggard.

"Joe, I've been trying to get hold of you. Hang on just a second."

The old lawyer turned his back to Joe, said something inaudible to Evan, glanced over his shoulder. His eyes flashed.

Evan nodded, then turned to Joe. "Better yet, Joe, I'll meet you in the Mint. Half an hour all right?"

Joe looked from one to the other, then left without answering.

The sun came from behind a cloud, its immediate heat

desiccating his eyes. He put back his sunglasses.

HALF AN HOUR later, Joe walked into the Mint. Backlit by the sharp summer sun, he couldn't see well at first, but knew the boisterous crowd could see him. The way everything fell silent. "That's him," he heard someone say, then noticed the turning of heads in a rolling wave down the length of the bar. Walking to the back, he sensed the not particularly friendly eyes follow him.

Evan was sitting at the end of the bar, playing blackjack with Marly who was behind the bar. Marly showed an ace for the house, Evan a two-eyed king of diamonds.

"Hmm. Should I stay or should I draw?"

He dabbed his finger in his scotch, tasting it, musing.

"I don't care, long as you don't do both," Marly said, avoiding any notice as Joe took a stool himself.

"Then I'll stay. Your bet."

Marly stayed also. Evan turned over a ten to her unburied nine; both had twenty one.

"All right, this time let's liven it up. One-eyed jacks wild?"

Marly nodded, reshuffled and dealt, still no eye contact whatsoever with Joe.

"Marly, while you're at it, why don't you bring our new arrival a drink, on me?"

Evan lifted the tip of his card.

"Evan, all's I want to know is about HRC land and the land above Sweetgrass Moraine. What're they up to? They thinkin about a dam up there now?"

Evan looked at his card again and this time motioned for a hit.

"Could be, down the road," he said at length. "There's enough demand for water to warrant another one." Now he looked squarely at Joe. "If they are, that's their business, not ours."

"Unless maybe they're thinkin to put the dam there *instead* of Bitterroot Gap?"

Evan took the second card Marly dealt. "Why on earth would you think that?"

"You said they got to build in a hurry. Could be that locatin it there would be a lot cheaper and faster to build."

"Damn!" Both Evan and Marly turned up 21. Evan shrugged, nodded at her to shuffle again, then turned back to Joe.

"Okay then, what's your point?"

"A dam at Sweetgrass Moraine, and the ranch right below, all that water, it'll grow crops thick as horsehair."

"Sure, if you can afford it, that is; I don't imagine they plan to give it away." Evan cut the deck. "Especially to someone with a history of getting in the way."

Over his shoulder, Joe could see Evan holding the jack of spades, its eerily beady one-eyed profile a little like Evan's own.

"You talk anymore like you're with HRC on this. What's with you?"

"What's with me?" Evan spun on his stool. "You talk like you want this deal to fall through. Second guessing dam sites now, what, so you can play rancher? Sure, Joe, great idea. Don't sell. Forget the money. Hang onto that worthless piece of property instead. That's your new half-baked numbskull plan?"

His voice rose, as he heated up. The many bar patrons turned their way, raptly attentive.

"Look Joe, maybe this is just the next in a path littered with endless screwball theories and being thrown off job after job because of them. Maybe I don't know why, maybe even you don't, maybe I don't even care, but when a maniac with a goddamn relentless compulsion to fuck things up starts in sabotaging the deal I'm working my ass off on, a deal that's the best, the fairest, and the *only* way to help us all out, including you, most of all, you, then I do what it takes to stop him."

Evan downed his glass of scotch and banged it on the bar.

"You think maybe you can understand that?"

He shoved his glass to Marly. She quietly filled it, and while Evan cooled off, drumming his fingers, she set one out for Joe too. It sat untouched. No one spoke. After a while the din returned to the barroom.

"One more thing." Evan's voice calm again. "Idiotic intrigues aside, still, it's been oddly helpful. HRC doesn't share my certainty you'll come to your senses, and frankly, if they are looking at this other site I'll bet it's because they're worried you'll drag your feet long enough that Arapahoe will pull their capital out, leaving HRC holding the bag. Which gives me some leverage, and since I've been unable to pin you down, I took the opportunity to use it. I just delivered Einar Leeds my final contract, which is for all the property Bitterroot Gap dam will inundate. It asks for more than I'd ever imagined asking when I first got involved. Whether or not you're even interested—take my word for it, it's a windfall even after it's divided among the Burchards, Gustafsens, and the Meeks survivors. With one stipulation: we close by the first of next month. Simply put, July 4th, you either sign over or the whole megillah is null and void. I cut my losses and get back to L.A and the hell with it."

He looked to Marly, laughing now.

"Jesus, you know? You need zero tolerance for all this thick-headedness, first Frances and now Joe. That, and find yourself the nearest chapter of Meeks Anonymous."

Marly smiled, halfheartedly, at Evan, then at Joe, then dealt Evan another card with a resounding click. For the third time, both had 21.

"Hmm," Evan said, "that's rare."

"Good things come in threes," Marly said, "Right Joe?"

But Joe had already left.

EVENING. JOE IN the lobby, wanting to check out. Marly at the front desk, on the cold vinyl of the stool, arms in her lap.

"I don't have enough cash, Marly; can I maybe owe you?"

She waved him off.

"I don't care about the bill, so much as your leaving. Wade's movin up with you too, I suppose?"

"He's there with Frances already."

"You're not still countin on keepin the ranch, are you? People'd never forgive you."

Joe studied the floor.

"I guess probably not. I don't know. But even if it's just another month out here, it'd be nice for Wade to have it at the ranch. He likes it there."

Marly lit a cigarette; the match arced smoke as she put it down, waving it, a useless wand.

"I hate to see you go," she said, surprised by her sudden candor. "I liked havin you here, even when I didn't see that much of you. I thought maybe you'd. . .get to feel the same. Ain't much, I know, but you liked it here a little, didn't you?"

"Beats where I came from, that's for sure."

She put her hand on his.

"Joe? The truth is—oh believe me I know it's silly of me—but havin you around, well, it kinda got my hopes goin. Is that why? Too much for you?"

"No but, it's not like that, Marly."

"Do you know what I mean, then? At all? Feel even a bit the way I do?"

"It was so long ago. We were just. . .too young."

"Two people right for each other once, don't you think they'd be always? Able to pick up where they left off no matter how long a time went by?"

Her chest rose, mushrooming confusion and hurt.

Joe bit his lip. "I don't know. So much happened."

"What? What did happen? All these years, and I still don't know. Did you blame me for Scotty? That's what I always thought."

"No. That's just. . .no, course not."

"But why else would you have just run off and left?"

Joe lowered his head, but had no answer.

"It might repeat all over again, that what you're afraid of?"

"Afraid?"

"Afraid, maybe like about what happened to Scotty will happen to Wade? Like that?"

"Marly, I just don't like draggin up what don't need to be dragged up. I know you got it into your head I'd make a nice addition to your plans for the Grand, but. . ."

Their eyes locked. She stood, anger rising in her.

"It better not have anything to do with Anne, then. She's her own girl, Joe, but she's the one got it into her head. That you'll get her out of here. Don't do it to her, Joe. You did it to me, and I can forgive that. Do it to her? I'd never be able."

"Marly, c'mon. It isn't anything like that. What's wrong with you?"

His hands went to his head, rubbing it, soothing it. Then he turned and left.

Marly, her cigarette out, pulled out another, but didn't light it. She didn't want to strike flame into the dark of the lobby. She put it in her mouth but didn't smoke. She didn't have the breath for it.

Chapter 20

WADE WRESTLING WITH sleep, tossing in Emma Meeks old musty bed. A summery breeze billowing the old lace curtains of the open window. Frances's hall clock tolling. This time he counted twelve.

Whether a minute or a year, he never had a real sense how long the headaches lasted, but since one wasn't ending, he got up. Walked noiselessly to the kitchen. Put a wet cloth in the icebox for freezing the forehead pain. Took a flashlight from the drawer and went outside. On the lawn, the ghosts of two dogs joined him, curious, sitting quietly at his feet. His calf, bawling faintly across the river, must have sensed him too.

Like always, his eyes popping and flashing imaginary lights He stared into the night sky, big with stars. It helped. He knew no constellation except the Big Dipper, and though he knew it was supposed to be a bear, he didn't think much of it, with its square stomach and dented tail.

Deer in the orchard eating the few leaves. Turning the flashlight on them, their eyes shone radium green. Fawns swimming with spots; does big with nervous ears. One lone buck, antlers coated with soft fiber. Did Wade's own eyes look green to *him?*

His gaze back to the sky again, Wade noticed this time that the Big Dipper had redesigned itself; its ladle was now a gargantuan torso, its handle an elongated massive arm, the triangle of quieter stars above it now a fearsome snout. It was no longer a dipper but a standing sprawling bear, whose immense twinkling outline had overtaken the entire northern night, encircling the earth. The smaller dipper was now her ferocious cub. Awed, Wade momentarily forgot the throb in his temples. And the vivid colored pain rimming his eyes. And the night silence hissing inside his head. In a way it was all normal.

Then a deep growl, a shower of white illumination like a roman candle going off. The darkness erupted, light burst on the leaves of the willows, pointed the blades of grass, flickered from his fingers and bare toes like sparklers. The yard a raging carnival of neons, with light show deer, a fire-tipped porcupine, two vibrating dogs.

And Wade? He was back in the night sky, He was light years gone.

Unconsciousness awhile, all black, all light extinguished. A slam. Gravel crunching, sparks underfoot of a large invisible walking thing. Wade looked hard right, moving the pain and blindness left, so and in the rim of his vision a face appeared, its teeth sparkling in the beam of his flashlight, its eyes shooting violet rays.

"Wade?"

The voice of Joe. Wade felt a force, a hand on his arm, lowering his flashlight. The face disappeared.

"Little cold to be out here in your undershorts, isn't it?"

A coarse-fabric jacket came over his shoulders. Then a hand came to his forehead. The wide warm palm sucked up some of the headache.

"You all right?"

Wade nodded. The nodding hurt.

A second or an hour passed.

The sound of deer feeding on the stackyard hay. No. The sound of Wade's own voice.

"There's a buck over there. He's in lavender."

The sound of a laugh. "You mean in velvet."

Wade laughed too and pain split sideways to let out his mirth, yellow spears in his temple.

"C'mon, sit down here on the porch a minute."

Joe talking. Wade answered something that meant okay, though it didn't sound like okay; it sounded underwater. The palm on his back guided him across a seaweed lawn. Grass sticking to his bare feet.

At the porch he stubbed his toe. "Ouch." His words. A yellow triangle pain joined the green pain; briefly the two canceled each other out. Then he could see a little. Sky. Joe. Dogs. He set his bare feet on their fur. He relocated the great starry she-bear, her pulsing umbra both awesome and indifferent. He could see why cave men looked to the heavens for strength.

"How come you aren't asleep, Wade? You're not still having headaches, are you?"

"No." His head shaking. "I just like it. Here."

Joe sat, leaned forward, elbows on his knees. He scratched Butter, who inserted himself between them, switching his head from one to the other for double pets.

"It's a temptation, this place. Half wish it'd be permanent."

"It's permanent for now."

"Permanent for now, huh?" Joe chuckling. "Well, I guess enjoy it while you can."

Wade felt a hand pat his hair.

"Growing out thick on top there."

"So's yours."

"Yeah, I guess it is." Joe stood up. "Let's get in. You hungry?"

In the kitchen, the icebox beamed out white. Wade stepped back. Joe dug out stewed mutton and scalloped potatoes. He ate ravenously. Wade did not.

"So I'm thinkin," Joe said, licking his fingers, "we'll go ahead an stay till the end of the month."

"Maybe even longer."

"Can't. Already late to get workin on your school."

He shut the icebox and guided Wade down the hall. The wall clock tolled. Once. Twice. Three times. They stopped at Emma's room, Joe waiting awhile at the door as Wade got into bed.

"I know I haven't quite been myself much. Have I?"

Wade nodded on is pillow.

"Me too."

Joe closed the door.

IN THE MORNING the window was brilliant with cold, clear sky. Wade woke, his head also cold and clear. He sprang from Emma's bed.

He stood on the porch. Everything was white.

"It snowed?" he squawked, his voice breaking.

Joe, sitting at the table, said, "Well it's not powdered sugar."

"But it's summer. And. . .how can it be snow?"

"Don't worry. It'll melt off by noon."

"Man, anything can happen here, can't it?"

Wade was starving. He found leftover stacks of pancakes, and those he didn't eat he took out to the dogs, who leapt eagerly at him, spilling the scraps in the wet dripping snow.

"Damn you dogs!"

Unlike Sorry, the dogs still weren't taking Wade's training seriously. As though they knew he was an adult and didn't present any threat. Even his profanity merely set both tails wagging, like he was playing some fun barking game with them.

"One of these days, you guys," Wade said, "you're. . ." His voice cracked again, sinking then rising like a girl's. He brushed their muddied snowy paw prints from his shirt. He felt like he was maturing the wrong direction half the time.

To feed his calf, he emptied the milk remaining in the peeling steel creamery can into the rubber nipple pail and lugged it toward the bridge. Butter, who ran out ahead, turned back and now was waiting for him, a furry troll, crouched on his front legs, ready to pounce. Wade stopped and planted both feet, lowering his milk bucket. Butter raised his rear end. Wade lifted his free arm menacingly. "No!" he boomed in his lowest loudest voice, the deep sound surprising him as much as the dog. Butter cocked his head, puzzled. For a minute it was a standoff, then Wade flinched in the manner he'd seen Frances do. Butter stood, and backed up. "Sit down," Wade commanded. Butter sat. Wade walked past, unimpeded. "Now come on," he ordered, and Butter amicably fell in escorting him to the loudly bawling calf.

AFTER BREAKFAST JOE and Wade drove down into town. Descending Bitterroot Gap, very slow going; the road slippery with melting snow. Coming down one particularly steep switchback, he saw a big cattle truck ahead. Saw it was stopped. Rounding out of the hairpin curve, saw that it was in trouble, its cab in the burrow pit, its trailer jutting across the road, jackknifed into both lanes, a mass of twisted steel.

Fast approaching, Joe downshifted, but it did not slow his jeep enough. He braked, but the brakes seized; pumping them merely locked the tires, throwing the jeep into a headlong slide straight at the wreckage ahead. Only a feebly low guard rail stood between them and the sharp drop-off into Bitterroot Gap. Joe's only hope, a very narrow gap between that and the trailer wreckage. He could only wheel straight and hope the jeep could squeeze through and not run off the road.

He felt eerily in slow-motion, aware of very little but a roaring in his ears and the oddly black red of the road.

"Hang on, Wade!" he cried as on both sides the jeep screeched metal to metal against the trailer and the guard rail, gouging it its entire length as it plowed through, slowed but still sliding, until, several hundred yards on, he was able to wrestle it to a stop.

Despite the din, Joe hearing a far off siren's wail in the distance.

Joe, Wade fast behind, running back toward the wreck, slipping on the red snow—red for being thick with the steaming blood spilling out from steers severed by the shards of the rent steel rails of the trailer, loud bellering steers still alive but pinned in.

The wheels on the upended side of the trailer lazily revolving, some one way, some the other. Steers thrown free shaking in the burrow pit; those still alive inside scrambling over one another, jamming pink nosed white snouts through the rails, snorting vaporous panicked breath.

A man weaving toward them, the driver, dragging a bum leg, his unshaven face embedded with loopy eyes, the reek of alcohol.

"Jesus, Harlo," Joe cried, "What happened here?"

"Hell if I know. Guess snow grabbed the wheels or somethin."

"Are you alright?"

Harlo swayed on his feet, a stupid smile on his face. "I been better, but I called in on the truck's radio. Law's gonna be along soon enough, so go on ahead, you don't got to stick around."

In fact the law arrived just then, the siren preceding Sheriff McComb's pickup as it came around the bend below, flashers throwing harsh blue across the snow as it pulled to a stop. McComb heaved out from the driver's side; his deputy, Jack Duffy, from the passenger's side.

"Shit almighty!"

Duffy appraising the situation, stomping muck from his boots. "Tyler's gonna shit gold nuggets when he hears about this."

Harlo staggered to him. "Yeah and he'll be burnin then, 'cause he's a golden flamin asshole anyway."

McComb shook his head. “Duffy, give a call for Ewing to bring up his tow truck. I’ll deal with Harlo.”

Duffy turned to Joe. “This is serious, I’m tellin you, Meeks. Way people’re feelin these days, they’re sure as hell goin to blame this on you, I hope you know.”

Joe was incredulous. “Blame what on me?”

“Folks here’ve always thought good of Harlo, and they’re goin to say that if you’d never showed up, this here wouldn’t’ve happened. They know Harlo ain’t ever goin to take anything serious long as he thinks that ranch might be around. That’s what they’ll say; I know em too well.”

Duffy got in the pickup to call in; McComb pulled Joe aside.

“Look, son, till I get Tyler calmed down, best thing is if you get Harlo on into town and sober him up quick. Take him to the Grand; Marly’ll look after him.”

“He’s free to go?”

“He ain’t never gonna work around here again; that ain’t enough for you?”

McComb stomped off, drawing his revolver, beginning the triage of putting down the steers who’d never make it.

WADE BETWEEN JOE and Harlo down to Meagher. Joe stone-faced, Harlo chatty.

“Yeah, that’s it for me. Tomorrow I was s’posed to start drivin regular out of Billings, now even that’s fucked up royal, ain’t it?” He swirled his head around to Joe, then out the window. “Fuck em all anyways, should’a knew better than to hire me anyhow.” His head swinging back then down to Wade. “See, kid, us Meeks just ain't cut out for the regular world."

Whereupon, Harlo, all yakked out, slept all the way to the Grand. He roused once the engine shut off.

"What the hell've you got the long face about, Joseph?"

The sky had cleared; sunlight glistened on the warming slushy street.

"Had a funny dream last night," Joe finally said.

"Well good for fuckin you, eh?"

"What about?" Wade asked.

"I was by a ditch, some irrigation ditch. It was brimming with water, real fast moving water . . ."

Harlo laughed. "That ain't much of a dream."

"Except that the water was running uphill."

"Yeah, that'll be the day."

Harlo opened his door and got out. "C'mon kid. Buy you a drink."

As Harlo limped off into the Mint, Joe sighed.

"What's wrong, Joe?"

"That does it, Wade. I'm going to find Evan."

"What for?"

"It's time to be done with this ranch mess once and for all. Look at Harlo. Evan's been right all along; I'm goin to screw everyone up, just like I always do. What more has to happen until I figure that out. I'm sorry, Wade, but it's got to be done."

Wade turned away.

"Now Wade, you knew this would happen."

Joe got no response. He sat, watching the snow melt. Marly's face appeared in the window of the Mint, looking at them, then was gone again. Joe looked at the clearing sky.

"That dream was so damn real; it's just like I feel all the time."

"What do you mean? Like what?"

Joe turned his door handle.

"Like I'm always trying to swim upstream."

Chapter 21

THE AIR BREEZY; the sun warm. Anne on the tailgate of her pickup, singing under her breath, swinging her feet, bootlaces flapping. Lazy excited, waiting for Norman to start the boys on the slope taping and get back down to work with her. Seeing a glint down valley, which became the jouncing daylight star of reflected sun off the windshield of a jeep—silver—grinding its way up the mining road, she fingered her bangs, aware of that same sun reflecting off the windshield of her face as well. And wondering. . .could Joe see her light, like she could see his?

It didn't matter to her why he was coming, it mattered to her only that it was still more to feel good about.

Dreamy alert, she waited for his jeep to turn off into the sea of mountain grass and sail her way. Which became the day's first bad turn, when his jeep did not turn, rather it continued bucking straight up the rutted road toward Independence Basin instead of toward her.

The second came half an hour later, when two four-wheel drives drove up and *did* turn her way, their thick tires knocking aside juniper shrubs and crushing the tall grasses as they cruised up alongside Norman's van. They stopped, quivering on their torsion bars. Inside tinted windows she could make out several figures.

Then, off the other way, she saw Norman's shock of white hair emerging from the timber. He clearly didn't know what to make of the new arrivals either, and tucking a clutch of maps under his arm, changed course to go greet them. As he approached, a team of men got out, all in new work clothes, and idly clustered together while one of them, a small size stump of a man in small size stumpy overalls and thick stumpy glasses, walked to intercept Norman. The two spoke, briefly, then the stumpy man returned to his team. Norman remained, strangely inert, arms at his side, the maps falling to the ground out from under them.

Anne's boots had hardly stopped swinging and she was running to him, demanding to know who they were, why were they here, what was going on, clearly aware that *something* was going on. He bent down to pick up the maps, ignoring her, telling her instead to go get the boys and bring them back down.

"What for?" Anne cried.

Norman pointed to the men from the two trucks.

"Because that there's the new survey team."

Anne looked at them, back at him, back at them, not getting it, whatever *it* was.

"Go on, Anne, call in the boys. We've been called off the job."

"But. . .what do you mean, off the job? What happened? I don't. . ."

"Can't give you an answer on that till I have one myself. C'mon now, pack it up. All of it."

The Roscoe boys whooped when they heard; dismissal, sudden or not, expected or unexpected, meant back to town, back to sleep, to sleep till noon, or even beyond. They were on their way the moment they were told. Anne, however, sat in her pickup, stunned with disbelief. Only once the new crew took the field did she start it up and drive off, not even knowing to where. She drove just to the turnout, and then stopped again, and sat again, unable to turn the wheel onto the road down to town. She looked at her feet, her unlaced boots. She looked at her watch; not even the 9:15 break yet. Her day—her last day?—hadn't even begun, and her job—over and done with? Just like that? She gripped the wheel. She looked left, right, then tore out in a flourish of spinning tires, not left toward home, but right, up toward Independence Basin.

JOE HEARD IT long before he saw it, sounding like a bushwhacking growling motor bear smashing through low hanging boughs, clambering over exposed blocks of shale, plowing through streams of runoff gushing out of the pine-softened crags that shadowed the last of yesterday's resilient snow, knowing it was Anne's red pickup well before it bounced across the boulder talus into the basin. He watched it shoot past the lakeside hunting cabin into the coulee up to where he himself had just parked, a few hundred feet below where he now sat, where he had come to be alone, to think, to figure things out. He watched Anne park and get out and scan the ridges in all directions, then began the scramble up the slope he himself had only just climbed, her calls drowned by the clatter of scree knocked loose as she climbed.

"Joe? I know you're there. Answer me, damn you!"

Knowing this couldn't be good, wishing he could wish her away, he nonetheless stood so she could see him.

"How's a person s'posed to get up there if she ain't a bighorn?" Anne yelled.

Joe pointed toward a crevasse an up an erosion-sculpted precipitous chute that led up to the outcrop to the impromptu aerie he had taken. Breathless and so wordless when she finally reached him, he waited while she caught her breath, patiently watching the shimmer of the distant ridges of the Absarokas receding to hazy sunlight, and the layering of their canyons surging like dark slow waves.

"God am I. . .I. . ."

Too winded to finish, Anne breathed deep then burst out in tears.

And cried and kept crying and cried some more, and, enraged that she couldn't quit what she hadn't intended in the first place, cried even more. She gulped and choked and held her breath and still couldn't stop. Flung off her jacket. Swore and stomped the ground. Buried her face in her forearms. Nothing helped. She slumped down on her knees in the muddy remaining snow. Gradually the sobbing abated, the tempo of her heaving shoulders slowed.

No idea why she was so upset, astonished that a person could cry like that, Joe had knelt beside her and did. . .not much more. Since there was not much more he could do. When she had about stopped, she raised her head, started to explain, then all at once threw her face into his shoulder and began all over again.

Still at a loss, Joe—tentatively—touched her hair.

"I guess just try an'. . .maybe take a deep breath or two?"

Nothing better to say came to him.

Ultimately she sighed, rolled up sitting on her ankles, pushed back her strewn hair, swiped the matte of dirt and pine needles from her face, and so revealed her eyes, watery red, and her cheeks, doughy white.

Noticing her laces loose, Joe pulled one boot off then the

other as she listlessly helplessly lifted her legs, one then the other, each boot a full pot of soil and scree, her socks a chiaroscuro of bleached white at the top, dirt black below. His hands, now each holding a naked foot, with a will of their own began to rub the instep of one then the other, sensing that doing so was releasing and freeing all her pent up dispirited gloom into the high altitude ethers of scrub pine forest. Quieting both the giver as well as the receiver.

Then for a time they sat, hip to hip, shoulder to shoulder, until Anne pulled the wet hair out of her mouth and settled her florid teary face into his neck.

"Joe?"

Her voice-breath like warm oil, her wet lashes flicking his cheek, Joe dreamishly let the fullness of his name, tuned by her voice, resonate in his head. Let the volume of her diaphanous blond hair occlude his eyes—familiar hair, thick, strawberry blond hair, not red, like Marly's, but yet. . .

Suddenly he turned away, dropped his head into his hands.

"What's wrong?"

"Nothin. My neck, it's a little sore."

"Then how come you're rubbin your forehead?"

Joe didn't explain.

"Here."

Anne spread her fingers over his forehead and pressed them into his head, his temples, then down to the base of his skull to the ropey tendons of his shoulders.

"That help any?"

Her touch radiating the heat of her palms, Joe nodded, which encouraged her to encircle his chest in her arms, and soon he was thinking of Marly. . .how sometimes she held him from behind, taking his hands in hers and pressing them all, hers and his, against his romping heart, how one of the hands, his, would break away and reach up behind him to touch her face, and how his fingers would find her mouth and somehow—who knew how?—they would lead his own mouth around to that same mouth and kiss the glossy lower lip, kiss it just barely. . .how his elation made his heart wallop into his ribs, his thighs jerk, his musculature go rigid in every root and limb, his eyes glaze. . .

He had shut his eyes, and when he then opened them, he was surprised to find Anne facing him. Averting them quickly, they fell and saw the rise and fall of a young woman's bosom, filling up the fabric of a work-shirt damp from tears, a breathing living chest lifting then subsiding—the closeness of it primed a carnal pump in him, a pump of desire so badly wanting what it wanted that the primal power of it ripped from his lungs any capacity for air they had left, and he was panting, feeling like a man who can't help but stop a lifelong denial of wanting what he wants and begin wanting what he wants like he never wanted it before. And filled with all this unwanted wanting, he couldn't breathe, and so struggled and wobbled up on his feet for air.

Anne also stood, slowly, brushing herself, pulling her wet shirt from where it was sticking to her skin.

"I got fired today," she announced, finally able to get off her chest what was so much on her mind.

"Oh you did? Meanin what?"

Anne visibly flared, silent, angry, defeated. "Meanin what? Meaning fired."

Joe now appreciating the seriousness in her but still not

getting it.

"Fired? You mean, like, let go?"

She doubled up in her shoulders, as though to burst out in tears, but with nothing left in her, she couldn't.

"But that can't be. Fired? How could Norman. . .he liked you, you were doin so well."

"It wasn't Norman. He got let go himself. The whole team got replaced."

"What for?" Joe paled. "Not for those loony ideas I had about that bein a better dam site?"

"I donno, Joe. I don't know anything."

She rose and stepped to the edge of the outcrop.

"What the hell. It was bound to happen. Mom was right, I never should'a got such fancy big ideas."

She gave an awful sigh and folded her arms around her.

"It's just that I. . ." she said, "I. . ."

And she choked.

Joe came to her side. His eyes took in the long dizzying drop from the precipice to down below, and he teetered until Anne leaned into him, nudging his arm so it came around her waist. And there they stood, at the height of all the rampant geology of Independence Basin, and the worked-over worn-out beautiful terrible landslide that had collapsed onto it, the magnitude of which Joe had hoped would shake off the crush of doubt and second thoughts and back and forth waffling, of his mind berating him, *What are you doing?* So as to somehow escape his always always always finding the something, whatever it was, that was wrong with everything.

Anne stretched her arms.

"Goddamn. You know? Who'd ever think such a pretty little stream in such a sunlit valley would empty down to such a miserable little cowshit town?"

Joe absently nodded; he no longer had an opinion one way or the other left in him.

"Do you ever wonder, though? About, what if you'd never left. Never got out?"

"Worse'n that. What I wonder is, what if, after all these years of believing one thing I did do right was get away, then I come back, only to find out that, no, I didn't, I never did get out."

"Don't tell me that, Joe. God. That's so. . ."

Doe elk grazing in the grassy ledge below, two young bucks fencing with antlers, the herd of them not fifty yards off yet not able to scent—because of updraft—the danger above, the humans. Joe picked up a rock and threw it down into the timber beyond them. As it clattered to the ground, coarse haired necks rose, rutilant heads stiffened, tall ears flicked back and forth, all sensing danger.

"Look at em," Joe said, watching the deer, picking up another rock. "Don't know whether to bolt or not. Just like us: you never know for sure."

"Know what?"

"Know anything. Nobody ever knows anything for sure."

A light wind rustled the tops of the jack pine below, which flickered the noon angles of shade, now hiding, now revealing the elk.

"You know, Anne? Just once, just one time in my life, I'd like to be right about something. Even only the once, I'd like to know what that's like."

He threw the second rock. It hit, and the shady grassy ledge erupted with elk instantly bolting into the trees and down out of sight.

THEY, JOE AND Anne, descended down the cragged crevasse, out of the weathered remnants of landslide to the shore of the sun-dappled lake it had created, over which now and then, as they edged around to the cabin, a breeze ghosted through the blanched dead white tips of the trees that it had so terribly drowned.

As they approached, Anne took Joe's hand and pulled him.

"C'mon."

Joe's hand reared almost from her grasp.

"What?"

"Just come on."

She jerked him harder, and led him up the draw to the hot springs.

"This time you're gettin *all* the way in. And no clothes allowed."

The languid billow of steam mirroring the water's surface, an invitation too compelling to resist, Joe removed the boots from his aching feet, while Anne pulled a fistful of his shirttail, rolled it up the sweaty lace of his ribs, and off over his head, airing his shoulders, his bony sternum, the oval of rust colored stomach hair to full sunlight. He stopped her when she went to ungird his pants, which, no, he would do, and did, dropping them, and—what the hell—waded in naked of all but the long shadow of his maleness. He submerged to his neck; the water's heat made his lungs bellow a low long-lasting OOOOO! His feet sighed relief; his calves thighs elbows fingers neck spine hair eyes spread away from him in a simmering loss of self.

Anne, also undressed, stood at the edge but did not join him.

"Joe? Would you just look at me?"

No, he would not. No. He instead followed two large blue dragonflies, their wings clacking as they skated the hot skin of water.

"Come on. Am I attractive to you at all? I just wanna know."

Sure she was. Obviously she was. Very much, very attractive. Everyone knew that. She knew that herself.

"Well of course you are, Anne."

"Yeah? So would you mind tellin me again, only while you're lookin at me?"

Joe shooed away the obstinate dragon flies.

"Anne. you're a real pretty looking girl."

"If you'd take a close look, asshole, you might notice there ain't no *girl* anywhere around."

The dragonflies returned, this time not as two but as one, an eight-winged, twin-torsoed double-blue buzzing mating dragonfly. Joe brushed to break them. . .it. . .apart. They, it, would not; it, they, the one thing of two, zipped like a flying motor toy in and out of reach.

A large rock kerplooshed in the pool at his feet, dousing him in heated mineral water.

"Well?"

Now, this time, Joe looked up, looked at this young unadorned woman, her leggy legs and shadowy thighs, rounded hips and breasts, her long strong arms and willowy hair. . .Anne's robustly female figure, maybe a bit too white of skin and thin of flesh, maybe ribs a bit too disclosed, her pearly smooth female flesh stretched on the lanky structure that suggested another year's maturation would fill it out to perfect softness, but for an average any age man, and particularly for Joe, she was a take-your-breath-away sight to see, a vivid reminder. . .how long since you felt the surge of that crushing desire. . .way too long. . .really not since the summer, so long gone, the summer of Marly, feeling that tingle in the chest, that boil in the loins, that heat of arousal when he heard water evaporate, heard the backs of his knees squeak, heard every throb of his pulse in every extremity, ears, fingers, toe-tips. Felt his legs quiver, galloping in place, which if he unbridled would bolt him right up to and onto her. How he would be beside himself, his steady incrementally thickening lust roiling the calm of the water.

"You say I'm pretty," Anne pouted, looking down the length of her figure reflecting in the water, "but how come you don't act that way?"

"Anne, I. . .you're just, you know. . ."

"Just a girl, that's what I'm just?"

His head shook no, his voice croaked something almost opposite.

"What's wrong with me then?"

Waifish, piqued, peeved, Anne waved away the thick steam stepping into the water.

"No, nothing's wrong with you. It's almost that. . ."

She waded to him, petulant, way too attractive. He looked away, up, skyward. The sun risen almost to its zenith.

"That, you're. . .you're awful attractive. How could you ever think you aren't. It's only that. . ."

. . .that all those many afternoons with Marly, palms on her face, fingers tracing her lips, her cheek, the curl of each eyelash. Her smooth brow, the slope of her nose, the rim of her eye. How their lips wet-whet each other, how they kissed fingers, eyes, cheek, more, falling, lying the moss banks, arms in arms. Clasping her and she him, sharp intakes of breath, cheeks welded, pounding inside hearts each as anxious to cleave together as the other. His undulating hand up and down, her hip to waist and up and back, under and around, the meadow of fine hair in the small of her back, the warm oozing cleft between her thighs, the quiet secreting wetness, without fail his touch rediscovering the dark glistening woman tissue. Hard for her, eager for him, the disintegration of giving in to the oblivion of pleasure, plunging hands grazing her marshy labial flesh, widening the tab of vital tissue anxious for his lust, haunches bucking involuntarily, in reflexive pelvic union, consummating, afternoon sun putting amethyst in her widened pupils, making her rising breasts flare, dizzily squirting feral glands. How he would moan, her name, God's name, any name, but barely, no longer able to hold on, when she would hotly whisper and beg him. . .

"Anne." Anne floating on her back in the water. "I have my own name, Joe: 'Anne'. Remember?"

Joe awash in memory realized he'd said something—not sure what—but had called her Marly.

"I guess it's a compliment of some kind. Comin from you."

Joe glanced at her, and as she began to laugh, he did as well, releasing it and letting it die down, an afterglow around the submerged nudity of their laughing bodies making a mosaic of intersecting steamy ripples on the surface.

After a while, Joe's eyes rose up from there to a scrubby whitebark pine, clinging to a boulder pile, the same stunted pine where Scotty liked to sit petting his sheepdog while down below in the same mineral springwater Joe pressed Marly to let him press against her, leg to her leg, cheek to her cheek, hand to anywhere and everywhere she would let him, but with Scotty's eyes on them she would guardedly rebuff his overtures, saying "no, not now, you," whispering, "later, Joe."

Those were special days, of living only to be close to and next to her, and he would often get annoyed about it.

"What's he like that for?"

Marly moving his underwater hands off her underwater leg venturing that Scotty "never seen you bein fond of anybody before, he's probly wantin to see if maybe you'll be fond of him too."

Joe laid back, hands behind his head, eyeing the mute young chaperone up on the rocks, wondering was she right and was that really what his brother might really want.

And they would sooner or later dress and walk up and sit with Scotty and pet his dog, and then all together return to the cabin. While Scotty poked around the mine tailings for chips of garnet or fool's gold, they the two of them in the darkness of the back room poked with one another, for new ways to kiss, for fresh places to touch. Joe taking her thick red hair, fistfuls of it; Marly guiding and pressing his fingers into her. Hours until leaving time they lay and touched and felt and murmured, unformed words pouring out of them, unmeaningful words, cries and cackles, oohs and aahs, giddy laughter and rapacious demands, profane scatological nasty, shouting whispers, tell me this or that kinds of things, tell me you love me words, say it do it tell me tell me again words.

Then, stroking the back of an arm or a slope of waist, they napped in a tangle of spent limbs. They emerged, rosy, relieved; in the lee side of the lowering sun, they sat together and with Scotty, Marly running her fingers through the boy's fine white-blond hair, eventually moving Joe to a desire to do so as well, and in time he did, and though tentative, it was good, petting Scotty's hair.

So of course it was always too late by the time he would finally have to say it: "I don't want to go." When Marly would reciprocate that she didn't want him to. When Scotty said the same, without words, since he couldn't speak. Always there was the extended silence; always the foreboding. About the coming fall, about what was going to happen, about how would they ever be able to be together. One or the other would shake their head. They didn't know.

"You're dad'll move back to town, right?"

"Even so, but still, we'll get all hell from everyone. We'll get in fights. We'll hate them, then each other. Just like before."

"No we won't. We're better'n any of em. They'll see."

"You're the one who'll see. See what they see. How I'm a wretch. A skank. You'll change, they'll make you. Sooner or later. An you'll give up and go on and one day won't have nothin to do with me."

"I won't ever want to have nothin to do with you."

"It's so goddamn awful in town. If only we could just stay up here."

"And at least we'd freeze to death together come winter."

Brooding, nodding, not speaking.

"What if we ran away then?"

"Ran away? Where to? We don't know no one."

Joe looked at Scotty, as if he had the answer but couldn't talk and couldn't tell it to him.

Shadows fell.

"Gettin dark and you need to go, Joe; you'll both get another whippin."

"You know I don't give a damn if I do, Marly."

"But I do."

Late in the summer, riding home, Joe thinking to himself out loud, worrying about the fall, what were they going to do. Asking Scotty, who didn't know either. Coming down out of Sweetgrass Moraine, Joe stopped. He remembered Marly's strange geologist friend.

"Hey now. You know, Scotty? We do know someone outside of Meagher, don't we? We know Vaughn Marlowe, that's who we know."

He smiled at Scotty, who smiled back, then strapped his horse for home, eager to finish chores and get his whipping.

TREES CREAKED. CLOUDS skirted Mount Contact. Now and then rock clattered down on other rock. Joe, taking a full big breath of sky, hazy valley, and dry pine-flavored wind, said,

"Whew!"

Anne lifted hot wet hair off her neck. They had dressed and now were basking in sun and heat.

"Whew what?"

"Scotty."

"Who?"

"I half expected to look up and there he'd be again."

"Oh. Scotty, your little brother?"

"Hard not to think you couldn't just roll away the boulders and there he'd be and out he'd walk. Back from. . ."

Anne shielded her eyes to him.

"What made you think of that?"

"I donno. I was thinking about why Norman was let go, too."

"Yeah. An here I thought he was so good at what he did. And givin me such good trainin."

"He was."

"How could it be, Joe. Else why would they of fired him."

"Probly wasn't for not bein good. I'm wonderin was it the other way round."

"What other way round?"

"That he was too good. Too thorough. It could be that. . ."

"That what?"

Joe sighed. "Forget it. I'm probly just, you know. . .I'm just like, here I go again, conjuring up mountains out of molehills, getting concoctions into my head, just like I always do, then how I can't leave it alone, I got to worry on it and worry on it."

"On what? For Christ's sake, Joe. "

"On. . .how maybe Norman, and me, we were actually on to something."

Anne sat up.

"So maybe you *are* onto something. He seemed to think you were, right?"

"I don't know. Maybe, but maybe not. . ."

"But, so what was it?"

Joe shook his head.

"If I only knew."

Chapter 22

ASSUMING JOE MEEKS'S imminent decision, the joint venture of Hellwater Reservoir Corporation and Arapahoe Oil Incorporated had begun in earnest, with plans to be off the drawing board and under construction by the end of July, and as summer settled in, Meagher began to teem with activity. In the Mint, dawn brought down new faces showered and ready for breakfast; evening brought new diners and drinkers at all hours of the night. On any given day the Grand was home to a bank officer or an oil technician, a geologist or a commissioner. Sales reps for contractors and engineering firms came and went. A planning conference took over the Grand for an entire week; the board of HRC, the R&D department for Arapahoe Oil, multiple state water resources agencies, and even the lieutenant governor, attended. The booths in the cafe were crammed with cost-accounting and project management teams. Problems arose, problems were hammered out, all of it attracting a variety of secondary business.

On the bluff south of town, the state highway department arrived to widen and pave the windswept field that on occasion had served as an airstrip. For the first time, charters and corporate jets would be able to land in Meagher.

A real estate company out of Denver signed Evan to a retainer as a consultant on an extravagant proposal to build a multipurpose ski-resort/mountain sports complex.

A delegation representing the nation's snowmobilers arrived to investigate Meagher as a site for their winter festival. Three hunting and fishing magazines sent reporters for features on the area. The state chapter of a national rodeo circuit came to solicit support for a special regional event, with a calf-cutting tournament, a pack horse competition, and a sheepdog contest.

The Loomises expanded the Chronicle to four bi-weekly pages with regularly occurring special editions. A photographer-writer team sent by a travel magazine to do an article on the newest most undiscovered town in America was unable to even find it. An organization for arthritis sufferers visited one of the abandoned Independence mines believing that the radioactive properties of the trapped radon would alleviate and possibly cure the affliction.

Along the ruts of Second Street, stumped Meagherites clustered around imported vehicles with license plates from unfamiliar states; some residents, never having ever been far from home, didn't know the country had so many.

One of several movie stars who visited, shopping for just the right ranch to be seen getting away from it all, was at a loss. Even without sunglasses, and no hat, not one fan accosted him. . .not one person at all even knew his name. "Everyone everywhere knows me," he complained to the men in McCauley's barber shop, "anyone who's ever turned on a TV or watched a movie." The men looked at him earnestly, wanting terribly to recognize him, but they just did not. It was the same in the Mint, the Timber, even Goosey's Drug, where the actor went in a vain search for celebrity magazines to prove his case. Finding none, he declared he would open Meagher's first movie theater just to show them all. After he left, the three women at the fountain asked the fat O'Donnell boy behind the counter about the strange good-looking man. He didn't know, he thought the man was an artificial inseminator Tyler had hired.

In the spirit of the new euphoria around town, Meagher's adults themselves held a reunion at the hatchery up Castle Creek; it was easily the most enjoyable time any could recall. Rejuvenated by the mirth and the unending fountain of beer, many diehards danced their odd dances late into the nights that week, around a never-dying bonfire blazing in the river rock fireplace. The two bald McNaulty twins, who had glued sheep shearings to their heads, got so drunk they somehow got their brass belt buckles entangled and like dueling elk could not get separated. Drunken wives called for a no-clothes dance and then those same women, who had castrated hundreds of steers, were surprised so many of their men were uncircumcised. One afternoon midweek, Walt Braughten, who hadn't stopped shuffling in place day after day, suddenly did, shouting that he couldn't feel anything. "Nothing at all," he laughed raucously, whereupon his sister Louise, taking bets on whether 'he'd feel this,' put a hot branding iron to Walt's naked buttocks. Walt jerked his head. Those who bet on him to feel it instantly chorused victory, but then Walt cried out that he smelled fire, and shouted imperatives for somebody to throw beer on it, wherever it was, then resumed his shuffling, to hurrahs so jubilant that thereafter the branding iron test was administered liberally, and any person flinching was served a mandatory drink.

At night the dark box elder brush surrounding the hatchery was, as it was with their teenagers, replete with copulating oldsters. Jim Decker, out to relieve himself under the stars, stumbled across an eagerly humping couple whose backside he did not recognize. He lay down beside them. "Pardon me, Bub, I don't believe I know your lady friend here," he said in his gentlemanly manner to the man on top. "Hell, Jim, you two oughta get acquainted then." Bud buttoned up while

Decker and the lusty woman picked up where he'd left off. Flesh flew, and afterward, on the way inside, Jim and the woman remarked drunkenly that they seemed familiar to one another, and by the time they reached the door had begun to recollect that they were husband and wife.

A shower of sparks shot continually from the chimney into the night sky, and on the last night of festivities, one of them ignited a fire. Jumping crown to crown, it was well on the way to becoming a thermal inferno that would have razed the northern Absarokas had it not been suddenly extinguished by a torrential cloudburst.

Of all the revivified Meagherites straggling back to town that last morning, only Marly was not among them. She had not attended. She rarely attended anything or went anywhere at all. Her business ran invisibly while she sat in her room, avoiding the guests and the nuisance of progress. Though her Grand was in ever-increasing demand, she agonized over the most tentative upgrade, unwilling to sign for any loan or commit to any contractor.

She wished she knew what to do. She wished she had a partner. She wished she could stop feeling sad about Joe. She had no reason to miss him, yet she did. She had every reason to feel angry, yet she didn't. Once he signed with Evan, losing the ranch, what would keep him here? What brought him here in the first place would now force him away, so the flurry of development was for her a hard reminder that she and Joe would be subject to a doubly cruel fate; for the second time in their lives, when their horizons seemed about to align and the world come closer to their doorstep, they would be thrown apart.

Not much of anything could ease the sadness, the helplessness, the despair. The hell with her big plans. What was so wrong with life as it was? Look what she had made of herself: A motherless urchin shivering night after night under a corner of a wool army blanket hogged by a half-wit shell-shocked vet and his mangy sheepdogs, yet she had become a respectable self-sustaining businesswoman, a hotelier for crying out loud, already a hundred times beyond what she had any reason to expect of her future. Wasn't it enough she was a good mother? Sparing her daughter her own experiences. Giving her everything. What was so wrong with that, that after all she had worked for, Anne didn't want it? Did that make Marly's life all a waste? No. It didn't. And Anne would realize that, one day she would. It was just taking her a long time.

So it was a relief, it did ease the sadness, when she learned Anne was fired. Finally things would turn for the better, the way they were supposed to. The way they were before, mother and daughter, Marly and Anne, since what good was prosperity unless they could share in it together?

Yet Anne seemed farther away than ever. Yes she quietly returned to waiting tables, yes now she kept her nails clean and her hair brushed, yes now she pleasantly accepted the endless flattery that came her way—Father Sterling holding her shiny hand, the chief of surveyors complimenting the rose in her cheeks, the gritty Ruth Loomis combing her hair, clucking on its healthy luster—but no, she was even more a stranger than before, utterly absorbed in her private thoughts, only God knowing what—or where—they were.

One night, another night wishing morning would come, hoping it wouldn't, Marly gave up and went down to start the coffee. She saw Anne out in the street, watching dawn rouge the sky.

"What're you doin up this early, honey? Can't sleep either?"

Anne didn't turn, letting sunrise shine her face.

"What d'you think is more beautiful, mom, the east at dawn or west at dusk? I can't ever decide."

Or on a dinner break one evening, Anne outside the lobby, staring down the darkening street.

"You alright, sweetheart?"

"Fine, mom. You ever wonder what it's like where you can't see the end of every street every direction you look?"

Marly didn't understand much but she did understand one thing: This had something to do with Joe. So one afternoon she took the photo of the windy laughing couple and sat next to Anne.

"I found this in Joe's room the other day."

Taking the photo, Anne smiled. "Mom, you look so pretty. And like you're really so in love."

Remembering the plans, about to run away with Joe, leave Meagher forever, she was now certain Anne wanted the same. Marly exhaled, purging all air from her lungs, then walked away.

She knew she was turning into a shrew, sometimes harping irrepressibly on everything her distant distracted daughter did:

"Anne, don't serve that! That plates's filthy dirty."

Anne looked it over. "It's just for McComb, mom; his taste buds are in his stomach anyway."

She laughed; Marly barked.

"Just please get it out before it gets cold. Is that too much to ask?"

"Okay, no sweat. Sorry."

She didn't even put up a good fight anymore.

One day heading out to the bank, Evan dropped in on his way to meet with county commissioners about opening vehicle access to the park.

"Good for you. Once you invest a bit in it, you'll have quite the first class lodging here, Marly."

"I didn't know it wasn't already."

She looked it over, her Grand, and now she saw, in contrast to her vivid imaginings, he was right; it was sad, it was old, it was tired.

"God, Evan. There's never any goin back, is there?"

"Life only goes one way, Marly. And that's forward. Whether you like it or not."

Pulling the heavy iron grate door into Treasure State Bank, her eyes leaden, her head heavy, she sat and was soon absently nodding as the loan officer leaned over his desk, like a snake-charmer with his important words: mortgage; equity; principle and interest; collateral; liability. In the end he sealed a large envelope with sheaves of forms, papers, pamphlets, worksheets and sample agreements. She rose, shook hands, and crossed the street. Damn. All these years thinking she was ahead of the game, now it was all she could do to stay even. Would it be so bad if things just never changed? If Meagher stayed just as it is was and really only ever ought to be?

Unsigned and unopened, she tossed the package on the lobby desk for Squash. Young and ambitious, let him deal; she didn't have a clue and didn't want one. She sat and leafed through her magazines. Their magic exhausted, she threw them aside. People drinking at her bar, people eating at her cafe, in the midst of the incessant noise of the world of people, she was alone and wanted to be more alone. Alone at the mirror in her room, toying with Anne's hairbrush, she pulled out a clutch of her own hair, twined it into a braid, thinking, whatever happened to the little girl with the pretty hair?

AFTER WORK, COMING into her room, Anne finding her mother, waiting on the windowsill, framed by new burnt orange satin drapes pulled aside with dark green sashes. Windexed windowpanes gleamed late day sunlight onto walls newly enameled white. A refinished bird's eye maple vanity set against the wall. A Persian style area rug covered newly lacquered flooring. A tall ceramic vase blooming big strands of lilacs at the side of the door where Anne stood.

"Somebody havin a baby?"

Marly laughed. "You like it?"

Anne took a tentative step.

"But why my room? I thought you were movin ahead with the kitchen first?"

"Oh I am, but this just seemed such a fun way for us to start off."

Anne nodding, "Yeah, but, really, this should all be for you, Mom. It's way more'n I need."

"I think it's just what you need, honey."

Anne ran her hand along the cast iron frame of the new bed, framing her next words.

"It sure will make for a good luxury guest room, though. If I, you know, have to move out."

"Move out?"

"Yeah, mom. See, Norman, he got hired up by Arapahoe Oil to survey these new water channels, and so, he was sayin how he wants to bring me back on. . .but it'd make more sense if I maybe got a place closer, since mostly the work would be. . ."

Marly noticed where a stain had bled through the new paint job, scarring the ceiling. She sighed.

"Mom, I know, but I'm not a little girl, an obviously. . ."

"Maybe not, but there's a lot of ways you remind me of one."

". . .obviously you're still my mother. . ."

"What a coincidence; that's what I think too."

". . .but why won't you ever see things my way once in a while?"

"Haven't I? Haven't I always given you free rein? Haven't you always done what you want, no matter what I think? All I'm doin is lookin down the road at how there's a great future here for you, but goddamn, Anne, there won't be if you don't grow up and help it along and forget this other nonsense."

"That's what you think it is?"

Marly looked away.

"You hate that I'm in love with Joe, is what I think it is."

"Love? You're callin it love now?"

"Yeah? Didn't you? Once upon a time?"

"Well pardon me for bustin your bubble, but hopin to get a man to get you what you want—what you think you want—don't make it love. You're so damn sure he's got a life out there with your name on it, well you tell me what happens a few weeks from now when he takes off."

"It's love when you laugh and feel happy to be alive. You just don't want me to ever have what you couldn't ever."

Marly laughed. "Anne, in case you hadn't noticed, bein in love with Joe Meeks is like drinkin water from a strainer."

"Okay so I ain't the all grown up expert, but are you? Maybe it never was him, it was you. You know so much what love is, so maybe that makes you too good for it. Too good for anyone. I don't even know my own dad, that's how good you are."

"I love my daughter, I know that. Even if she don't."

"You had your chance, mom, don't take it out on me."

"Well, I see this is goin nowhere fast."

Marly went to the door.

"Mom, why didn't you just go off with Joe when you could of?"

"Why?" Marly turned. "I'll tell you why. He left me. The only boy I ever loved and who ever really loved me, and he just up and left. I never knew why, or where to, an even if I had, there'd of been nothin I could'a done about it."

She stood lost in her thoughts a while.

"Honestly, Annie? Just thank God you're not really in love with him. I'd feel very sorry for you if I believed you were. Trust me, I know."

She looked once more around the darkening room.

"As for movin out, I guess I don't care. You'll do what you want anyway."

Chapter 23

WADE IN HIS boundless energy outside working on the tractor, the same old Ford 500 that Joe years before would have been out working on, the same old Joe who now sat in the kitchen only observing it, pumping dry axles with the grease gun, scraping corrosion from battery terminals, duct taping frayed distributor wires. The Joe who otherwise would be listless waiting for Evan to finalize the deal with HRC, the Joe who otherwise would be busy convincing himself that once again only he knew the right thing from the wrong thing and should be doing it, only now he wasn't.

Frances, never the observer, bored with complaining she had nothing to live for after all these wasted years, hobbled out to oversee Wade's project, hovering like an old blue heron while Wade grease monkeyed around on the long idle engine.

"For Chrissake, you didn't bring out the spark plug wrench? Go on back to the tool shed for it then."

Wade, no idea what he was looking for, knew by now most things Frances said eventually became clear, and sure enough, he knew it when he saw it, the long steel handled tool, knew it as if he had known all along. Taking it back to the tractor, going at the first plug, he could not loosen it whatsoever. He pushed, pulled, pounded, kicked, hung on the handle, no matter; he couldn't make it budge.

"Why ain't you squirted oil on it? I got to do every damn thing myself around here?"

Miffed now, Wade slopped on motor oil and lunged with renewed vengeance.

"Come on, yank the son of a bitch."

He did yank, again, but this time was rewarded with a loud screech. He yanked again, and harder, the plug gave, and was out in no time. Surprised, he went straight on to the next, and, as though he had grown stronger, each one was all that easier to remove.

"You goin to change the oil, or do I have to think of everything?"

Wade looked up at her, and in that instant, Frances, sitting spread legged on a fallen cottonwood, had drifted off to sleep. A puff of breeze fluttered the still standing cottonwoods, which shook their leaves and powdered them both with cottony seeds, which in time made her sneeze but until which time, before she roused, Wade had changed the oil, put water in the radiator, emptied a gas can into the fuel tank.

"Well then go on an start the damn thing if you want."

Wade grinned, hopped on the tractor seat, turned the key, but. . .nothing.

"What'd you expect? Battery ain't been charged since before Leonard died."

Finally Wade protested. "Well how the hell was I supposed to know that?"

"Same way you're s'posed to know you got to take it out of gear and push start it."

"Oh."

Wade hopped back down, unblocked the wheels, put his shoulder behind a rear tire taller than he was and shoved. Shoved again. And continued to shove, Frances helping out, flailing her cane like a mad sorceress yelling "Harder!" and "Put weight into it!" and smiting the tire so hard her cane bounced and flew out of her hand. And with the shoving and rocking, the wheels, little by little, helped out by the down slope position of the tractor, gave it momentum enough to start rolling on its own.

"Get on now, goddammit!"

Frances teetering on her feet, Wade jumped on from behind.

"Put it in gear!"

He clutched and ground the shifter into first gear; when he let up, the massive engine stalled, sputtered, coughed, smoked, and finally caught, and by that point the tractor was careening straight into the field where Sorry was pastured.

Joe leapt from the table and ran out, but the action was too far away.

"Give it some damn gas!"

Wade grabbed and pulled the accelerator lever, too hard, too far, so that it chattered fiendishly up the metal nibs of the gauge, flooding the engine, causing the tractor to roar forward. He threw an apologetic glance back just as it burst through the barbed wire fenceline, shattering the row of old posts, and rocketed out into the field.

The sorrel filly sprang into a gallop alongside, sporting with the machine. Wade couldn't hear what Frances was yelling, could only see her black hat waving, but it didn't matter, none of it mattered, all that mattered was he was in control and driving. He pushed the accelerator lever up, and slowed to a manageable cruising speed.

Joe began laughing, laughing he didn't know why, but laughing. Frances stopped waving her hat.

The rest of the day Wade drove the field. He shifted and steered, sped and braked, jousting with Sorry who lunged and feinted as he motored over the field, crushing worthless timothy, withered alfalfa, dead yellow clover. He churned up and down slopes overrun with dandelions, mashing the stems and strewing up seed puffs behind him. As the tractor sped so did his heart. His lungs swelled and thickened inhaling the fumes of billowing blue exhaust. He stood and drove; air swirled into his nose. He straddled the chassis and drove one-handed, waving his free hand like a bronc buster. Banging into a dry gulch, he was hurled off his feet and bounced back in the seat as the free-wheeling machine charged out like a tank on maneuvers.

He exulted, yelling out cries all lost to the wind, thinking, "If only Joe could see me now!"

Joe could see him now, Joe had seen it all, then hurried after Frances, seeing she had become crazy, confused, lost. He reached her stumbling back to the house, cursing that she couldn't remember things, who was the damn kid on the tractor, whose house was she headed for, who was the asshole holding her arm.

The dogs sat up on alert, keeping their distance, as she wobbled into the yard, muttering that it didn't matter, there was hay to stack, cattle to move, sheep to sheer, all of it for damn sure had to get done whether her mind was slipping or not. Damn em, damn all of em, year after year she took care a things while they all left and she stayed and for what? For never getting anything, not a damn thing, when the place should have gone to her, something should have, something should have made it worth working away her entire life over.

She stopped at the front steps. She couldn't breathe. She trembled precariously, the dogs groveling at her feet, puzzled but—expecting to be thwacked—they scooted away quickly when her knees buckled and she toppled down.

She lay not knowing where or how long. A man, some man, appeared over her; a man she had to suffer lifting her and carrying her into some house. She cursed him with no lungs, no air, no sound, thinking she never needed em, not a man, not any of em. Never had. Never would.

Joe carried her to bed. She slept for hours. Joe sat in watch in her room, thinking. Joe sat in the kitchen in watch over Wade, thinking. He was still thinking the next morning when Wade offered to make breakfast. It took him two trips to carry it all, a plate of fried beef briskets covered with thick melting cream and scrambled eggs, fried potatoes, a pitcher of milk and a pan of coffee. "Is that going to be enough?" he asked, noticing Joe eyeing him funny.

"Yeah, Wade, more than enough."

Joe started to eat, noticing how Wade's pants wouldn't quite button; he had improvised with a belt of old bailing twine. His fraying cuffs ended six inches above his ankles. His old t-shirt rode up his back and was ripped around his armpits. His toes stuck out of his shoes. His hair sprouted out in weed-like licks.

Joe pulled out several bills from the coffee can in the kitchen and laid them on the table.

"What's that for?"

"You need a haircut."

Wade stuck a forkful of food in his mouth. "Makes two 've us."

"Yeah. So anyway, get to town. Have McCauley trim you up. Buy some clothes too."

"What clothes?"

"All clothes. See how every damn thing's been shrinkin on you?"

"Oh." Wade tugged at his shirt. "Maybe go now then?"

"You, not me. I don't feel all that much like being in town."

Wade set down his glass and pocketed the money. "How am I supposed to get there then?"

"Take the tractor. You drive it now. Right?"

"Really? You mean it? It's legal?"

Joe shrugged but Wade didn't wait for an answer. Forgetting all about breakfast, he was already on his way, and soon rattling up the lane.

JUST ABOVE BITTERROOT Gap, passing the vacated Burchard place, Wade saw a black sedan parked just off the road, and out in the adjacent field clustered around a black 4-wheel drive, a group of men; he recognized first Evan, then the two Japanese men who had been with him at the Grand, but not the small stumpy man with heavy black glasses. Evan was pointing his arm, sweeping it up and down the valley while the others listened and looked on.

Wade waved, unseen, and tractored on, reaching town at noon. He had visions of a flag-waving crowd on hand to welcome him which of course was not the case. In fact strangely the opposite: not a soul out on the street. He sauntered into the Mint, legs wobbly from the long drive, still half hoping for a fanfare; here again, no one, not even Marly. Squash clattering in the kitchen didn't count. Back outside, he now noticed all the stores were closed; no way to buy clothes, he considered his next move.

He heard sounds and walked in their direction, toward, up to, and into the church. It was Sunday, he realized, and happy to see everyone, he joined the boisterous congregation.

Clearly Father Sterling had lost no time capitalizing on the success of his Graduation Week service. Overnight, communion had become a popular summer event, townspeople happily quenching their palettes on the plentiful 'refreshments', as he now called it, the reduction of gin and blood 'wine' and the 'foie gras' pâté, a mash of lamb liver donated by the town abattoir that Squash Maloney spiced up with lavender and wild mustard and served with his specialty fried barley dough 'toasts'. In that vein, and as inducement to encourage more generous tithing, Father Sterling began stocking the contribution plates with cash before passing them down the pews. Initially a setback—he hadn't counted on Meagherites making the logical assumption that, just as the communion was free, so too was the money in the plates, and would meekly then gratefully then fullfistedly help themselves to that as well— even this monetary loss turned profitable: By inadvertently helping congregants to 'help themselves', word spread, and the suddenly swelling attendance reports delighted the diocese, which began providing more and more support funding, more than making up for the monies lost priming the contribution plates. Father Sterling relished his success while humbly appreciating its temporal limitations, fully aware that this was, essentially, burning bridges at both ends. In fact, it all had a certain existential, if not perfectly Kierkegaardian, harmony.

Now Meagherites and visitors alike thronged to the sanctuary, kneeling and drinking, gossiping in the pews and returning for refills while Father Sterling preached. Wade, to get away from all the deafening festive chatter, moved near the pulpit. Above him, Father Sterling's baritone voice rose and fell, sermonizing this day on the topic of free will, citing a parable by a man Wade had never heard of, about two travelers, how every day each would ride from one town to another, both riding a horse that unerringly knew the route and infallibly carried each man to his destination. The first traveler always slept, utterly content to let the horse take the lead, while the second traveler persisted in guiding the horse himself, each and every time no matter how often he went. The point being, Father Sterling said sonorously, that it was the second man, he and only he, that had free will. It was difficult to hear, much less understand, but Wade loved the ring of the phrase, 'free will'. It seemed important, essential, and worth listening to.

Then he caught sight of the new acolyte, standing complacently in the sanctuary, and recognizing the bare feet, the marbled brown eyes, Wade was first startled then pleased when he realized who he was. After the service, Wade back in the Mint, Father Sterling burst in the door, wearing sunglasses and church garb, followed dutifully by the new acolyte wearing *his* church garb, a white frock and ragged levis. They took a booth, and Wade joined them.

"God Almighty, the sprout has sprouted; I hardly recognized ye," Father Sterling said grandiloquently, motioning Wade to sit. "Please feed at our trough, Wade. You look like you not only could eat a horse, you look like you did. I trust you devoured my sermon too?"

Wade nodded. "I tried. But I don't really get free will, though."

"Ah, then you do. To understand nothing, that's free will. John, this is Wade. Wade, meet John, my new aide de camp."

Wade nodded hello, though he could see the acolyte did not remember him at all. Clean-shaven, not so hungry looking, the former possible felon seemed more at ease, and Wade was glad for that. Though his desire to find and join Harlo at

Independence had been thwarted, he had at least found himself a home some place other than jail.

"Ho, the fair Opheliac," Father Sterling said, hailing Anne. "Give us this day our daily doubles."

Anne was already bringing two Bloody Mary's; every Sunday afternoon was the same. Father Sterling tucked his napkin under his stained collar. "One lamb medium rare, and no fancy stuff this time."

"Same," the former possible felon chimed.

Anne plopped down a menu for Wade and went to shout an order through the doors to the kitchen. Wade caught a glimpse of Squash, happily tossing his pots and pans. He hardly recognized the new menu. Squash, lost more than ever after his total failure with Anne, had thrown himself into his cooking. Taking cues from Marly's magazines, he brazenly expanded his repertoire by substituting native foods where he could not identify the foreign. Reading avidly to forget his heartache, he improvised one homemade creation after another, sprucing them up with his own elegant names. Dried Indian Paintbrush petals he named Northern Saffron. Grouse he named Yellowstone Plover. Cut-throat trout eggs became Caviar Sangle. Curdled milk from the vats at Malarkey's DairyGold became Buerre Anglais. Mule deer became Venison de la Compagne; white tail, Venison de la Neige.

He served rice fried with chopped pine needles substituting for rosemary. He braised young rattlesnake and served it in a warm salad of dandelion greens and minced root. He prepared soufflés made with sage hen eggs called Oeufs du Prairie. He invented Whitefish Bisque with Alfalfa. Blue Sucker Langosta del Pobre. Cattail Tempura. Ringneck Pheasant Terrine. Shanks of Lamb in Wild Timothy.

Sagebrush Ragout. Meadowlark Egg Drop Soup. Loin of Wapiti Roti. Pronghorn Cutlets with Glacier Lilies. Crab Apple Tarte Piquante. Rhubarb Mousse. And the more he found the art in his work, the more Squash began to forget about Anne.

Wade closed the menu; exotic cuisine maybe, but not for him. As he was about to get up, the bar suddenly emptied, everyone thronging out the door onto the hot summery street. He joined Anne at the door to see what was going on: The highway department had arrived to prep First Street, the first street ever to be paved in town.

"Where's Joe?" Anne asked.

"He didn't come in."

"Then how'd you get in?"

"Drove."

"Drove? Drove what?"

Wade pointed down Second Street where he had parked.

"That tractor?"

Anne laughed; Wade shrugged.

Around them, the crowd, applauding a large tanker truck passing by with twin spigot lines spraying the gravel street with hot oil, parted as Evan and the men Wade had seen walked by into the Mint. Evan did not notice, or acknowledge, Anne or Wade.

"What's he doin with that guy?" Anne wondered after they went inside.

"What guy?"

"That short guy in those ugly glasses. He runs the survey team who replaced us."

"Evan's been with him all morning. I passed them at Burchard's place on the way to town."

"What were they doin there? On a Sunday?"

"They missed a good sermon."

Hot fumes roiled the street, the oiler completing its last pass. After the hurrahs, people swarmed back into the Mint, proudly blackening the floor with the tracks of progress. Wade stood to the side, smiling; Anne looked off in thought, then abruptly spun and followed in after them. As soon as she spotted Norman's replacement, who had taken a booth by himself, she sidled over with the best brightest smile she could muster.

"Hoo boy, some heat; only good thing on a day like this is hang out in here."

The man looked up. "That's for sure."

"Everyone's got pretty much the same idea." She made an exaggerated survey of the tables. "Mind if I share your booth?"

"No, I sure don't. My pleasure."

Now recognizing her, the man's sunburned cheeks reddened the thick lenses of his glasses. "You're the girl from that survey team up the Hellwater."

Anne nodded. "Ah I was just a go-fer for them. How're you doin?"

"Oh, much better, now my lunch hour took such a nice turn for the better."

Anne smiled, lifted the back of her hair, "Phew, it's so hot though. Why d'you have to be out workin today?"

"Oh honey, you wouldn't believe the heat we're under and I

don't mean sun. Overtime is about killing me, especially now those InterPacific big shots are here breathing down my neck."

"InterPacific?"

"Yeah, the company that hired us." He put forward his hand. "Dick Janney, Janney Engineering. Out of Seattle."

"I thought you were workin for HRC."

"In a way. InterPacific, HRC, Arapahoe, it's all connected. And you are. . .?"

Anne leaned forward, puzzled. "But you're up surveyin HRC's land, aren't you?"

Janney removed his glasses to clean them, and his wall-eyed pupils narrowed as he leaned forward himself.

"And they're all sensitive as hell about publicity, so I can't really go into it. . .though now we're done, I don't get the reason for it."

"Done with what? Who's done?"

"InterPacific, I mean. They've got a big land deal working here, and need to ease in quiet, being that they're, you know, foreigners. There's problems whenever Japanese get seen taking things over. No need to give anyone a chance to make trouble, especially so close to all the approvals."

"Oh well sure, I see," Anne said, not seeing at all. "So there is a second site at Sweetgrass Moraine, I guess."

Janney smiled, picking up the menu. "Sorry, I didn't mean to bore you about work. Let me buy you lunch why don't you?"

"Aw, na" Anne smiled, "I couldn't let you do that."

"Sure you could. Just so there's no hard feelings. Believe me, I had nothing to do with you getting laid off."

"Oh forget that; I hated surveyin work anyway. But you're awful nice to offer."

"I am? I think it's more you. You're the nicest thing about this town."

"Well thanks." She touched his hand. "Maybe I will join you, if you mean it. You seem like an interesting guy to me."

She knew he didn't know how interesting.

HOT LIKE THE sun itself had set down on the field. Smoke so thick it couldn't be seen if it had. The burning pyre, carcass of the mother cow and corpse of the long dead bull, thundered flame and ash high overhead high up the bench land where Joe had hauled them, drenched them with gasoline, and set them afire. With the roar of the inferno and the thick black particulates of their blazing bodies blotting the sky, Anne's pickup appeared out of the air. He quickly grabbed his shirt and pulled it over his naked blackened shoulders. Sooty tears trickled down his face.

"Joe, you okay?"

He nodded, waving away the heat. "Fumes are makin my eyes water."

Anne covered her mouth with her shirttail.

"Can we get out of this bon fire? I have to talk to you."

He pointed to a flat boulder nearby where they could sit out of the heat and smoke.

"What's goin on?"

"You know anything about a company called InterPacific?"

"InterPacific? No. Why?"

"It's this huge Japanese company out here looking for a big cattle ranch to raise beef. That's who Norman was hired by, and who hired this new outfit to replace him, Janney Engineering. I was just talking with him, Joe; you ain't goin to believe it."

"Believe what?"

"You were right. There's no dam goin in at Bitterroot gap now; it's Sweetgrass Moraine they're surveying for. That's where the dam's goin."

"What? Of course there is."

"No, think about it. InterPacific is, and Evan's getting ready to sell it to em. The whole upper Hellwater now. If that ain't one goddamn big cattle ranch, I don't know what is."

Joe let out a long slow whistle, it fully dawning on him now that a dam at Sweetgrass Moraine, not at Bitterroot Gap, all that ranch acreage and the water to irrigate it. . .quicker and cheaper to build, something for everyone, once it dawns on someone, like Evan Gallantine, HRC down river, Arapahoe for the water intensive technology, InterPacific for their high end beef. . .it wouldn't take more than an idea to have so much capital it'd be financed before ground was broken, and by then, who would give a damn if they changed the site to Sweetgrass Moraine?

"That makes a shit load of money behind that dam. And Evan figured it out all along."

And realized it had to be kept quiet until all the land was secured. If Frances or the others had known, they'd have no reason to sell their land, and wouldn't have.

"That's why they sacked us, right, Joe?"

"Norman saw what I didn't, went asking questions, about what it was he was really surveying for."

He shook his head, how Evan was pressuring him to ink the deal, knowing he wouldn't have if he had known, Evan's face that day in the Mint. The one eyed jack.

"Plain as my the back of my hand. . .and I never saw it."

He turned over his hands and started laughing.

"What're you laughin for?"

Joe lay back in the dirt, laughing harder.

He was on his back, smelling sweetgrass, staring up into the blue bowl of sky. A few sprinkles hit his face, though there were no clouds above him. A sunshine shower.

He sat up. His vision so vivid, a photograph of a dream you had all your life: The upper Hellwater valley, a long fertile crescent laced with irrigation canals and steel headgates feeding quarter sections waist deep in hay, automatic sprinkler units walking the fields, the river flow regulated like clockwork, stackyards brimming, third even fourth cuttings, livestock grazing everywhere, all new wide lane roadway all the way over Independence Basin into the park, black asphalt lined with red gravel shoulders, new split-level ranch houses, scarlet barns, brand new pickups and gleaming farm equipment.

"Too bad it all couldn't be ours."

"It is. You can get it back. They cheated you."

"Even if I could, I'd never be able to turn it into anything they could. It'd almost be a shame if they didn't. Jesus, the more we get to wantin it—me, my dad, Harlo, Frances—the more we end up wantin to just finally be done with it."

Another drop touched his cheek. The clear blue sky was still lightly raining.

"You know, Anne? Evan? You think what all he had goin in his head. . .I mean, you got to hand it to him. You really do."

They sat.

"Well at least you got one thing you wanted, Joe."

"What? The ranch?"

"No, not that." Anne looked off. "Remember how you said you'd just once know what it'd be like bein right about something?"

He smiled.

"Looks like you were really goddamn right this time."

It was cloudless but still lightly raining. He could see the drops catching the fire of the sun as they fell.

Chapter 24

EVAN, LEANING OVER the ink-blotted counter at the Chronicle, talking to—trying to talk to—Jack Loomis, almost unable to hear even himself, hating having to repeat and repeat things drowned out by the loud clanking offset presses, knew nevertheless, without hearing a sound, who had just come in the front.

Joe. Nodding hello, indicating, in his Joe-like way, that he 'wanted a word'. Evan, knowing he knew, nodded back, to wait one sec, he'd join him outside, then motioned to the right, meaning to make sure: Did Joe mind if Harlo came along?

Till that moment Joe hadn't noticed him, Harlo, standing to the side, preferring to be an afterthought.

And so it was moments later, the three of them out walking the imprecisely parallel tracks of the old rail spur, heading left, which was south, in the direction of the simmering snow-peaked Independence Basin. Walking not quite together, Joe's pace subdued but ahead of Harlo's amble, his swaying limp leg keeping him behind, Evan's self-satisfied easygoing stride a little forward, jingling the loose change in his khakis, calm, whistling, purposely elongating the time before they 'talked', not about to let Joe, however much he might want to, rip loose with his haranguing about whatever he knew or thought he knew.

Then, at the right time, enjoying the splash of sunlight on his face, Evan turned, swept his long light colored hair behind his ears, and began reflecting, now that his work was almost done, on life in general and his own in particular.

You wouldn't think it, he mused—to Joe, and Harlo, and to anyone who he imagined would be interested—but actually, in truth, he'd never been one for common pleasures: travel, society, high living, marriage and family. No. Rather, what he lived for, what gave him most pleasure in life, most often, was success: the satisfaction that came of completing a good deal. Really, it was; it was the greatest joy, to find and uncover the common denominators that made for bringing all sides to the table for the good of them all. Mating up those with something of value to sell and a need to sell it, with those in need of something of value to buy, and a desire to buy it, ferreting out the good faith of all parties. To Evan—yes, he knew it was eccentric—this was not work, not a job or a career, but an art, and that's what, in his own way, he was, and what he strived to be—an artist, the best he could be. He clasped his hands, describing it, how he felt now, at this moment in time, which was this: That this deal he'd orchestrated here in Meagher, over the course of the past many months, was, in his humble opinion, his masterpiece. Because—whether he did say so himself or not, nevertheless, no matter what, it was. A success, more than any other he'd ever put together. And that, to him, was the reward. The payoff. Not money—he hadn't made much; some, of course, but not a lot. Not what he could have made, it certainly hadn't been the best next project, not for him, not when he undertook it; there were several more lucrative deals in the pipeline back in Southern California. But this was different for him. Far different. There were family interests at stake, it was personal, at heart. That alone, reason enough. But in addition, to be able to get a return on the value of property that had no value, get it not for himself, and not only for his own immediate family, his mother, but for them all, all the hard-working lifelong impoverished Meeks: Frances, Leonard, Harlo, even Joe, and now Wade, and not just family but others, the natives, the Burchards and Gustafsens, the HRC ranchers, and Marly, and for Anne. And furthermore, it wasn't easy, not whatsoever, though it might look that way, to some, to some it might look as though it all just came together all on its own. He understood how his business acumen might make it seem otherwise, still, success didn't happen invisibly. Not at all; on the contrary, it was hard, it took constant dedication, it took effort, it took battling back each day's turns for the worse, facilitating the ever new, ever increasing complexities, pursuing multiple dead ends, forging novel solutions that had to be hammered out and worked through. It took compromising. It took pouring himself into it, focusing exclusively on it, it was not at all predestined to be successful. Few if any really knew the extent of it, pressuring high placed legislators, hard knuckled back and forth negotiating with powerful interests, Arapahoe, HRC, InterPacific, courting the state legislature and pressuring the governor's mansion, all of it went far beyond just a putting up a new dam, it was about a new economy, it was about tapping the wealth of modern technologies and tourism and advanced market economics. And of course, it took overcoming the big sticklers, like persuading Frances Meeks, as he correctly anticipated, and then Joe Meeks, which he hadn't.

Evan then stopped, and turned, and gauging Joe's reaction, considered his next words.

"Joe, I don't expect you to understand the magnitude of what we've accomplished, much less accept it, but whatever you're here to say, there's nothing I can tell you that you don't already know."

He lit a cigarette. Grandly wafted away its smoke.

"I would have liked to do it. . .to have done it. . .differently. . .transparently if I could have, but the constantly changing variables, it was all too complex. I know an opportunity when I see one, and I wasn't about to jeopardize it by having to accede to too many people with such irrational attachment to that fucked up land. Fair enough?"

"Yeah, fair enough, I guess."

Joe looked at Harlo. Harlo looked down at his feet, balancing on one of the track rails.

Evan exhaled. "The Meeks tribe. . .it's like there's genetic encoding in our roots to twine them into and around that rock-burdened waste land and, no matter what, make do with it above all else. Worthless as it may be. Fortunately there's one of us enough in the real world who can see more tangibly. I know I sound arrogant, but so what. It's obvious I know how. . .and why. . .to do the right thing here. And I did. How I did it, how it all came together, despite so many ways it almost didn't. . . at this point? It's irrelevant, it seems to me."

Joe nodding but not meeting Evan's gray eyes. "Yeah I s'pose then we should thank you. For deciding what's right for us."

"I wish you meant that, Joe. You should. And once I make the final disbursements, you will. Eventually."

"I already do. Considerin how we're all so irrational, it was the least you could do, right? Sell it right out from under us." Joe wiped a drop of sunbaked sweat from his brow. "Who'd know better what was best for that place other than someone who it never meant anything to?"

"It's been a long time, if ever, that it had any reason to mean anything to any of us. It's dirt. Whether HRC builds a dam over it or InterPacific makes a cattle factory on it, it isn't ours anymore, and in some ways, I believe it never really was. What's ours—yours, mine, Harlo's—is our future. So yeah, go right ahead and knock yourself out moralizing and rethinking every goddamn little thing; I get that it's what you are compelled to do, but ask yourself, has it ever made things better? Ever?"

"Don't see why I'd bother, Evan. You don't deserve it. You got your hands full enough as it is, playin Santa Claus."

Sunlight flared in Evan's sunglasses. "As though that's not why you're here? To take your best shot at undoing anything good I've done? I'd be surprised if not. How could you ever resist such a golden opportunity to make a stinking mess of everything?"

Joe put his hands in his pockets.

"Yeah. Well. It seems pretty much done."

"Yeah it is, it's what we call a done deal. And InterPacific owns it all now, at least they will come this weekend, at the closing. So anything from here on out is just wasting time. For me, the only to-do left is write the rather healthy check I'll be handing you. Feel free to include Harlo, or not, and Wade of course, or blow it however you want."

Evan looked at Harlo. Harlo shrugged.

"If you're interested; InterPacific will be here Fourth of July sponsoring a big closing celebration as part of the rodeo weekend. Drop by. Harass them all you want. But I'm out of here."

Evan left, heading back to the Loomis's. Joe stared down the other direction, down vanishing length of rust worn tracks.

Harlo sat down on the sun-hot steel track.

He chuckled.

"What's so funny?"

"Na, I was just imaginin, like one of them Sunday cartoons way back when, where the old timer's got his ear pressed to the track, facing up to his horse, sayin he hears somethin comin, and right there behind him is the locomotive right about to run him over."

Joe sat down next to him.

"It does actually kinda feel like there's a long off tremor in the rail. Of somethin comin. Like how it would've felt back when them old ore trains were coming down one after another from up at the mines."

"Uh huh, only today, it's just the one, full of all the riches Evan has got comin for us."

And they both laughed.

MORNING. JOE NOT up yet. Wade at the table with Frances.

She jerked suddenly.

"Another one?" Wade asked.

Another one, another pain, out of nowhere, this one shooting from her hip down her right leg. But she didn't acknowledge it. She pushed back her chair, straightened her leg out, rubbed her thigh.

"I hate the numbness far more than the sharp pains."

Every day, losing more and more feeling, in more and more places. Sometimes, impossible to walk. Or even think. Like now, all of a sudden she realized she couldn't recall why this young man was at her table, eating her food, asking her was she okay. She couldn't remember his name or if she even knew him.

Wade turned. Then she heard it too, driveway gravel crunching under tires, somebody coming to visit. She was about to go to the window to see who, just as Joe came in from the bathroom, and just as suddenly as she forgot, she remembered things again.

She tamped her cane, irritated, hating these lapses.

"What the hell does Harlo want now?"

Joe walked to the window. "It's Evan's pickup, but no sign of him."

"It's probly Harlo. Evan don't have no need to bring him beggin like Harlo does."

Sure enough, the pickup door swung open and Harlo got out, and, like he'd never seen the place before, like he was in no hurry to come inside, he looked around, then circled the pickup, around and back, his limp worse, his whole body moving more like an assemblage of spare parts than a healthy man.

"He's got a new hop to him, I see," Frances said, joining Joe at the window.

Joe nodded. They watched Harlo step into the shade of the weeping willow, and its filtering leaves speckled him in morning sunlight, so that he looked to Joe like an apparition of. . .a man with no hope. The wall clock tolled eight. Frances prodded Joe with her cane.

"Better go see what's up his sleeve."

Joe sighed. He didn't want to talk to Harlo. He looked at

Wade. He was eating, of course; Frances had brought him another plate of pancakes. And, as if for the first time, in contrast to this motherly gesture, he thought of how little motherliness she had ever been able to allow inside her.

And he went out.

Harlo had left; Joe saw his path of trampled nettles leading to the tool shed, where Joe found him, inside, picking old dead wool from a currycomb with all its fine pointed teeth broken. The shed's dark air reeked of dingy mortar and timber rot, its dirt floor like an archeological dig, all strewn with half-buried junk, rust caked screws, dull axe heads, broken mower blades, hay hooks, pitch forks, a crosscut saw. . .and mesmerized, they each stood a long time, just looking, examining it all.

"Kinda like we're two ol grandmas in some bargain basement store lookin for good deals."

"Yeah. All helpless without Evan here with all his *acumen*."

Harlo tried to straddle a worn leather saddle set on a makeshift buck, but couldn't lift his leg.

"Goddamn trick knee actin up again, ever since that truck wreck."

He instead hoisted himself onto a castoff cast iron stove.

"There, that's more like it. Back on the hot seat now."

Joe nodded. He stepped out the back door and looked out onto what was really a graveyard, a final resting place for farm equipment junk—flatbed wagons, horse-drawn plows, a spoked hayrake, a baler, a depression era motorized tractor unused for so long its spiked steel wheels were sunk halfway into the earth.

All of it, all thick with the sienna red dust of oxidized iron.

Harlow standing next to him now.

"Though, you know, there could be life in this old place yet, Joe. Maybe get some of this equipment back workin."

He walked to the baler, kicked at one of its flat tires, which shattered the old rubber and sent black flecks of it flying. He picked at the engine mounts, digging the gunk of hay dust and oil from the housing. He fashioned a loop of twine around the flywheel, pulled it taut.

Something about it, his manner, his rangy body, his loopy thinking, something about Harlo now beginning to agitate Joe.

"You lost that truckin job with Tyler?"

"Yeah I did."

"So what're you thinking you'll do now?"

"Guess get another job."

They nodded, nodding that they both knew that would never happen.

"Goddamn, how many bales of hay we threw usin this old piece a shit. It was old even then. Remember me teachin you to run it?"

"Yeah, so you wouldn't have to."

"Lotta good that did me. Probly one reason alone you run off when you did. Goddamn, I should of run off right along with you. Maybe made somethin of myself. But I been thinkin, I might still yet, make somethin of myself. A guy can always pick up where he left off, can't he? All's it might take is the right break."

"Meanin?"

"Meanin nothin; just how it's funny. . ." Under the baler's chute, a large anthill, which Harlo toed at, watching the inhabitants start rebuilding it even as he ruined it. "Funny how things twist around over time. Take how you run off, never to come back then years later you do an find yourself ownin the goddamn place."

"Owning it but not a thing you can do with it, an all when you didn't ever want it to begin with. Except sell it for whatever it'll get."

Harlo braced his legs against the baler chassis, pulled at his cord, testing it. Then for the first time he looked at Joe face to face.

"Joe? I know you'll be more'n generous with me, once things get settled. . .but I gotta say, an maybe it's just convict's sense, but just listenin to Evan, I get the idea he ain't got the shells in his clip he thinks he does. I been in court enough over the years, I suspect you an me, we could start up some kind of injunction or desist order. I may not know any particulars, but I do believe there's other ways."

"Why would I ever even want that?"

"Well, yeah, I'm with you on that, but on the other hand, you can't tell me a person, the right person, couldn't still suck out a livin out of this place. A normal person, no. Wouldn't bring him much but trouble. . .but a person like me, y'know? With some years left in him? He might could tough it out. If it was his, of course."

He yanked on the cord. The flywheel spun. The engine coughed.

"Yes sir! I think this baby might just start right up. Given some grease and TLC."

"So Harlo? You're askin me to give the place over to you."

"Now there's an idea. Maybe not actually 'give'. . .but it was your idea too, y'know, a few weeks ago. Remember?"

"Yeah. I know."

Harlo rewound the twine and pulled again. The flywheel spun from the might of his pull, the motor turned over twice, then clicked and died. Harlo full choked it and tried again. Fumes swirled around him, puffs of white smoke escaped the perforated exhaust pipe, but it still failed to start.

"Fuck it. This piece a shit? I give up."

He leaned back on the chute, eyes tearing from the exhaust.

"The way I see it, as long as Emma was alive, this place was never owned by the people workin it. Like Frances. Like your dad. I know better'n to think you might wanna partner with me, I know you wouldn't want to be in that position, and I do get it. Neither would I. But all's I'm thinkin, is. . ."

"I know, Harlo. I see how maybe it makes sense. You sure deserve it, by rights, and by need, I know that. But. . .I don't know. We can talk about it, but I have to think that's pretty much out of reach by now."

"Yeah, I know. Sure. It's all right."

They stood, looking off, not at one another, but away, in different directions. Both nodding absently, knowing it would never happen.

They walked back to the pickup.

"So you're driving Evan's rig now."

"Yeah, he lent it to me, since I ain't got nothin."

Harlo got in.

“He ain’t a half bad guy at heart, really. Just that, he’s pretty much full of it, you know?”

Joe nodded.

“Well, see you around.”

Harlo turned the ignition. The pickup’s big engine roared with power.

WADE WITH ONE of Frances’s old legs across his lap, rubbing her feet.

“What’s the use? It ain’t gonna change nothin.”

“It feels better, doesn’t it?”

“How do I know if it feels better, I can’t feel anything anyway. I don’t know I even want it to. Most things in life, you’re better off to just get used to it.”

Frances jerked, another jolt of pain up her leg, knocking her cane to the floor. She clutched the table until it passed.

“Oh I sure never imagined I’d ever let myself go soft like this.”

Wade set down her thin leg; she eased back in her chair. Closed her eyes.

Outside, Joe and Harlo, Wade watched them, how they talked, then didn’t, then did.

“Frances? How come Harlo looks so much like Joe but not like you. Not like you’d think, for being your son.”

Frances opened her eyes, looked out the window. Kept looking out the window, a long time, something out there only she could see.

"Well obviously he don't, 'cause he ain't."

She sat up suddenly. "Well that's funny, now I can feel clear to my toes. Everything's all clear all of a sudden."

"But, Frances, what do you mean?"

Frances leaned on the table, bracing herself on her swollen blueish knuckles.

"What do I mean? About what?"

"What you just said."

"What'd I just say?"

"You said Harlo wasn't your son. Didn't you?"

"Damn, Wade. Don't Joe ever tell you nothin?"

She began smoothing the grip of her cane with the palm of her good hand, at the same time she began recounting, for Wade, the story of the Meeks family, from Peter and Mary Meeks, who weren't her real parents, weren't Lillian's real parents either; only the one girl, the simple slow girl, Emma, was their own. Frances and Lillian were orphaned when their father, Peter Meek's mining partner, was killed by a bandit who jumped his claim. And because there was nowhere else, Peter Meeks brought them both down to his wife and daughter on the homestead on the upper Hellwater. Frances remembered, so lucid to her even now, how he'd told his wife how he felt like, at last, he'd finally found pure gold up at Independence, no, it was better than silver, what he found was two more daughters, the prettiest ones in the world. And Frances admitted, she loved this new poppa far more and far better than she had the real one, who never had nice words like that. And though Frances feared that Mary Meeks would be angry about it, she wasn't, she took both girls in and raised them as her own, even when, shortly thereafter, Peter Meeks himself died in a cave-in. She was a one hard-working determined woman, for Frances, the one person in life who you want to live up to. She sure did, anyways. When Mary Meeks went out to work the fields, Frances worked. When Mary Meeks was dying, Frances wanted to die. And swore to her, like to a real mother, to reassure her, that she'd do anything she could to keep the place going, to take care of Emma like her own sister, and Emma's poor sons Leonard and Harlo.

"I swore to be a real Meeks, always, and goddamn if I didn't always think I was."

"Because you are, Frances."

"Goddamn right, son."

Frances smiled, the clarity of her past returning with such vividness. She reached for her wine jar though it was long empty and stained with grainy residues.

"Even after she willed the place to Emma so it'd stay with real Meeks blood, I never wavered. She had to do that. . .though all those years, silly me, I did kinda keep thinkin one day the place'd go to me. That's how much a Meeks I thought I was." She put the jar to her mouth with both hands and drank. "But you can't go and make yourself somethin you ain't, can you? Now here I am. No ranch. No children. No nothin."

FRANCES LIFTED HER legs; there was no pain.

"You know Wade, I feel so good, I think I could go for a nice long sleep."

As she started to get up, Joe came in.

"So, here he is. Just look at him, Wade."

"What about me?" Joe said.

"What about you?" She rose slowly. "Just how you're a misfit Meeks if there ever was one. Like all Meekses. . .except you'd be the last. Seein how Wade's the exception what proves the rule. Right, Wade?"

Wade nodded. He wondered if all families were this complicated.

She planted her cane and slowly hobbled to her room.

Chapter 25

THEY—ANNE, WITH Wade tagging behind—found Joe sitting out back in the silver-green shadow of dew cast by the weeping willow. He looked up as, announced by the rustle of sunlit fallen leaves, they sat in the wild grass on his either side.

Anne pulled a long blade of grass and bit the tender stem.

"What're you doin?"

"Watching that plane. Wonderin what it's up to."

Anne shielded her eyes. Far off, just above the cottonwood lining of the Hellwater, a bright white-silver flash, a small plane, swept across the canvas of valley wall, then disappeared into Bitterroot Gap.

"How'd it go with talkin to Evan?"

"About how you'd expect. What's done is done; can't change anything."

Anne spit out the chewed stem. Neither with anything more to say.

Wade said, "Out riding yesterday, I came across these couple of cows. Their brand was Bar-Slash-Heart. That means they're Frances's, right?"

Joe um-hmmed.

"They got through some broken fence, right? Want me to ride up and bring them in? I don't mind."

"Oh I'm sure you don't."

"Yeah, Joe," Anne said. "Let's you and me get the Jeep an drive alongside."

Joe arched his eyes at her.

"What?" she said, "you got something better to do?"

He looked up, the plane again, whisking back upriver for another run.

"So. . .Joe? I'll go saddle up then?"

"Yeah Wade, go saddle up then."

Wade already striking out for the barn, keeping at bay the two canine cohorts, who immediately joined and jumped him.

"Frances's dogs sure do love having him here for play dates, don't they?"

Joe shook his head, the sun higher, hotter, making the wet turquoise dew recede, and desiccating the beads of moisture from blades of grass as they were exposed.

"I'm afraid Wade's getting too attached."

"Yeah, you should have heard him when I told him they changed the dam site. He's all, like, now for sure you'll find a way to keep it."

"Anne, don't go tellin him all. . .you go gettin his hopes all up an. . .it's not good. For him."

"He's fine, you ol grouch. It's just you it's not good for."

She swatted Joe, resisting doing more than that, then turned to watch Wade approach the sorrel, halter hidden behind his back, wagging a handful of wild wheat.

"Got awful lanky awful fast, didn't he?"

"Awful fast."

"Won't be long till he's as hot lookin as his dad."

She tossed a clump of wet dirt at him.

"Why'd you come, Anne?"

"I missed you. That a problem for you now? You gonna tell me I'm getting too attached now too?"

Joe wiped his hands on his pants and stood up.

"We better go."

WADE COULDN'T HOLD Sorry in step alongside the jeep. Hard as he reined her back, the headstrong filly battled ahead, and he was waiting at the gate to high pasture well before the pickup caught up. Anne got out, wanting a turn on the young horse. Dismounting, Wade stepped in prickly pear, and spent the time riding in the cab pulling out the cactus spears which had lanced his new sneakers.

Joe pulled up, cocked his head out the window, scanned the sky.

"Listen, Scotty. Hear that?"

Wade—wondering if he looked like Joe's little brother, and that was why Joe called him Scotty—wished he had a picture, of himself and of Scotty, so he could compare and see for himself.

"You and Marly went in a plane like that, right Joe?"

"How'd you know that?"

"That picture Anne has. Of, you know, when you were kids. Right?"

Joe didn't answer.

"I guess it was Scotty who took that picture. Was it?"

Wade thinking it had to be someone who liked Joe and Marly and who they liked too.

"No, it wasn't him."

"But he got to go up with you guys too? Didn't he, Joe?"

"No, Wade."

Joe started driving ahead again, following Anne.

"Scotty never made it."

Then for a long time he didn't answer any more of Wade's questions. . .

. . .Endless, the land leading up to Independence, uninhabited, wild, empty, especially in a hurry, to get to Marly, and he passed the time tugging the mane of his horse, fretting out loud as though Scotty, beside him, was listening and understanding and liking all the new ideas Joe had had churning inside him, how he couldn't wait to get out in the world, how he might never get another chance, how he couldn't stand what little he knew about anything, how bad he wanted to know at least as much as Vaughn Marlowe knew. Since the day he had thought of it, Joe blazed with the notion, that they could go where Vaughn went, he and Marly, do what Vaughn did, learn what he learned. God what he wouldn't give for that.

He hoped Vaughn would have returned now, and like last time, sit outside and talk like a know-it-all about the tropical climates that existed here millions and millions of years ago, thick rainforests of sycamore, redwood, breadfruit, magnolia, and mangrove, along shallow seas that got higher and then drowned those forests in layer after layer of sediment and how, between the pressure of the seas above and the hot earth below, they were hardened and transformed into vast basins of lignite and coal, then uplifted (there was so much Joe couldn't possibly understand) so that, exposed by erosion, some of those fields caught fire in lightning storms, furious fires that lasted thousands of years, baking the underlying shale to brick-hard clinker, and kept uplifting so that mountains like Mount Contact were made, seafloor lifted so high that now you could find a rock like this, and Vaughn broke off a chunk of rust red rock he found and there were prehistoric, perfectly pressed carbons imprints of leaves fallen from those ancient forests into the swampy mud. He put the fossil rock to his nose and smelled and gave it to Joe, saying he was smelling aromas from millions of years ago. Joe's legs had fallen asleep from not wanting to move, because Marly had her head in his lap; it was nice, the geology of Vaughn's imagination and the sun floating down and Marly's warmth and Scotty playing with his dog.

Since that last day, many more days had passed without seeing him, Vaughn Marlow, and Marly missed him, though she wouldn't say so, and Joe knew, but wasn't jealous, once he realized he missed him too and wouldn't say so either, because he didn't want to think he might have gone for good. But this time when Joe and Scotty rode up, Vaughn was there, laughing his laugh, even more when Joe jumped down and laughed his laugh too.

"You're leaving, ain't you?"

Vaughn leaned back. "Day after tomorrow, yep. But tomorrow itself, I'm flying. Arranged a twin engine to take me up, get the ten thousand foot view on things."

His eyes gleamed with memory. "You see such things from a plane. It's like God turns on a light for you."

Joe looked at him, envious, and yet, it was good to have him back.

Marly looked almost in pain, from the desire she felt seeing Joe again, and from Vaughn's being about to leave. She sat up.

"Last night, the funniest thing. I woke up, pots an pans all rattlin and the cabin creakin, I thought it was a grizzly, but when I got up, it was like somebody pulled the ground out from under me. I fell right over."

"Yep,' Vaughn said, "I felt it too, just before dark, I was at a fire lookout near the park, and the ranger there said he's been calling these tremors all day long. Said they told him to stop, weren't interested, told him it was just wind shaking his tower. Fools had any brains, they'd at least notify the seismology department at the university."

"Why? It was an earthquake?"

"It was seismic something or other, I don't care what those Forest Service paper-pushers said. There's at least ten known faults all across Independence Basin, and probably others. It hasn't been mapped except by the Emmons survey, and that was 1908."

He stood up, clapped his hands, grinning.

"Too bad I can't stay. I'd sure as hell hate to miss the big one."

Joe toyed with his fingers. "Where you goin, anyway?"

"Alberta. There's all that oil and pipeline work there, which is about the only thing that pays these days." He stretched. "Now, if you'll excuse me, I'm about to spring a leak."

He walked out into the nearby aspen thicket, and Joe followed, leaning against a tree while Vaughn relieved himself.

"Something on your mind there, kid?"

Joe shrugged 'no', and nodded 'yes', both at the same time.

"Shoot."

"What if we went along with you? I mean, to Alberta? Tomorrow?"

"Go with me? Tomorrow?"

"Yeah, take us along, me and Marly."

Vaughn Marlowe, incredulously, "Joe, you know I can't. . .you're not even. . .and still in school? I mean. . ."

"School? We don't learn in school; I learn more from you in one afternoon. There's nothin but nothin here for us. We'd work hard. We'd learn."

Vaughn looked down, away, at Marly, at Joe, down again.

"Joe, it's a. . .an interesting idea, I understand how you feel, but it's. . .I just can't do that."

But Joe, now that he'd got it out, couldn't stop, give up, walk away.

"Just get us started, then. We got to get out in the world, Vaughn. There's just no other way, we're goin to go, one way or another, somewhere, out of here, we will. . .an all we hoped was if you could help make it easier for us."

Vaughn Marlow shaking his head, rubbing his jaw, and, nothing more to say, watched as evening sunlight sharpened the summit edge of Mount Contact.

"And what's so wrong with it anyway? Only reason I'm even here is some boy same age as me, even younger actually, my grandpa Meeks, run off from his own family an stowed away from back in Europe, an I don't see why I can't do the same, only in reverse."

Vaughn put his foot on a fallen pine and took a long breath.

"First thing tomorrow morning, that plane I told you about, is landing at a field south of Meagher, to do a final reconnaissance, then it's contracted to get me up to Alberta."

His voice slow, even, quiet, but his eyes betraying him.

"Now, if. . .if. . .two young people were to happen to be there, and if there happens to be room enough for two more, and if the pilot happens not to say anything, well, who the hell am I to say anything. That's the best I can do. Don't count on any more than that. I can't take that kind of responsibility."

Vaughn, starting to walk off, turned back.

"Oh, and. . .you drive, right? Farm equipment, tractors, like that?"

"Sure I do. What about it?"

"I'm not saying one way or the other, but could be they're hard up for equipment operators up there."

He left, to his tent outside, where he turned in, and it grew night, and late, stars beginning to pop the thick ink of dusk. Scotty asleep in the cabin; Joe and Marly outside, talking it over, in low voices.

"You really mean it, Joe? Really do it. Run away?"

"Not run away, just go to where Vaughn's goin. Yeah, Marly, I really want to. I got to. But I can't go without you goin too."

Marly, folded into a ball. Hands tremoring.

"So, just leave then. Just like that. Tomorrow, we just. . .you an me. Jesus, Joe. I can't barely imagine."

Joe nodding, "I know, yeah, but we got to, don't we? What if we never get a chance like this, ever again?"

Marly turned, eyes big and uncertain and all over him, weakening Joe in his own certainty.

"Maybe I'm nuts; I don't know what I'm talkin about. . .I. . ."

Marly reached her hand to his lips, smoothed them nervously, to console not him but herself, asking him, Did he really want her with him?

And he thought, of summer ending soon, of returning to town, to school, to chores.

To home.

Did he mean it?

"Yeah, Marly. What do we got to lose?"

And on it went. Joe didn't get up and head home, he remained, hours into it, that hot night, its bowl of sky brilliant with stars. Sleeping, not sleeping, fretting, waking, Joe put his arms around Marly, her face with diamonds of dream sweat on it, and, eventually, he roused himself, waking her.

"Joe? What's wrong?"

"We better go, Marly. Vaughn's getting up. We don't want to miss that plane. I'll get Scotty."

She held his arm.

"What?"

"Joe, we can't."

Joe not understanding.

"We can't take Scotty with us. You know that, right?"

"No, course we can't, I only meant to go get him to take him back. . .on our way to town."

"But you know him; he won't get it. He'll want to go. He'll be so. . ."

"We can't just leave him. . ."

But no, he knew, they could leave him, and would; they had to, she was right, and it was obvious. That in leaving him, with no way to explain, no way to ever get him to understand, Scotty would follow them, no matter what they said, or did, he would, and Joe couldn't face it, he knew that, Marly knew that. They would just have do it, have to leave, and go. Go without him. Better for him not to even know. Much better.

"He'll just get home, maybe he won't even know what. . .you never know what he knows and don't know. He'll get back all right. "

"Yeah." Marly nodding, wiping her eyes. "Yeah but. . .I'm goin to miss him. He's the closest thing to a brother I ever had."

"I know, but, we're goin to make money, right, have work, and. . .first thing we'll do? Come back and see him. Even bring him with us. Right?"

There wasn't much to get together, and soon they quietly approached Loner, muzzling him with clumps of grass and slow soothing hands so he made no noise. They walked him through the ghostly buildings of Independence and up to the divide, where they stopped to get mounted. Marly turned to look one last time.

"Bein up here, havin you around, goddammit. It changed my life. Changed everything."

"It's only the beginning, Marl."

"Long as you're sure, I'm sure. You know that, right, Joe?"

And they found Vaughn Marlow, and joined him, and were on their way.

WHEN THEY LOCATED the two strays, Anne was still riding Sorry, driving them homeward ahead of her. A shadow swooped overhead, the motor whine of the plane, cutting into the heat of the day.

Wade's head out the jeep's window, watching the plane rise, descend, disappear again.

"Joe? You know that picture of you and Marly, the one of you guys, in front of the plane?"

Joe turned, having forgot Wade was there.

"Yeah. What about it?"

"Where were you guys going?"

"Where? Just taking a little plane ride, is all."

Anne now and then having trouble keeping Sorry in check, when they reached the river, the sorrel was relentless, eager to run the two cows across. When they balked, Sorry reared, and Anne, wanting no part of that, yanked the reins back hard, The filly bristled, but obeyed, and—as though calmed being under the cool of river-lining cottonwoods—settled into an easy gait. Wade admired Anne, how she let herself sway with the rhythm of Sorry's pace, keeping alongside the jeep.

Now and then the three would talk, or not, thinking their thoughts.

"Joe, do you know what free will is supposed to be?"

"Free what?"

Wade told them Father Sterling's parable of the two travelers. "So if the horses know the way by heart, and the first man goes to sleep and lets his horse go on his own, but the second man steers his horse no matter what, how come it's the second man that's got free will?"

Anne, lazing back in the saddle, volunteered, "You ask me, the second guy is just a know-it-all. If anybody's got free will it's the horse."

Joe, considering it, interested in it, said, "Might have something to do with how a person sees his life, maybe, like, how do you think of your life; do you lead it, or does it lead you? Are you just along for the ride, or do you try to take charge somehow. What do you think?"

Wade shrugged. "I think nobody ever cares what I think."

"Huh?"

Wade blushed, and to cover his outburst, said, "I mean, like about me going off to some proper school, I just meant, well, everything is fine here just the way it is, and. . .but like, what difference does it make anyway? What I think? That's all."

At that, they all went silent again. The jeep, the horse, all stopped mid-river in the long shade of the cottonwoods, barely a ripple of river water lapping against the tires, more a trickle of foam and crud than a river. Moss baked on the hot white domes of the larger boulders.

"Awful damn low," Anne said, and Joe said, "And not two months ago, it was a near flood."

"It's same as every year, two or three weeks of snowmelt and spring rain, then, bam, dry as a bone."

"Just when hayin season needs it."

Sorry, aware Anne had let the reins go free, started off toward the far bank on her own, splashing the ankle deep water.

"Look at this one. Wade, your filly's got more free will than any of us. Put together."

Overhead, the white plane had cut its engine, and as it was gliding silently over them, Anne waved. The pilot, in response, dipped the wings.

"Hey," Anne cried, "that's Norman." She flailed her arms again. "I bet he's started that job. Surveyin how they plan to feed all that water to the liquid fuel plant they're buildin."

The plane's engine roared, it sped away, a hand flash behind the small cockpit windows waved. Joe watching Anne, waving back, laughing, happy. A momentary bolt of hope crackled within him.

LATE, MIDDLE OF the night, Frances in her room, Wade in Emma's old room, Joe on a cot in the front room. Again, a night of the usual tossing and turning, though this night with moonlight glimmer filling the window.

A tail swished his face, he rolled over. A wet nose touched his ear, he batted it away. A weight settled on the end of his cot.

"Damn you. How'd you get inside?"

Butter, one of Frances's dogs. He thrashed at him with his foot; Butter jumped down. Joe settled back down.

"Joe?"

Now a hand, rocking his leg.

"Joe?"

Anne, now sitting where Butter just left.

Joe's head went bolt upright.

"Jesus. Anne? What d'you think you're doing here?"

"Oh, great, thanks a lot. I want to be with you, what's it look like."

"But you can't. . .you can't just. . ."

Joe skootched back as she stood suddenly. The cot flipped up, and over, landing Joe in a heap.

"Ow!" he swore, untangling, getting to his feet, pulling his blanket over his underwear.

Lowering his voice, he asked, again, What was she doing here?

Anne raised a bottle—wine—took a long drink. Its strong fumes wavered the moonlight.

"I just told you."

She offered it to him, he waved it away. Righted the cot. Rubbed his eyes.

"What time is it?"

"Time for you to stop bein a wimp, pretendin you don't care about me, an. . ."

"Jeez, Anne, lower your voice, you're wakin up the whole valley."

"Fine," she retorted, and plopped in a huff on the floor. Joe sat carefully positioning himself in the dark, back on the cot.

"Anne, c'mon now, you can't just expect. . .you know, to. . ."

"To what?"

"To come an. . ."

"Expect what?"

"Expect to, you know, come in and just like that, get. . .you're not. . ."

"Not what, young enough for you?"

Joe, surprised that he couldn't help but laugh, shook it off, and said, "It's that, what you think is love is only. . .only just what you somehow got into your head is somethin me and your mother had and don't want you to have."

"Yeah, well, that's a pretty dumb shit way to make it my fault when you're in love with me and don't wanna be."

"It's not. . .that's not what it is. You know as well as me."

"What I know? That you keep sayin all that 'cause you can't stand that you *are* in love. With me. An' that you can't put it all in a picture frame on a shelf and expect it to sit there and rust. You sound just the same, you an mom, big shot know-it-all grown-ups. Anymore, neither of you'd know love if it kicked you in the head. Which is what it did me. But at least I know what it is."

Butter leaning against her leg, Anne scratched his ears, then went on.

"She told you to keep away from me, didn't she?"

"No. She didn't have to."

"She did. I know why she did. She's still in love with you too. So now? You're all guilty 'cause you used to love her and now you love me."

Joe shook his head. "No, that's not how it works, it just. . .we were kids, Anne, but. . ."

"Yeah? Kids? So love, that's somethin you outgrow, that what you mean?"

In the dark, and not easy to see her face, it made her voice omnipotent. He gave up, he sighed, and he was surprised how much of a sigh he sighed.

"What's between us, Joe, whatever you want to call it, call it blue sky, call it dog shit, don't tell me you don't want it the same as I do."

"I don't. What you want isn't. . .what I want is. . .ah never mind."

Anne leaned over Butter.

"He lies like a rug, don't he? Why's he doin this to me, huh?"

Butter stretched out his legs, she stretched up her arms. She yawned then sleepily curled herself onto the cot, head on his leg.

"You can't stay here, Anne."

"Okay, sure, I know. I can't stay. Fine, I just ain't leavin, though."

A standoff, quiet, during which Anne curled closer, during which, Joe almost unaware of it, his hand began stroking her hair, his voice saying, how she was such a beautiful girl, had so much more on the ball than he ever did, her age or even now, how if she really did love somebody it'd be impossible not to love her back, meaning that she didn't, didn't love him anyway, and how it was late, and she was drunk, so he'd go ahead and sleep on the floor and she could go ahead and sleep there on the cot, how this other stuff, all of it, had got to end.

The dog squeezed between his legs, panting, smiling up at him, mostly happy teeth all Joe could see in the dark, his tail switching Anne's face. She swatted it away, murmuring how, All right, Butter, they had to leave it alone now, how Joe didn't want loving creatures around much, how that ruled out him and her. Butter rolling his happy eyes at her as she smoothed his flat ears.

"Aw, nice doggie, Butter; you're better lookin anyway. Plus, you got a lot bigger heart."

She let the weight of her head fall full onto Joe's thigh. When her breathing became rhythmic, he eased out, replaced himself with his pillow, smoothed the blanket over her, lay on the floor with a coat over him, and though he didn't go back to sleep, he was no longer restless. He knew everything would get cleared up soon enough.

Shortly before morning, he got dressed and drove off in the jeep.

Chapter 26

TO INAUGURATE MEAGHER'S First Annual Fourth of July Rodeo and Sheep Drive, the InterPacific company, in conjunction with their purchase of the upper Hellwater valley and to foster good will for the project, rented out the Grand for an open-bar and free buffet banquet the entire weekend. The first morning, in advance of the chartered jet which was bringing the silver-haired Harada and several of his subordinates, three vans arrived with the caterers and all their supplies; soon the head caterer, a Latin man, who opened many an eye with his diamond earring, was airily waving his assistants on their mission. Almost in no time he had transformed the kitchen into a pavilion of restaurant equipment as fancy as any Squash had seen in any magazine. While the caterer barked in Spanish to his help, he bantered with Squash in stilted English, suiting him up in chef whites and encouraging him to mingle with the other chefs. Whereupon Squash did, tasting the veal cutlets, swirling the Teflon pans full of sauces, studying the prep cooks as they sliced up their intricate floral garnishes. Meanwhile, the industrious caterer was everywhere at once, diplomatically marshalling the setup effort while Father Sterling pestered him about wine and pâté, searching for some culinary common ground to angle for a donation or discount of some kind for the grand church bazaar Father Sterling was just now conceiving.

Marly Croft surreptitiously ducked in, meandering among the tables of pewter banquet ware and silver-plated warming bins, fingering the lace and table linens, marveling at the fine cutlery and exotic tropical flowers blooming in cut-glass vases. The caterer, learning she was the proprietor, immediately fell all over her, lavishing and complimenting and admiring her with such aplomb that she even let him have fifteen minutes for the honor of doing her makeup. They went off together, and when she made her appearance, she was radiant; the shades and hues of his masterful work boosted the auburn of her hair and highlighted the cream of her skin. The kitchen was hushed, then burst into applause. Not only her premises but even Marly herself had been beautifully and adoringly rendered by the robust touches of the caterer.

In the street, preliminary events were already beginning. Dozens of children herded, pushed, kicked, dragged their prize calves, lambs, colts, piglets before a panel of judges seated in lawn chairs under the shade of Major Thomas F. Meagher, the statue itself fluttering with blue, red, white, green satin prize ribbons.

The Tyler family organized a barrel racing event, arranging First Street in a slalom of canary yellow drums provided by Arapahoe Oil. The event was won by their nine year old daughter, because most of the older girls (who were in fact fine riders) were boisterously drunk; they knocked over more barrels than they turned, and drove laughing bystanders from the street.

Stodgy backcountry guides loaded their pack horses with the heaviest gear they could find—rocks, chairs, drunks from the bar—anything to add weight for the pack horse contest, in which each guide would try to lead his horse the fastest the farthest, packed with the most and losing the least. At the gunshot, they filled the road south in a chaotic scramble; by sundown, few had returned. Most of them had lost their way.

Hordes of people milled along First Street, thronging to

makeshift booths selling everything from home brew to mutton burgers. An impromptu parade began, joined by anyone who felt like walking, a parade celebrating the residents themselves, because as McComb had remarked, "Who else would?" For a good part of the afternoon old ranchers and sheepherders, itinerant loggers and ranch hands, cooks and wives and clerks and shopkeepers, all cheered one another for being nobody. They cheered whenever the spirit moved them, which was constantly, because it refreshed their hearts; they had never before had anything worth cheering for. Everybody was a crowd pleaser; every man woman and child of Meagher walked in fame the entire length of First Street, then rejoined their beer-can waving, shoulder-jostling neighbors. McComb drove his sheriff's pickup with makeshift kilts on its wheel wells. Jack Loomis tossed papers from two satchels full of Chronicles printed especially for the occasion. Brad Angstman drove his new International Harvester farmhand, forklift stacked with kegs of beer. Jack Duffy helped Ben Faw start the original town fire-truck; they made it halfway down First Street before a fire broke out under the hood. It sat smoking like a Chinese dragon and people hoo-rayed and doused it with beer. The Berg twins, Ollie and Orville, with beards dyed red with wine and wearing loincloths and breastplates, paraded as Vikings in a cutout canoe emblazoned with the words "Sons of Norway".

A legion of girls, five to fifteen, wearing swimming suits and chaps and white cowboy boots, twirled leather cattle crops to lead off the Sheep Drive. Behind them, a swarm of over a thousand dirt-gray animals turned line by line onto the street and like an unruly bustling living carpet rolled down the gauntlet of jabbering humans who cleared to the side. Escorted by grizzled sheepherders, the bewildered animals became a leaping river of thick fur bounding one over another, bolting leaping bleating nosing their way, herded by their somber, woolen-clad masters to makeshift pens on the outskirts of town for the next day's sheepdog cutting contest.

JOE MEEKS WANTED to go home, though he had none, but then at least to hole up, keep quiet, see no one. And no more going over and over and over it all over again. Only get the money from Evan and bolt from Meagher for good.

Instead, he was walking into the Mint, into a rowdy festival of complete foreigners and reveling strangers, fingers worrying the already frayed one way plane ticket in his jacket pocket. Here, he was to meet the head of InterPacific, at Evan's insistence. Who now appeared quickly at his side to intercept him.

"Nothing to worry about, Joe. Mr. Harada asked me specifically about making your acquaintance."

Joe followed Evan into the new banquet room, to a senior looking Japanese suit and his younger looking aide standing at a greeting table shaking hands. Evan made introductions. Formal gestures, stiff half bows and limp handshakes, exchanged. Mr. Kato, the aide, incapable of ever not smiling, offered each—Joe, Evan, Mr. Harada, and himself—a small ceramic cup. In it, a liquid that was as clear as, but probably was not, water. Mr. Harada raised his in a toast, Evan and Mr. Kato followed suit, but Joe, anxious, thirsty, and not noticing, gulped his down.

It was not water. Or, it was, but more accurately, fire water.

He reddened. Held back a choke. Coughed. Some silence, just

a moment, Evan warily monitoring his guests for any sign of insult. . .

"Pretty good," Joe said.

And Mr. Harada smiled. And nodded to Mr. Kato, who smilingly refilled Joe's cup. And once again, with particular pronounced solemnity, the international trading titan raised his cup.

"For appreciation, we very much like honor you, Mr. Joe Meeks, with small Japanese gift."

Before Joe could throw back this drink too, Mr. Kato quickly keenly grandly presented to him a large package artfully wrappered in decorative rice paper. Joe, no choice but to take it, held it tentatively, anxious, puzzled, looking to Evan. Who grinned and shrugged and was of no help. Meanwhile Mr. Kato intricately removed the rice paper, uncovering a beautifully glazed porcelain pot, and planted in it, a plant—a miniature tree, an infant ornamental full foliaged pine.

"Is bonsai plant, made by my daughter," Mr. Harada intoned. "We hope you will accept."

Mr. Harada, uneasy about his English, looked to his aide.

"Bonsai," Mr. Kato explained, "is art to grow small tree in container, create by cutting roots and wiring branches, to restrict growth of it. It is very ancient custom. Maybe one day in America too, we hope."

Mr. Harada, with happy eyes now, nodded to Mr. Kato, who nodded, and continued, "A small thank you for your help in our purchase."

Then he, and Mr. Harada, stepped back. Then another round of stiff bows. Then Mr. Harada turned aside to Evan, while Mr. Kato, on cue, turned to Joe.

"We have great hope for your valley. And as we have been your guests, we hope you come too, be our guest. Often visit. You please have invitation anytime."

"Well yeah; I don't know what to say," Joe, knowing not what to say, said.

Mr. Kato nodded vigorously, not fully understanding, then trailed dutifully behind as Evan took Mr. Harada deeper into the crowd to meet and greet the various shit-kicker clad patrons.

Behind the bar, three bartenders slung amber liquor and bubbly mixers into plastic glasses which disappeared as soon as they were set on the bartop. Outside, car horns blared. People on hoods and tailgates laughed and fell off. All of Meagher either jammed the Mint or spilled out front.

Joe worked his way through the room, trying to leave, to get away from the vaguely familiar names wafting out of the crowd—Tyler, McComb, Habeger, Braughten, Springer—faces he knew and half knew smiling approvingly at him, shaking his hand, passing him drinks he didn't want. He felt congratulatory eyes on him—the narrow eyed Loomises, the round faced Duffy, the fat eyes of the Malarkey woman from the clinic—and had to look down.

He saw a flash of red hair—a woman—in the corner of his eye. He changed course and veered toward it, curious, thinking it was Marly, but then, no, it was somebody famous. A movie star, a. . .but then saw anew, and it *was* Marly. . .but Marly like he'd never seen her, all done up, stunning, glamorous. He stopped short. Their eyes met; their eyes looked away.

And Joe moved on. Encumbered and assaulted. Nods and handshakes. For each gesture Joe felt more and more uneasy.

He smiled, looking in each taut round face for a sign of suspicion. He felt for the ticket in his pocket again.

"So Joe."

He turned. Harlo's lanky body standing next to him.

"Everything's all okay then?"

"Okay?"

"With how this's all turned out?"

Joe shrugged. "I guess okay's an okay way to put it."

"Wasn't much else could have been done, anyway. Right?"

"Right."

"All there is left is take the money and run, I s'pose."

Joe searched Harlo's face.

"You mean. . .you're sayin that's what you're gonna do, with your cut of the money?"

"My cut?" Harlo shook his head, half a smile. "Aw I ain't takin any money, I guess."

"Sure you are. Why not?"

Harlo pushed back his stringy hair. "Tell you the truth, it just don't seem right somehow. Can't say I can say why, but. . ."

But now Wade appeared, holding out two overfull cups, sloshing their boozy contents on the floor.

"Hey. I bought you guys a drink."

Harlo laughed. "Oh, real generous of you, Wade, given how it's an open bar."

Wade, his eyes wild and white, pressed Harlo, then Joe, to take the cups he offered. Harlo looked at Joe; Joe shook his head.

"Wade, put those down. You shouldn't. . ."

"Okay." Whereupon Wade downed the drink and crumpled the plastic cup. . .then downed the second.

"Hey chief, I'd lay back a little if I were you." Harlo said.

"I get to celebrate, don' I?" Wade's voice cracked. "Being on my own."

"Hope you shape up before you get to your new school, Wade. Else you won't last a week."

"I can act how I want now, though." Wade shrugged, grinning drunkenly. "Didn't you say, Joe?"

"I get the feelin Wade don't quite go for that fancy pants school you got him goin to."

"He'll be fine, soon as he gets there. Gettin used to things comes easy for him."

Harlo tousled Wade's hair. "C'mon there, Wade, no one's pullin out on you here. Just doin what's best. All anybody can do, right?"

Wade didn't hear, staring excitedly off into the mass of people.

"Harlo, I'm doin all this for him; nobody gets that?" Joe sighed. "I can't do anything right?"

"Aw I don't know bout that. Lookit all these folks wantin to fall over their selves thankin you for sellin out."

"Yeah. I'm like the grim reaper at a baptism."

"Mr. Joe Meeks? Must not forget this." Mr. Kato reappeared, carefully handing Joe the bonsai tree. "Remember, very very delicate."

The aide bowed and left.

"Wha's that, Joe?"

Wade, despite his goofy smile, looked sad, reminding Joe of someone, he wasn't sure who. He handed the bonsai to Wade, who puzzled over it, eyes glazed.

"Wade, you're good with delicate things. How bout you put this somewhere safe."

Wade held it, teetering, focusing, and Evan arrived to join them again. He clapped Joe's shoulders.

"Harada is very pleased, Joe. In case you're interested."

"You sayin, or askin?"

"What do you mean?"

"Your radar's on full alert, seems like. Still lookin for somethin to worry about?"

"Well, no, I wasn't. Now I'm not sure. Is there anything more I should know about?"

"Don't know what. You got all what you wanted, didn't you?"

Evan nodded. "We all did. I hope we did. Or is that why you're in such a rush to leave town?"

"I did what you brought me out to do, didn't I? So, why not?" Joe pulled out the plane ticket in his jacket. "Though I do sure wish my flight was tomorrow instead of havin to wait."

"Okay. But, really, why? Do you actually have anywhere to go back to?"

With Wade's hang dog face wavering in and out of paying attention, Joe shook his head.

"Wherever I can get this all behind me."

He put the plane ticket back in his jacket.

“Come on, Wade, let’s get home.”

“Home?” Wade said. But Joe had already walked away.

Chapter 27

THE RODEO BEGAN the next morning in a milkweed infested oxbow of the Hellwater. An arena was created out of an abandoned sheep corral, reinforced with pickups parked tightly into a circle. Events happened haphazardly, and though it little resembled a conventional rodeo, the spectators didn't mind. Meagherites hadn't had a rodeo in so long anything was fine with them, and of the many curious visitors, few had any idea this wasn't the real thing.

The sheep cutting contest lasted until noon, as one old master after another stood to the side whistling specialized commands to his one best sheepdog, who was tasked with driving a herd of sheep through a maze of fences and cut them all into a pen. As the morning progressed, betting circles did a brisk business in the back of nearly every pickup.

Bronc riding started terribly. The set of young geldings, more interested in eating than bronco-ing, couldn't be bothered; the minute the chute opened, they stupidly poked a head out and lay down. Riders leapt off, kicking and cussing, but with no result. After several successive disappointments, a hand from the Tyler outfit strategically mixed locoweed into their oats, bringing about a much more desirable result, and now when the chute flung open, the horse spun out, hallucinating wildly, and when the unsuspecting rider dug his spurs into its flanks, his horse, as though struck by a jolt of lightning, arced ten feet in the air, hurling the rider another ten feet above that. Thereafter, bronc riding was an acclaimed success.

Calf roping had mixed results. On several occasions, a horse, racing after the quixotic scamper of its smaller prey, would cut sharply and reverse direction, leaving its rider midair, more than one ending up landing headlong among the drunken scrambling onlookers. One cowboy, throwing his lasso with great flair, accidently snared a spectator who was then treated to a whirlwind manure-softened drag around the arena before the stampeding horse could be reined to a halt.

In bull riding, one notably egregious performance was given by a champion-sized Hereford which thundered straight out of the chute to a young woman sitting on the pickup hood with that weekend's boyfriend. The bull then did nothing but beller and stomp and paw the dirt before her, his solid muscle all but shaking several pounds from its rider's already skinny frame. The young woman on the hood, a ravishing blonde, was uncertain whether to be flattered or indignant, and nudged her passed-out boyfriend for an explanation. "Jinx," she said, "is that a male or female cow?" Rousing himself, Jinx Conner took one look at the bull's lower quarters, its long and mighty pink needle dripping with white fluids, quivering in and out of its sheath, and yanked her off the hood and ran off back to town. The overstimulated beast then tore into a rampage around the arena, throwing his startled rider off like a leaf. The bull was rewarded with thunderous applause, which the cowboy mistook for himself. He took several deep bows before being shouted from the arena.

EVAN GALLANTINE SKIPPED the rodeoing; he now had little desire to be among people. Shortly after noon, finding Marly alone behind her bar, he asked her on a walk. They went nowhere in particular. Meandering. It was hot, the air thick with heavy pungent ripening hay, and quiet, but for the buzz of grasshoppers and an occasional melody of the meadowlarks.

Evan picked some wild bitterroot and fashioned it into a bouquet.

"Marly, the way you look lately," he said, handing her the flowers, "you won't be able to fend off all these new bachelors in town much longer."

"We'll see about that." She put the flowers behind her ear. "You look a bit down in the mouth yourself."

"Long in the tooth maybe."

He was unshaven, wearing yesterday's shirt, his hair a tangle of gray streaks and blond flips.

Marly stopped and turned. "So?"

"So. . ." Evan inhaled. "So now that this is over, I should be relieved. . ."

"So, are you?"

He shrugged. "I've been thinking, but. . .I feel rusty in that regard."

"Oh boy. Lots of *that* goin around."

She sighed. A breeze rustled her hair, she pushed up a loose spray, the flower bouquet fell out of her hair.

She picked it up and their walk resumed.

"What are you thinking then?"

"I don't know. What I'm trying to think is, what was ever I doing here? I thought I was here to make the perfect deal.

But, why? So I can walk away swell-headed, how I had everyone's best interest at heart, doling out profits and a few hopes? So. . .am I really just kidding myself? That I'm so different than Joe. . .or any of us? When it comes to half-baked, self-important fantasies, no; I'm every bit a Meeks as the rest. It's really like. . .what is it with this family? And, for that matter, is it even really a family?"

Marly turned her face into a cooling gust of air. The afternoon was summer warm, although high up the valley there were storm clouds suggesting winter was far away but not that far. She looped her arm in his.

"Evan, far's I'm concerned, you only did one thing wrong. But I can't ever forgive you for it."

He stopped. He thought. He smiled.

"I brought Joe back?"

"Oh, worse. You made him go away."

Evan pulled his arm around her waist.

"Ah Marly, there's only one thing to know about Joe. You never know what the hell he's going to do."

THAT SAME DAY, the whole day, Anne kept to her room. With Joe flying out soon and forever, and not with her, she was avoiding everyone. She went out once, down to the bar, to fetch the nearest bottle that wasn't full of something sweet or fancy or green, and returned. That—drinking alone in her room—made her feel better.

Later in the day, her eyes fluttered open. Almost dark. Her mother at her door. Just like her, to come stand wait. . .and not say a goddamn word.

“S’pose you can hardly wait to throw in your two cents.”

Marly holding a small picture frame prominently sitting on the dresser. In it, the photograph of her, and Joe, and the plane in the background.

“You got the picture back, I see.”

Anne saying nothing, Marly folded her arms and leaned her head against the door jamb.

“Why’re you here, Anne?”

“What d’you mean? Where else am I s’posed to be?”

“Not here. You’re movin out. Ain’t that what you told me?”

“Yeah I did, but. . .never mind. I ain’t. You happy now?”

“You can’t stay here, Anne.”

“What?” Bourbon backed up in Anne’s nose. “You been saying how much you needed me here. To help out. To. . .”

“I know. But I’ll be fine. I’m a big girl now.”

“Just like that, now you don’t need me all of a sudden.”

“I was wrong. You were right. An you should go, wherever it is you’re goin.”

“Goddamn, mom, what’d you want from me? What am I s’posed to say? ‘I’m sorry’? All right, fine. I’m sorry.”

“Sorry for what?”

“For. . .what d’you mean for what? I don’t know. Everything I’m s’posed to be sorry for. I get it. I’m sorry. Can’t you just leave me alone an have a little sympathy about it?”

Marly came to the bed, sat with hands tucked between her knees.

"Anne, I mean it. You don't belong here now."

"But you. . .what about all your big plans?"

"Oh I still got my plans. And you got your own. And. . .they're just very differnt."

"Dammit, Mom, you're makin me. . ." Anne pulled the hair from her eyes. "Why're you doin this? It's 'cause of me and Joe, ain't it? Well you can stop. . ."

"It's got nothin to do with that."

Anne started to tear up.

"Okay, I know how awful I was. I didn't mean those things I said, I never should of. . ."

Marly reached to wipe an eye, then the other, then took her daughter's hand.

"No, Annie, I'm the one sayin 'I'm sorry'." Marly looked away. "I knew better. I knew day one I saw Joe back. When things started goin off in my head, how now everything'd be so perfect, how we'd be just, well, happy again, how we'd just pick up from before, just like that. But see, tellin myself all that? I knew better. If from nothin else than from how it got me so goddamn scared."

"Scared?"

"Yeah scared. How I got to thinkin how I needed Joe for it to happen. An needin Joe for somethin? That's damn scary just that alone. An. . .goddamn how I felt myself startin to go crazy—and not sure why—wakin every mornin feelin just plain at a loss. Here a whole world of opportunities are comin my way, but the more they did, the more I felt like I was bein thrown into somethin I didn't want. A bottomless pit. The day I come across that damn photo you always loved, but in his room? Rememberin that day, Joe an me, us laughin an happy an runnin away to a new life. . .God, it near killed me. You know why? 'Cause now, lookin at it, I seen what I couldn't before. What I had let die in myself. What I lost."

She wiped her own eyes now. Reached to pick up the framed photo on the dresser, fingered it, her young smiling face, next to Joe Meeks' young smiling face.

"And I don't mean just the good sex."

"You mean it was?"

"Well, yeah, honey. It sure was that."

She smoothed Anne's hair.

"Oh my. That summer. Me an Joe. Like for the first time ever I felt how I could have a life. A better one. One so big and wild an right there in front of us you could touch it, and, I tell you, I never felt that before. Not anything like it. I was excited, all right. . .but Anne? We had so much between us and even so. . .goddamn I was so scared. I can't even tell you how scared. An I just don't like feelin scared. I don't, I hate it. To even dare think I might. . ."

"But why didn't you? What happened?"

"You know damn well what happened."

"He left an you didn't. But. . .I don't get why?"

"He felt to blame of course. Who wouldn't? I know I did. Felt to blame too, I mean. I figured he blamed me too. I thought he'd get over it. I thought he'd come back. I thought that for a long long time. Even after you came along, I was sure. I wanted it too much, honey; once you want somethin that much, you don't want to ever give it up. Once you finally do, let me tell you, you don't never want to let it happen again."

Anne leaned her head against her mother's shoulder.

Marly held out the back of her hands; picked at a chip in her nail polish.

"Must be awful strange, your own mother, talkin this way, sorry poor old flesh and blood silly human being if there ever was one."

"I'm sorry, mom. Really sorry."

"Ah no, forget that. I'm the one who's sorry. For you."

"For me? For what?"

"For bein a mother who decided what growin up means is learnin not to ever want what you really want. It wasn't that surveyin job or how you thought you were in love with Joe. Oh I knew better'n that. It was seein you want somethin that I gave up on. What I didn't want to see was, I was doin to you exactly what I done to myself. So I didn't. Until now. Maybe that's what scared me."

She ran her fingers through Anne's hair.

"You know, there's times I just can't believe anything as alive as you ever come from me."

Anne put her face in her mother's neck. "It's goin to be so nice here though. Real soon. I can tell."

"Well, who can ever know?"

"We can't give up on it."

"Never mind we. You go on and go after it, whatever it is you're after. Don't give up on it. That's why I want you out, Anne. Okay?"

Anne nodded.

"Just one thing."

"What?"

“Stay away from Squash. Him I can’t do without.”

Anne grinned.

“Oh, that’ll be a bitch, mom, but I’ll really really try. I promise”

They sat very still, breathing as one. Marly stood to go. Then sighed and reached out her arm.

“Oh hell. Just let me have a hit on your bottle there, before I go.”

Chapter 28

JUST DAWN. JOE alone, waiting for Norman at the airstrip outside Meagher. Standing alongside the dark twin-engine propeller plane resting on the near end of a long grassy runway that stretched west for a good length of the benchland. Down in the still dark Hellwater flood plain, under the early light, croplands shimmered like an arctic front had swept down and glazed them mercury blue. Other than the crimson line of dawn streaking the east, the extremities of sky were luminous dusty black from the summer's forest fires hundreds of miles to the west. What little remained of the aurora borealis, its faint diaphanous green orange curtains, waned in the north. . .

. . .A similar sky. . .Joe with Marly, hurrying to the rendezvous with Vaughn Marlowe and the flight to Alberta, tense, quiet, driving Harlo's old Chevy that they had furtively push-started, undetected, from the driveway onto the road, and now had it racing toward the air strip.

The car suddenly jolted.

Joe swerved, regaining control just before it flew off the road.

"What was that?"

"I don't know." Joe flashed his eyes in the rear view then back on the road, wheeling ahead. "Nothing, I guess. Strange though."

Marly looking unconvinced, he grinned.

"It's okay, Marle. Take a last look around; all this's behind us now. Ready for what all lays ahead?"

Calmed by his smile, she turned her eyes front, nodding.

Dawn-light stratified the sky as the bluff with the airstrip came in sight. But again, without warning, the car lurched to the side, jumped the edge, leaving the ground, spinning laterally in the air, into the burrow pit traveling backwards. Joe wrestled it to a stop.

"Be careful, Joe."

"I didn't do anything. It just. . .Jesus did you see that? Like we were flyin."

"What happened? Is the steering broke?"

"I don't know. Let me see what's goin on."

Just as he got out, the ground heaved sideways, hurling Marly against the door, and tossing Joe flat on his back. For only several seconds, the earth gyrated, then stopped as abruptly as it began. Joe leapt back in the car.

"We got to get to Vaughn, quick!"

He spun the car around, and banged back up onto the road. At the airstrip, Vaughn Marlowe charged out to them, his face blazing, a camera swinging around his neck.

"Thank Christ you're early! Come on!"

"What's goin on?" Marly yelled. "Is it an earthquake?"

"You better believe it is! One hell of an earthquake, and it's all ours!"

They ran to the plane, rocking on its wheels, propeller spinning madly, whipping air into their faces.

"Get in," Vaughn shouted.

"Wait!"

"What?"

Joe grabbed Marly. "Take our picture."

Vaughn hesitated only a second. "No, we don't have. . .oh all right, just hurry the hell up!"

He unshouldered his camera. In the viewfinder, Joe, holding Marly tight, her hair flying, both laughing, wind from the roaring propeller driving tears from their eyes. Behind them, the first sprays of sun tinging the morning clouds pink and splashing their face. As Vaughn snapped the shutter, Joe inhaled, sucking air, like breathing for the first time.

"Marly, we're really goin, aren't we?"

"Together!"

"And it's only the beginning."

"Get in" Vaughn yelled, "Time's wasting."

"Joe, say you love me!"

"I love you, Marly, I can't believe how much I do."

"No, Joe, say it like you really mean it."

Laughing. Hearts racing.

A FEW WEEKS later, an envelope, from Alberta, from Vaughn Marlowe, arrived for Marly, the developed photograph and a short note, about that day, the greatest day of his life. Give regards to Joe, it said at the end, but Joe, already long gone, was never to see it.

WITH DAYLIGHT CAME Norman's vehicle up the road pulling up next to the plane.

"Bright and early," Norman said, shaking Joe's hand, "Good to see you. Give me a few minutes to check things out here, and we'll be all set."

To Joe, eager to get airborne, the few minutes seemed an hour that Norman monkeyed with the plane.

"You were smart, learning to fly."

"Comes in dang handy, tell you that."

"So, bout finished up?"

"Yeah, that should about do it."

"Guess we may's well go then?"

"Sure." Norman rested his foot on the wheel. "Soon as they get here."

"They?"

"Fact, that must be them here now."

Joe turned. Another vehicle, a dust-caked chalk red pickup plowing up the hillside, jerked to a stop. Wade popped out one side, Anne Croft the other.

"You didn't. . .they're comin with us?" Joe exclaimed.

"Why not? Just as I was finishing breakfast, I was talking with Anne, and she mentioned how much you had wanted to take Wade up along with. . .heck, the plane seats four; no problem at all. So what d'you say, let's go. Wade, you first."

As Wade climbed in, Anne stuck her smiling face in Joe's. "So thoughtful of you, Joe," she whispered as she climbed in behind.

Once airborne, Norman turned and yelled, "All right, folks,

anywhere you want to go, just say the word. I only have a few flight strips left to do, so this run, I'm all yours."

"How about Independence?" Wade shouted. "And over that landslide and past Mount Contact?"

"Easy peasy. Independence it is. Heck of a sight from the air, for dang sure."

The plane banked south and they were on their way, quiet but for the drone of the aircraft zipping over tawny summer grassland.

"What's all this?"

Anne leaned forward, indicating the equipment between the seats.

"Aerial photogrammetry. Use it to get estimates for right-of-way costs on them water canals."

"Oh. But then. . .what about regular surveyin?"

"Start terrain surveys any day, since the new site got prelim approvals." Norman smiled wryly. "Means a lot of work for me."

"What about me?"

"Well I don't know." Norman scratched his chin, perfectly serious. "What I need right quick is a photographic interpreter, someone who'd wanna take on some fast learnin up on aerial displacement formulas."

He winked at Joe. Anne sat back.

"Be careful, your face might break," Joe yelled. Anne jabbed an elbow at him; Joe flinched.

"You okay there?"

"It's just a spasm; he gets em sometimes," Anne called back.

"Right, Joe?"

Joe turned his attention out the window.

The canyon of Bitterroot Gap flashed below. Norman nosed the plane higher in order to crest the upper ridges. The engines roared, and all at once they sailed out over the upper valley, glowing like a hot lake of dry range. . .recalling another flight over the same valley. . .

. . .Joe holding Marly's hand in back, Vaughn in the co-pilot seat next to the pilot.

"Head for that!"

Vaughn pointing ahead where the morning light was just then illuminating the peaks surrounding the upper Hellwater. He turned back.

"That fault system I told you about, that I guessed runs under Independence Basin? I'll bet that's where the quake hit."

"You think it's over with?" Joe yelled.

"Hard to know. Could be more. Aftershocks, or maybe the main strike hasn't even occurred yet. That's why I want to get there."

The plane swept up the valley, the sun behind, rising quickly, speeding it on, they soon crested the divide and soared out over Independence Basin.

"Will you look at that!" Vaughn cried.

He pointed to a light-colored line across the north face of Mount Contact. "There, you see, orogeny in action."

"What's that?" Joe yelled.

"Lusty mountain building," Vaughn laughed, "From here, I'd

say the displacement is ten to fifteen feet. Crustal slippage at that rate, every couple thousand years, that's a mile over a million years, there's your mountain range. A geological instant. Incredible!"

Joe, eyes pressed to the windows, amazed at the power that could move a block of earth like that, caught sight of something, a movement in the trees. Then nothing.

Vaughn snapping picture after picture, hollered, "Go lower there; follow that scarp there."

The pilot, not as fascinated by the moment, balked. "I don't know, Vaughn."

"It's okay, get lower," Vaughn ordered, and the pilot reluctantly dipped them nearer the ground. "Look at that rock, for crying out loud! It's shaking like jelly."

Joe noticed a ripple shoot through the trees, eerily silent, then suddenly, a whomp of noise, and something threw the plane up and sideways.

"Jesus God, what the. . .that's no cross-current!" the pilot cried as the plane spun and whined, while below, the ground buckled. Trees bent sideways. Puffs of dirt spewed along the fault line as though a gaseous flour were venting from the bowels of the earth. Vaughn yelled something but it was lost in a deafening roar. Then Mount Contact's north face exploded.

For less than a split second, a lull, a moment suspended, then the entire ridge blew out laterally into the sky, and as percussive shockwaves of air tossed the plane, the shattered mountainside fell in a torrent down upon the basin floor.

The pilot grappled with the controls, crying out, "I got to go up!"

"No!" Vaughn countermanded, "not yet."

In minutes the avalanche of boulders had plummeted over the basin headwaters and shot high up the other side. Swirls of residual slides clattered in every direction as the mammoth rockslide settled. A storm of rolling dirt obscured everything but the high peaks and the gaping wound slashed across out of Mount Contact.

In the plane, silence but for the roar of the engines. Joe thunderstruck. A landscape so permanent, fractured then destroyed in seconds. He thought, in the shadow of such calamity, how inconsequential he was, and yet his life, in its insignificance, seemed more valuable to him now than ever before. He felt like he had been given a second chance.

Vaughn turned to say, "You two? You remember this! You'll never see anything like it again. Ever!

Joe could feel Marly shivering, and realized his body was shaking in the same frequency, like they were one. Like he didn't know himself anymore. He gripped her hand tight.

Vaughn, hurriedly writing notes, turned to the pilot. "I'd love to see the looks on those Forest Service smart-alecs now."

"Lucky it's so remote," the pilot said. "No people, no casualties."

Joe dropped Marly's hand. A hammerblow hit inside against his chest, like a boulder had landed on his lungs.

Scotty.

"SURE IS OBVIOUS from up here, isn't it?" Norman mused, the plane now directly over Sweetgrass Moraine, the ridge a perfect roll of boulders and glacial till across the narrow breadth of the valley. Tall blue stands of jack pine colored the base, flourishes of red alder on the higher slopes, ripening chokecherry thickets blackening each draw. And bisecting it, the slice of river falls where the Hellwater cut a lazy channel through the moraine.

"What's obvious?" Anne called from behind.

"It's perfect. Just like Joe said before, that moraine ridge? Alls they have to do is plug up the falls and build the causeway."

"But you said they ought to do some other surveys, not rush it through like they were doin? What about that?"

"That's right, I did. I thought that moraine, well, it's loose, and so's just bound to fail. That's why I went to the Corps of Engineers."

"You did? You went to them?" Joe said, now interested.

"Yup, and I had it all wrong."

"Why is that?"

"Because moraine is all glacial rounded rock jammed up and glued together with finer and finer grades of till. You put fifty thousand acre feet of water up against it, pressure locks that damn stuff up tight as steel. Impermeable. Couldn't get any tighter if you welded it."

Norman looked back at Anne. "So I sure felt like one heck of a fool. That new outfit knew their hydrology darn good after all. A dam there'll last till kingdom come. Just so long as nothing ever gives it a good jolt."

Joe leaned forward. "Why, what would happen then?"

"Well, 'cause what locks up that loose till so tight is steady pressure from the weight of a reservoir. If something were to set it vibrating, break the surface tension, then that water would seep in a little here, little there, then whoosh, there goes your dam collapsing like a sand castle. They had a dam just like that fail over there in Idaho, he told me. Dang fools built it on top of a fault."

"Well Jesus," Joe exclaimed, "don't they know about that Independence earthquake?"

"Oh sure. Asked that first thing. They said no, it'd pretty much have to be right on a fault itself to have to worry about it. And that Independence Basin fault is miles further up."

Joe sat back, blood pounding, new sweat beading his brow. Looking down over the slow trickle of the Hellwater Falls, the river so low it ran brown, that same muddy brown it ran in the aftermath of the landslide. . .

. . ."That's odd."

Vaughn Marlowe noticed it on the return flight down the river.

"What is?" Marly asked.

Neither had yet noticed Joe's ashen face.

"Down there, how the Hellwater is perfectly clear flowing into Sweetgrass Moraine, but it's completely muddy where it spills out." He tapped his pencil on his notebook. "That has to mean that's where the actual fault is. Under Sweetgrass Moraine."

"I don't see."

Marly only half listening, thinking about Alberta.

"No, there's no scarp because the moraine overlays and obscures it. But obviously it slipped, quite a bit, that river's loaded with soil. Hell, so that's why the cataracts are there in the first place. Damn!"

"What?"

"Just wish I was staying; I'd document it all up. Nobody knows. Hell, I'd get to name it."

Joe not listening. Not even thinking. His stomach knotted, repeating to himself, Scotty would have got up and gone down. . .he'd have been well out of there. He'd have left at dawn. He'd have seen them gone and left, and. . .he'd have left.

Joe looked down, searching, scanning, how the Hellwater turned from clear blue whitewater to black brown murk, but he didn't see what Vaughn saw. Vaughn saw geology. Joe saw his hopes churning ominously foul.

"I gotta go back, Vaughn."

"Joe?" Marly said, only then noticing his colorless face. "What's wrong?"

"No I. . .really, I gotta get home."

"I told you, Joe," Vaughn said, "You can't just. . ."

"Take me back down! You have to."

Vaughn turned, angry, but then saw Joe's face.

"What is it?"

"Scotty. My brother. We. . ."

Marly recoiled, her face bloodless.

JOE'S HEART RACING. He knew. A major fault ran under that

moraine. . .he knew but no one did. Vaughn Marlowe had never had the chance to document it. The new survey crew, in its hurry, wouldn't have been obsessively accurate. Or even if they were, there were multi-million dollar reasons to overlook it.

Man oh man. He felt weak. He felt. . .

"The Corps, though, they got to still evaluate the site, right?"

"Na, only when it's public land. That down there's all private, like I told you. Bought up by HRC."

"But wouldn't they want to bring them in anyway?"

"Well, to play it safe, but it would slow things down considerably."

"What about the state engineer? They have to review it."

"Just the construction plans for the dam, which they already did, since it's been approved. I guess they didn't find anything wrong."

Joe's head was pounding. He had certainly been right; by flying up here, everything had become clear. Everything, he thought, except what he was going to do about it.

Chapter 29

WADE STANDING AT the window. Storm clouds blackened the sky. Dead quiet but for the rumble of thunder now and then. What had been a hot summer morning had turned bizarrely cold.

The long slopes of sage brush from ash blue to silver green.

The dogs come back to their shelter.

A chilling breeze turned up the heavy long leaves of the willow. He buttoned his shirt.

In the window itself, the darkened afternoon as background light, the reflection of an unfamiliar strapping young man. He breathed on it and fogged the image, then used the sleeve of his shirt to rub it out. Wondering, how many times would you breathe in your life? How many breaths already taken, how many more to come? Day in day out, hour by hour, minute after minute, your life just one breath after the next. Like Father Sterling's parable about the sissy who had to roll a boulder up a hill every day, only to have it fall back down again at night. Day after day.

Boring.

He felt sad. He was used to this place; he was part of things here. The land, the weather, the machines and animals. The taste of beer and scalding black coffee. The silences. Like he'd always lived here. And in a few days? Like none of this would have even happened.

He felt sad, and—even worse—now another headache coming on.

"You still here?"

Frances, at the table, hadn't said anything in so long Wade had forgotten about her, so lost in thought he reminded himself of poor old Emma Meeks, how she spent all those hours, just staring out the window.

"I don't want to go. . .no matter what Joe says. I don't see why I don't have any say in anything, ever."

"That's Joe for you."

She drank from her ever present jar of wine.

Wade watched the silver-black clouds cover the peaks up the Hellwater. The center of what he could see was slowly fading, which soon would mean flashing lights, spinning, nausea.

"Think I'll go lie down.

"What about the jeep?" Frances said. "You pull it up like I said?"

"Pull it up?"

"Got to tell you every damn thing, I guess."

Wade looking at the jeep out front imagining it running over Joe Meeks.

"Oh man," he said.

"What?"

"I was imagining something terrible."

"Oh yeah?"

"Joe getting killed."

"Ah. So what was the terrible part?"

She raised up on her cane. Wade went to help but she flinched at him.

"Never mind that; let's get goin."

"Going where? I'm not leaving till I have to."

"Quit the back sass, you. I about had it. Bring that along too like I told you."

She pointed at the old shotgun resting on the rack of antlers hung on the wall.

"I don't got to tell you to get shells, I hope," she said, caning her way out the front door.

"Shells?"

"You're deaf now too? What good's a .12 gauge if you don't got shells. They're in the box in the closet. An my wine, don't forget that."

He left and returned, catching up to Frances at the jeep, toting the almost empty shell box, the jar of wine, the shotgun.

"There's only one shell left," Wade said

"Well how damn many do you think it takes?"

"For what?"

Frances hobbled to the passenger's side, pried open the door, and struggled in.

"Are you gettin in or waitin for Christmas?"

"I'm supposed to drive?"

He got behind the wheel without an answer. Though the only vehicle he'd driven was the tractor, from that, and from watching others, he knew more or less what to do. He started it easily, but driving was something else again. He lurched it forward, stalled it, choked and killed it, and did it all over again. Frances sat wordlessly and not even aware.

Concentrating hard, he got down the lane and made the main road. He pulled out in the direction of town.

"Where you goin?"

"I don't know; I thought you. . ."

"If you don't know, what're you doin drivin? Can't you men keep a damn thing in your head?"

She shifted irritably in her seat.

"Where the hell am I? Damn I hate not knowin where I am."

While she got her bearings, Wade turned on the heat, and soon warm air began to pour from the vents.

"Then just turn around and go up toward Independence, I don't give a damn."

Wheeling up the road, squinting and rubbing his eyes, it took so much concentration, all the worse as the road and his vision narrowed. As they gained elevation, the storm clouding out the sun, Wade felt for the headlight switch and pulled it. His eyes erupted with light in the rim of his vision.

Frances directed him off the mining road onto an open ridge, which he followed up as far as he could go. She said stop. Managed to get herself out. Wade trailed her as she grabbed her wine, hobbled to a boulder, and sat down against it.

"Well?"

She glared up at Wade.

"Well what?"

"The .12 gauge? I still got to tell you every little thing?"

Wade, walking back to get the shotgun. felt tiny pricks of cold falling on his face. He cocked his eye skyward, seeing the most incredible thing: fine white snow crystals, glinting in the horizontal sunlight streaking through the low clouds. He leaned his head back and cackled, his mouth open, his eyes full of blue and falling snow.

By the time he returned, Frances already had a wreath of snow on her hat and shoulders. Wade knelt down, startling her.

"Jesus, you still here?"

Wade nodded. He felt better. Even good. The air, minty with sage and pine and cold, helped clear his head. He had an inkling this headache would pass mildly. He took a healthy swig of her wine, then another. Maybe he was finally outgrowing the headaches, maturing, becoming the young man in his reflection. Driving. Free to do what he wanted. Ready for anything.

He took another drink, aware despite his darkened vision that Frances was watching him.

"Look at you," he heard her say, "another damn foundling. Is that all it ever is for me, raising other people's kids? What a lotta shit life was. Goddammit anyways."

Wade sat beside her. "Yeah I know," he said.

She took her wine back and had another drink.

"Look down there, Wade. All I ever wanted. I raised everything—hay, livestock, children—and here I am, no more left of me than the little that's in them barren fields. An what do I got? Not a damn thing of my own, no child, no crops, no livestock, not even a square foot of dirt."

She laid the shotgun across her lap, quiet for a long time. It continued to snow. They passed the bottle back and forth. It grew dark and turned even colder.

When Frances spoke again, it was without looking up.

"All right, Wade. Time you got the jeep back home."

"But what about you?"

"Never mind me. Just go on."

"What are you going to do?"

"Hunt," she finally said. "I'm goin to hunt."

"Hunt what?"

"Birds. Sage hens. Grouse. Come on now, an git. You're scarin em away. All your blatherin."

Wade stood uncertainly.

"When do I come get you then?"

"You don't. And don't say nothin to Joe. He'll be up here claimin that all the game birds are his too. I'll come back when I'm good and ready."

Wade shrugged doubtfully and wobbled a few yards off. He knew she wasn't about to let him stay. He felt flush with wine, so stuporously sad he wanted to cry, so drunk he didn't care. He looked up at the range of mountains, glittering with snow that was much heavier at the higher elevations. He looked back at Frances. She sat sheltered against her rock, shotgun across her lap, dirty hat crunched back on her head. The powdery snow had coated her, blending her in with the rock.

It was a perfect camouflage.

He admired her for that.

Chapter 30

THE AFTERNOON'S SUMMER snow high up Independence Basin fell in town as a quiet rain. The final rodeo events ran into early evening, by which point the makeshift arena was awash with mud and wet manure. The closing ceremony was held in premature darkness, with pickup headlights for floodlights. Undaunted by the rain, hooting spectators remained to the end as a stream of contestants in numbered pie tins slogged out to a central booth to receive their dubious awards. It was only when the last battery wore down that the rodeo marshals called a halt and everyone clogged the road back to town.

Waiting for the coming of the mob, Marly stood behind the bar, rubbing white polishing paste onto a silver pot. Joe Meeks came in. Silently took a stool.

"Well look who's back. A little early though, ain't you?"

"Early? How so?"

"Didn't expect you to drop by again for another twenty years. Or so."

Joe hooked his heels on the boot-rail. Other than Marly, the place was empty but for two cowboy hats in a booth in back. He spun a quarter on the waxy bar, staring into the flaking silver mirror behind the bar until Marly stepped between him and his image.

"Happy to get you somethin, though. What'll you have?"

"Anything's fine."

She pulled a glass from a sink of suds, burdened it with

straight whiskey and set it in front of him. He rubbed his finger slowly circling the rim. Making a lonely hum. Reminding Marly of the touches of that same fingertip.

"You're lookin none the worse for wear," she said.

"Still the same. Hair's longer, maybe."

"It is. But somethin's differnt. Not sure what though."

She took the stool next to him.

Joe laced his fingers together.

"So. . .I hoped to talk. If you're done usin me for a dartboard, that is."

"Sure, I can bite my tongue, ain't all that much venom left in it. What'd you want to talk about?"

"It's that damn ranch. How I still can't get straight if I want it or not."

"Joe, c'mon. It's kind of a bit late for that now."

"Yeah, maybe so, but. . .just s'pose the dam didn't go through. Like, say someone had a way to stop it."

"S'pose they did."

"Then, it falls through, obviously. Everything falls through, pretty much, and then, what do you know. I still got the ranch on my hands."

Marly noticed her image in the moist sheen of the bartop; she wiped it away.

"Guess I was wrong. This ain't just an idle chat bout old times an what mighta been."

He nodded, studying his glass like a crystal ball. After a while, he looked up.

"You ever wonder. . .whether if someone ever does get a chance to pick up where he left off, could he?"

"What's it matter to you what I wonder, Joe?"

"Just s'pose it does. Matter. What d'you think?"

Marly pulled her hair back, running it through her hands, heavy and darker red from being unwashed.

"Might be a man could. If it's you—the one doin the pickin up where he left off—I don't know, Joe. Where would that leave Wade?"

"Wade? What's he got to do with it?"

"Seems like bout everything, to me. How's a guy s'posed to pick up where he left off, if he lives life like everyone he ever gets close to is just goin to turn into another Scotty?"

Joe swung his head around, glaring at her, but decided not to share the thought and turned away and while he sat thinking about it, she sat thinking about it, then put her hand on his arm.

"Wade and Scotty, Joe? It's a big difference. Just so happens Wade's still alive."

Behind them, just then, a vanguard of the muddy crowd on its way from the rodeo began to throng in.

"Feel like getting a little wet?" she said.

THE OVERCAST SO low, the lane to the cemetery had barely enough light to see. They stood under dripping poplars, listening to the quiet hiss of rain.

"Where's Wade, anyway?" Marly asked.

"Up spending his last day at the ranch."

"He's leavin tomorrow?"

Joe nodded. "Got him in a school with a summer program. He'll be late but only a little. "

Marly nodded. "And then what about you? Where you off to? As far from here as possible, I expect?"

He didn't answer. His thoughts unclear, she fell silent. Then not.

"Not that it makes any difference, Joe, but. . .I was kinda hopin you wouldn't. Take off. Not right away."

She reached to wipe trickles from his forehead. He looked down.

"Well, never mind."

She took his arm, started walking again.

"So what was that you were sayin, bout stoppin the dam?"

"Yeah. That was. . .it's nothin. Just me bein. . .me."

"You know somethin though. There's a problem with somethin. Somewhere. I see it in your eyes, plain as this rain."

He ran his hands through his hair, long enough to slick back now when it was wet.

"It won't matter. It's not my problem. Not once I get that check in my hands."

"That don't quite ring true, Joe. You don't need the money, not that bad."

"Wade needs it."

"Wade? Why him?"

"That way at least he's got a chance."

"Chance of what?"

"I don't know." Joe shook his head. "I'm done talkin about it; there's really nothin more to say."

"About all that, yeah, it might be. But seems to me there's still somethin to talk about. . .and I'd guess you know what about just as well as me. Ain't that why you came by in the first place?"

Joe looked at her, puzzled.

"What happened that day, Joe?"

"What happened? What day?"

"The day you left."

Joe wiped the wet from his hands; they glistened of being newly cleansed.

"You know what happened, Marly. What do you think? I couldn't have very well. . ."

"Have what? Run off with me like we planned?"

"Well how could I? My own brother dead and I caused it? Could you have?"

"Course not. I never could of done that, not then, not after. . .but you did. You did it anyways, goddamn you, Joe. Without me. And why? I could never understand. How could. . ."

They had stopped, facing one another. Joe stooped, picked up a rock, raised his arm to throw it. But didn't.

"I can't see what difference it makes anymore."

"Well none, I guess. If you can't see, you can't see. Forget it. Like you said, what difference can it make?"

Joe looked at her, not sure if the wetness on her face was all rain. And whether it was or not, he saw how it made her face shine.

"I just always wished I knew why," she finally said. "Only 'cause I mighta been able to let it go. That's all, Joe."

He lowered his arm. Dropped the rock. Rocked his boots into the mud a long time before he began to talk. . .

. . .The phone ringing, yet again, but no one answering, yet again. They all knew it could only be one person.

When it stopped, silence again, loud, louder than ever. None of them, Harlo, Leonard, Frances; no one telling Joe what had happened to Scotty. And they knew, he knew they knew, and he hated that they wouldn't just say it. But they wouldn't. They just picked at their dinner, sawed their liver, stabbed their potatoes. Scotty's chair empty, his dog underneath, curled up, tail thumping rhythmically. Through it all, Emma grinning her simple-minded grin. Like nothing had happened. For her, nothing had.

The phone ringing again. The sound like a sword in his brain.

His dad put down his knife and fork and closed his hands into fists.

"You might tell that gal of yours there's been a death here so she'll quit her damn callin."

So this time Joe reached for the phone.

"Joe?"

Marly in his ear, her voice urgent; scared.

"Yeah?"

"Oh god, Joe. How is it? How are you?"

"All right."

"You want me to do anything? You want me to be with you?"

"No. It's okay."

"I don't know what to do. I feel so terrible. I. . ."

Joe staring outside, a deer Harlo had killed, its carcass hanging from the eaves of the tool shed.

"Joe, say somethin, can't you? What's wrong? Are they all listenin?"

"Yeah. I gotta get goin."

"Wait, Joe, just. . .maybe you can get to town later? We'll figure somethin out. Okay? Joe?"

"Yeah okay."

He pressed the receiver into his ear even as he hung up. Silence returned; utter resounding silence. At a loss what to say, he said, "I wish Scotty was here instead of me."

His dad scraped his chair back.

"Maybe if you'd of stayed put 'stead of always runnin off tail waggin up to Independence for that half-baked Croft girl, he would be."

Leonard rose and stalked into the kitchen.

"Poor little son of a bitch," Harlo said, the first thing he'd said all evening.

Frances wiped her sleeve across her mouth to remove a trickle of liver blood.

"You figured on runnin off with that girl then?"

Joe shot her a look, wondering what she knew, but she

ignored it if she even noticed.

"Might as well get on and do it, then. Can't go on all worryin about it. People die, you don't, you go on."

Leonard returned with a beer. Sat down. Said nothing.

"Lucky your dad didn't die with him," Frances continued.

"What d'you mean?"

"Once I seen you and that gal stealin off in Harlo's car this morning, I thought, the hell with you. But with Scotty not in bed and his horse still out, I knew I better send your dad up to have a look."

"You went back up to Independence?"

Leonard leaned back, laced his hands behind his head.

"Got just about there when all of a sudden it hit," he said. "Trees swayin and the ground shakin like mad. Bout the same time, there comes Scotty's dog scamperin toward me. No Scotty though; nowheres in sight. There was a lull, and me and the dog kept goin, that's when I found him."

Harlo shook his head. "I don't see why Joe's got to hear all that."

"He don't got to," Frances said, "but he might want to know."

"What happened?" Joe burst out.

"He'd been headin down, I guess once he seen you two'd left him. Must have been when the quake hit, a big chunk of boulder size of a car broke loose. Somehow it knocked him from his horse an pinned him to the ground. Crushed in his chest. Time I got to him, he couldn't barely breathe. He wasn't gonna make it, that was clear. Poor little fella. Scared shit. I seen in his eyes he knew it, too."

"But. . .so you just left. . ."

"Goddamn, Joe, I'm sorry it wasn't you there so you could'a moved that boulder all by yourself an pulled him on out, then brung him. . .but no, you'd run off by then I guess."

Leonard sipped his beer.

"I did hear this plane somewhere above but no way to signal it, so what choice I had was just get back down quick for help. . .I'd just got up to the divide when all holy hell broke loose. Goddamn it was like a thousand freight trains. Ground just plain rose out from under me, and the wind whipped me clean off my feet. Air got blacker'n midnight. And the dirt? Never seen anything like it. I thought I was bein buried alive."

For the first time ever, Joe saw tears fill his dad's eyes.

"Turns out Scotty was."

Joe's tongue soured. He gagged. He fixed his eyes on the plastic gingham table, the plaid patterning on his eyes, dizzying.

After a long silence, the longest yet, Frances leaned back.

"Years ago, this bad red fever was goin around hereabouts. I was just a girl, I remember it bein winter and I was out choppin ice from the pump, with that Hellwater wind whistlin through my bones just about as cold as cold could ever be. All of a sudden I got just plumb weak, all swoozy and swayin so bad I had to put down the ax like a cane to hold myself steady. I seen my hands, near to all blue. I went to blow on em an all of a sudden I pitched forward right onto the ice. Next thing I know I'm shakin in mother's bed, sweat freezin on my forehead, eyes rollin back an forth, heart knockin against my ribs. I never really knew how long, but it was a long while I was out, wakin up delirious, dyin of thirst, moanin and talkin to myself. Somewhere in all that, I remember: there was this loud trompin woke me up. The door'd creaked open, a blast of wind shakin the place near to pieces, and this. . .shape. . .this somethin. . .big an dark. . .comes in. It's got on a dirty ol hat an sheepskin coat. An that's it. Next thing I know it's mornin and mother's shakin my leg, wantin to know why I was still in bed with no chores done.

"An I sat up. An I tell you, I felt like, who am I to be layin sick, givin mother even more to do, when it wasn't one time at all in her life she wasn't out there workin, day in day out, just to keep us all goin. I tell you, Joe; a fierceness took grip in me then. I got up, walked out back, pumped me some water, drank my fill and got back to doin my chores. I broke that fever, broke it for good, an from that day I never had another day sick in my life."

She leaned back and kicked Scotty's dog out from under the table.

"Don't ever give in, not for nothin. That's just how you survive. You don't ever learn that, you can't ever expect to live much of a life."

NOW AND THEN, the rain letting up, the cemetery glowed with its luminous after-mist.

"I sat at that table, each person there like a mirror of myself, of what it meant to be a Meeks. And I knew right then I wouldn't wish that, ever, on anyone. Includin you, Marly. Especially you. Next day I was gone for good. I should've stayed that way. An never come back."

Joe fell silent a while, pushing back the images, despite their long reach, to what was the far past.

"I did learn one thing, for all that."

"Just one?"

Joe laughed.

"Oh don't mind me and my bad jokin. What was it?"

"That. . .the fact is, Marly? I never did leave. Not really; I left town, but I just kept myself in the very place I tried to get away from."

"No, you can't say that. It's a lot more. . ."

"It doesn't have to be the same for Wade, though. It's not written out anywhere. The one thing he for sure doesn't need is to ever be a Meeks like me. An that's why I won't let myself get any more involved. I don't need that money, but he does."

Marly shook her head.

"No, you got it backwards, Joe. What Wade needs is for you to be the person he needs you to be."

Joe shook his head, almost violently, but didn't speak.

"Believe me, I know. Once you got a child, the way you love thinkin oh so poorly of yourself. . .from then on it's a luxury you can't afford. Otherwise, they turn out just as coldhearted and given up as you. As us. No matter how good a school you send em to, you can't pretend to be surprised."

Joe's face was dark, whether from the low light, or not, she couldn't tell. But still, he didn't speak.

"You already got one child on your conscience, Joe. That's not enough for you?"

Mist beaded on his face. Like wet on cold white marble. Then.

. .

He sighed. And hung his head.

Marly took his hand. When he looked up, seeing her smile, the hard marble glaze dissolved.

"You can't allow that dam to go through just to get the money. That kind of money won't pay for savin Wade. It'll pay for abandonin him."

He lifted his shirt trail, dried his face. She realized, she still had his hands in hers. He was idly soothing her fingers. And she was his.

Chapter 31

MUSIC FROM THE jukebox resounded throughout the Mint. Clusters of young kids outside listening at the windows while adults crowded the booths. The throng reached clear through to the lobby.

Joe bulled his way through, scanning the faces, pushing ahead. People drank his health; he kept moving.

"Too much of a rush for a quick one?"

Harlo behind him, offering him a drink. Joe shook his head, but Harlo insisted.

"Piss poor rodeo, wasn't it? Used to ride better myself."

"You did?"

Joe continuing to move through the people, Harlo trailing along.

"Hell yeah. Guess it wasn't much after you run off, I hit the bull ridin circuit for a time. Never won nothin, 'cept for this particular limp I got."

Joe searching the crowd, half listening.

"Yeah, Wolf Point, was where that was; they let any poor asshole have a go up there. I was hardly out of the chute and that bull got him a hoof right here where she lives. Cracked my pelvis three places, mashed all hell outta my groin. Ended more'n my rodeo ridin days, believe you me."

"That's too bad."

"Yep. In more ways'n one. Anne's as close as I'll ever get to havin a kid."

"What?" Joe stopped short. "What do you mean, Anne?"

"What d'you mean, what d'you mean? Hell, Joe, you'd be the only one in the state if you don't know that."

"Jesus, Harlo; know what? You sayin you're the father?"

Harlo grinned.

"Well, there's a little more to it than that. After that final rodeo injury, I come back here to lay up a while. Marly was around, and she sure was a different gal than that wild girl I'd known before. We started seein each other; kind of to help patch each other up, I guess. By then she was takin things over at the Grand, not doin too bad, and she had some flings now and then, gettin over you. Anne come along, and well, Marly kind of wanted to keep her. Then after she got clear you wasn't about to ever come back, she figured I'd maybe stick around and play papa. An I did for a while, but it wasn't my kind of situation in the long run."

"What are you saying? Anne's your daughter or not?"

"I sure's hell don't see how she could of been my actual daughter. I couldn't of even sired a ball of spit after that bull ridin injury. But I seemed to be the only one who knew. Town folks all just assumed, and pretty soon even Marly did too. I swear, women have a peculiar way they can both see things the way they are and the way they want em to be, and it don't make no difference to em. I don't know, I figured let people think whatever the hell they want."

"If you aren't her father, who is?"

"Hell if I know who. I half think maybe she just spawned herself."

"Doesn't Marly know?"

"Maybe, maybe not. Far as I can tell, Anne could be most

anybody's, Joe. What them hippies call a love child, I guess."

Joe shook his head. He felt dizzy, the bar whirling with dancing couples, dark hats bobbing and loose long hair swirling. Outside on the oily new blacktop, the overflow were dancing too.

"Hey, lookit here. Now it's an official Meeks' family reunion."

Evan Gallantine, clearly obviously pleasantly drunk. And before he could say anything, Ruth Loomis, a shit-eating grin on her face, drew up to him, dropped her cigarette to the floor, pulled off her baggy knit sweater, gathered her white streaked hair with a handkerchief, and reached her arm round Evan's waist. He was dancing with her before he could even beg their pardon. While, at the same time, Jack Loomis came up, happy, cheery, wanting to shake Joe's hand.

"Mr. Meeks! You're looking awfully proud."

"Proud? I don't think I'm anywhere near that."

"Yessir. You must be particularly happy how things turned out."

"Most everyone is, I guess."

"You bet. Though now it's all said and done, there's a feeling around."

"A feeling?"

The printer rubbed his chin.

"Yeah, I can't quite put my finger on it. And not that everyone thinks like me, but. . .this town, you know, it won't ever be the same now. So much progress, change, and all at once? I have to wonder it won't be quite all what we wanted as much as we thought we did."

"Things change, you can't stop that."

"No you sure can't."

They stood shoulder pressing shoulder as the make shift dance floor continued to fill. Evan and Ruth swung past. Evan, though disheveled, looked good, dancing with Ruth; to Joe, it seemed a kind of warmth had come into his face. He glowed, and Ruth did too, when he drew her close and kissed her.

Jack Loomis blushed, smiling at them. He leaned into Joe.

"Been years since she's smiled that way."

But Joe hadn't heard, spotting his quarry standing off by the back door.

"Hey there, Joe." Norman said as Joe approached. "I hear you're leaving us tomorrow."

"Could be."

"Could be?"

"I don't know. Can I talk to you about that? About the Sweetgrass Moraine site, I mean. In particular."

"Free country, you can talk about anything you want. But I don't know what I could tell you. I'm sure as heck no construction engineer like you."

"Never mind that. You're plenty professional enough, at least for me to bounce some notions in my head off you."

"Notions about what?"

Joe, about to begin, then saw Evan break away from Ruth Loomis and come straight for him, clearly distressed.

JOE RUNNING OUT before Evan could finish, splashing up

First Street, a channel of water up to his ankles, oblivious to the dark storefronts teeming with people taking shelter from rain as it changed to a light snow. The swirling, fine grained micro-flakes amplified the light beaming out from the Mint enough for Joe to see Wade sitting at the foot of the town's eponymous bronze Major Thomas F. Meagher standing high in his saddle, waving his saber, or so it seemed, the statue still slightly swaying from the impact of the jeep that Wade had only just crashed into its base.

He'd got out, and now at Joe's approach, stood, stumbling and swaggering erratically.

"Wade!"

Joe's cry more of a whisper, as though keeping a secret from the shadowy orange halo of faces here and there lit by a cigarette puff. Wade cocked his jaw, his eyes searching wildly. He couldn't see.

"Wade?"

"I'm not talking to you. In case you didn't notice."

Joe reaching him, bounced up against the reek of alcohol. Wine. Frances's wine.

"Wade, it's Joe. C'mon. Let's get you inside."

"No you don't. Don't get me anything but out of my way."

Joe took his arm, gently.

"Here, let's go."

Wade shook him off. "I *am* going. Going going gone."

"Wade, settle down. I'm going to help you. Now just. . ."

"You?" Wade squinted, his eyeballs rolling. "You aren't even there."

He looked sidelong in the direction of the voice he was hearing, then suddenly swung his fist. Not expecting it, Joe took the punch full in the mouth, and stepped back, more in surprise than from the blow. The momentum of the swing, however, spun Wade completely around and he fell to the ground, landing sitting up.

Joe felt his lip, moist with blood.

"Wade," Joe said, mad and more than a little scared. "You had an accident. We got to let somebody have a look. Come on now."

"Quit calling me Wade. It's Mister now. Mister Wade. Besides, I'm not talking to you."

He weaved away toward the glitter of light emanating from the Mint. Not seeing the steps, he stumbled and fell flat, but Joe caught his fall. Marly already there to help, she and Joe grappled Wade into the lobby, where he abruptly threw up all over himself.

"God somebody stinks," he said, and passed out.

They laid him on the sofa, dimmed the lights. Marly found a quilt while Joe wiped vomit from his face. They listened to him breathe. Watched his eyes move under his eyelids. Watched them flutter open.

"What?" Wade asked, smiling sickishly.

Marly sat, putting his head on her lap. She put her hand on his forehead.

"How you feelin, sweetheart?"

"Frances."

"Frances?"

Wade's eyes fluttered shut.

"Wade? What about Frances?"

He rolled his head, stupidly. "She's gone, but she's fine there."

"Gone? Gone where, Wade?"

"Hunting birds."

"Birds?"

"Partridges. In pear trees." He grinned and winced simultaneously. "Christmas lights. And firecrackers."

He continued, incoherently, then passed out again.

"Marly, we have to get him down to a doctor. He could have cracked his skull. He could have. . ."

"Joe, the way he smells, all he has to worry about is a wicked hangover. We can see if Edna at the clinic can. . ."

"No; no way. This is more than just him drinkin too much. Something's wrong."

"Oh so you're an expert doctor now too?"

"I'm not an expert anything. Just do this, just. . .get Evan, anybody. Drive him down to Billings, find the best doctor. Tell em about the headaches he's been having. Whatever it takes."

"Joe, if it's so bad as that, you need to take him yourself. Just 'cause you're leavin tomorrow, you can't. . ."

"Never mind. I'm not leaving tomorrow."

"But. . .I thought you. . ."

"Please Marly, not now. Something's happened to Frances, I don't know what, but I need to get up there."

Wade's eyes rapidly clicking under his eyelids.

"This needs somebody I can trust. And I trust you more than I trust myself."

Marly looked up, studied Joe's face, then stood.

"All right then go on an take Anne's pickup; she leaves the keys in it. I'll get her an Evan to help with Wade. Just. . .just go on, Joe."

Joe ran out, found the pickup, spun up the street out of town. The snow changed back to rain, and that rain was pouring heavily again.

Chapter 32

JOE GLANCED DOWN; the dashboard's cold glow, the orange dial of Anne's speedometer jittering at its limit. Then up and ahead, in the weak headlights piercing the black rain, a blinded jackrabbit streaked in front and stopped. Joe swerved but not in time.

"Damn you," he swore at the lifeless animal in the rear view.

Where the graveled road ended it become mud; he fought the steering wheel to keep the pickup on the road. Finally reaching the Meeks ranch, he caromed right up in front of the porch. The house was eerily and entirely dark. The dogs sauntered out, curious, quiet. Deer stood motionless in the orchard, eyeing him, the snow iridescent on their silky hides.

But no Frances.

A gunshot.

Muffled, and far-off, but Joe knew the sound at once, not percussive like the blast of a rifle, but the whomp and pingless decay of a shotgun. He was back racing up the road before it died out.

He knew it was Frances, but not where, exactly, to find her, only that the gunshot had come from up into Sweetgrass Moraine. And he also knew he could follow the snow-muddied ruts, which could only have been left by Wade driving the jeep to town. They led up a steep logging road to a small meadow flat, and there, a confusion of tracks. Where they must have first come, then turned around. Joe stopped and jumped out. When his eyes adjusted, in the direction of a weak trickling sound—a small spring— he saw a dark shape that looked out of place.

He ran.

She was leaned up against a rock outcrop, wearing only a black sweater over her old woolen dress, and jeans underneath. Her bare hands lay loosely in her lap. Joe knelt, throwing his skimpy jacket around her.

"What the hell are you doing?" he said, just to say anything, in fear that she might not answer.

"Ah just never mind all that."

She spoke without movement. He pressed his palm to her cheek, cold, and still, as ice. Sitting so near the spring, ground water had frozen the back of her legs; he couldn't get his hands under to lift her.

Fumbling for a grip, he felt instead a glass jar, laying by her feet. Half full of wine. He poured some onto his fingers and wet her lips, then again more, into his cupped palm, which she managed to sip from, spit out, sip a little more.

He nursed her in this way, whisking the slushy drool of wine from her old chin, until she raised her eyes.

"What the hell, all this damn snow? Does make things look nice, though, don't it?"

Her head drooped back down again. The wine jar now empty, he filled it with spring water and poured it onto the frozen mud encasing her legs, softening it enough to work it loose.

"I didn't come up to just sit and do nothin, you know."

"Yeah I know, course not. You're gonna be alright now."

"I only had the one shell. Figured that's all I needed."

Joe took her hands in his, massaging them briskly.

"Can you feel this?"

"Not hardly."

"Are your fingers numb? Frances?"

"Don't matter; those ol claws, what's left of em, I can afford to lose a few more. You know it got so chilly I couldn't barely pull the trigger as it was."

Little by little, scraping rapidly, keeping her talking, he got her free.

"That Wade. Where's he at, anyway? Wish I could of had a boy like that. One of my own, I mean."

"Hang in there, Frances." Joe hurrying; her breath was weakening, issuing only now and then from her nostrils in a faint dusty sparkle. "For once I prefer you talking."

"But no, instead, all I ever thought about, how I just had to have that ranch. Had to have it more'n anything else on earth, and for what? For this? That's what I just come to realize, Joe. An that all up and changed my mind. You know? Hell, there's a thing or two I could still do."

"That's right, Frances. Let me just get you. . ."

"After that, well God knows how long I must of been here till I seen your headlights way down at the place. My one worry was if you didn't hear the shotgun fire. I wouldn't of had another shell, an no way to put myself out of my misery."

"You did fine, Frances. Here, we about got you free."

Both arms under her, lifting, she was so light he felt she might fly up out of his arms.

"Bout time, too. Joe, I got to get on with things. Figure why not live it up while I still can. An it's all right now, you go on ahead an put me in one of those homes. They say there's dancing there. You know I never danced?"

"You will, Frances, every night. Just save your breath now. Save it for all that dancin, okay?"

"Dancin. Ha. You know, when I was a girl, there was a time or two when I'd think someday I'd meet a boy. I'd've like to've been kissed, Joe. Just once. So maybe find me a place where men ain't too old and sour to kiss."

"I will, Frances, lots of them."

"But if them sons of bitches don't keep their hands off me, I'll smack em. They'll learn, quick; they won't ever. . ."

Her breath failed, she couldn't finish. Joe running now, to the pickup, Frances lighter and lighter with each step.

"Frances? Hang in there. Almost there."

"You come by, Joe. And that Wade too. He'll make all them other old biddies turn green. He'd do that for me; I know he would."

"Sure he'll do that."

Joe could barely hear her now. He hoisted her, muscling open the door, laying her as carefully as possible on the passenger seat. She was nearly weightless.

"He likes me, Joe. I know he does."

"I know, Frances. He does. A lot."

"Probly the only one ever did."

"Just hush up now; don't talk. Save your strength. We'll get it all figured out soon enough."

"At least someone liked me. It's more'n I could say before. Thing's're lookin up already, ain't they?"

She began to slump sideways; Joe let her ease down onto her

side. He set her head in his lap as he jumped behind the wheel. As he turned on the pickup and put it in gear, he looked down. She was smiling. Eyes bright. Lips slightly parted. And then, in her face, the dark blending out the age, feathering out the shadow of her leathered skin, he could see her, Frances, young again.

How she was.

How she died.

Chapter 33

HERE, IN THE long shade of the dolomite monolith that crowned the landslide, above him, the summit of Mount Contact blazed the blue sky, around him, golden green coins of aspen leaves flickering. All over, everywhere Joe Meeks looked, lay the sun-soaked Independence Basin. Frances's two dogs, or rather, Wade's two dogs, the black with his head on Joe's foot, the tawny golden anointing surrounding stones with his precious urine. They heard it although Joe didn't, both dogs instantly on alert, noses forward, tails rigid. In minutes, in the direction of their point, a lanky man came picking his way up the talus rubble.

On reaching the shade, he leaned against the large cool rock, catching his breath. He did not offer nor receive a greeting, though it had been days since they'd seen one another.

"What brings you up?"

"Oh, a few things, I guess," Harlo said. "To say so long, for starters."

"No need. I'm not leaving."

"Maybe you ain't. But I am."

"Oh?"

"Yeah I am. An also I wanted to see Independence one more time before I do. Closest thing to a home I got left. . .not countin the big house. Which I don't plan to ever return to."

"There's a good plan."

Joe rose to his feet. A spurt of breeze rustled the aspens,

making children's whispers of the air.

"Sorry that foreman job for InterPacific didn't work out."

"Why're *you* sorry?"

"Well, it weren't for me and my big mouth. . .anyway, I'm sorry about it all. It would've been a good fit for you."

"Hell," Harlo said, blue eyes dancing, "that's one other thing I come up for. To thank you for that good word you put in for me with that Mr. Harada fella."

Joe looked at him, puzzled. Harlo grinned.

"You ain't heard, seems like."

"Heard what?"

"Well, turns out that InterPacific outfit had its eye on a coupla backup places for their operation, case things didn't work out. Soon as all this trouble with the Sweetgrass Moraine fault lines, they pulled out an closed on this other place. It's over a ways west a here. I tell you, Joe, them Japanese are some crafty wheeler-dealers. Don't miss a beat."

"What's that got to do with you?"

"Oh well so now they figure to still make use a me; I train em in ranchin and they learn me to raise beef Japanese style. Kobe it's called, I believe. Somethin like that."

Joe laughed.

"Damn, Harlo. Now I really do feel sorry for you."

"Hey, it's a job ain't it?"

"That's what I mean. Now you're going to have work for a living."

"Oh no sirree. I never said *that,* did I? See, the way I see it is, soon's I get the hang of it, my job's goin to be to get other folks to do the work. I'll be whatcha call a manager."

He eased his long limbs down, sitting alongside Joe.

"Anyways. Figured I'd find you here, since I knew you was back from the hospital, and no one'd seen you around town."

Joe nodded. "Guess I don't feel too welcome there, being the one that put the stop to things. Lot of people were pretty eager for that deal to go through."

"Aw well, ain't too many of em'll care that much after while. HRC figures to salvage the Bitterroot site, an if they go like sixty buildin it, which you know they're hot to do, to keep that Arapahoe company int'rested, well then, I guess everyone'll come out okay in the end."

Joe leaned back his head, studying the high scudding clouds.

"Not like if I hadn't kept quiet."

"So what, that ain't your problem. It was a poor enough site for a dam to begin with, what I hear. You responsible for Mother Nature too?"

Harlo picked at the dirt in his nails.

"Hell of a thing, how you could know about that goddamn fault. Even that bald-headed four-eyed surveyor didn't know nothin about it."

"People get in just too big a hurry to bother lookin into things for a better way."

"Aw, bullshit to that. With all that was ridin on that dam? Na, them people knew. They had to know, whether they was sayin so or not. We both of us know it wouldn't be the first time somethin like that ever happened."

Butter shifted from Joe, who'd stopped rubbing his belly, to Harlo, who absently pushed him aside, so he returned to Joe, for continued attention.

"Maybe you're right," Joe said. "Still, a lot of land is going to get flooded that wouldn't've been. Includin yours."

"You mean *ours*?"

"Yeah. Ours."

"Hell, Joe, you know better'n anyone, that ranch was never ever goin to do any one of us any good. An somewhere, every one of us knew it, and always did."

He turned a sidelong long look over Joe.

"Besides which, I don't get the idea you're too all broke up about it anyhow."

Joe shaking his head, suppressing a slight but merry grin.

"Not that it matters none, but, well, you did what you had to do, Joe."

Joe nodded.

"Same thing Norman told me. . .the surveyor Anne worked for? He said how there was no other choice, how that kind of information, that I knew, it had to get public."

Harlo nodded. "Yeah, an let the rest of em sort it out."

Butter back at him again, Harlo tossed a nearby branch for him to chase and leave him be.

"So what's happenin with The Wade?"

"Still under observation. But looks like he's going to be fine."

"Had some kind of bad concussion or somethin?"

"That, and a fracture."

"Fracture huh? Now that's somethin I know about. Probly had one of those in every bone in my body. Cept where I need most: in my head."

"Yeah. Well, that's where Wade had his."

"Poor goof ball. Hope they fixed it right up."

Butter now back at Harlo, drooling with the stick in mouth. Harlo pushed him, Butter persisted, Harlo relented, patting his head.

"Turns out it wasn't from the jeep accident after all," Joe said. "That fracture was pre-existin. They said if we'd got him in too much later, it could've been. . ."

Joe sighed.

"So, yeah, it was close, but he's going to be fine."

"When's he gettin out?"

Joe shrugged. "I said to keep him there till everyone's a hundred and fifty percent positive he's okay."

"Too bad. I'd hoped to say good-bye to him."

Once again, the dogs raised ears and stiffened. Harlo sat up straight almost immediately.

"That'd be Anne's pickup. Busier'n hell up here today."

He got himself to his feet.

"So I'm goin to skedaddle. Ain't really no one else I feel like seein."

"Especially Anne?"

"She ain't here to see me, Joe. Better if I just duck out now."

He stuck out his banged up hand.

"Good luck to you."

Joe took it. Leveraged himself to standing.

"Thanks, Harlo."

"Expect I'll probly see you again soon enough."

"Hope so."

"Take care'a Wade for me." He turned to go. "And yourself too. You ain't all too good at that neither."

He laughed, and left. Leaving Joe thinking how, though his limp seemed worse, he moved much faster going than coming.

HOPING ANNE, SEEING no one at the cabin, would turn and leave, while also hoping she'd stay, Joe clambered grappled up the boulder gravestone to where he was high enough to reach Harlo's rusty plaque for Scotty. He took it down, then having done that, he felt unsure why, and asked himself, Did he think something would happen? Like the huge rock would roll aside and Scotty would come walking out.

So he put the plaque back. And as he did, it struck him then that no photographs of Scotty existed, none that he knew of, which meant that he, like his image, would never exist again, except in the chemistry of Joe's memory.

A clatter of rock, and at once the dogs shot off barking and racing down the slope. Joe smoothed back his hair. Straightened his shirt. He rehearsed what to say once Anne got to him.

But it was not Anne.

It was Wade.

Both dogs poised to leap and lick his face, Wade pointed the walking stick he carried, first at the black, then at Butter.

Both dogs sat. Tails flapping expectantly.

"They said it was okay, Joe," Wade explained, heading off the inevitable reproach. "They said to just take it easy."

"Wade, for cryin out loud, you call this taking it easy? Climbing all the way up here, alone? You know I oughta. . ."

"Brain me?"

"Yeah. Brain you."

Joe smiled. He had to, Wade looking so well, so alive, so happy. Bushy sandy hair. Rosy blushed cheeks. Smiling lips. All enough to make Joe wonder, as he never had, where did such a boy come from. Which led him to wonder, as he never had, whether he himself could have looked so good at that age.

"It's good to see you, Wade."

Wade nodded, and sat, as Joe's arms started to lift, to reach, to hug, to. . .he didn't know what. To applaud.

Wade began to draw in the cool loamy soil, his walking stick his stylus; he petted one dog then the other in their turn.

"So you came all the way up here just to draw in the dirt?"

Wade continued his drawing, as he spoke.

"I was thinking, you know, about that school?"

"What about it?"

"I don't even know where it is. Where I'm supposed to go. Or when I'm supposed to be there."

"Minnesota, somewheres. Don't worry, we'll get you there."

"But, like, you know, are they expecting me? Because, I mean, we didn't get the ranch money. So how would we afford it?"

Joe bit his lip.

"Sounds like maybe, for all you were wantin not to, now you do want to go?" A moment of anger flashed through him, as a bitter thought took momentary hold: The minute you care about someone, you lose them. "I guess now I want him around, a certain someone wants to be out on his own."

"What?"

Wade shielded his eyes up.

"Ah, never mind me. It's all goin to be okay."

Butter pestering him for attention, Wade relented, and turned to scratching him behind the ears how he loved.

"You know, Wade, I was thinkin. . ."

"What about?"

"I owe you a birthday present, don't I, since I never did give you a proper one before."

"You don't need to. Plus you get another chance next year. And the year after that."

Joe laughed now too, as he joined in scratching Butter's ears.

"Look, Wade. You want to go that school, I'll get you there. I be findin some kind of job soon enough. An we'll get somethin out of the ranch—I don't know what but somethin. We got that calf we could sell for starters. And your horse, what's her name, she'd get a good price."

"Sell Sorry?"

"Well, or not. I just mean. . .never mind. I'll figure it out."

Wade nodding.

"But Joe? What if I don't go till fall? Couldn't we could just stay here, like on the ranch, just till then? Like we first wanted?"

"Yeah Wade, we can stay till then. Sure. Like we first wanted."

Wade's earnest eyes, Joe couldn't help smiling, and forgetting whatever had been weighing on him before.

"Why don't we head down, then?"

"Okay."

"Just take it slow; no more emergency rooms for you."

The dogs trotting eccentric circles around them, two mountain goats, old and young, picking their way down the landscape of an aging softening landslide.

When the old cabin came into sight, Joe stopped for breath. He saw someone leaning on the wheelwell of Anne's pickup.

"You didn't drive up by yourself, I see."

Wade shook his head. "Didn't you know she was here too?"

"Nope. Not her, I didn't."

Marly's hair was the reddest shade of red in the entire basin.

JOE VEERED AWAY from the cabin and instead clung to the water's edge, where he stood, hands against his back, looking around, not wanting to face Marly. Behind him, the footprints along the lakeshore where he and Wade had approached. In front of him, a smooth rim of bright turquoise water, calmed by a blanket of summer air and the whistle of a million invisible insects, the only movement now a mountain butterfly flitting over the shimmering surface, and a fire orange leaf falling and drifting in the imperceptible air currents left to right against the backdrop of granite cliffs.

Pine and spruce, rock and water. Despite, even in ways because of, the massive destruction of that long ago earthquake, this place was by now far and away the most serene of any he'd ever known.

"Brought you somethin, Joe."

He hadn't heard Marly come up. She stood alongside him at the water's edge, holding an envelope.

"Evan gave this to me to give to you just before he left."

"Evan left?"

"Back to L.A. Went late yesterday."

Joe took the envelope. "He should've said somethin."

"Maybe he did. Open it."

Inside was a newspaper clipping, stapled neatly together. Joe read it, reread it, then folded it up and put it back in its envelope.

"Well? What's it say?"

He stared at the water.

"Joe?"

"Just a news article. About a building I worked on back in New York. He must've cut it out of one of those financial papers he reads."

"So what about it?"

"Some controversy about it. Lot of trouble with how the building's settled, upper floors buckling, stress-fractured windows falling to the street. Contractors suing each other all over the place. Guess Evan thought I'd be int'rested."

"I s'pose that's all your fault too?"

Joe looked up from the article, then cracked a laugh. "Marly, this here is probly the one thing I know for damn sure isn't my fault."

He crumpled the envelope, turned to throw it in the lake, then, deciding against it, stuffed it in his pocket.

"Brought you somethin else, too."

Marly held out a bottle of whiskey.

"From Anne. She said it was for whichever of us wanted it more."

Marly cracked it open, tasted it, knelt to cup her hands in the water and splash some on her face.

"When I heard the pickup," Joe said, "I thought it was Anne coming up herself."

"Not hardly. She's down in Wyoming."

"Wyoming?"

"Workin with Norman again. He's got some pipeline project down there."

"Well, good for her."

"Yeah. Thought I'd never get her out of my hair."

They shared a smile. Looked down over the water that blazed back their reflection, standing alongside one another. And Joe realized, then, there was at least one other person who carried Scotty inside her.

"Marly, remind me, will you, first thing back in Meagher, I need to buy a camera. I want plenty of pictures from now on."

"Why's that, Joe?"

He shrugged. "Everyone's gettin out of town; seems like it

anyway. Anne. Harlo. Evan. Wade."

"Well they should. Here's a toast for em all, then. I bet they all of em do just fine."

"And a toast for you, Marly."

Joe took a drink himself.

"Better be a long one. God knows I need it."

Marly slipped her arm around his waist; Joe's own arm dropped around her shoulders. They exchanged the bottle again, one to the other.

"I sometimes wonder, whatever became of that Vaughn Marlowe?" Joe said.

"No doubt still out somewhere nosin around, lookin for more geology. God knows there's plenty to go around."

They stood a while, Joe's fingers spreading through the rich head hair cascading over his arm.

"Know what I could use now?" she asked.

Joe shook his head.

"A long soak in a hot pool."

"That does have a certain appeal at that," he smiled.

She moved her body, womanly warm, closer into his, her arm, her strong feminine arm, gripped him tighter. His own arm reflexively, with a will of its own, pulled her into him, as though to purge out any emptiness between them.

"Listen."

The sound of dogs, Wade running them somewhere deep in the timber. Joe, looking behind them, noticed how Marly's set of footprints had mingled with his own, all of them leading right to where they now stood.

"Marly?" he said quietly.

She leaned her head back, giving him all her hair.

Also by the author

ARTIFACT

ABANDON

THE CHOSEN ONE

SADDLE BUTTE

Made in the USA
Columbia, SC
25 April 2017

3